P9-DJL-475

A Road Through Mali-Kuli

A Novel

By

Agi Kiss

© 2001 by Agi Kiss. All rights reserved.

No part of this book may be reproduced, stored in a retrieval system, or transmitted by any means, electronic, mechanical, photocopying, recording, or otherwise, without written permission from the author.

ISBN: 0-75964-992-8

This book is printed on acid free paper.

1stBooks - rev. 8/20/01

Dedicated with love to my mother, Klara and my father, Kornel

This book is a work of fiction. The Republic of Rumura, the Mali-Kuli Forest Reserve and the characters and events are products of the author's imagination or are used fictitiously. Any resemblance to actual people, places or events is coincidental.

PEOPLE AND PLACES

Tabitha Akello: sister of Margaret Waiyala

Greg Allen: a Biologist, Director of the Mali-Kuli Primate Research Center, husband of Lisa Othieno

Juma Ayala: a resident of Mwatumi, working for V.J. Singh

Gideon Bashega: Commissioner of Police in the Republic of Rumura

Jean-Louis Benoit: the French Ambassador to the Republic of Rumura

Peter Bergen: an agent of the U.S. Fish and Wildlife Service, International Division

Boku: a young Pygmy boy from the Mali-Kuli forest

Bonaventure: Andre Delacroix' house servant

Sanjit Dawari: proprietor of the Cock and Bull pub in Mwatumi village

Andre Delacroix: head of a French logging company operating in the Republic of Rumura

Phil and Melissa Drayton: Director of the United States Information Service office in Rumura, and his wife

Cheeya Ethungu: an old man, resident of Mwatumi, Mary Mayama's husband

Emily: daughter of Ethungu and Mayama

Laura Handley: Administrator of the Schooley Foundation

Celeste Hartmann: a member of the Green Brigade, Jasper Reijksen's former partner

Joseph: a waiter at the Cock and Bull pub

Captain Kamundu Kamanga: Police Chief of Mwatumi village

Honorable Ignatius Kulibani: Minister of Forests and Environment in the Republic of Rumura

Samuel Liumba: a research assistant at the Mali-Kuli Research Center

Father Emmanuel Loretto: a missionary priest from Mwatumi

George Mahoney: Chairman of the Board of the Schooley Foundation

Thadeus Maleke: Director of the Forest Department in the Republic of Rumura

Jonathan and Pat Marshall: Political Officer at the U.S. Embassy in Rumura, and his wife—old Peace Corps friends of Carol Simmons

Mary Mayama: an old woman, resident of Mwatumi, Cheeya Ethungu's wife

Brian McCallister: U.S. Ambassador to Rumura

Elkannan Mojio: Assistant Chief of Mwatumi, half brother of Margaret Waiyala and Head of the Clan

Mjuju: a young Ruahya boy living in Mwatumi

Mr. Ndaye: Maitre d' at the Norfolk Hotel in Nairobi

Thor Nilssen: a freelance Norwegian journalist

Wanjiku Nkako: Director of the Nairobi Office of Women's Coalition for Action

Wangeru Odege: a resident of Mwatumi, husband of Margarat Waiyala and father of David Wangeru

Lisa Othieno: a Biologist at the Mali Kuli Research Center, and Greg Allen's wife

Muna Rabukoko: a young Rumuran woman, partner of David Wangeru and Juma Ayala

Rasputin: Greg and Lisa's African Gray parrot

Jasper Reijksen: a Dutch sociologist at the Mali-Kuli Primate Research Center

Carol Simmons: an American woman working for the Women's Coalition for Action

Neil Simmons: Carol's husband, a medical researcher

V.J. Singh: a reclusive business man

Constantine Sotiropoulos,: proprietor of the Acropolis Hotel in Mwatumi

Elena and Nico Sotiropoulos: Constantine's wife and teenage son

Margaret Waiyala: a resident of Mwatumi, President of Mwatumi Greengoods Women's Cooperative

Faith, Hope, Patience, Grace and Nelson Waiyala: the other children of Margaret Waiyala and Wangeru Odege

David Wangeru: a resident of Mwatumi, oldest son of Margaret
    Waiyala and Wangeru Odege
Camilla Wong: Neil Simmons' graduate student
Truman Yates: an American evicted from the Republic of
    Rumura as a conman

Acropolis Hotel: a hotel in Mwatumi village
Ankara Hotel: a hotel in Kobani
ba'shyamba: a local (Ruahya) term for Pygmies (literally,
    "children of the forest")
ba'shyamba kipu: Ruahya name for bonobos (literally, small
    "small children of the forest")
Bola: a town located east of Mwatumi, on the road to Kobani
Bonobo: *Pan paniscus*, also known as the Pygmy
    Chimpanzee—a real and highly endangered species
Green Brigade: a environmental activist group based in the
    Netherlands
Kobani: the capital city of the Republic of Rumura
Mali-Kuli Forest Reserve: a fictional forest reserve in western
    Rumura
Mali-Kuli Primate Research Center: a research center devoted
    to the study and conservation of the Mali-Kuli forest and the
    bonobos
Mwatumi: a village in western Rumura
Mwatumi Greengoods Cooperative: a women's horticultural
    self-help group in Mwatumi village
Norfolk Hotel: an elegant hotel in Nairobi, Kenya
Rendesha: a sizeable town located west of Mwatumi
The Republic of Rumura: a fictional country located at the
    intersection of Uganda, Rwanda and the Democratic
    Republic of Congo Zaire (formerly Zaire)
Ruahya: a tribe found in western Rumura (also their language)
Schooley Foundation: an U.S.-based foundation that supports
    projects in developing countries

Women's Coalition for Action: a Non-governmental Organization funded by the Schooley Foundation

PROLOGUE

Mary Mayama padded barefoot down the steep trail carrying an old plastic jerrycan in one hand. On the way back up she would balance it on her head, filled with twenty-five liters of sweet water. It was very early in the morning, cold and damp. The stream at the bottom of the gorge was hidden in the mist.

Mary's back was bent from nearly fifty years of digging in the fields with a short hoe, and her bones and joints ached terribly in the morning. Fetching water was really Emily's task. But that morning, Mary had glanced at her daughter's swollen figure wrapped in her blankets and decided to let her sleep. Emily's time was so close now, and she needed her rest to keep her strength.

Mary sighed deeply as she picked her way over the stones and roots in the trail. It was not so much that Emily was pregnant and unmarried. That happened to many girls, even if the priest did say it was a terrible sin. What was bringing such shame on the family was that no man had stepped forward to claim the baby, and Emily stubbornly refused to name the father. The village gossips were smirking and pointing fingers left and right. Mary defended her daughter in public, even while nagging at her in private. Mary's husband, old Ethungo, had taken no interest in the matter at first. But lately he had been going around muttering hints just like the worst of their neighbors— things that a God-fearing man should not say.

At the bottom of the trail a clear spring bubbled from a crack in the rocks into a small, shallow pool. It was the headwaters of an anonymous, meandering little stream that eventually emptied into the Kiryambura River about seven miles away. Mary removed the top from the jerrycan and squatted beside the spring, ready to catch the sparkling flow.

Suddenly she heard someone shouting her name from the cliff at the top of the trail. She straightened up and strained to see who it was, shading her eyes against the morning sun that was beginning to break through the mist.

"Mama Mayama!" It was the young son of her neighbor, the midwife, shouting in a shrill, cracking voice through cupped hands. "Mama, come quickly! It is time!"

Mary waved up at him to show that she had heard. Then she sighed and squatted again to finish scooping water. The boy was excited because he was young and because he had been entrusted with the responsibility of finding her. But she knew that there was no need to hurry. The baby would not come so quickly, and the midwife was already there.

Finally, when the jerrycan was full, she balanced it carefully on her head and straightened up again, steadying the can with one hand.

She turned and began the long, slow climb, already tired at the beginning of the long day. Soon enough she would be washing Emily's baby and laying it on her daughter's sinful breast. Soon enough she would see what color her first grandchild turned out to be.

CHAPTER 1

1

Carol Simmons stepped inside the darkened auditorium, letting the door creak closed behind her. She edged her way past the knees and handbags and irritated looks and slipped into the empty seat beside Camilla Wong. At the front of the room a huge projection screen showed a slide which might have been an abstract painting but was actually a brightly stained cross-section of brain tissue.

"Am I late?" Carol whispered to Camilla.

"You just made it," Camilla whispered back. "He's up next."

Carol peered through the darkness to see who was at the podium. "How's Fred doing?"

"Okay, I guess," said Camilla, shrugging her slender shoulders. "It's the exact same talk he gave in Denver last month. He could probably give it in his sleep by now."

The screen went blank and the room lights came up. Carol saw Neil sitting behind the table onstage, stiff and solemn in his dark blue suit and burgundy striped tie.

When the smattering of applause faded away, the Chairman of Neil's department stepped up to the podium and gave a short speech introducing the winner of this year's Bellingham Prize in experimental neurobiology. As Neil stood to accept the award, Carol saw his eyes scan the audience, seeking and finding her. She smiled encouragingly, fighting down the impulse to wave at him like the mother of a kindergartner in his first Christmas pageant.

"That's one hurdle down," she sighed to herself gratefully, settling back to listen to Neil's acceptance speech.

The next one came sooner than she had hoped, in the car on the way home.

"I didn't see you come in," said Neil, as they headed up Wisconsin Avenue. "When did you arrive?"

"Just after Fred started in on his slides," said Carol. She preferred Neil not to know how close she had cut it.

"What did you think of his talk?"

"I don't know...wasn't it just the same paper you told me he gave in Denver last month?"

"Damn right," said Neil. "And in San Francisco last January, and in New York before that. I don't know how he gets away with it. He hasn't done anything new in years, but he still gets invited everywhere."

"But he didn't get the Bellingham Prize, did he?" said Carol, squeezing Neil's arm.

"I guess there is a God, after all." Neil looked over at her and grinned. "So, how did I look?"

"Very solemn and dignified, and absolutely adorable. I was so proud—I wanted to run right up on stage and give you a great big hug. Camilla had to hold me back."

"Thank God. Too bad she won't be there at the awards banquet tomorrow, just in case you lose control."

Carol didn't answer. As usual, Neil picked up on it right away.

"What?" he asked.

"I didn't say anything."

"So say something."

"It looks like I won't be able to make the banquet after all."

Carol could sense Neil's jaw and lips tightening as he kept his eyes firmly on the road.

"You've known about this for months," he said.

"I know, sweetheart, and I'm really sorry. But something's come up."

"All I'm asking for is two hours, over lunch."

"I know, but I have to go to Baltimore. Laura Handley called this morning and asked me to come to a meeting at the Schooley Foundation tomorrow at two o'clock."

"So tell her you've got a prior commitment. Why should she expect you to just drop everything and run over to Baltimore any time she calls?"

"You know Schooley is our biggest supporter."

"So what? Tell her to reschedule and give you more notice next time."

"I did try—she said it's just not possible. The Chairman of the Board is flying in from Chicago, on his way to Paris tomorrow night. Laura said she couldn't tell me much ahead of time, but it's essential that I be there. It sounds like they're threatening to cut off funding for our Rumura project."

Carol waited for Neil to ask her why, but he didn't. She knew he didn't want the conversation to be diverted from his problem to hers.

"It's got to have something to do with that letter they sent, about the accusations being made against Margaret Waiyala," Carol went on. "You remember, I showed it to you."

"Yeah, I remember," said Neil grudgingly. "But you got that letter a couple of weeks ago, and you already wrote back saying you're going to investigate. So why this sudden emergency meeting now?"

"I don't know," said Carol, "but if the Chairman is flying in for it, I have to be there. I really am sorry, Neil. But it's just a lunch, isn't it? I did make it for the actual award ceremony."

"Yeah."

Carol looked out her window, letting his sullen reply hang in the air between them. Neil turned off the main road and navigated the quiet, leafy streets to their house. He punched the remote control button to open the garage door and pulled the car inside.

"I guess I can ask Camilla to go with me," he said as he turned off the engine.

"Why do you need anyone to go with you?" asked Carol.

"You know I don't like going to these things alone. I like to have someone to talk to."

3

"You're the guest of honor. Everyone's going to talk to you."

"Are you saying you don't want me to invite Camilla?" he challenged her.

Carol refused to rise to the bait. "No, of course not. Go ahead and invite her if you want to. After all, she deserves her share of the credit for the work anyway, doesn't she? Have a great time. I just wish I could be there with you, sweetheart, I really do."

2

The Schooley Foundation offices were on the eighth floor of a newly refurbished office building near the waterfront. Carol arrived a few minutes before two and waited in the reception area, admiring the tasteful artwork on the walls, until the phone on the receptionist's desk buzzed and she was shown into Laura Handley's elegantly furnished office. Four people were seated in deep leather chairs around a low coffee table. In addition to Laura, Carol recognized two long-time members of the Schooley Foundation Board, whom she considered to be friends. The fourth person was a short, square man in his early sixties, whom she recognized from his photograph in the Foundation's latest Annual Report.

Laura greeted Carol with a peck on each cheek. "Carol, I don't believe you've met our new Chairman, George Mahoney. George—Carol Simmons, Director of the Washington office of the Women's Coalition For Action—the WCA."

Mahoney's handshake was hard and dry, and he fixed Carol with a look of unnerving intensity. She cast her mind back to his brief biography in the newsletter. He was the President of his college alumni association, a pillar of the Rotary, served on the committees of countless other worthwhile organizations and charities, and a devout Catholic. All that in addition to heading up one of the biggest banks in Chicago.

As soon as they had all sat down, Mahoney took over with the air of someone with no time to waste. "I presume you know the purpose of this meeting, Mrs. Simmons?"

"Laura mentioned that it's about our WCA project in Rumura," said Carol.

"I'm sorry to say we've been hearing some very disturbing allegations about that project."

"I did receive a letter from the Foundation a few weeks ago, but it was a bit vague," said Carol. "As I understood it, our local project coordinator, Margaret Waiyala, is being accused of financial mismanagement. And there was also something about the project itself causing environmental damage, although it wasn't clear what that was about. I wrote back asking for more information."

"We weren't prepared to put the details into an official letter just yet, Mrs. Simmons, but I can give them to you now. Mrs. Waiyala isn't just being accused of mismanaging project funds. Our informant charges that she's embezzling them and using them to finance a smuggling operation."

Carol wanted to laugh, but the faces around her were too serious. "I'm sorry, Mr. Mahoney, but that's absolutely ridiculous. You'd have to know Margaret..."

"Of course, I sincerely hope you're right, Mrs. Simmons. But we can't just dismiss allegations like these. We have the reputation of the Foundation to consider."

"May I ask who your informant is?"

"For the moment he prefers to keep his name out of it, but I believe you'll have the opportunity to meet him soon. In the meantime, take my word for it that he's a very credible witness and I would be very surprised if there wasn't something to what he says. And with regard to the environmental aspects, he's given us these to back it up."

Mahoney passed Carol several snapshots of fires burning through patches of tall, buttressed trees. One picture was taken looking downward onto a dense forest canopy, showing spires of smoke rising up from the middle of it. In another, a woman in a headscarf stood at the edge of the flames with a hoe in her hand.

"Do you know that woman?" asked Mahoney.

"I really can't tell," said Carol. "You can't see her face in the picture."

"According to the note on the back of the photo, she's a member of the Greengoods Cooperative in Mwatumi village in western Rumura. Does that mean anything to you?"

"Yes, of course," said Carol. "It's the women's horticultural cooperative WCA is funding in Mwatumi. But this doesn't look like the area the Coop is cultivating."

"The photograph suggests that it is."

"For all we know, this wasn't even taken in Rumura," protested Carol. "It could be almost anywhere in Africa."

"I think we can assume that the photo is just what it says it is," said Mahoney curtly. "We seem to have a very serious problem on our hands, Mrs. Simmons."

Carol glanced at Laura, who shrugged almost imperceptibly.

"It certainly warrants looking into," Carol said cautiously.

"I'm glad you agree. And the sooner the better."

"Mr. Mahoney was saying that he's putting the Rumura project on the agenda for the Board meeting at the end of the month," said Laura.

"Our informant will be attending the meeting to present his evidence in person," said Mahoney. "If the Board is convinced his concerns are justified, we will of course have to discontinue funding immediately," said Mahoney.

"I'm sure it won't come to that," said Carol. "Mwatumi Greengoods is one of WCA's best projects. It would be a real shame to cut it off just when it's starting to get off the ground."

"I'm not talking only about the Rumura project," Mahoney told her. "A foundation like Schooley has to have total confidence in the organizations we support. Our reputation depends on it. If these accusations turn out to be true, I'm afraid we'll have to end our association with the WCA altogether."

6

3

Neil laid his fork down on his plate with exaggerated care, as though he didn't trust himself to make any sudden movements. Carol worked on another mouthful of her spaghetti bolognese, which suddenly felt and tasted like cardboard.

"You're kidding, right?" said Neil.

"Please, Neil, let me explain..."

"What's to explain? You just got off the plane after a month in India, and now you want to go right off again to Africa, for God knows how long."

"I didn't 'just get off the plane.' I've been back nearly three weeks."

"Oh, *excuse me*! Has it been three weeks? It's so hard to keep track."

"And I don't *want* to go to Africa, I *have* to go. I told you, I have to find out what's going on before the next Schooley Board meeting. It's not just the Rumura project at stake—it's WCA."

"Schooley isn't the only foundation in the world."

"You think anyone's going to touch us if Schooley dumps us? Especially with Mahoney going around telling everyone they cut us off because our projects are stealing money and destroying the rain forest? Can't you see how important this is, Neil?"

"Sure, it's important," said Neil. . "Everything's always important. Everything but me, that is."

"Christ, Neil, could you please try just for once to think about something other than yourself?" exclaimed Carol.

"I happen to be thinking about you, too. Has it ever occurred to you that this trip could be very dangerous?"

"What are you talking about? I've been to Rumura before."

"Not to investigate smuggling, you haven't. Sounds to me like there could be some big money and some very bad people involved in this."

"Don't be ridiculous. Nobody at Greengoods Co-op is involved in gold smuggling."

"Mahoney seems to be pretty sure they are."

"Only because of this mysterious 'informant' of his, who won't even show his face. I know Margaret Waiyala, Neil. She's as honest as you can get."

"You know what they say—where there's smoke there's fire."

"Is that supposed to be funny?" Carol demanded. "I told you, there's no way to know if those photos were taken anywhere near Mwatumi."

"Lighten up—it's just an expression," said Neil. But look at it this way—why would someone be making all this up?"

Carol sighed. She had been asking herself the same question all day. All she had been able to come up with was that some of the men in Mwatumi might be upset because the project money was going to the women instead of to them. She told Neil they could have accused Margaret out of spite, or in the hopes that if she were gone they could get their hands on the money somehow.

"How could a bunch of disgruntled husbands from a little village in Africa have gotten to someone like George Mahoney?" objected Neil. "It just supports my hypothesis that there's big money involved."

"Or it could be some kind of political thing," said Carol. There were some people in the Rumuran government who had been annoyed when WCA had chosen to support Mwatumi Greengoods instead of some of their own pet projects. "But what good would it do them for Schooley to cut WCA off altogether? There's just no way I'm going to get to the bottom of this without talking to Mahoney's informant. I've got to meet him face to face."

"But why does it have to be in Nairobi? You said he's coming here for the Schooley Board meeting anyway."

"That'll be too late. I have to talk to him and then go to Rumura to check up on his story before the meeting."

"So, there you are, in a secret meeting at some some dive in Nairobi, with a guy who's probably some kind of international gangster..."

"Don't be ridiculous, Neil. Laura said he's willing to meet me at the WCA office in Nairobi. And I'm sure he's not a gangster."

"We don't know what he is. What I do know is that we agreed you were going to spend more time at home, so we could think about starting a family. You promised the India trip was going to be the last one this year."

"I know, Neil, but what can I do?"

"You can try taking your promises to me more seriously. We had an agreement."

Neil picked up his fork and stabbed viciously at his ravioli. Carol watched him gnashing at the soft pasta as if it were shoe leather. His hurt and anger dismayed and infuriated her. Really, he left her no choice.

"All right, Neil," she said finally. "I've tried to explain why this is important to me and why I need to go. But, if after everything I've said, you really don't want me to go, then I won't. I'm leaving it up to you."

"Shit," said Neil. "Why do you always do this to me?"

CHAPTER 2

1

Carol forced her way forward through the thick, steamy jungle, pushing aside curtains of dripping leaves and tearing at the clinging vines. Towering tree trunks rose up all around her like cathedral arches. Shafts of light breaking through the dense forest canopy threw golden stripes on the dark ground in front of her. Somewhere ahead a strident trill rang through the stillness, summoning her, more urgent and insistent with every step she took. The underbrush gave way to a soft, pale mist and she pressed forward, moving faster and faster, her feet barely touching the ground. Straining, grasping, she was almost there, had almost reached it, when suddenly the trill turned into the ringing of a telephone, dissolving the dream around her.

With one hand she groped around and found the receiver just as the ringing stopped. Sighing, she pulled her hand back under the covers. The memory of the dream slipped away, leaving only disconnected images and a vague, uneasy feeling. She cracked her eyes open, and saw nothing.

Fighting a sudden surge of panic, she lay very still and took stock. She was lying naked in a soft, strange bed, surrounded by darkness. Images drifted through her mind: Neil dropping her off at the departures terminal, the tedious seven hour stop-over under the glaring lights of the airport in London, the all-night flight through pitch blackness giving way to a brilliant dawn over Egypt, and the clamor and jostling of arrival in Nairobi. And finally, the smiling doorman in top hat and tails opening the door of her taxi, welcoming her to the Norfolk Hotel. She had checked in, drawn the heavy curtains, dropped her clothes in a pile on the floor, and slipped gratefully between the cool sheets. Checking the softly glowing dial of her watch, Carol saw that it was three o'clock. She had been asleep for about five hours. She curled up on her side and let her mind wander, letting herself sink back into sleep. Her thoughts began to disassociate. Random images formed and dissolved in her mind's eye and another dream began to take shape. The telephone rang again.

"Hello?" Carol let her voice sound like she felt—groggy and irritated.

"Mrs. Simon?" The voice was high pitched and raw, with a pronounced African accent. She thought it belonged to a man, but she couldn't be sure.

"Close enough," she said. She herself got the African names wrong often enough. "Who is this?"

"We have expected you before. I pray you met no trouble on your journey?"

Carol frowned to herself. She still didn't know the identity of the man she had come here to meet, but that meeting was set for the next day at the WCA office. But who else would know she was coming?

"I'm sorry," she said, "I've just woken up. Could you please tell me who you are, and why you're calling?"

"I am the one to apologize for waking you," he said smoothly. "You can be very tired. So maybe we can set to meet for the evening, yes?"

Carol's confusion gave way to annoyance. "Look, would you please tell me who's calling?"

"It is better I can tell you when we meet, madam. You understand—in our business, it is best to be a little bit careful, yes."

Carol sat up. "What's this all about, anyway?" she asked sharply.

"We know what you are looking for, Mrs. Simon. We can be of very good...*service* to you." The voice had taken on an irritating, insinuating quality.

"Listen, I think you must have the wrong room after all. My name is really Simmons, not Simon, and I honestly don't have any idea what you're talking about—."

"Please, madam," the caller cut in. "We know you have already...*contacts*...in Rumura, yes. But you Americans believe

11

in competition, isn't it? You can give us the opportunity to show why we can help you in your...*business*. And our price will be the best."

"I told you, you've got the wrong person. Goodbye!"

Carol slammed the receiver back into its cradle. She could actually hear her heart pounding in the quiet room. She told herself it was ridiculous. After all, the man hadn't said anything threatening. And it probably was really just a mistake. But how many women staying at the Norfolk, with names that sounded like Simon, could possibly be on their way to the tiny little Republic of Rumura? And the annoying voice lingered like an echo in her mind, particularly the way he had emphasized words like "business" and "contacts" and "services," as though loading them with surreptitious meanings that she was supposed to understand. Just what kind of "business" was this Mrs. Simon supposed to be in? Neil's warning about gangsters and gold smugglers suddenly came back to her.

Then another thought occurred to her. Maybe the call really was for her, and the man was offering to sell her information— something related to what Mahoney's contact was going to tell her tomorrow. If so, maybe he would call again. But should she even consider dealing with someone like that?

She lay in bed, tense, half-hoping and half-fearing that the phone would ring again. Going back to sleep was clearly out of the question. Finally she reached over and turned on the bedside lamp. She felt better as the light revealed the room, comfortingly familiar after so many visits: the solid brown furniture with its shiny, brass knobs, the batik prints on the walls and the basket filled with mangoes, bananas and a pineapple on the table. Home away from home.

Carol stepped out of bed and slid the floor-length curtains open, letting the white sunlight pour in. Outside, the wide green lawn was dappled with the shade of tall acacia trees. A few tourists were strolling across the landscaped courtyard, admiring and photographing the exotic birds in the aviary and the antique tractors and wagons that lay artfully scattered around the lawn to evoke the Norfolk's colorful colonial past. Overhead, a cloud of chittering swallows wheeled tirelessly, darting and swooping like bats, plucking flies from the air. Just in front of her, a sleek black-and-white wagtail bobbed past like a mechanical toy, its head cocked as it searched for grubs and worms under the grass.

Now that she was out of bed, Carol weighed her choices. A swim first, then a beer at the terrace restaurant? Or a shower first, then a swim and then a beer? Or, how about forgetting the swim, and just doing the shower and the beer?

Halfway to the bathroom, Carol caught a glimpse of herself in the full-length mirror. The squarish, open face that gazed back at her didn't look much different than on her first stay at the Norfolk almost fifteen years ago. Her cap of salt-and-pepper hair might have added ten years to her age, except that the simple, Dutch-boy cut shaved them off again. On closer inspection there were a few creases around the corners of the eyes and mouth that hadn't been there before, but nothing too noticeable. She let her gaze move downward and saw a few pounds that hadn't been there fifteen years before either. 'Well, nobody stays twenty forever,' she thought to herself. 'Who would even want to?'

Suddenly, from nowhere, a clear image of Camilla Wong's willowy figure and sleek black hair popped into her mind. She banished it brusquely and turned on the shower.

2

In a noisy, basement bar in downtown Nairobi, David Wangeru and Juma Ayala sat together over a well-earned beer. Tall and gangly, David was draped over the high barstool with one foot firmly on the floor and the other propped on the tarnished brass railing. He wore narrow black trousers that stopped too far up on his ankles, and a red and white striped shirt with the sleeves rolled up over his forearms and the tails hanging loose. His hair was cropped close to the skull and his high, narrow forehead was decorated with scars—a design of three parallel lines etched into the skin above each eye. He rested his chin on the pink palm of one slender, dark hand and savored his beer in long, slow swallows.

Juma was very short, with a short neck and a head that seemed too big for the rest of his bony body, giving him a hunched and stunted look. His eyes protruded over sharp cheekbones, their prominent whites making a startling contrast to the brown-black skin of his face. He was dressed in a gray, pinstriped woolen suit jacket with broad padded shoulders and wide lapels, flannel trousers in a different shade of gray, and an open-necked shirt with a colorful paisley pattern. The toes of his polished, ankle-high black boots were fashionably pointed. Juma twisted on his stool, his two-inch heels wedged behind the crossbar, and took short, quick swallows of beer as he talked. He didn't bother to lower his voice. No one in a Nairobi bar was likely to understand Rumuran.

"Of course she's going to say she doesn't know what I'm talking about," Juma was saying. "What did you expect? She's got to be cautious. She doesn't know who we are—it could be a trick. The important thing was to make contact."

David said nothing. He drained his beer and placed the empty glass on the counter where Juma could see it.

"It all fits—it has to be her."

David nodded, and gave his empty glass a nudge, as though by accident. Juma didn't appear to notice.

"But we can't afford to make a mistake. We have to be sure." Juma drummed his fingers on the sticky bartop. "Muna said she's supposed to spend two days in Nairobi before she goes on to Rumura. We'll follow her, watch where she goes and who she meets. And we'll call her a few more times, leave messages, keep her curious, and let her know we know all her movements. It'll make her take us seriously."

"Maybe we can drop his name, too," suggested David. "so she won't be so suspicious about us."

14

Juma shook his head in exasperation. "Maybe we should just ask him for a letter of reference," he snorted.

David looked sullenly down at his glass. For some reason his suggestion must have been very stupid, but he was not sure why.

Juma noticed David's pouting and ordered another round of beer to mollify him.

"We leave him out of it," he explained wearily, as if for the hundredth time. "That's the whole point. We're big-time, remember. We don't need him."

"But how can we leave him out of it? Won't she ask him about us?"

"Not if we play our cards right. And even if she does, what can he tell her? It's not like he knows who we work for."

"No," crowed David, gleefully slapping his long palm on the counter, "for sure he doesn't know who we work for!" He laughed out loud.

"Aieh," agreed Juma, smiling tolerantly at his partner.

3

After a short swim, Carol felt refreshed and virtuous and ready to face the lively scene that was the Norfolk Hotel's Lord Delamere Terrace on a sunny Sunday afternoon. She showered and slipped on a lightweight Indian cotton dress and a pair of well-worn sandals, grabbed the novel she had not quite finished reading on the plane, and headed out the door.

She found a sunny table on the street side. "A Tusker Premium, please, very cold," she told the waiter.

Settled comfortably in the big, wooden chair, Carol opened her book, but she felt too lazy to begin reading. Instead she listened to the voices around her carrying on spirited conversations in half a dozen languages and all the different flavors of English. At the next table two couples who had to be from New England were talking about seeing baby elephants tumbling in the mud like puppies in Amboseli "Pahk." At another, three weathered-looking Scotswomen exchanged complaints about their tour guide: "Eeww, he's a cheeky one. I dooon't knooow if I liyke his attitewd..." The twangy vowels booming over from an exuberant, red-faced crowd at the bar sounded Australian, or maybe South African.

"Carol?"

She looked up to see Pat Marshall waving vigorously as she wove around the tables toward her.

"Pat! What on earth are you doing here?" Carol hadn't seen Pat in years, but she was only a little surprised to bump into her here. Everyone knew that if you sat on the Delamere terrace long enough, everyone you knew in Africa would eventually pass by.

Pat explained that her husband Jonathan had come to Nairobi to meet an important visitor from Washington—'some mucky-muck' as she put it—and she had tagged along to do some shopping. The waiter arrived with Carol's beer, and Pat ordered the same.

"I'm really beat," said Pat. "I've been walking around all day looking for car parts and makeup and clothes for the kids."

"Just like the old days, coming in to Nairobi to stock up," said Carol. The four of them—Carol, Neil, Pat and Jonathan—had been Peace Corps volunteers together in Kenya back in the seventies. "Where are you guys now?"

"In Rumura," said Pat. "It's a tiny little country just east of the Democratic Republic of Congo—you've probably never even heard of it."

"Not only have I heard of it—I'm going there in two days," said Carol.

"You're kidding! Whatever for?"

"We've got a project there, but it's a long story. How are you all doing? Is Jonathan an Ambassador yet?"

"Not yet, just a Political Officer, but he's working on it. The kids are fine. Kobani's more like a small town than a capital city, but there's a good international school. And they're not old enough yet to complain that there's no place to go at night, thank God."

"How about you?"

"I'm getting by," said Pat. "I do a bit of consulting work every now and then for USAID. Mostly I try to keep Jonathan and the kids in shape and survive the Embassy parties. But tell me about your project in Kobani."

"Actually, it's in a little village called Mwatumi in the western part of Rumura, in the mountains."

"I've been there," said Pat. "That's a beautiful area— reminds me a bit of Costa Rica. You remember, that was Jonathan's first posting after he joined the State Department—" suddenly she interrupted herself. "Speaking of Mwatumi, look who's here!" She waved at someone at the entrance.

Carol turned to look and saw a tall, angular young man who glanced briefly in their direction and then quickly away. Then he looked back again and let Pat's eye catch his and nodded slightly. Pat's wave turned into a cheerful beckoning gesture. The man hesitated, then shrugged and began to work his way around the tables towards them.

He was somewhere in his thirties, raw-boned and almost skeletally thin, with narrow shoulders and a long neck with a prominent Adam's apple. All his features seemed somehow oversized, exaggerated like a puppet's. His thin, pale blond hair was swept carelessly sideways and back from his high, sunburned forehead. A patchy beard didn't quite cover his sharp jaw and sunken cheeks. He wore a wrinkled khaki shirt with patch pockets, and loose khaki trousers that barely clung to their purchase on his narrow hips. The trousers ended in a pair of drooping green socks that disappeared into worn suede desert boots. This was the authentic version of the spotless, neatly pressed cotton-blend safari outfits that many of the tourists around the terrace were wearing. Carol thought that he looked uncomfortable, as though even those clothes were too much and he really belonged in jeans and an old T-shirt. The narrow brown tie knotted loosely around his neck seemed completely out of place.

"You know," said Pat, confirming Carol's impression, "I don't think I've ever seen him in a tie before." She glanced down toward his feet. "Or wearing socks, for that matter."

"Who is he?"

"Oh, no! Now I can't remember his name."

"Don't worry," said Carol. "I'll handle it." When he reached their table she immediately extended her hand and said, "Hi, I'm Carol Simmons."

"Jasper Reijksen," he said, in a rough Dutch accent.

"Hi, Jasper," said Pat. "Remember me? Pat Marshall, from Rumura."

"Yes, of course, the American Embassy."

Pat turned to Carol. "Jasper is at the primate research camp in the Mali-Kuli forest, right near Mwatumi." She turned back to Jasper. "Carol is with the WCA."

"Women's Coalition for Action," explained Carol. "It's an international non-governmental organization. We specialize in helping women set up small business cooperatives."

"Carol just told me the WCA has a project in Mwatumi," added Pat.

"Yes?" asked Jasper, looking distracted and a bit bored.

"Are Greg and Lisa here in Nairobi too?" asked Pat.

"No, I came alone to collect supplies."

"I'm surprised to see you at the Norfolk," Pat teased him. "I wouldn't have thought it was quite your style."

"I am not stopping here." Jasper stood stiffly beside the table, making no move to sit down.

"Are you meeting someone? Why don't you join us for a beer while you wait?"

"No, thank you," said Jasper. "I am not waiting for anyone. I am just leaving. It was a pleasure to meet you," he said without sincerity, shaking first Carol's hand and then Pat's.

"We'll see you back in Rumura," said Pat. "Carol is going there too in a few days."

He acknowledged her remark with a slight nod, already striding off. Pat continued to look after him.

"Nice guy," remarked Carol, grimacing.

"That's funny," said Pat. "He said he was leaving, but instead he went inside."

"I guess he just wasn't interested in our company," said Carol.

"I still wonder why he's hanging out here at the Norfolk," said Pat. "Greg and Lisa and their crowd usually stay somewhere a lot cheaper, like the Boulevard or the Milimani."

"Who are Greg and Lisa?"

"Greg Allen and his wife, Lisa Othieno. They run the research station where Jasper is working."

"Are they as unpleasant as he is?"

"No, they're very nice. I have them over to dinner sometimes when they come to town, and I've taken the kids out to visit them at the research station. They're doing some fascinating work there, studying pygmy chimpanzees."

"I've never even heard of pygmy chimpanzees. Are they like miniature chimpanzees?"

"No, they're a completely different species, and they're actually about the same size as regular chimps. The real name for them is 'bonobos.' They look different—longer legs and smaller heads and flatter faces. A lot more like people. They're very rare. Apparently the ones in the Mali-Kuli forest are the only ones that have ever been found outside the DRC. Lisa studies their social behavior and Greg studies their feeding habits and physiology."

"And Jasper?"

"He's one of the students they always have hanging around the place—I think he's from some university in the Netherlands. Lisa told me he's a sociologist, looking at people's attitudes towards the forest and the chimps."

"Aren't sociologists supposed to be friendly and outgoing, sort of 'people' people?"

"You'd think so, wouldn't you?" said Pat. "Oh, there he is again. I guess he really is leaving now. He doesn't look very happy, does he?"

They watched Jasper as he passed by the terrace, heading toward downtown, walking fast with his face set in a grim mask.

"I wonder what's with him," said Pat.

The Maitre d' had come up to their table, a stout man in a tight black suit. "That one, he does not stay here or buy anything," he said. "He looks for messages at the desk, then he goes away. May I bring you a menu?"

"That's a very polite way of asking us to order something else, or go," Carol told Pat. "Tell you what...if you're free, how about dinner at the Three Bells tonight, for old time's sake?"

"You're on," said Pat. "We'll see if you can still handle your curry, or if Washington life has made you soft."

When Carol returned later that evening, she found the lobby jammed with newly arrived tourists. They milled around and gazed in the gift shop window while porters unloaded their piles of luggage from zebra-striped minibuses and their tour guides struggled to match names and room assignments. She squeezed through to the desk and caught the eye of the receptionist.

"Room 321, please," she said.

The young woman pulled the room key from its pigeonhole and handed it to over along with a sealed envelope. Carol eased her way back out through the crowd, tearing open the envelope.

It contained only a business card, which read:

V.J. Singh
Export and Import

At the bottom someone had scrawled: "We will contact you."

Carol turned and pushed her way back to the reception desk.

"Excuse me," she said, "I'm Carol Simmons. Could you please tell me who left this card for me?"

"I am too sorry, madam," the receptionist answered in precise, schoolgirl English. "It was here already when I began my shift. Perhaps my colleague knows."

She turned to the man beside her and spoke to him briefly in Swahili. He shook his head without looking up from his work.

"He says he did not take the note. Is there a problem, Mrs. Simmons?"

"No, it's all right. Thank you." Carol turned thoughtfully away from the desk and walked through the fragrant courtyard back to her room.

Once inside she examined the card again. The edges of the print were blurred and bleeding into the rough, poor quality paper. She looked again at the envelope: there was no name, only her room number. She laid it on the desk, thinking she would decide what to do with it later.

She checked her watch and saw that it was only ten o'clock. Seeing Pat had brought back memories—being young and idealistic, the Peace Corps, all the close friends she had made in her life and then somehow fallen out of touch with. And Neil, the way he used to be when she first met him. She thought about calling him, but he would probably be in the lab and he hated to be disturbed there. It would be better to wait and call him at home later.

She checked the in-house film schedule and found that a James Bond movie was about to begin. It was better than nothing. She slipped into a loose cotton *kitenga*, chose a bottle of tonic water from the mini-bar, propped some pillows against the headboard and settled back to watch 007 face off against another unlikely villain and his harem of lethal, leggy side-kicks.

21

CHAPTER 3

1

Carol dozed through the night, waking up every hour or two, paying the price for her afternoon nap. She finally fell into a deep sleep just before dawn, only to have it shattered by the rapid-fire beeping of her alarm clock. She grabbed it and fumbled with the tiny buttons until the infuriating noise finally stopped.

As she crossed the room sleepily toward the bathroom, Carol spotted a white envelope that had been pushed underneath the door. Once again there was nothing in it but a single business card from V.J. Singh, but this time there was a telephone number written at the bottom. She threw it onto the bed and went in to the bathroom.

After breakfast, Carol went to the front desk and slid the card over the counter to the receptionist.

"Good morning. I think you must have a Mrs. Simon staying here. Could you please pass this card on to her? It came to me by mistake."

"Mrs. Simon? I will check. How is it written, please, S-I-M-O-N? Sorry, I do not find that name."

"Are you sure? I've been getting messages from someone that are meant for a Mrs. Simon."

"The name is very like your name. Are you quite sure the messages are not for you?"

"Yes, I'm very sure. I have no idea what they're about. And frankly, I don't want to know."

The receptionist's face grew concerned, and Carol realized she must have spoken more emphatically than she had meant to.

"Do you wish to speak to the Manager?"

"No, that's all right," said Carol. "I'm sure it's nothing—just a case of mistaken identity." She slipped the card back into her pocket, left the key on the counter, went outside and turned left on Harry Thuku Street toward the center of town.

The concrete and glass towers of Nairobi could have belonged to any city in the world, but the scene at street level was typically African. The dusty pavement and concrete walls formed a gray backdrop for an explosion of color, the boldly patterned dresses of women competing with the violet and crimson bougainvillea that spilled over walls and out of pots on every corner. Ears of corn, goat kebabs and cauldrons of tea smoked and sizzled and bubbled over small open fires, beckoning the passersby. The wood smoke mingled with diesel fumes and a pervasive, sulfurous undercurrent of sewage to flavor the air like a pungent stew.

Along the crowded main streets, shop windows tempted passing tourists with woodcarvings, sisal baskets, T-shirts, gaudy batik prints and jewelry made of malachite, lapis lazuli, tigers' eye, silver and brass. The narrow alleys were crammed with rough stalls displaying the same goods, with prices varying with the buyer's bargaining skills. Ragged vendors squatted on their heels behind straw mats spread with cigarettes, candies, cosmetics, books and magazines. Passing in front of a flower shop, Carol had to step down into the street to go around two men perched on low stools in the midst of a mound of red and white carnations, patiently weaving them into funeral wreaths and crosses.

Tiny barefoot children ran up to Carol to beg for coins and pens, following along and plucking at her skirt for awhile, then attached themselves to the first white person they found heading back the other way. On one corner, a group of young men lounged idly against the wall, talking and joking, holding hands in the casual African way. Waiting to cross the street, Carol glanced down as something brushed her skirt, and then looked awkwardly away again, trying not to stare at the man on the ground beside her. His broad hands were thrust into a pair of plastic sandals and his legs, just shafts of skin-covered bone, were twisted in front of his chest like a pretzel. He swung himself over the curb, using his powerfully muscled arms like crutches, and wove his way across the street through the slow-moving traffic along with the other pedestrians.

After crossing the busy main thoroughfare of Kenyatta Avenue, Carol turned down Standard Street to the entrance of Muinde House. She joined the crowd waiting in the lobby for one of the building's two elevators to inch its way downward. When the doors opened at last, the flood of passengers trying to get out had to force their way through a wall of those trying to crowd in. Carol let herself get swept along and was soon packed tightly into the elevator with twenty other bodies. She tried to imagine Nairobi in twenty years, when the population would have doubled: two people for every one pressing up against her right now. The elevator started its slow climb, stopping at every floor.

The WCA office was on the fifth floor. Carol opened the door into the small reception area, whose walls were covered with posters and photos of women of every race milking, planting, marketing, sewing and building.

"*Hodi!*" she called. "Is anyone home?"

Wanjiku Nkako appeared in the doorway of her office, nearly filling it. Unlike western clothes that tried to conceal and camouflage a large figure, her gaudy blue and yellow African dress was drawn in tightly at the waist and flared dramatically above and below with folds and ruffles, to accentuate and celebrate the swells of her broad hips and huge bust. Her matching headscarf was twisted into an elaborate turban that added another six inches to her already substantial height.

As a Peace Corps volunteer, Carol had been assigned to Wanjiku's village to help develop a community health care program. During those four years she had watched Wanjiku start a small women's trading cooperative, which had since grown into a company that supplied medicines to rural clinics across the country. After joining WCA, Carol had persuaded Wanjiku to hand the running of the company over to her sister and open the first WCA office in Africa. Wanjiku ran the office with a big heart and an iron hand. Anyone with a project that was in tune with WCA's philosophy of cooperative action, self-reliance and hard-nosed business sense could be sure of her invincible support. Those who came looking for hand-outs were quickly shown the door.

"Carol!" cried Wanjiku. "You are here! I am too happy to see you." She rushed over and enveloped Carol in a bear hug. "When did you come?"

"Yesterday morning," answered Carol. "How are the girls?"

Wanjiku sighed and threw up her hands. "These days do I see them anymore? Between their school friends and the club, there is no time anymore for poor old mother. But they will stop at home tonight, so you can come for supper and meet them."

"It's a deal, especially if you're making your world-famous fish stew."

"It is already waiting for you on the cooker. But now there is somebody waiting for you in my office."

Carol dropped her voice. "So our mystery man showed up, did he? What do you think of him?"

"I think this you must come and see for yourself," said Wanjiku, raising her eyebrows dramatically. She beckoned Carol to follow her.

Whatever Carol had been expecting, it was not the strikingly handsome, muscular young man who rose to meet her.

"Carol, meet Father Emmanuel Loretto," said Wanjiku.

2

David shifted his weight impatiently as he sat on the hood of a car parked across the street from the Norfolk Hotel. From time to time he glanced at Juma, who was leaning on his elbows beside him, the smoke from his cigarette curling lazily over his head. Finally, Juma straightened up, tossed the stub of the cigarette onto the ground and started toward the street. David hopped off the car and started to follow him. Juma turned and shook his head.

"You'd better stay here," said Juma.

"Why?" protested David, "It's too cold."

"You'll attract attention in there dressed like that," replied Juma, looking disparagingly at David as he straightened his own jacket and brushed a speck of dust from his sleeve. "Anyway, it's better if I meet her alone."

David settled sullenly back onto the hood of the car.

Juma hurried across the street, slowing to a dignified walk as he approached the hotel. The doorman looked him over with professional suspicion but let him pass. Inside the elegant lobby, Juma strolled nonchalantly past the reception desk and over to the house phones, where he quickly punched in a number. As it rang, he glanced up to meet the level gaze of the security guard standing discreetly off to one side of the lobby. Juma looked away and made a show of checking his wristwatch and drumming his fingers on the countertop—a busy man who has been kept waiting for an important appointment. Finally, after letting the phone ring twenty times, he put down the receiver and strolled over to the window of the gift shop, pretending to be absorbed in the display. He could feel the security man still watching him from across the lobby.

Suddenly he felt a tap on his shoulder. He jerked and turned around, ready to face the guard, but it was only David.

"What are you doing here?" Juma demanded in a hoarse whisper, "I told you to wait outside."

"I had to let you know—he's here." David was breathless, lowering his voice to match Juma's.

"What!"

"Look—over by the reception. He came in right after you."

Juma glanced over his shoulder and spotted the familiar profile. He quickly turned and slipped into the gift shop, pulling David after him. The sales clerk behind the counter watched them with narrowed eyes.

"You fool," snapped Juma under his breath, "what if he'd seen you?"

"I waited until he was busy at the reception, looking the other way," David whispered back. "I thought you'd better know."

"Bloody hell. She's probably on her way here to meet him. That's why she didn't answer the phone."

"What are we going to do?" asked David.

"We have to get out of here without letting him see us."

"But what about her? You said you were going to meet her tonight."

"Too risky now," replied Juma. "We'll wait for tomorrow."

Still conscious of the sales clerk's suspicious gaze, Juma clasped his hands behind his back and bent to examine the silver bracelets inside a glass display case. He kept one eye on the reception desk just visible through the window of the shop. David nervously started fingering postcards on a revolving rack.

After a while Juma straightened up and spoke pleasantly to the sales clerk in English. "How much are these bracelets, please?"

"Two hundred and fifty shillings for the small ones, three hundred and fifty for the larger ones."

"Thank you very much," said Juma. "Very nice." He went over to David and whispered, "He's gone into the restaurant. Let's go." In a normal voice he added casually in English, "Do you find anything you want?"

David shook his head without speaking, and they walked out of the shop.

3

Carol turned off the water and heard the phone. "Damn it!" she muttered, and stepped out of the shower, wondering how long it had been ringing. She rushed around the bed to the night table and snatched up the receiver, and stood dripping water and listening to the dial tone.

She pressed the disconnect button and dialed the number for the front desk.

"Reception, may I help you?"

"Yes, this is Carol Simmons in room 321. Did someone just call and leave a message for me?"

"One moment, please...No, Mrs. Simmons, sorry there is no message."

Carol hung up the phone slowly, wondering whether it might have been her mystery caller again. And if so, who could he be? She had been startled at first to discover that Mahoney's informant was a priest, but actually it made sense. At least it explained why Mahoney placed such faith in the truthfulness of his informant. The connection had turned out to be a church-based environmental group called the "Keepers of the Garden." Mahoney was a member of the Board of Trustees. When a letter had arrived from Father Loretto complaining about the WCA project, the Director had passed it on to Mahoney, knowing about his connection to WCA through the Schooley Foundation grant. Somehow, Carol doubted that her mystery caller was anything like a priest, and she wasn't very happy about the idea of doing business with him. But she might have to, if he could offer her some ammunition to counter Father Loretto's strong indictment of Margaret Waiyala and Mwatumi Greengoods. Her word against his was clearly not going to be enough.

By the time she had dried off and finished dressing, she had decided that it couldn't hurt to at least find out whether the caller and the cards were related. She found the card that had been slipped under her door and nervously punched the number into the telephone.

"Scotts Hotel."

"I'd like to speak to Mr. V.J. Singh, please."

There was a pause on the other end, then the receptionist came back on the line. "There is no Mr. Singh here," he said.

"Are you sure? This was the number he gave me."

"Sorry, we have no Mr. Singh," he repeated.

"Oh. Could you please check to see whether you've got a reservation for him?"

"Hold the line, please. No, no booking for Mr. Singh."

"I see. Thank you." She laid the receiver down thoughtfully and slipped the card into her pocket. All that struggling with her conscience, for nothing.

There was still nearly a half-hour before Wanjiku came to collect her. Carol decided to have a beer while she waited.

The Delamere terrace was crowded with dusty tourists just back from safaris and well-dressed locals having a sundowner on the way home from work. Carol stood at the entrance, peering into the semi-darkness, searching for an empty table. She didn't find one, but she did spot Jasper Reijksen sitting alone at a table against the wall. Their eyes connected momentarily, and a watchful waiter hurried over and pulled out the empty chair across from him. Feeling a bit foolish, Carol wound her way over to the table.

"Good evening," she said, "I hope I'm not disturbing you."

"Not at all," he answered, in his usual disinterested voice.

Carol sat down, explaining, "It's so crowded tonight. I'm waiting for a friend to meet me for dinner, and I thought I'd have a quick drink."

Jasper motioned to the waiter. "One Tusker Premium and another Whitecap, please." He turned back to Carol, "I hope that's right? You were drinking Tusker yesterday."

"Yes, thank you." Carol was surprised that he had noticed. He had acted so distracted the day before that she hadn't even expected him to recognize her again.

"So," she said, "have you been able to finish your shopping?"

He looked at her vaguely. "Shopping?"

"You said you were here in Nairobi picking up supplies."

"Yes," he said.

"I'm scheduled to go to Rumura on Wednesday, but I may go tomorrow if there's a flight," said Carol.

Jasper didn't answer and Carol began to regret having sat down. Trying to converse with Jasper was worse than pulling teeth, she thought. It was more like trying to yank the marrow right out of the jawbone.

"Pat told me a bit about your research," she said. "How long have you been working in Mwatumi?"

"A few months."

"This will only be my second visit. We have a project there, assisting a women's horticultural cooperative. It's called 'Mwatumi Greengoods.' Maybe you've come across it?"

"No."

As they fell back into an awkward silence, Carol saw a small, dapper man in a well-tailored suit working his way across the terrace, stopping to shake hands and greet people at several of the tables. Eventually he reached them.

"Ah, Mrs. Simmons. *Karibu sana*—you are very welcome back to the Norfolk."

"Thank you, Mr. Ndaye. It's nice to be back. I see you're out making your rounds." She turned to Jasper. "Mr. Ndaye is the Assistant Manager. That's what keeps us old timers coming back to the Norfolk," she said, "the personal touch. Mr. Ndaye, this is Jasper Reijksen, visiting from Rumura."

"Mrs. Simmons, Nwanze told me you mentioned a problem this morning—a matter of receiving some unwanted messages?" Mr Ndaye's voice was concerned.

"Oh, it's really nothing. Whoever it was has probably figured out he's got the wrong person by now. She shouldn't have bothered you about it."

"Nwanze said you sounded distressed."

"Really it was nothing. People are always mixing up my name. I just hope he finally found this Mrs. Simon he was looking for."

Jasper's gaze, which had been wandering around the crowd, snapped back and fixed on Carol. He raised his glass to his lips thoughtfully as Ndaye said goodbye and moved on to the next table. Carol turned back to Jasper and caught him scrutinizing her with apparent interest for a fleeting moment before lapsing back into his habitual distant manner.

"You are receiving messages meant for someone else?" he asked, casually. "What were they about?"

Carol looked at Jasper curiously. He still sounded distracted and bored, but she could sense a glimmering of interest behind it.

"Some kind of a business deal, I think," she said, "A man called me in my room yesterday, looking for a Mrs. Simon. I told him he had the wrong room, but he didn't seem to want to believe me. And then I also started getting these strange cards."

"Strange in what way?"

"Well, they're like business cards, but there's no information—wait, I think I've got one here." Carol pulled the card out of her pocket and held it up. Jasper took and it glanced at it in an off-hand way.

"Singh," he remarked. "Was the caller also Indian?"

"No, he had an African accent," said Carol. "And a very high-pitched voice. I've just been assuming that the phone call and the cards are related—I don't know even that much for sure."

"Have you tried to call the number?"

"No, why should I?" said Carol. She saw no reason to take Jasper into her confidence.

Jasper handed the card back to her.

"I don't want it," she said, and tossed it into the ash tray.

"You don't seem very concerned."

"There's not much I can do about it. Anyway, with any luck they've finally found the person they're looking for or given up. I haven't gotten any more calls or cards since this morning. Oh, there's my ride. Nice chatting with you. Maybe I'll see you in Rumura."

As soon as she was gone, Jasper picked up the card again and slipped it into his shirt pocket. He laid a hundred shilling note under his half-finished glass and left without waiting for his change.

4

Moses, the night clerk, came in to start his shift at ten thirty. He found Koigi sound asleep behind the desk.

"So, you're here," said Koigi grumpily after Moses shook him awake. "You're supposed to come at ten."

"And you're supposed to stay awake. What if the manager sees you?"

"He's in back, drunk as usual. Say, did we have a man named Singh staying here? I had two calls for him tonight. Two *mzungus*—one man and one woman."

"Singh? You're supposed to pass calls for him to room number three. Didn't Alisha tell you?"

"No, nothing."

"Stupid girl, she must have forgotten. I told her to pass the message when you took over."

"Say, I remember the guys staying in number three—they're not Indians."

"So? What business is it of ours?"

"It's just a bit funny, that's all. Well, when they come in, tell them there were two calls."

"Are you crazy? Then they'll just be cross we didn't follow their instructions. Better not to say anything."

A light of understanding dawned in Koigi's eyes. "Say, how much did they pay you?"

"Why should they pay me anything? We're here to take calls, aren't we?"

"I don't believe you. They gave you something. And now you're afraid they'll take it back if they find out what happened."

"You're crazy. Now go on home."

"I can tell them tomorrow that you screwed up and made them miss their calls," said Koigi.

Moses glared at him. "I told you, they didn't pay me anything. But I don't want them to get me in trouble with the manager. Here's a hundred to stop your bloody mouth."

Koigi grinned as he pocketed the money. "Huh—I'll bet they gave you five hundred," he said.

CHAPTER 4

1

Carol was just finishing breakfast on the terrace when a shadow fell on her newspaper. She looked up to see Jasper. His shirt and trousers were even more wrinkled than before and he had taken off the tie.

"Good morning."

"Good morning." Jasper was absentmindedly folding a piece of paper into smaller and smaller squares. His bony face looked even grimmer and harder than usual.

"Bad news?" she asked.

"Pardon?"

"The fax," she said, indicating the wad of paper in his hand.

"No, nothing important," he answered.

Whatever it was, Carol could see that he didn't want to talk about it. She decided not to invite him to sit down. The magazine was better company.

Jasper pulled out the chair across from her and folded himself into it without a word. Carol poured herself some more coffee and spread jam on another piece of toast. Jasper continued to fiddle with the wad of paper while looking at and around her in his usual, distracted way. The waiter came by and Jasper asked for tea. He sat back in his chair and lit a cigarette.

Carol grimaced as the smoke drifted across the table toward her and waved her hand once in front of her face. Jasper noticed and held the cigarette off the edge of the table, blowing the smoke expertly off to one side.

"Have you decided when you will go to Rumura?" he asked.

"I still hope to leave this evening," answered Carol. "I have a few more people to see today, but I think I'll leave the rest until I come back next week."

Jasper nodded and narrowed his eyes in a thoughtful way.

34

"I will take the same flight," he said. The waiter returned and placed a pot of tea, a small metal pitcher of milk and a cup in front of him. .

"So you've been able to finish up your business in Nairobi," said Carol.

"Yes," Jasper answered. He put down the paper and poured out the tea and milk, adding three spoons of sugar. "Everything is taken care of." He took a few sips from the cup, then rose from the table, dropping a few bills beside the cup.

"I will meet you this evening, at the airport," he said.

"Aren't you going to finish your tea?"

"I have to go."

Carol watched him stride quickly off the terrace and out of sight.

'What was that all about?' she wondered. Had he really stopped by just to find out when she was going to Rumura and tell her that he was on the same flight? The prospect left her cold, but at least she could probably escape his company on the plane by hiding out in the non-smoking section.

Carol slipped the newspaper into her briefcase and signed the check. Then her eye fell on the paper that Jasper had left behind. Despite what he had said, she was sure it contained some kind of bad news. Had he meant to discard it, or had he just forgotten it? Feeling guilty, she unfolded the paper and read:

> "*Het spijt me maar ik kan niet komen. Te riskant. Ik hoop dat je nie het niet kwalisk neemt. Celeste.*"

The only thing she could make out was the woman's name at the end.

'Serves me right,' she thought to herself, as she crumpled the paper and tossed it back onto the table.

2

Juma lay on one bed with his eyes half closed and a cigarette dangling in his hand. He raised his arm and opened one eye to look at his wristwatch. He sat up and swung his feet down to the floor.

"Half six," he said. "Time to try again."

David sat on the second bed in the small bedroom, leaning against the wall. He held a deck of cards in his hands, shuffling them, spreading them and snapping them shut again, cutting the deck with one hand, trying to keep the Queen of Hearts on top. Every now and then some cards flipped out of his fingers and fell on the worn bedspread. He picked them up without a word, put them back in the pack, started again. He looked up briefly when Juma spoke.

Juma picked up the receiver and dialed the old-fashioned black telephone. "Good evening, Norfolk Hotel."

Juma cleared his voice and said, in careful English, "Room 321 please."

At the other end of the line the telephone rang three times.

"Werner." The voice was male and elderly, with a heavy German accent.

Juma was startled. "I want Mrs. Simon, please," he said.

The line was quiet for a moment, then the same voice spoke again, more insistently. "Hallo, Werner here."

"Is this room 321? I am looking for Mrs. Simon."

"Yes, correct, 321, but here is Werner. You haf called a wrong number." Juma heard a loud click and found himself listening to the dial tone. Frowning, he dialed the number again.

"Norfolk Hotel."

"I wish to speak with Mrs. Simon, please."

"Do you mean Mrs. Carol Simmons, sir? I am sorry sir, she has checked out."

"What!"

David looked at Juma, the fan of cards frozen in his hands.

"But, where did she go?"

"I beg your pardon, sir?"

"I mean to say, is she coming back?"

"Let me check for you...no, sir, she has made no booking."

Juma slowly replaced the receiver. "She's gone," he said. "Checked out."

"But she was supposed to stay in Nairobi until Wednesday," protested David.

"What happened today?" demanded Juma. "Who did she meet?"

"I don't know," David's tone was defensive. "She went inside some more buildings and I waited outside. She went back to the hotel at about three and I left to come back here. That's it."

"What was I thinking, leaving this to you?" groaned Juma, "I should have followed her myself."

David shrugged. "She didn't meet anybody," he repeated, under his breath.

Juma picked up the receiver again and dialed the hotel operator. "I want to be connected to Kenya Airways," he said, and hung up. A moment later the phone rang and Juma snatched it up.

"Hello, Kenya Airways? Do you have any flight to Rumura this evening?"

David's eyes opened wider. Juma listened, scowled and replaced the receiver. "I thought so," he told David. "There's a flight that leaves at six for Kigali. It makes a stop in Rumura first."

"But she was supposed to stay in Nairobi until Wednesday."

"Well, she changed her mind."

"How do you know? Why didn't you ask if she's booked on that flight?"

"She's got to be on it. Whatever she wanted to do in Nairobi, she's already done it. Or something's happened so she has to go to Rumura early."

"Now what do we do?"

Juma was already pulling on his jacket and heading for the door. "Let's go," he said. "We're going back to Rumura."

3

Flying south from Nairobi, Carol gazed out the window and watched the savanna unfolding beneath her. Rows of tin-roofed houses and plowed fields on the outskirts of the city soon gave way to open bushland dotted with Maasai bomas, their circular thornwood fences like dark necklaces tossed carelessly across a golden brown carpet. The dry grassland was etched with the winding green tracks of small river valleys. She could see herds of cattle and goats, irregular splotches of white, black and brown clearly outlined against the muted background. Much harder to see were the wild animals, whose stripes and lines and countershading melted into the mottled vegetation. She could only spot them when they were moving. Standing still, even the elephants disappeared from view.

By the time they began their descent it was dark. Kobani was visible as a scattering of winking lights across the shadows of the rolling hills. As they got closer to the ground she could see three large, brightly lit buildings which she knew were the Presidential palace, the Parliament and the Intercontinental Hotel.

The plane taxied toward a stop near the small terminal building and the cabin erupted into activity as passengers leaped from their seats to grab their bags and parcels from the overhead compartments. They stood impatiently in the aisles, waiting for the exit ramp to be rolled up and the doors to open.

Carol stayed in her seat, letting the crowd thin out. When she finally stepped out into the warm, humid night air and made her way down the shaky stairs, she was surprised to find Jasper waiting at the bottom. He fell into step with her as they walked across the tarmack to the terminal.

Inside, he was right behind her as they passed through immigration control and stood silently next to her at the baggage carousel. He didn't say anything to her the entire time. Carol thought how much they must have looked like a tired, married couple who no longer had anything to talk about.

The customs official reached out for Jasper's papers as Carol handed him hers.

"We're not together," Carol said firmly.

The official gave a bored shrug, stamped her currency declaration, scribbled a chalk mark on her suitcase and waved her on.

As she stepped outside the terminal, a crowd of taxi drivers and porters surrounded her, fighting for her suitcase.

"Let me drop you," said Jasper's voice behind her. He slung his duffel bag over one shoulder and retrieved her suitcase from the porter who had managed to take possession of it.

"Is that all you have?" Carol asked, looking at his duffel.

"Yes."

Carol wondered what supplies he might have gone all the way to Nairobi to get, and then been able to tuck into such a small bag.

"I have my car here," said Jasper. "I'll be happy to drop you at your hotel."

"Thanks," said Carol a bit uncertainly. "I'm at the Intercon. Are you sure it's not out of your way?"

"No, not at all. My car is just over there. If you will wait here I will bring it." He headed out across the dark parking lot, dodging the ancient taxis.

As Carol waited, a late-model, midnight blue Mercedes-Benz with tinted windows pulled up directly in front of the terminal a few feet away. The driver jumped out and held the back door open for a prosperous-looking, middle-aged African in a well-tailored western suit, who strode out of the terminal without glancing to either side. A statuesque white woman walked beside him, dressed in an elaborately embroidered *kinanga*, which swept from her shoulders to her ankles in a series of complicated folds and gathers. Usually Carol thought these beautiful African dresses looked silly on western women, whose long strides seemed better suited to jeans than to flowing, floor-length skirts. But she had to admit that this woman carried it off well, and her porcelain-white skin and rich, black hair set off the dress' vivid green, red and yellow pattern.

As the driver closed the doors of the Mercedes behind the couple, a porter came up with a handcart loaded with a set of Louis Vitton suitcases. The driver supervised as three young boys rushed forward to load them into the car's spacious trunk. Dropping a few coins into their outstretched hands, he slammed the trunk shut and pulled smoothly away as the boys counted their take.

Jasper's car turned out to be a battered, 2-door Suzuki jeep, painted dark green. Stenciled in white paint on each side was a stylized silhouette of a long-legged chimpanzee, framed by a circle of words reading "Mali-Kuli Primate Research Project" above and "Eastern Colorado University" below. The back door was covered with decals of international conservation groups. Carol guessed that these must be the groups that had donated money to the project.

Jasper opened the back door of the jeep and laid Carol's suitcase on top of a worn spare tire which took up most of the floor of the compartment. He reached for her briefcase.

"No, thanks, I'll hang on to it."

Jasper slammed the door hard to make it catch. He unlocked the passenger side and walked around to the driver's side. Carol climbed somewhat clumsily up into the jeep.

"Who was that getting into the big blue Mercedes?" she shouted over the roar of the Suzuki's engine as they left the airport.

Jasper shook his head.

"Very distinguished looking man," Carol added. "An African, with a *mzungu* wife. At least, I guess it was his wife. She was very pretty—dressed in a *kinanga.*"

"I didn't see them," said Jasper.

"The car had blue license plates, with white numbers. Doesn't that mean a government car?"

Jasper nodded.

"How many couples like that could there be in Rumura?" asked Carol.

Jasper shrugged and Carol gave up the effort at conversation. They rode the rest of the way into Kobani in silence and finally pulled into the long, semi-circular driveway of the Intercontinental Hotel. Jasper jumped out and opened the back of the jeep to hand Carol's suitcase to the doorman. He walked over to where she stood by the door and gave her a brisk, business-like handshake.

"Good night, then," he said abruptly, and immediately turned away. He climbed back into the car and pulled away.

"Good night, and...thanks again," she called after him, feeling a bit foolish. He certainly was peculiar.

Like many African countries, Rumura had been gradually sliding into disrepair since independence. The Intercontinental had once been an elegant hotel, a costly showpiece intended to demonstrate that Rumura could hold its own against any country in the region. Now the bright lights of its lobby exposed the rough edges of neglect, from the worn carpets to the sagging curtains and old-fashioned furniture. Nevertheless, as Carol went through the familiar routine of filling out the registration card, she felt the relief of a voyager arriving at last in the harbor. Remembering the layout of the hotel from her earlier visit, she asked for a garden room, near the swimming pool.

The receptionist glanced at the card. "One moment, please Mrs. Simmons," he said. "I believe there is a message for you."

A knot formed in Carol's stomach as he handed her a sealed white envelope. Something must have shown in her face because she saw him looking at her curiously. 'Don't be so paranoid,' she scolded herself. Still, she was relieved to see that the envelope was addressed to 'Ms. Carol Simmons.' She tore it open and read the note inside:

"Welcome to Rumura! Can you come for dinner tomorrow night? Meet Jonathan at the Embassy at 5:30 and come home with him. Everyone's dying to see you. Cheerio, Pat."

"Is everything fine, madam?" asked the receptionist.
"Yes, just fine," she said, with a relieved smile.

CHAPTER 5

1

Carol handed her business card to the young woman behind the desk and took a seat on the sagging velveteen sofa in the waiting room. She was pleasantly surprised to find that the Minister was in, and that his secretary knew about her appointment. She was even more surprised when she was ushered into the Minister's office after only fifteen minutes of waiting.

The Honorable Ignatius Kulibani, Minister of Forests and Environment, was a big, bulky man with mocha-colored skin, a long, rubbery face and a heavy, square jaw. Despite the heat, he was dressed in a dark, pinstriped woolen suit. He rose to meet Carol as she came into the room.

"Good morning, Mr. Minister," said Carol.

"Good morning, Mrs...Simmons," he said, consulting the card his secretary had handed him. He motioned for her to sit down in a high-backed armchair and settled himself in another across a low coffee table. An electric fan propped in the window drew in hot air from the outside and stirred it around in the room.

"I must apologize. The air conditioning is out of order." Like many high-level African officials, the Minister's English suggested a stint at a solid British public school. They exchanged small talk about the heat and about Carol's journey. When he learned that she lived in Washington, he requested her to pass his greetings to George Bush, whom he had once met at a diplomatic function.

The secretary returned with a tea tray and poured out two cups of sweet, milky tea. "Your meeting with the President is at eleven, Minister," she reminded him as she was leaving.

Kulibani nodded briefly in her direction and then looked at Carol.

43

"I appreciate your agreeing to see me, Mr. Minister," said Carol. "I'll try not to take up too much of your time."

"Not at all. I am acquainted with the Schooley Foundation, and with your organization's project in Mwatumi. What is it I can do for you?"

Carol explained that she had come to look into some complaints and criticisms the Schooley Foundation had received about the Mwatumi project.

"What sort of criticisms? Something to do with the finances? I seem to remember hearing some rumors about that myself."

"I'm sure we'll be able to straighten out that aspect. What I wanted to ask you about is some concern that's been raised about the environmental impacts of the project. There have been allegations that the project is causing the destruction of a tropical rain forest—in a Forest Reserve. That would fall under your mandate, wouldn't it, Mr. Minister?"

"Yes, certainly. The Forest Department is within my ministry. But I can set your mind at ease, Mrs. Simmons. There is no truth in these allegations."

"I'm very glad to hear that, of course. But maybe you could give me a bit more information? Why would someone have made these accusations if they aren't true?"

Kulibani sighed as he set his teacup on the table and settled back in his chair, crossing his legs. "The fact is, Mrs. Simmons, this is an accusation we in the developing countries hear all the time. We have growing rural populations who need land to grow food and fuelwood to cook it. We don't have the luxury to set aside all of our forests for nature conservation, like the West seems to want us to do. Some of these resources must be used to meet the needs of our people. But we do also recognize the importance of maintaining some areas as forest reserves. You may report to the Schooley Foundation that the project in Mwatumi is in fact helping us to preserve the Mali-Kuli Forest Reserve, by allowing the local community to cultivate their own

44

land more intensively and sustainably. In this way, they are no longer forced to encroach into the Reserve to clear new land."

"But is it possible that some people are actually using our support to expand their cultivation inside the Reserve?"

"That is not the case," said the Minister. "The cultivation is all strictly outside the forest. But, have you met Dr. Thadeus Maleke, the Director of the Forest Department? No? You should certainly meet with him. And perhaps if you have time, I am sure that Dr. Maleke will be pleased to arrange a trip to the area for you to see the situation for yourself."

"I certainly do plan to go to Mwatumi," said Carol. "And of course I would like to meet with Dr. Maleke."

"My secretary can set an appointment for you."

"Thank you, Mr. Minister. There was just one other thing I wanted to ask you about. There's been a suggestion that our project is stimulating plans to build an ecologically destructive road through the forest reserve."

"That is also quite untrue," said Kulibani. "But again, I think it will be best for you to discuss the matter with Dr. Maleke. He can answer your questions much better than I can. Now I am afraid, I must ask you to excuse me. Our President is not quite so easy-going as I remember Mr. George Bush to be. He does not like to be kept waiting."

2

As the old Peugot rattled down the road, Juma leaned back in the front passenger seat and tossed the stub of his cigarette out the window. In the back, David stretched out his long legs and tried to get comfortable. It was late afternoon but still very hot.

"We were lucky to get here today at all," complained Juma. "We had to go from Nairobi all the way down to Burundi to get a flight back here. Cost me plenty. Why didn't you tell us she'd changed her travel plans?"

In the driver's seat, Muna Rabukoko took her eyes off the road to glare at him. "How could I tell you when I didn't know myself?" she demanded. "She didn't book the change through us."

"I thought you could get the information through your computer," said Juma.

"Not if she changes her ticket at the airport at the last minute," answered Muna. "By the time it came up on the computer it would have been too late to tell you. Anyway, what's the difference? You're here aren't you?"

"The difference is she's had all day here in Kobani while we were stuck in bloody Bujumbura. Who knows what she's been up to?"

"Well, why didn't you get on the same flight with her? It wasn't full—I checked."

"We were going to—we even went to the airport..." began David, leaning forward to join in the conversation.

Juma looked sharply over his shoulder and shot a frown at David, who immediately fell silent and slouched back onto the seat.

"So?" Muna prodded.

"Nothing," said Juma. "Don't pay any attention to him. It's got nothing to do with you anyway."

Muna snorted and pushed the gas pedal to the floor, straining the Peugeot to pass a dawdling pickup truck.

"So where are we going?" asked Muna.

"My place," said Juma. "You can drop us there."

3

Somehow, Carol wasn't surprised to see Jasper's green jeep in the parking lot when she returned to the hotel at five o'clock. She had come to think of him as the proverbial bad penny, always turning up. As she collected her key at the front desk, she heard loud music and laughter spilling through the doors of the Volcano Bar. From five to eight each evening, the bar played pirated music videos and accepted local currency, attracting a boisterous crowd of Kobani's young elite. She guessed that Jasper must be inside somewhere, conducting sociological research over peanuts and beer.

After a quick shower, Carol walked the few blocks from the hotel to the American Embassy. The gate was guarded by a fresh-faced young Marine, who glanced inside her handbag and waved her through. In the entrance lobby another Marine politely examined her identification from behind a window of bullet-proof glass and asked whether she had an appointment.

"Yes, with Jonathan Marshall," answered Carol. "He's expecting me at 5:30."

"Okay, ma'am," said the Marine, returning her passport. "Please sit down and I'll let him know you're here."

Carol heard Jonathan before she saw him, issuing instructions to someone on the other side of the door in an irritated tone. Then the door opened and he came halfway out, then stopped to call back over his shoulder, "...and tell Washington I need it on my desk first thing in the morning, before I go to see the Police Commissioner," he was saying. "How am I supposed to sort things like this out if I can't get even the most basic information?"

"Hi, Jonathan," said Carol.

"Carol! Great to see you. I hope you haven't been waiting long."

"Nope, just got here."

They embraced awkwardly, both feeling the changes and the distance that had grown between them over the years. Jonathan's hair had retreated from his forehead and gone gray around the temples and he had put on some weight, but he was still solid and athletic, thanks to a strict regimen of morning runs and weekends on the tennis court. But what Carol noticed most about him was the well-tailored suit, the business-like way he carried his heavy briefcase and his cool nod to the Marine as they left. Even in their old, free-wheeling Peace Corps days, she

47

had always suspected that he carried the seeds of a bureaucrat within him.

They walked out into the parking lot and climbed into Jonathan's silver Land Cruiser.

"We have a driver for Pat and the kids, but I like to drive myself," said Jonathan, as he pulled out onto the main road.

"Pat's filled me in a bit on what you're doing here in Rumura," said Jonathan a short while later. "If you don't mind my saying so, I'm a bit surprised you didn't alert us at the Embassy officially about your visit."

"Really? I don't normally do that anywhere I go. You know, we're not funded by the U.S. government."

"Maybe not, but Schooley is a well-known American foundation. If any problems come up, of the kind I understand you're looking into, we're the ones that have to deal with them."

"Deal with them how?"

"Smooth things over with the government...answer questions from the press...things like that. It just makes sense to keep us informed so we're not caught unprepared."

"As far as I know, there's nothing to smooth over, and I certainly hope there won't be anything coming out in the papers," said Carol. "This is supposed to be a very low-profile visit."

"But you went to see the Minister this morning, didn't you? Kulibani?"

"How did you know that?"

"I got a call from Thadeus Maleke, Director of the Forest Department. Seems the Minister's office called him to set up an appointment for you."

"That's right, but his office said he wasn't in. They said I might be able to see him tomorrow morning. But why would he call you?"

"To check you out. He gets a lot of people from American and European environmental organizations through his office, a lot of them looking to make trouble. So he wanted some background on who you are and what you're doing here."

"What did you tell him?" Carol asked uncomfortably.

"Just that I knew you, that you're a friend of Pat's and mine, and that your organization is legitimate. I suggested that he should go ahead and meet you."

"That's all?"

"If you're worried that I passed on what you told Pat, about the accusations being made against the project, I didn't. I figured that's your business. Anyway, officially speaking, I don't even know why you're here. But it would be a good idea if you filled me in a bit. I might be able to help, you know. For example, who was this fellow you talked to in Nairobi—the one who wrote to Mahoney? If he's from Rumura, I might be able to give you a low-down on him."

"I'm sorry, but I really can't tell you that right now, Jonathan."

"I see."

"Only because we've promised to keep his identity a secret for now," she explained quickly. "But other than that, I really would welcome your advice. At this point I'm not quite sure who I should be talking to about what."

"Everybody's a suspect, right? You don't know who might be mixed up in what. Particularly when it comes to people in the government."

"That's about it."

"Well, you're going to have to confide in some people, otherwise you're not going to learn anything. Thadeus Maleke would be a good person to level with. He's honest, he's well-connected, and you can trust him to give you the straight scoop. Pretty unusual combination around here."

"I'll keep that in mind," said Carol. "I hope to see him tomorrow morning before I leave for Mwatumi."

Jonathan turned off the paved main road and they bounced along a washboard dirt road for about a mile. On both sides, behind the high stone walls, Carol could glimpse spacious houses set in elegant gardens. The suburb was originally built to house colonial officials. It was now an enclave of diplomats, wealthy businessmen and high-level government officials, many of whom would have had some trouble explaining how they were able to afford the houses on their government salaries.

Jonathan pulled up in front of a tall, wrought iron gate and gave a short tap on the horn. The uniformed guard hurried to open the gate and gave him a snappy salute as they drove through. The garden was lush and rich, blazing with bougainvillea, flamboyants and frangipani trees and beds of richly colored flowers. The house itself was shaded by jacaranda trees and had a screened veranda running along two sides.

"This country is amazing," said Jonathan, in response to Carol's compliments on the garden. "You can put a dry stick in the ground and a week later it's a tree."

There were already two cars parked at the end of the driveway in front of the house. Carol recognized the Mali-Kuli primate project's logo on the door of a green Suzuki jeep that looked a bit newer than Jasper's. The other car was a small, somewhat battered white Renault.

"Looks like you've got some other company," remarked Carol. "Is that Jasper Reijksen's jeep?"

"Who?" asked Jonathan. "No, it belongs to Greg Allen and his wife Lisa. They're friends of Pat's. I don't know who the other car belongs to. Pat's always picking up strays and bringing them home for dinner."

Carol sensed that Jonathan was not entirely happy to find that dinner seemed to be turning into a dinner party. She imagined that he liked his social engagements planned well in advance, and preferably with other respectable diplomats, just as Neil seemed to have developed a preference for catered dinners with tenured professors and department heads over potlucks with graduate students and junior faculty. She could imagine Neil complaining to a friend that his wife tended to 'pick up strays.'

As she climbed down from the high seat of the Land Cruiser, two black Labrador Retrievers came running up to her, baying with excitement. They nuzzled her hands and swung their thick tails eagerly back and forth.

"Great watchdogs," laughed Carol.

"They make a lot of noise—that's what counts," said Jonathan. "We don't want vicious dogs with the kids around. We brought these two back with us from the States last year. Our old spaniel died soon after we got here—someone threw poisoned meat over the wall."

"That's terrible," said Carol. "The kids must have been heartbroken."

Jonathan shrugged. "It's a bad idea to get too attached to dogs in Africa. They're always getting poisoned or killed by snakes or something. Some friends of ours in Kenya had their dog eaten by a leopard. It came out of Nairobi National Park right into their garden. Well, let's go in and see who's coming for dinner."

The house was spacious and airy, with polished wooden floors and sleek modern furniture. The walls and bookshelves were filled with artifacts from Latin America, Asia and Africa, from delicate silk wall hangings and painted porcelain bowls to an enormous drum made from a roughly carved tree trunk and covered with spotted goatskin. On one side of the living room large sliding glass doors opened onto the garden.

Pat and the others were outside, half hidden in tall wicker armchairs at the far end of the long veranda. A couple was sitting side by side on the sofa with their legs pressed cosily together. The man was about forty, broad-chested and muscular with thick, curly, strawberry blond hair and a dense, reddish gold beard and matching fur on his arms. The woman seemed to be at least ten years younger, a tall, slender-waisted African with very dark skin and full, wine-colored lips. She wore her hair in thin, tight braids pulled together into a ponytail at the back. The fourth person in the group was also somewhere in his forties, with straight brown hair beginning to recede from his forehead. He was talking animatedly and gesturing with his free hand.

"Well, here they are, finally," said Pat. "Everybody, this is Carol Simmons, my old and dear friend from the Peace Corps, about a hundred years ago."

The two men started struggling to pull themselves out of the deep cushions.

"Please, don't anyone get up," said Carol. "You all look so comfortable."

While Jonathan went to change, Carol sat down and accepted a Margarita. Pat introduced Greg Allen and Lisa Othieno to Carol. "You remember, Carol, I told you about their research camp. Lisa is from Kenya, originally."

Carol guessed immediately that Lisa had been Greg's graduate student before becoming his wife. Inevitably, it made her think of Camilla and Neil.

"And I am Thor Nilssen." Thor stretched forward to extend his hand over the coffee table. He had a Scandinavian accent, pronouncing his name with a hard "T" and a long "o" and an upward lilt at the end.

"You might have seen Thor on the plane, Carol," said Pat. "You came in on the same flight from Nairobi."

"Pleased to meet you, Thor." Carol tried to pronounce his name the same way he did, without making it sound like she was mimicking his accent. "Are you Norwegian?" she guessed, thinking that ironically it was Greg and not Thor who looked like a Viking.

"Yes, that's correct."

"Thor is a journalist," said Pat. "I met him today at the French cultural center and he was so charming that I just had to invite him to dinner."

"Who do you write for?" asked Carol.

"I am what you would call a 'freelance,'" he answered. "Sometimes I receive assignments for articles. Other times I write them and then try to sell them."

"What do you write about?"

"Anything interesting that I come across. To be honest, it is really only a way of paying for my travels."

"Well, there's always something going on in Africa."

"But I don't write about wars and famines. I try to write the stories of the people I meet, how they live from day to day."

"Thor was telling us about an article he's just finishing up," said Pat. She turned to him with a smile, inviting him to continue. He went on with a description of a burial party he had recently attended in Madagascar, where the deceased was the guest of honor.

"It is a wonderful celebration. The family digs up the beloved relative after a few years and throws a big party for him. They dance and feast, and he sits at the table with his plate loaded with food. Then they wrap him again in a brand new burial cloth and put him back into his grave for another few years. The Malagasy believe that simply because somebody is dead, it doesn't mean he can't have a good time."

"I'll drink to that!" said Greg.

"Do the Malagasy worship their ancestors, like the Shintos in Japan?" asked Carol.

"Perhaps not quite the same," answered Thor. "But they do believe the dead play an active role in the lives of the living. And the forest is sacred as the sanctuary of their spirits. They call it the "cloak of the ancestors.""

"The people around the Mali-Kuli forest used to believe something like that too," said Lisa, "but now that is changing. They're losing the old taboos that once protected the trees and animals. Most of the local people would probably like to see the whole forest cut down. All but the Pygmies."

"I didn't even know there were Pygmies in Rumura," said Carol. "I'd love to see one."

"There are a few left in and around the forest," said Lisa. "They rarely come out except to trade with the villagers, who are always cheating them. They are very poor and everyone discriminates against them. If someone tries to help them, the village people become quite annoyed."

"Like that priest who was running the mission near Mwatumi," said Greg. "He was trying to do something for the Pygmies—start up a school, get them a bit of land, that kind of thing. He wound up getting run out of town."

"I heard he got a girl pregnant, and then fled the country," said Jonathan.

"That was probably a frame-up," said Greg. "The baby turned out to be pretty light-skinned, but there are other white guys and Asians in Rumura, you know."

There certainly are," said Lisa pointedly.

Greg grinned and put his arm around her shoulder, sqeezing her against his side before letting her go again. "Someone was just using it as an excuse to get rid of him. It's too bad—I'm not big on missionaries in general, but Father Loretto was okay."

"I don't know about that," said Jonathan. "If it was a frame-up, why didn't the Church authorities defend him instead of just spiriting him out of the country?"

"If you ask me, it's because he knew too much," said Greg darkly. "Somebody big probably told the Bishop to stay out of it. I've always wondered whatever happened to the good Father."

"He's in Nairobi," said Carol.

Everyone looked at her in surprise.

"I happened to meet him at the WCA office," Carol explained.

"So that's who it was!" exclaimed Jonathan.

"Who what was?" asked Greg.

Carol shot Jonathan a frown.

"Oh, nothing," said Jonathan, lifting his eyebrows back at her slightly. "I saw someone on the street when I was in Nairobi a few days ago, and I couldn't place him. I just realized it was this priest—you remember, the newspaper ran a photo of him."

"Greg, what is it you think the priest knew too much about?" asked Thor.

"Poaching and smuggling," said Greg promptly.

"Do you mean gold?"

"I wouldn't be surprised, and maybe drugs and guns, too. But I'm mainly concerned about the poaching—ivory, cat skins, birds...that kind of thing. There's a steady stream coming in across the border from the DRC, and stolen cars and illegal logs going the other way. It all goes through the forest."

"You don't really know that's all true, Greg," said Lisa uncomfortably.

"Of course it's true—everyone in town knows it. What you mean is, I shouldn't be talking about it. But why not? We're all friends here, right? Anyway, I'll bet the U.S. Embassy already knows all about it. Isn't that right Jonathan? Unofficially, that is?"

Jonathan was saved from answering by the arrival of the houseboy, announcing that dinner was ready. Thor gave Carol a hand to get out of the deep chair.

Greg stood up and stretched luxuriously. Carol glanced appreciatively at the way his T-shirt strained across his broad chest and shoulders and outlined his washboard belly before tucking neatly into the narrow waist of his faded Levi's. With the sun setting behind him, his curls glowed like gold shavings, setting off his deeply tanned face and startling blue eyes.

Standing next to him, Thor suffered somewhat in comparison. He was a head shorter and there was the hint of a paunch above the belt of his rumpled khaki trousers. But, Carol observed, his straight back and squared shoulders made the most of his five feet eight inches, and his face was strong and intelligent, with warm brown eyes. 'All in all,' thought Carol, remembering a saying from her college days, 'I wouldn't kick him out of bed.'

Thor turned and looked at her with a quizzical expression. She felt a quick flush of embarrassment, sure that somehow he knew what she was thinking. At the same time she suddenly became very conscious of Lisa standing beside her, slender and graceful and looking very young in her cut-off jeans and leotard top. Carol felt chunky and awkward and very middle aged by contrast. As her eyes met Thor's she blushed, thinking that he must have been making some comparisons of his own. He gave her an ironic but friendly smile and, despite her embarrassment, she found herself smiling back.

55

"I'll be right with you," said Greg, "I just have to check in with the office." He pulled a two-way radio out of a holster on his belt and went off towards the back yard as the others headed for the dining room.

Thor fell into step beside Carol. "I am anticipating an all-American dinner," he said. "A lettuce salad, a large and bloody steak and French fries. Would you like to make a bet?"

Carol shook her head. "No bet," she said. "Except maybe baked potatoes instead of French fries."

"Anyway, it will make a change from fish stew and rice."

"Your English is excellent," Carol said as they sat down at the table. Pat seated them side by side facing a picture window looking out over the back garden. "Have you spent a lot of time in the States?"

"On and off," he answered. "I spent a few years at the university in Berkeley many years ago and sometimes I write for American magazines. My ex-wife is also an American."

Through the window Carol could see Greg standing out on the back lawn, alternately talking into the radio and holding it up to his ear to listen.

"Where is this office Greg's trying to call?" she asked Lisa.

"That's his idea of a joke," said Lisa. "He is trying to get the Embassy to patch him through to Nairobi, to the African Wildlife Foundation office."

"Why is that?" asked Thor, with a journalist's immediate interest.

Lisa started to answer, and then checked herself. She picked up her glass and sipped it casually.

"We just like to stay in touch," she said. "It's not easy to keep up with the news out at Mick-Pick. We're so isolated."

"Mick-pick?"

"That's our nickname for the research station. It comes from Mali-Kuli Primate Center. You know, M-K-P-C."

"Where is it exactly?" asked Thor.

"It's in the forest, about twenty kilometers west of a village called Mwatumi. Twenty long kilometers on old logging roads.

It takes about an hour and in the rainy season you can't get there without a four wheel drive. We love it."

"Did Pat tell you that my organization is supporting a project in Mwatumi?" Carol asked Lisa. "It's a women's horticultural cooperative, called Mwatumi Greengoods. We've set up a revolving loan fund so they can buy tools and seeds and fertilizers to grow market vegetables."

"Can only women borrow from this fund?" asked Thor.

"That's right," said Carol. "That's the whole purpose behind the 'Women's Coalition for Action.'"

"Now *that's* sexist," put in Jonathan.

"Absolutely," said Carol. "It's a sexist world, and we're just trying to level out the playing field a bit. In most developing countries women are treated as minors under the law. Like here in Rumura—legally, women aren't even allowed to take loans under their own names. They have to get their husband or father or brother to co-sign."

"Then how is it possible for WCA to make loans to women in Mwatumi?" asked Thor.

Carol explained that WCA's policy was to support organized women's groups that were legally registered with the government. This gave them the legal status to borrow money as a group, rather than as individuals.

"And it also makes it possible for them to hang onto the money they earn," she added. "The problem with a lot of development projects is that the women wind up doing all the work to earn money, but once they take the money home, they have to hand it over to their husbands. But in this case the profits belong to the cooperative as a whole, so no individual member's husband can get his hands on it to spend on beer and prostitutes."

"That's a bit hard on African men, isn't it?" objected Jonathan. "They're not all boozers and spendthrifts."

"Of course not. But the people who set the WCA policy obviously see it as a problem, and they should know—they're all women from developing countries."

The cook emerged from the kitchen carrying a tray loaded with glass bowls of tossed salad. Thor nudged Carol with his elbow, surreptitiously pointing to the salad and holding up the steak knife that lay beside his plate. Carol smiled back at him, just as Greg arrived and took his seat at the table.

"Did you get through?" asked Lisa.

"Yeah, but the signal was very weak," he answered, gathering up a generous forkful of salad.

"Was there any news?" asked Thor.

Greg glanced quickly at Lisa, who shook her head almost imperceptibly.

"Nothing much," said Greg gruffly as he pushed the mound of lettuce and tomato into his mouth.

The cook reappeared with a heavy platter of thick steaks and baked potatoes, which he placed in the center of the table. Carol nudged Thor and made an invisible mark in the air in front of her: 'score one for me.' He accepted defeat with a smile.

Lisa turned to Carol. "I'm glad to have a chance to meet you, because I think you should know that this project of yours is helping to create a very big problem."

"What do you mean?" asked Carol.

Lisa told her the same thing she had heard from Father Loretto, that the women from the cooperative were clearing land in the forest to plant vegetables. She also described the plan to upgrade the road from Bola to Mwatumi and extend it to the town of Rendesha on the Congo border, cutting across the southern end of the forest reserve on the way.

"The Mwatumi villagers want the road because it would put them right on the main trading route to Zaire, and they think they could sell all those vegetables they're going to be growing through your project to the truckers passing through. But it would be a disaster for the forest."

"You'd have huge diesel trucks going back and forth on it all day," added Greg, "scaring the animals and running them over. And it would make it that much easier to smuggle timber out of the Reserve."

58

"So, in your opinion, the people of Mwatumi should stay isolated and poor forever," said Jonathan.

"Of course not, but there are alternatives," countered Greg. "They could build the road direct from Bola to Rendesha, bypassing the forest, and run a trunk road up to Mwatumi. It would even be cheaper that way. The problem is, they *want* the road to pass through the forest."

"Who does?" asked Thor.

"Kulibani, Maleke, you name it. They're all in it up to their eyeballs."

"Just between us, I won't argue with you about the Minister," said Jonathan. "But you're wrong about Thadeus Maleke."

"That's exactly why Maleke is even more dangerous than Kulibani himself," said Greg. "He's got all you diplomats eating out of his hands."

"There's a *dudu* in that mango for sure," agreed Lisa.

"What's that?" asked Carol.

"A *dudu* in the mango. It's a local expression, meaning that someone is not what he seems to be. When I was at school in America, they used to say 'a worm in the apple.' Bugs are called *dudus* here, just like in Kenya. The saying comes from the mango weevil. It lays its eggs under the skin of the green mango fruit and the larva develops inside. When the mango becomes ripe, from the outside it looks smooth and perfect. But when you cut it open, inside you find a slimy, stinking mess."

"That's Maleke," said Greg, "smooth and perfect on the outside, slimy on the inside."

"It would be better not to go around spreading these kinds of rumors unless you've got some kind of proof," said Jonathan.

"Where do you suppose Maleke got the money for that big house and that flashy car?" demanded Greg.

"Not that it's any of your business, but I believe his wife comes from a rich family," said Jonathan archly.

"Wake up, Jonathan," said Greg. "The man's got you completely snowed."

"All right, that's enough, you two," said Pat. "Let's talk about something else."

"You said you're meeting Thadeus tomorrow, before heading up to Mwatumi." Jonathan said to Carol, "So you can judge for yourself. Just keep an open mind."

"If you're going to Mwatumi, why don't you come and visit Mick-Pick?" suggested Lisa. "We can show you around the forest, so you can see for yourself what's going on. And you can also go and see the bonobos—the pygmy chimpanzees. We've got a couple of groups that we're trying to habituate for tourists, as they've done with the mountain gorillas in Rwanda and DRC and Uganda."

Greg looked sharply at Lisa, then went back to sawing at his steak without a word.

"I'd love to," said Carol. "But I don't know exactly when I could arrange it. I think Dr. Maleke is supposed to make arrangements for me to visit the forest."

"Then you absolutely must come to visit us," said Lisa. "He won't show you anything. How are you coming to Mwatumi? Do you have a car?"

"No, I was planning to book one through the hotel."

"I could take you," suggested Thor. "My friend has lent me his house and his car while he is in Norway for the month."

Again Greg looked up from his steak, first at Lisa and then at Thor. His expression was unmistakably disapproving.

"You're going to Mwatumi, too?" he asked.

"I was thinking perhaps I would," said Thor.

"We're pretty full up at the research station right now," said Greg. "We don't have a lot of room for visitors."

An awkward silence fell over the table. Everyone seemed relieved when Pat suggested that they go to the living room for coffee. Sitting together on the sofa, Lisa and Carol made plans for Greg to pick Carol up at the hotel in Mwatumi on Saturday morning to take her to the research station.

"You can always radio us from the Acropolis hotel if you change your mind," said Lisa.

Carol stifled a yawn. "I'm afraid I'm still a bit jet-lagged," she apologized. "I think I'd better call it a night."

Thor offered her a lift back to the hotel, which he insisted was directly on his way. As they started up the dark driveway, Carol glanced backwards to see Greg and Lisa coming out of the house and pausing on the front steps to watch them leave. There was no mistaking the scowl that darkened Greg's face as he looked after them.

4

David Wangeru sat at a table beside the small dance floor, watching the couples sway and sweat to the lively *Lingala* beat. The club had only four records, which the disk jockey played over and over, sometimes varying the order of the songs to keep things interesting. The dancers, lost in the pleasure of movement, hardly noticed as long as the music kept playing. They stayed out on the floor as one song blended into another, practicing their moves in the long mirrors lining the walls.

David swayed to the rhythm and looked longingly at the girls clustered around the bar. There was one in particular, with long legs and high, firm buttocks barely covered by a white miniskirt. He wanted to ask her to dance, but he didn't even have enough money to buy another beer for himself. The girls could always tell who had money and who didn't. Clothes were only part of it; it was also the way a man moved and talked and looked at people when he had money in his pocket. Some, like Juma, had no money yet but were so sure they would be rich someday that they felt it in their guts and acted like rich men, so that others treated them the same way. It was this confidence that had drawn David to Juma, leading him to take orders from the smaller man and to swallow his patronizing attitude and his insults. Juma was going to be rich and powerful someday, and his friends would share in that wealth and power.

The deal they were working on now was just the beginning. Soon David would have enough money to swagger into a place like this and take his pick. The same eyes that now looked disdainfully away from him would seek him out, hopeful and inviting. The girls would work their way across the floor to dance in front of him, swaying and striking provocative poses. They would sit down at his table and lean forward, enticing him with the deep shadows between their pushed-up breasts. He would let them dance and pout and compete with each other, and then he would choose one. A different one every night.

Lost in his reverie, David didn't notice Juma until he swatted him on the shoulder.

"Hey, what's with you?" Juma leaned down to make himself heard over the music. "Didn't you see me at the door?"

David shook his head to clear it.

"Come on, let's go. We can't talk here." Juma turned and headed for the exit without looking back.

David drained his beer and followed after him regretfully. In the street outside the club, Juma was pacing in an agitated way and devouring his cigarette in short, impatient puffs.

"I don't like it," said Juma.

David said nothing, wondering what he had done wrong this time.

"Everywhere she goes, there he is. In Nairobi, on the airplane, at the hotel...he sticks with her like mud on a pig."

David nodded, relieved that he was in the clear.

"I've had to be on guard all the time so he doesn't spot us. We came that close to getting on that bloody plane with him in Nairobi." Juma held up his hand with a gap between the thumb and forefinger illustrating just how close.

"What would have been so bad if he'd seen us?" asked David.

"Stupid. He would have wanted to know why we were in Nairobi."

"We could have made something up."

"Like what? Anyway, he would have been suspicious," said Juma. "We can't afford that right now. We need more time."

"How much more time?" complained David. His resentment at being pulled out of the club made him reckless. "This is taking too long."

"You're right."

David looked at him with surprise.

"We've waited long enough," said Juma. "Tonight's the night."

CHAPTER 6

1

The dim yellow circles cast by the headlights were hardly brighter than the pale moonlight washing across the road. Thor did his best to swerve around the potholes, while Carol let her body relax to the swaying of the old car.

"Am I mistaken," Thor asked thoughtfully, "or did Greg specifically *not* invite me to visit the research station?"

"It did seem like it," Carol admitted, remembering Greg's abruptness and the expression on his face as he watched them leave. "What was the problem between you two?"

"I don't know," said Thor. "I must have offended him in some way."

"I didn't notice you doing anything wrong."

"He did seem annoyed when I asked about the news from Nairobi, didn't you think?"

"But that was a perfectly innocent question. If you hadn't asked someone else would have."

"I suppose some people are simply suspicious of journalists. It's a pity. The research camp sounds very interesting."

He sank into a glum silence.

"Maybe he'll change his mind," said Carol sympathetically. "I could talk to Pat tomorrow and see if she can do something."

"I wouldn't want to place you in an awkward position..."

"It can't hurt to ask. Pat won't mind, and she can always say no."

"Well, if you are sure...thank you very much."

When they arrived at the hotel, Carol noticed with some surprise that Jasper's car was still in the parking lot. As they approached the entrance, she saw a crowd of elegantly dressed African men and women streaming inside. Thor pulled the car into a parking space near the door.

"Here we are," he said. He turned off the engine, turned to Carol and smiled. He really did have a very nice smile, she decided. "I will just come in to check whether I have any messages. I've arranged to receive them here."

Together they walked in through the revolving door and went up to the reception desk.

"Good evening, Theresa," said Thor. "Any message for me?"

"No, Mr. Nilssen, I am sorry, there is nothing," the young woman behind the desk replied with a flash of very white teeth. It was clear that Thor was popular here. "But I believe there is a letter for you, madam." She reached into the wall of cubbyholes behind her and pulled out Carol's room key and a small white envelope.

Carol looked at it and gave a small gasp.

"What's wrong?" asked Thor.

"I don't believe it," she exclaimed. "Look at this!"

She pointed to the name 'Mrs. Simon' handwritten on the front of the envelope.

"Is that how you spell your name?" asked Thor.

"No, my name is *Simmons*," said Carol, angrily. "With two "m"s."

"Oh, I see. A mistake." He looked at her curiously.

"You don't understand," said Carol. "This started in Nairobi two days ago. He must have followed me here to Rumura now!"

"Who?" asked Thor, bewildered.

"I don't know. I got a phone call in Nairobi—a man with an African accent. He seems to have me mixed up with someone named Mrs. Simon. I told him he had the wrong person, but he just won't quit."

"He called you again?"

"No, he started to leave these cards. Or someone did."

"Which cards?"

Carol tore open the envelope and reached inside.

"I thought so," she said. "This is getting ridiculous." She pulled out the crude business card and handed it to Thor distastefully.

"'V.J. Singh, Export and Import'," he read aloud. "'Welcome to Rumura'. This is strange. No address and no telephone number. Who is V.J. Singh?"

"I have no idea," said Carol grimly. "But this is the third one I've gotten. It's really starting to get to me."

"Maybe somebody is playing a joke." Thor suggested.

"Who would follow me all the way from Nairobi to play a stupid joke?" asked Carol, sharply. A few people in the lobby turned to look at her. Thor rested his hand briefly on her arm and turned back to the receptionist.

"Theresa," he said. "Do you remember who left this message for Mrs. Simmons?"

The receptionist had been listening and watching with concern. "I am sorry, Mr. Nilssen," she said. "It was left here at the counter. I put it in Mrs. Simmon's box because there is nobody named Simon who is staying with us. I am too sorry if that was not correct."

"Never mind, it's not your fault. But if there are any other messages for Mrs. Simon, please try to find out who leaves them." He turned back to Carol. "Perhaps you should change to another room."

Carol sighed. "I'm shouldn't be so paranoid—it's probably all just a silly coincidence. Anyway, it's late and I'm tired, and I'll only be here one more night. I think I'll just go to bed."

"Well, if you're sure. But fasten the chain on your door, and don't let anyone in," said Thor. He reached into his shirt pocket and pulled out a small spiral notebook and a ball-point pen. He scribbled something, tore out the page and handed it to Carol.

"This is the telephone number and address for my friend's house, where I am staying," he said. "Please, if I can be of any help, don't hesitate to telephone me. Or just come to the house."

"Thanks," said Carol. "That's really very nice of you."

They stood for a moment, each waiting for the other to say something.

"Well, goodnight," said Carol, finally.

"Good night," answered Thor. "I hope we will meet again soon."

"Yes, me too," replied Carol. They shook hands a bit awkwardly. Finally, with a last smile over his shoulder, Thor stepped back into the revolving door.

Carol watched until he disappeared in the darkness and then started across the lobby toward the doors leading out to the garden. Out of the corner of her eye she spotted Jasper Reijksen near the reception desk. She was in no mood for him, so she turned and walked quickly away and worked her way into the middle of a small group of people walking toward the garden rooms.

No one in the busy lobby took any notice of the very short, hunched-looking man in a mismatched suit and pointed boots who had been leaning casually against the wall near the entrance of the Volcano Bar for more than an hour, deeply engrossed in the newspaper. As the last of the small group disappeared through the doors and out into the garden, Juma folded the paper, tucked it behind a potted palm tree and hurried out after them.

2

Outside in the garden, Carol slowed down and let the others pull ahead of her toward the pool-side restaurant, which was decorated for a wedding reception with flowers and Japanese lanterns. She continued on toward her room, along a dark flagstone path lined with trees and shrubs illuminated from below by muted spotlights. She passed a bush full of large, white night-blooming flowers and took a deep breath, enjoying the rich, fruity fragrance. Soft, rhythmic music spilled over from the wedding party, drifting toward her on the warm breeze.

Halfway to her room, Carol suddenly became aware of the sound of footsteps behind her. She told herself that it was just another guest walking to his room, but she began to walk faster anyway. She gripped her room key tightly, ready to unlock the door the moment she reached it.

As she turned off the main path and stepped up to her door, the footsteps sped up. She fumbled with the key in the lock, wishing there were more light to see what she was doing. The lock finally gave way and she put her hand on the doorknob.

"Mrs. Simon." The voice came from close behind her.

Carol swung around sharply and found herself facing a very short, thin man, with hunched-looking shoulders. His face was almost invisible in the darkness except for the startling whites of his eyes, which seemed to pop out of his face.

"Who are you?" she demanded.

"You remember, we have talked before, one time," said Juma.

She recognized the high pitched, nasal voice. "You're the one who called me in Nairobi," she said.

Juma nodded, pleased and encouraged. "Yes, Mrs. Simon," he said, baring his teeth in a tight smile. "We try to meet with you in Nairobi, but you came too soon to Rumura. But it is fine, now we meet here."

"I told you on the phone, I'm not Mrs. Simon," said Carol.

Juma raised both his hands, palms forward, in a placating gesture. He lowered his voice confidentially. "Of course, you are very right to be cautious, madam. But it is fine. We know you very well."

The way he kept saying 'we' was unsettling. Carol glanced uneasily beyond him into the darkness, wondering who else might be out there. Part of her wanted to yank the door open and rush inside and bolt it. But the strange little man didn't seem particularly threatening, and she wanted to get to the bottom of this.

"I asked who you are," she said firmly, with her hand still firmly on the doorknob. "And what do you want?"

"My colleagues and me, we are ready to provide what you are looking for," said Juma. "Most assuredly it will be to your advantage to talk with us. Most assuredly," he repeated, rolling the words on his tongue.

"Who is this 'we'?" demanded Carol. "And who says I'm looking for anything?"

"Mr. Singh is a very great man in Rumura," said Juma. "He can be a very great help to you in your business."

"I can't imagine how," said Carol. "But if this Mr. Singh, whoever he is, really wants to talk to me, tell him to meet me in the hotel lobby tomorrow morning at eight o'clock. I'll be happy to hear what he has to say."

Juma clucked his tongue. "It is not so easy," he said. "First we two must talk together. Then I can tell him you are serious."

"Serious about what?"

Juma licked his lips nervously. "The money," he said. "You understand, it must be enough for a great man like Mr. Singh."

"I thought so," said Carol. Any ambivalence she might have had, had disappeared. She was not having anything to do with these people. "You can tell your Mr. Singh that he's wasting his time. Whatever it is, I'm not interested."

"You cannot listen only to this man in Nairobi," said Juma, almost beseechingly. "You can hear also what we can offer."

"What man in Nairobi?" demanded Carol sharply.

Her reaction restored some of Juma's self-confidence. "Now, yes, you are interested, isn't it?" he said, nodding with satisfaction. "We know also very well this man," Juma told her. "It is better you leave him out. He is foolish and too greedy— soon he will be finished."

"I've had about enough of this nonsense," said Carol tightly. "You tell your Mr. Singh that I don't want anything to do with him. And if you're not gone in two minutes I'm calling hotel security." She jerked the door open and stalked inside, slamming it hard behind her.

3

Greg pulled his T-shirt over his head and sat on the bed to unlace his boots. He could hear Lisa brushing her teeth in the adjoining bathroom. They were spending the night in Kobani at a friend's house before leaving for Mwatumi in the morning.

"I didn't say I didn't like her," said Greg. "I just don't know why you had to invite her out to Mick-Pick. What are we running, a research station or a resort?"

Lisa spit a mouthful of toothpaste into the sink and came to stand in the doorway. She was wearing one of Greg's old T-shirts, which reached to the middle of her slender, dark thighs and stretched across her full breasts in front. "Don't exaggerate," she protested. "We don't have so many visitors."

"We get more than I want," he responded, standing up to slip off his jeans. He took his toothbrush out of his backpack and squeezed past her into the bathroom. "It's one thing to have researchers, or even people who might bring in some money. But do we have to let ourselves be over-run by a bunch of tourists?"

"I was just doing Pat a favor. She's done lots of things for us, and besides it's a good idea to stay on good terms with the Embassy."

"You think inviting Carol Simmons out to Mick-Pick is going to win us points with Jonathan Marshall? Don't count on it."

"You never know, it might," answered Lisa. "Besides, how else are people like Carol Simmons and the Schooley Foundation going to understand the kind of damage they can do with their well-intentioned development projects?"

"Oh, right," scoffed Greg, jerking the toothbrush out of his mouth, "you think if she spends a weekend climbing around in the forest and sees some bonobos, she'll cancel the project?" He began to brush vigorously again.

"It can't hurt for her to know that there's more than one side to it. Anyway, what do you care? I'll be the one taking her

70

around. All you have to do is be polite to her for a few hours one evening."

Greg rinsed his mouth and walked back into the bedroom. He stripped off his underwear and climbed into the bed, pulling the sheet up to his waist. He lay back, crossing his arms behind his head.

"How much you want to bet she shows up with that Norwegian?" he said. "That's the last thing we need right now—a journalist sniffing around."

"I thought you made it pretty clear that he wasn't invited," replied Lisa, climbing in beside him. "In fact, my darling, you were downright rude."

"Good," said Greg. He switched off the bedside reading lamp and slid his arm around her shoulders to draw her toward him. "I hope he got the message."

4

At one in the morning Carol was still wide awake, thanks to jet-lag and jangled nerves. The hunched man had disappeared from her door but still haunted her mind, along with his mysterious Mr. Singh. She felt lost and disoriented in the pitch blackness of the room and achingly alone in the queen-sized bed. She closed her eyes and tried to imagine that she could feel the circle of Neil's arms and the firm warmth of his body against hers.

Finally she gave up and switched on the bedside light. She blinked against the sudden glare and reached for the telephone.

"I'd like to place a call to the United States, please," she said. She gave the operator the number, replaced the receiver, turned off the light and sank back onto the pillow.

The sudden jangling of the phone a few minutes later made her heart leap.

"You are through to Washington, DC," said the operator.

"Carol? Where are you calling from, Nairobi?"

It was comforting to hear Neil's voice, although Carol wouldn't have minded if he'd sounded a bit more excited to hear hers.

"No, I'm in Rumura already."

"It must be the middle of the night there."

"It is. I couldn't sleep."

"I hope it's not a bad time," she said. "Can you talk?"

"I've got a procedure running and I'm taking readings at three minute intervals."

Carol's need to talk overcame her fear of sounding pathetic. "It's okay, I don't mind waiting."

"Okay, if it's that important. What's up?"

"I finally had my meeting with the 'mystery man.' You'll never guess who he turned out to be..." Carol stumbled through a disjointed account of the past few days, broken off every three minutes as Neil took his readings. She tried to be matter-of-fact, but she could tell that her voice sounded shaky. Meanwhile, Neil said nothing and it seemed to take him a few moments to realize she had finished.

"Sounds like this guy gave you a real scare," he said, finally.

"He didn't actually threaten me or anything."

"I thought you said the guy warned you to steer clear of the priest, because he's getting too greedy and they're going to finish him off. That sounds a lot like a threat to me." Neil's tone was coolly analytical, as though he were reviewing some routine laboratory observations, looking for a number to fill in an equation.

Carol fought her exasperation. "I didn't take it like that, exactly."

"Okay, what do you think he meant?"

"I don't know! I don't know what any of it means. I still think they've got me mixed up with someone else."

"Come on, Carol, be realistic. What are the chances of that? Obviously, someone there knows who you are and what you're doing in Rumura. Or, they *think* they do," he added ominously.

"What's that supposed to mean?"

"The way I see it, these guys not only knew when you arrived in Nairobi and all your movements there, but now they've followed you all the way to Rumura. How much money is involved in this project you're supposed to be looking into?"

"About thirty thousand dollars, so far."

"Peanuts. This has got to be about something a lot bigger than that. I tried to warn you."

"Neil, are you purposely trying to scare me?" demanded Carol.

"Why the hell would I do that?"

"Maybe to get back at me for coming out here when you didn't want me to."

"Jesus, Carol!" exclaimed Neil. "I don't have time for this. You called me, remember? Do you want my advice or don't you? There's the timer again."

Carol took a deep breath. This was ridiculous; she wasn't spending four dollars a minute to fight with Neil. In fact, she wasn't sure why she was spending four dollars a minute, except that she couldn't bring herself to break the connection and be completely alone again.

When Neil came back on the line he accepted her apology grudgingly. "You've got to look at the situation logically," he said. "The first thing is to figure out who these guys are and what they're after. Who knew you were going to Kenya and Rumura?"

Carol named a few people at the Schooley Foundation and the WCA office in Nairobi.

"And this priest, of course," said Neil. "How about people in Rumura? Did you set up any appointments in advance?"

"Yes, with a few government people, but I didn't say why I was coming. Only that I was going to visit our project in Mwatumi."

"That could be enough to make someone suspicious if there's something in Mwatumi they're trying to hide."

"But they're the ones who came to me," Carol pointed out. "Why would they do that if they're trying to hide something?"

73

"That's even worse. I think these gold smugglers or drug runners, or whatever they are, have gotten the idea you're in the same business. You're getting sucked into something way over your head. If I were you I'd get out of there fast."

"I can't," protested Carol. "I haven't even gone to Mwatumi yet."

"You don't mean you're still planning to go out there?"

"I have to. This Father Loretto is making all sorts of accusations against Margaret and the Co-op. I've got to get the other side of the story."

There was a brief silence on Neil's end of the line, and Carol could almost see him scowling. "Well, you asked what I think and I told you. Do what you want, like you always do."

Carol bit her lip hard. It had been a mistake to call Neil. She'd been aching for comfort and reassurance, but it was much more his style to give blunt advice and then become impatient if she didn't immediately appreciate and accept it. Add his pre-occupation with his procedure and his readings, as well as his simmering resentment over her trip, and it was a recipe for relationship disaster.

"No, you're right. I should think about it. I know, maybe Jonathan will lend me one of those hunky Marines as a bodyguard," she said lightly.

"Yeah? Who's Jonathan?" Neil asked distractedly.

"I forgot to tell you. You remember Jonathan and Pat Marshall, from the Peace Corps? They're here in Kobani now—Jonathan's with the U.S. Embassy. How's that for a coincidence? I had dinner with them tonight—they send their love."

If Carol was hoping to spark warm reminiscences, she clearly failed.

"So what did Jonathan have to say about this?" asked Neil.

"I haven't told him about it."

"Probably because you know he'd tell you the same thing I am. But if you won't listen to him either, at least he might be able to help keep you out of trouble. Maybe he knows who this

Mr. Singh is. I'm sure the Embassy keeps an eye on criminal activities."

"That's a good idea. I'll talk to him tomorrow." The problem with Neil was that he actually often was right, but every time she agreed with him it somehow felt like losing another round in a game she didn't even want to be playing.

"Hi, Camilla. Wait a minute, Carol." The background noise of the lab disappeared suddenly as Neil covered the mouthpiece of the phone. He came back on the line a moment later, sounding even more distracted than before. "Sorry, something's come up. I've got to go. Take care of yourself."

"I will. I'll try to call you tomorrow before I leave. Love you."

The click of the phone being hung up carried sharp and clear across six thousand miles to echo in the silence of her room.

CHAPTER 7

1

The sun was already bright and high in the sky when Carol awoke, still groggy from her restless night. She dressed and packed simultaneously, throwing things into one bag to take to Mwatumi and another to leave in storage at the hotel. She left them in the room to be collected later, and stepped outside into the warm, fresh morning. A gardener was hosing down the flagstones and the concrete deck of the pool, raising a fragrance of rich, moist earth. Someone was swimming slow laps in the pool, which was still hung with streamers and lanterns from last night's party.

The sign on the door said the travel office in the lobby was open from eight to six o'clock every day except Sunday. It was now past nine, but the door was firmly locked with no sign of life inside. The receptionist at the front desk couldn't tell her when it would open. "It is meant to be open now," he assured her. She used the telephone at the front desk to call the Embassy, and learned that Jonathan had come to the hotel for a breakfast meeting.

As she entered the coffee shop, Carol spotted Jonathan near the window, talking with the man she had seen getting into the midnight blue Mercedes at the airport. They seemed to be chatting casually, so she went over to their table.

As she came within earshot, the African was saying, "Jonathan, the trouble is they are undermining my authority. My rangers all seem to think they work for Allen now. And they are also spreading very damaging lies and rumors. You will admit that I have been very tolerant up to now, but this must change, or I cannot be responsible for the consequences."

Carol hesitated, since their conversation seemed to be more serious than she had thought, but Jonathan spotted her and waved her over. Carol saw that Jonathan's companion was in his early fifties, with a strong, handsome face distinguished by a neatly trimmed mustache. His double-breasted charcoal gray suit fit him like a second skin and his club tie was knotted in a perfect double Windsor.

"Carol, this Dr. Thadeus Maleke, Director of the Forest Department. Thadeus, Carol Simmons is an old friend of mine and Pat's from our Peace Corps days." Since Jonathan seemed to be pretending that Maleke didn't already know that, Carol assumed she was not supposed to know that they had already discussed her the day before.

Maleke grasped her hand firmly. "*Enchante,*" he said, in a low, well-modulated voice. "I am delighted to meet a friend of my good friend Jonathan. Also, I believe my Minister mentioned your name to me just yesterday." The accent was distinctly African with its long vowels and richly rolling R's, but refined and polished by college years in England and with a lilt that suggested a stint in Paris as well.

"He suggested I should meet you," said Carol. "By the way, didn't I see you at the airport the night before last?"

"Yes, quite possibly. My wife and I were returning from Nairobi."

"Are you just coming for breakfast?" Jonathan asked.

"Terrible, isn't it?" agreed Pat. "But I was up very late last night. I just couldn't get to sleep."

"I hope it wasn't due to our festivities by the swimming pool," said Maleke.

"No, not at all," said Carol. "The music was very nice. Were you at that party?"

"I was the host. It was a wedding reception for my niece, who is sitting over there with her new husband." Maleke indicated a young couple at a corner table. They smiled back shyly before turning their attention back to one another.

"The honeymoon couple," smiled Maleke with a good-natured wink at Carol. "They have eyes only for one another."

"I can't keep track of your family, Thadeus," complained Jonathan. "There are just too many of them."

"You know how it is with African families. She is actually the daughter of one of my cousins, but we don't make these distinctions. When I was a boy, three of my aunts lived in our compound with their families and I called them all 'mother.' All their children are like my own brothers and sisters."

"That kind of family closeness is something we've lost in the west," said Carol, thinking of her sister in Oregon and her parents in Florida.

"Of course, sometimes it is not so easy," said Maleke. "When all the nieces and nephews come for money for school fees at the same time." He laughed ruefully, but Carol also detected the strong note of pride.

The waiter arrived and began to lay a fresh setting at the table for Carol.

"I didn't mean to interrupt your meeting," said Carol.

"In fact, I was just leaving," said Maleke, picking up a slim leather briefcase. "I have a meeting with my Minister in a few minutes."

Before he left, Carol arranged to meet him in his office later in the morning.

"I leave the matter in your hands, my friend," said Maleke as he left.

"I'll see what I can do," sighed Jonathan.

On his way out, Maleke stopped to speak briefly with his niece and her new husband, saying something that made the girl look down at her plate and giggle behind her hand. He also shook hands at several other tables.

"Dr. Maleke seems to know everybody," observed Carol.

"Kobani is a small town, and Rumura is a small country," said Jonathan. "I find it's safest to assume that whoever you're talking to is somehow related to whoever you're talking about."

"That must put a damper on the gossip," said Carol.

"Not necessarily. Just because people are related doesn't necessarily mean they like each other."

The waiter returned with two golden croissants in a basket and small metal pots of steaming coffee and hot milk. Carol broke one of the flaky rolls in half and dabbed the end with jam. She took a bite and closed her eyes in appreciation. "Delicious," she said. "You can tell this used to be a French colony."

"Fortunately, they didn't change their cuisine along with their language when the British took over." Jonathan took a sip of coffee and glanced at his watch. "I should be getting back to the office, too."

"Do you have just a few more minutes? I need your advice."

"Sure, what's up?"

Carol told the story again as she had to Neil, starting with the first telephone call in Nairobi and finishing with last night's meeting with Juma.

"I have to admit, it's got me a bit jumpy," she said. "I told Neil I thought I'd finally gotten rid of these people, but then I found this under my door this morning." Carol took another of the crude business cards out of her pocket. This one had a telephone number scribbled at the bottom. "Does it mean anything to you?"

Jonathan looked at the card, turning it over and back again. "Not really," he said. "Every second businessman in this part of the world seems to be named Singh. It's like being named Goldschmidt in the diamond business. This looks pretty amateurish."

"So, not something that a member of an international gold and drugs smuggling cartel would carry?"

"I agree Neil is letting his imagination run away with him. But all the same, I wouldn't dismiss it too lightly. You've obviously stumbled into something."

"Neil thought you might be able to help me figure out what."

Jonathan continued to finger the card thoughtfully. "Maybe. But it could take some time. Of course, it could just be some kind of stupid joke."

"That's what Thor said," said Carol.

"Nilssen? What does he know about it?"

"He was with me when I found another of these cards last night, so I told him what's been happening."

"The first thing you've got to do is stop confiding in everybody," said Jonathan sternly. "What do you know about about this Nilssen, anyway? I'll see what I can do, but meanwhile I don't want you talking to anybody else about this. Nobody."

"Sure, okay."

"Now, tell me again about this man last night. What did he look like?" Jonathan pulled out a small, leather-bound notebook and a gold-plated pen and jotted down a few notes as Carol described Juma.

"Okay," said Jonathan, slipping the card into the inside pocket of his jacket along with the pen and notebook. "That's enough for now."

"What are you going to do?"

"Leave it to me. Why don't you give me a call later this afternoon at the office?"

"I was hoping to leave for Mwatumi right after my appointment with Dr. Maleke at eleven," said Carol.

"I think you should hold off on going to Mwatumi until we get this cleared up. Especially since there are people here who know about your plans."

"But I haven't told anyone else."

"What about the hotel travel office? You said last night you were going to book a car and a driver."

"I hadn't thought of that," sighed Carol. "I guess I'm really not cut out for this kind of thing. But I've got to get to Mwatumi as soon as I can. If I can leave after lunch today I could get there before dark."

"That may not be possible," said Jonathan. "But give me a call around lunch time and I'll let you know if I've got anything." He signaled the waitress for the check and placed a few bills on the table. "Don't worry. We'll get to the bottom of it."

Carol watched Jonathan leave, looking professional and competent in his dark blue suit and heavy briefcase. Much as she hated to admit it, she did feel better knowing he was on the case. She drained the last of her coffee and went out into the lobby, where she saw that the travel office was finally open.

"Good morning," she said to the young man seated behind the desk. "I'm Carol Simmons. I had a car and driver reserved to go to Mwatumi this morning."

"Yes, madam. The driver is ready—I will summon him directly."

"I'm afraid something's come up. I won't be leaving until at least after lunch."

"Very well, madam." The man's face was courteously impassive. But remembering Jonathan's warning, Carol found herself wondering whether this fresh-faced, polite young man was going to pick up the phone the moment she left and report to Mr. Singh on her change of plans.

2

Jonathan Marshall and Gideon Bashega faced each other across the Police Commissioner's wide desk. It was a familiar scene for Jonathan. Somehow he had become the one the Ambassador called on to straighten things out when an American citizen fell afoul of the local authorities. Half the time, Jonathan believed, his countrymen and women were up to no good and deserved whatever they got. A stint in the stinking cells of Kobani prison was enough to make any con-man or drug runner think twice about coming back to peddle his trade in Rumura again. But he also had no illusions about the saintliness of the Rumuran police force or its Commander-in-Chief.

"We caught him with a hundred grams of heroin," said the Commissioner. "That is a very serious offense." He tilted back in his tall leather chair and folded his stubby fingers comfortably across his pot belly. He looked at Jonathan out of the tops of his eyes, which gave him a humorously ironical look. With his round cheeks and gold rimmed glasses, he looked like a school teacher waiting for a student to explain what had happened to his homework this time. The baby face and a slight stammer had led many people to underestimate Bashega as he worked his way up through the ranks, but there weren't many who made that mistake anymore.

"I understand he claims it was planted," said Jonathan.

Bashega shrugged dismissively. "They all say that. Anyway, now he has signed a confession." He tossed a paper across the desk. Jonathan didn't look at it.

"I'd like to talk to him," said Jonathan.

"Sorry, that is not possible. Not until we complete our investigation."

"And when will that be?"

"In due course, Mr. Marshall. In the meantime, he is in perfect health. You have my word."

Jonathan's face was expressionless as he opened his briefcase and pulled out a manila envelope. He removed an eight-by-ten photograph and laid it on the desk in front of the Commissioner. "I've seen healthier," he observed.

Bashega picked up the photo and examined it with interest. "Regrettably, Mr. Yates resisted arrest. My officers were forced to subdue him. I am satisfied they exercised restraint, under the circumstances. Incidentally, how did you get this?"

"Commissioner, I am registering an official protest on behalf of my government over this deplorable treatment of a U.S. citizen, and I repeat my demand to see him. I must warn you that we are prepared to pursue this matter to the highest levels."

Bashega put the photo down and leaned across the desk. "Why are you so concerned about this Mr. Yates? In the past you have been more sympathetic to our strict treatment of drug traffickers."

"We have reason to believe Mr. Yates is innocent of the charges, Commissioner."

"What reason?" growled Bashega.

Jonathan reached into the manila envelope again and pulled out a letter. Bashega looked it over quickly. The muscles of his round cheeks bulged as he clenched his jaw.

"A forgery," he scowled, tossing the letter back to Jonathan.

"There is that possibility, of course," said Jonathan. "As I said, we're prepared to pursue this matter, and we're ready to carry out our own investigations."

Bashega narrowed his eyes. "I hope that will not be necessary."

Jonathan met the Commissioner's gaze steadily. "Of course, if Mr. Yates were to be released and allowed to leave the country without further harm, our interest in the case would be finished. From there, we would regard it purely as a matter for the Rumuran authorities."

For a moment the only sound in the room was the tapping of Bashega's fingernail on the desk. Then he picked up the photograph and the letter and slipped them into his desk drawer.

"Perhaps we shall review the evidence against Mr. Yates again," he said. "Now, I have a question for you, Mr. Marshall. There is an American woman who has just arrived from Nairobi. She had dinner at your home last night. She is a friend of yours?"

"My wife and I have known Carol for many years."

"What is her business in Mwatumi?"

If Jonathan was surprised at the extent of the Commissioner's knowledge about Carol's plans, he didn't show it. "I believe it's a routine visit to review a project her organization is funding."

Bashega took off his glasses and polished them with his handkerchief. "You are quite certain she has no other business there?"

"Not that I know of. Why, is there a problem?"

"I am glad to hear it," said Bashega, "as she is a friend of yours..."

"I trust that if you have any concerns about her or what she's doing, you'll raise them with me? We wouldn't want any unfortunate misunderstandings." Jonathan's voice was mild but his eyes were fixed firmly on the Commissioner's.

Bashega hooked his glasses back over his ears. "Of course, Mr. Marshall," he said. "You are quite right—we must not have any misunderstandings." He stood up and extended his hand to signal that the meeting was over.

A short while later, Jonathan settled into the back seat of his car as the driver guided it through the mid-morning traffic. Not so long ago he would have walked the few blocks to the Embassy, but lately he had gotten in the habit of using an official car and driver for his appointments. He felt that it was more dignified and commanded respect. He also appreciated the air conditioning since the day was getting hot and sticky.

The meeting on Yates had gone exactly as expected. His spy at Kobani prison had proven once again to be a good investment. He was confident that Bashega would find some pretext to release Truman Yates and let him slip quietly out of the country, rather than risk letting it become known that the two of them were partners in a jewelry exporting business. No doubt the enterprise was a lucrative one, enjoying strictly unofficial exemptions from the usual export duties and similar inconveniences. He had no idea what sort of falling out had led Bashega to employ his favorite strong-arm tactics on Yates. Maybe the American had gotten greedy and needed to be taught a lesson, or maybe Bashega had simply decided he no longer needed a business partner. Either way, the important thing was that Yates would soon be on his way home, as the Ambassador had wanted.

Bashega's interest in Carol, on the other hand, had taken Jonathan completely by surprise. Since he didn't believe in coincidences, he assumed that it must be related somehow to this Singh business. He took the dog-eared business card from his pocket and looked it over again distastefully. In Africa, even the seediest briefcase capitalist or con-man usually had a beautifully printed business card with a fancy company name and an important-sounding title. This one was clearly an amateur and probably not even worth bothering with. But Jonathan was cautious by nature and experience. So far, with the help of a few well-placed, carefully cultivated connections, he had managed to avert trouble and even score a few modest successes that had brought him favorable recognition back in Washington. He knew his name had begun to surface in water-cooler gossip as a man on his way up. He wasn't about to take the risk of underestimating this situation and letting it blow up in his face. It would be simple enough to give these people a good scare and get them off Carol's back. But that wasn't enough, particularly if there was a chance that Bashega might be mixed up in it somehow. He had to find out what was going on.

By the time the car pulled up at the front door of the Embassy, Jonathan had come to a decision. As he stepped into his office he was already rehearsing in his mind what he would say to this mysterious Mr. Singh.

3

Juma sat on the windowsill in the small, steamy office, watching the smoke from his cigarette drift out the open window. Muna sat at the desk, behind an old black rotary telephone and a computer screen blinking lines of numbers. The drab plaster walls were covered with travel posters depicting quaint central European villages and beautiful people soaking up the sun on glistening beaches. The lights in the office were off to make the room seem cooler, and a fan in one corner rotated slowly, stirring the air and lifting the corners of the papers on the desk.

"I'm hungry," said Muna. "What's taking David so long?"

Juma shrugged and blew another plume of smoke.

"Mr. Patel's coming back the day after tomorrow. Then you won't be able to use this office anymore."

"How many times are you going to remind me?" asked Juma irritably. They spoke an urban and slangy Rumuran, with many English and Swahili words thrown in. David sometimes had trouble following it, but he was determined to learn to speak the same way.

"I don't like this, anyway," complained Muna. "What if Mr. Patel calls? He'll be mad if I don't say, 'Big World Travel, may I help you?' when I answer the phone."

"He's not going to call," said Juma in a bored voice.

"Well, he might."

"We won't need the office after today anyway. She's going to call."

"That's what you say." Muna scowled and turned her attention back to the magazine laid out on the desk in front of her. Juma closed his eyes and leaned back against the window frame, waiting for the fan to come around to blow on his face.

There was the jingle of a cowbell as the door opened and David came inside. He flopped down in one of the swivel chairs in front of the desk. His shirt was soaked through in large, oval spots under the arms and another down his back. He pulled out a dirty handkerchief and wiped the sweat off his forehead.

"It's hotter in here than it is out there!" he complained.

"Where's my lunch?" asked Muna.

David gave her the greasy paper parcel and she started to unwrap sandwiches made of flat bread rolled around chunks of roasted meat and tomatoes. She handed one to Juma.

"You forgot the pili-pili," said Juma, looking at his sandwich with distaste.

"You didn't say you wanted any," said David.

"This stuff tastes like old boots without pili-pili sauce."

"Leave him alone," said Muna. "Next time tell him what you want or go get it yourself."

"Just give us your report," said Juma. "Has she gone yet?"

"Isaac said now she's not going until later."

"The bloody woman is always changing her plans," grumbled Juma. "You have to watch her every second."

"We already know where she's going," said Muna. "What does it matter when she leaves?"

"It matters to me," said Juma. "I'm the one who has to do all the planning."

Muna snorted and tore a small bite out of her sandwich.

They all jumped when the phone rang. Juma motioned to Muna to answer it.

"You don't have to tell me," snapped Muna as she lifted the heavy receiver.

"Good afternoon," she said in English. "May I help you?"

The voice on the phone was low and gruff. "I vish to spick vit Meester Seenk."

Muna quickly covered the mouthpiece and turned to face Juma. "I think he wants to speak to Singh," she hissed in a stage whisper.

"*He?*" exclaimed Juma. He jumped off the windowsill and came to stand beside her.

"What should I tell him?" said Muna nervously.

"Tell him Singh's not here, then pass the call to me. But calm down and make it sound natural."

Muna took a deep breath and uncovered the mouthpiece. "I am so sorry, Mr. Singh is not available at this moment," she said in her receptionist voice. "Please hold the line while I pass you to his associate, Mr..." her voice trailed off. Juma hadn't thought of giving her a name to use. She quickly handed the receiver to Juma and rolled her chair back out of the way. David sat forward intently and leaned his elbows on the desk.

Juma cleared his throat. "Good afternoon," he said, also in English. "Can I help you?"

"I vish to spick vit Meester Seenk," said the caller. "It iss a matter of business."

"I am Mr. Singh's business partner," said Juma. "You can speak with me, yes."

There was a pause on the other end. "No. I vant Seenk," said the caller. "I haff his name from an associate. He iss in Kobani?"

"Yes, yes, Mr. Singh is in town," said Juma hastily. "He has only stepped out from the office. He can return very shortly. Maybe you will like to leave a message?" he suggested.

"Yes, good. I leaf a message for Meester Seenk. You tell him I vish to meet vit him for a matter of business. Iss very urgent."

"What is your telephone number, please?" asked Juma, motioning to Muna for a pencil and paper.

"You haf no need from my telephone number," the caller said curtly. "You tell Meester Seenk I meet him today, at five o'clock in Ankara Hotel."

"One moment, please, I will refer to his diary to see if he is free..." "Five o'clock in Ankara Hotel," the caller repeated firmly. "And you tell Meester Seenk also, he can forget now the voman. From now, it is me he deal vit. You tell him, yes? It is finished now vit the voman."

Juma placed the receiver slowly back in its cradle.

"Who was it?" demanded David.

"He wouldn't give me his name," said Juma.

"You didn't recognize the voice?" asked Muna.

Juma shook his head distractedly. "He had a funny accent. European, I think, but I don't know what kind—I never heard it before."

"But who is he? How did he get this number?" asked David.

"From Mrs. Simon, you idiot," said Juma. "How else?"

"So they're working together?" asked Muna.

"Maybe," mused Juma, lighting another cigarette. "Maybe."

CHAPTER 8

1

Carol tossed her briefcase onto the bed and turned on the air conditioner. She stood for a moment directly in the blast of cold air before pulling off her sticky blouse and going into the bathroom to rinse the sweat off her face. The cool, blue depths of the swimming pool beckoned, but first she had to check in with Jonathan.

"I haven't found out much yet," Jonathan told her. "But I don't think they'll bother you any more."

"Why do you say that?"

"I've put the word out, as they say."

"Out where? With whom?" asked Carol, perplexed.

"I really can't go into the details right now," said Jonathan. "The main thing is that you shouldn't worry too much about it."

"Does that mean I can go ahead to Mwatumi?"

Jonathan hesitated for a moment. "I don't see why not. As long as you keep a low profile."

"What's that supposed to mean?"

"I know you're here to check up on some specific allegations about problems in the WCA project. Just make sure you stick to that, and don't let it look like you're digging around for something else."

"What on earth are you talking about, Jonathan? Is there something you're not telling me?"

"No, not about you..." Jonathan hesitated again. "Look, here's the situation. There's an American that I've just been working on getting out of jail here. He seems to have gotten himself mixed up in some business with illegal exports, and I happen to know he spent some time in Mwatumi before he was arrested. It's got nothing to do with you, of course, but there's a chance it could have something to do with this Mr. Singh. And since you're also an American, and not many Americans go to

Mwatumi...you just need to be a bit careful, that's all." Jonathan decided there was no need to worry Carol by mentioning his meeting with the Commissioner. "Just so you know, the American's name is Truman Yates. If anyone seems to think you know him, just play dumb and then let me know about it. You can call me from the Acropolis Hotel. But remember, somebody could be listening in, so be careful what you say."

"Got it," said Carol. "Maybe we should work out some kind of code. If anyone asks me about Yates, I'll call you and say something like, 'The hound bays at midnight.' And then what will you say?"

"It's fine to joke about it, but remember what I told you—don't go around talking to anyone about any of this, including the business with Singh. You never know who you can trust."

"I understand," said Carol. She was going to have to tell Neil that Jonathan had definitely lost his sense of humor.

"By the way, how was your meeting with Thadeus Maleke?"

"He was very nice, but he didn't really say much except to confirm what the Minister told me—that our project isn't causing any deforestation in the Mali-Kuli Reserve. He offered to have his Head Forest Ranger show me around when I get out there."

"Did he happen to say anything about Greg Allen?"

"No, we didn't talk about him at all. Why?"

"Are you still planning to visit them at the research station?"

"I hope so. But I decided not to mention it to Dr. Maleke, since I got the idea last night at dinner that they're not on very good terms."

"If you do stay with Greg and Lisa, you could do me a favor." Jonathan paused. "I've been getting some complaints and I want to find out if there's anything to it."

He explained that people were saying Greg had started acting as though the Reserve belonged to him, discrediting and undermining the authority of the government officials.

"Greg has money from his research grant, and the Forest Department has almost none. So he's been supplying the wardens and rangers with food and fuel and uniforms, and he tops up their salaries, so that in effect the guys are working for him. Of course, this gives him a lot of influence. I hear now he's decided that all the Pygmies have to be kicked out of the forest because they're hunting some of the animals. Thadeus was telling me he's been getting heat about that from some human rights groups, who think it's a Rumuran government policy, when it's actually a Greg Allen policy. He's also managed to get a couple of the rangers fired, claiming that they were poaching. The next time, maybe he'll go after the Warden or someone even higher up. Next thing you know, he'll be up to his neck in local politics."

"Like that woman who studied the gorillas in Rwanda?" asked Carol.

"Right, like Dian Fossey," said Jonathan. "And you know what happened to her—she got herself killed."

"But what exactly do you want me to do?"

"Just keep your eyes open and see what Greg and Lisa are doing out there—how they interact with the rangers, what they say about the Forest Department...that kind of thing."

"I wouldn't feel right spying on them," said Carol.

"I'm not asking you to spy," said Jonathan. "Just be observant. And you can tell them exactly what I've just told you—I'd like to know what they have to say about it."

"Is it Dr. Maleke who's been complaining to you?" asked Carol, remembering the tail end of the breakfast conversation she had interrupted.

"It's not just him. The Minister himself told me that Greg's going around telling anyone who'll listen, that the whole government is completely corrupt. He's apparently accused the Minister himself of being involved in poaching and timber smuggling."

"Maybe it's true."

"Maybe it is, but I haven't seen any proof. And these things can cut both ways, you know. I've heard some interesting rumors about Greg, too."

"What," exclaimed Carol, "that he's involved in poaching? I can't believe it."

"Why not? Because he's an American and claims to be a conservationist? The story I've heard is that when he was in Cameroon a few years ago, he got caught trying to send some baby chimpanzees to the U.S. illegally."

"From Dr. Maleke, again?"

"I'm not saying I believe it—just that it's easy to make accusations. Anyway, the point is that Greg's on thin ice here, whether he knows it or not. If he's not careful, he's going to get kicked out of Rumura for good. At the very least, he's likely to find it hard to get his research permit renewed next year."

"Have you told him this yourself?"

"Of course I have," said Jonathan. "Aside from his being a friend of Pat's, it's part of my job to look out for Americans working here. But Greg's so damned arrogant—he just denies that there's anything wrong with what he's doing and accuses me of being hoodwinked by Maleke. I'm hoping he might be willing to listen if an objective observer backed up what I'm saying."

"I'll see what I can do, as long as it's all above-board," said Carol.

"That's all I'm asking. Have a good trip to Mwatumi."

"Thanks. By the way, do you mind if I give your number to Neil in case of any emergency? I don't know whether he'd be able to reach me in Mwatumi."

"Sure, you do that. And tell him not to worry—we'll keep you out of trouble."

2

Carol hurried gingerly across the baking concrete to the edge of the pool, took a deep breath and braced herself for the delicious shock as she hit the cold water. She swam a few easy laps to warm up, then pushed herself hard for ten more, churning the water with her flip turns. Then she turned over on her back and let herself drift, paddling lazily with her hands and feet and closing her eyes against the glare of the bright sun.

"Be careful, or you may float out to sea."

Carol opened her eyes abruptly to see Thor Nilssen standing beside the pool, wearing khakis and a well-worn Panama hat. She turned herself right side up and swam over to the side.

"Hi," she said. "How long have you been there?"

"Not so long," he answered. "The girl at the front desk said maybe I could find you here. I'm happy to see that you haven't left yet for Mwatumi."

"Why is that?"

"Because I have decided to go, and I wanted to try again to persuade you to travel with me."

"Still hoping to charm Greg into letting you visit the research station?"

"That would be nice, of course. But in any case, I wanted to take the chance to see that part of the country. I'm told the mountains are very beautiful."

"When are you planning to come back?"

Thor shrugged disarmingly. "I am not planning" he said. "That's the beauty of it. My car and I are entirely at your disposal."

"That's a hard offer to turn down," Carol admitted. "Why don't you tell me more over lunch?"

Thor bent over and extended his hand for her to grasp. Carol had a sudden whim to brace her feet against the side and pull him in, but instead she let him help her lift herself out of the water. He was stronger than he looked.

They found a table under a striped beach umbrella. Carol felt self-conscious in her bathing suit and dripping hair, but Thor didn't seem to mind. They ordered sandwiches and iced tea.

"In addition to the pleasure of your company, I have another motive for suggesting that we go to Mwatumi together," admitted Thor.

"You're short of money and want me to split the gas?"

"I wouldn't hear of it. But I am hoping you'll let me come along to visit this women's cooperative of yours. I would like to write a story about them if they are willing."

"Not quite as exotic as a Madagascar funeral party, I'm afraid. But if you're really interested I don't mind asking them for you."

"Then it's agreed. We can leave whenever you like."

"I have to shower and change, and cancel the hotel car and check out...anyway, don't you have to pack?"

"My bag is already in the car," he grinned. "Why don't you go and get ready? I'll wait for the bill and meet you in the lobby."

Back in her room, Carol checked the time and did a quick calculation. It would be just after five in the morning back in Washington. Neil never went to bed before midnight and he hated to be woken up before seven, but she might not be able to talk to him again until she returned from Mwatumi. She picked up the phone and asked the operator to place the call.

The call went through a few minutes later, just as she had finished drying her hair. Carol listened to the phone ringing and braced herself for Neil's early morning grumpiness.

"Hello—"

"Hi, Neil, it's me," she said quickly. "I'm sorry to call so early, but I'm about to take off for Mwatumi—"

"—can't come to the phone right now. Please leave your name and number and a short message after the beep."

"Neil? It's Carol. Please pick up the phone, honey. I know it's early, but I have to talk to you. Neil? Are you there?"

Carol waited a few more seconds, listening to the silence. Finally she left the contact numbers for Jonathan at the Embassy and at home and slowly hung up the phone.

Carol gave Thor her bags to carry out to the car and went to the travel office.

"Your car is ready, madam," said the clerk, as soon as she walked in the door. "The driver is waiting just outside."

"I'm sorry, but I'm afraid I'm going to have to cancel my booking altogether," said Carol.

"Ah, then you will not be traveling to Mwatumi?"

Under normal circumstances, the question would have seemed perfectly innocent, but Carol found herself wondering once again whether the man wasn't just a bit too interested in her movements.

"That's right," she said. "I've decided to spend a few days with some friends instead. In Lihari," she added, naming a town about fifty kilometers east of Kobani, the opposite direction from Mwatumi. "I hope it's not a problem."

"There is no problem, madam. I will inform the driver."

"I feel terrible that he's been waiting around all morning," said Carol. "I'd like to pay him for his time."

"It is not necessary, madam."

"No, I insist. It's only fair. It was two thousand rimands for the day, wasn't it? How about if I pay half of that?" she counted out the bills.

"That is very generous, madam. I will see that he gets it."

Carol stopped by the reception desk to check out and make a reservation for when she returned. While she was waiting for the receptionist to confirm the reservation, she heard someone call her name. She turned to find Jasper Reijksen coming up behind her, a bit out of breath.

"Jasper? What a surprise. I thought you'd be back in Mwatumi by now."

"I am driving back now," said Jasper. "Greg and Lisa told me you wanted to go there today, and so I came to offer you a lift." He spoke with his usual stiffness, his hands hanging awkwardly at his sides.

"Thanks, but I've already got a ride. Oh, here he is now."

"Ready?" asked Thor as he came up to them.

"Jasper just offered me a ride to Mwatumi," Carol told Thor as they walked to his car.

"Did he? Then I'm glad I thought of it first."

"Me too."

Thor opened the car door and held it while Carol sat in and pulled her skirt in around her knees.

As they pulled onto the road, Carol said, "To tell you the truth, I'd find it hard to imagine spending five hours in a car with Jasper Reijksen. I don't know why, but he gets on my nerves."

"It's his eyes, I think," said Thor thoughtfully. "I noticed when you introduced us. When he looks at you, his eyes look at your eyes, but somehow they don't meet. He looks through your eyes, like a spy looking through a window. You wonder what he could be searching for on the other side."

"That's a writer for you," said Carol. "I'd just have said he gives me the creeps."

Isaac Msumba watched the Renault pull out from the parking lot and went back to the travel office. He put his feet up on the desk and fingered the bank notes in his pocket with satisfaction. It wasn't every day that money came pouring down from heaven. He wondered why so many people wanted to know where the American woman was going and when. First the Rumuran yokel had given him a hundred rimands, and then the European had paid four hundred for the same information. It made him feel a bit bad for accepting the thousand she had given him herself. As a sort of atonement, he'd even passed two hundred of it on to the driver, for which the man had been pathetically grateful. "These *mzungus*," Isaac thought contemptuously. "Money flows from them like water from the Nile."

2

Jonathan climbed the crumbling concrete steps and opened the peeling wooden door of the Ankara Hotel. He paused to let his eyes adjust from the dazzling sunlight to the fluorescent gloom inside. It was his first time inside the Ankara, a squat, decaying structure which catered mostly to local businessmen and the occasional shoestring tourist. The lobby was empty except for one stooped old man in a dirty uniform who was listlessly sweeping the threadbare carpet with a hand broom and dustpan. A radio mounted on the wall above the reception desk provided tinny background music. An ancient air conditioner in one window droned loudly but did nothing to ease the stifling heat. The only relief came from two large fans rotating slowly on the ceiling.

Jonathan touched his upper lip self-consciously. Once again, he cursed the sudden impulse that had led him to adopt that ridiculous accent over the phone: now he would have to keep it up, and he already felt foolish enough in the fake mustache he'd borrowed from his son's Halloween costume. He almost began to hope that Singh wouldn't show up.

The receptionist glanced up from his newspaper as the door opened, but turned back to it when Jonathan walked past sank down into a dusty sofa at the far end of the lobby. Jonathan realized that he had set the rendezvous too early—an hour later, people would have been coming in for drinks at the bar and he wouldn't have been so conspicuous. And though he had purposely come half an hour late, Singh was apparently playing it even cooler. He settled in to wait.

Across the street and about fifty yards down from the Ankara, Juma and David sat up in Muna's car and watched the well-dressed white man step out of the taxi and tell it to wait. "That must be him," said Juma.

"I think I've seen him before," said David.

"Where?"

"It could be the same man Mrs. Simon left the American Embassy with yesterday. They drove away together in his car."

Juma turned a hard stare on him. "Are you certain?"

Juma's insistence rattled David. Most *mzungus* looked pretty much the same to him. "I'm almost certain," he apologized.

"What kind of car was it?"

"A Land Cruiser," said David firmly. If there was one thing he knew it was cars. "A silver one with an orange stripe."

"What kind of number plates?"

David sagged again and avoided Juma's eyes. "I don't know," he muttered.

Juma hissed his disgust and turned back to gaze at the hotel door. He frowned. "The man who called wasn't American—I know an American accent."

"Isaac from the travel office said she left the hotel with a European," said David. "Not Reijksen—another one he'd never seen before. Maybe he's the one who called."

"How many partners does she have?" exclaimed Juma in exasperation. He lit another cigarette to help him concentrate. David maintained a respectful silence.

"All right," Juma said at last, "here's what we do. We can't take the chance of making contact until we know who he really is. If he's with the Embassy it could get sticky. I'll wait here and keep an eye out. You go inside and use the phone to call Muna. Tell her to dress up fancy and get over here fast. She can go inside and see if she recognizes him—she knows lots of *mzungus* from working in the travel agency. If not, maybe she can get friendly with him and get him talking. And try to get a good look at him when you go in, but don't make him suspicious."

David scowled at the thought of Muna cozying up to this *mzungu*, but he got out of the car and started across the street to the hotel.

By six o'clock there was still no sign of Singh, and Jonathan decided that waiting any longer would be out of character for the role he was playing, of a man who was used to seeing people jump when he spoke. He would call the number again tomorrow and demand an explanation.

Just as he reached the door it opened and a striking young African woman in a short, tight black dress and heavy make-up walked in. She seemed to be in a hurry but slowed down when she saw him. He looked her over appreciatively, but looked away when she gave him a bold smile. He nodded briefly and edged past, closing the door firmly behind him. She was sexy, but he knew better than to have anything to do with a girl who worked a hotel like this one. The last he heard, the HIV infection rate among prostitutes in Kobani was about seventy percent.

He stepped into the waiting taxi and told the driver to take him back to the American Embassy. A moment later, he changed his mind and directed him to the Intercontinental instead. He would call the Embassy from there and have his driver pick him up at the back door of the hotel, just in case Singh was having him watched. He pulled the mustache off his lip, rubbing the adhesive from his skin with his fingertip.

Chapter 9

1

Navigating the obstacle course that was the main road westward from Kobani, Thor concentrated on weaving around the deepest potholes and dodging the oncoming traffic. Drivers sped by each other on the narrow strip of crumbling blacktop in a never-ending game of "chicken," equally at home on either side of the road, showing no concern for their own safety or anyone else's. A quick flash of the headlights was all the warning they gave oncoming vehicles to get out of the way. Sometimes cars were forced to swerve right off the road, scattering gravel and pedestrians, to avoid a head-on collision.

On both sides the roadside was streaming with people. Crowds of young children in school uniforms dawdled homeward, their pencil-thin legs protruding from under baggy shorts and skirts. Some men pedaled slowly along on heavy bicycles piled with mounds of hay or green bananas, but most people were on foot, walking steadily to and from distant markets and fields. Many, particularly the women and girls, carried loads of firewood or burlap bags full of grain on their heads. On almost every woman's back a baby's head bobbed above a sling made from a *kanga* cloth knotted in front above her breasts. The cattle and goats walked alongside the people with the same deliberate, plodding patience. Even the powerful, hump-backed bulls, their wicked-looking horns spreading out from their ponderous heads like heavy tree branches, swayed along as placidly as docile old dogs.

Thor slowed to a crawl to let a small herd of cattle cross the road, urged on by a small boy whacking at their hindquarters with a thin stick.

"Do you suppose this car used to have shock absorbers?" asked Carol after they hit a pothole that threw them both up out of their seats like bronco busters.

"Probably once, a long time ago," answered Thor. "Is it like this all the way to Mwatumi?"

"Only as far as Bola, where the main road turns south toward Rwanda. After that we'll be on a dirt road. It'll be bumpy, but at least we won't have these craters, and we'll lose most of the trucks."

Bola consisted of two gas stations, a seedy hotel and a line of dingy shops and open-air stalls catering to the long-distance truckers. Past the Rwanda turn-off, the landscape began to change from open plains to rolling foothills cresting like green breakers toward a wall of dark mountains in the distance. Carol gazed out the window at the bright green and yellow patchwork of maize and beans fields alternating with dense groves of banana trees holding up their broad, fringed leaves like the blades of green windmills.

They reached Mwatumi just as the sun sank behind the peaks, casting the village into a twilight shadow. The bare bulbs and kerosene lanterns hanging in the open storefronts along the road drew people like moths. Men stood or squatted in small groups, smoking cigarettes and drinking banana beer. Women loaded their bundles on their heads and started up the narrow footpaths toward their homes on the hillside, where their daughters were stirring up the cooking fires and pounding the hard kernels of maize into coarse meal for porridge.

The concrete walls of the Acropolis Hotel were a faded blue with green trim around the windows and door. A low wire fence, almost hidden beneath bright orange bougainvillea vines, separated the stretch of hard packed dirt that served as the parking lot from the road. More bougainvillea climbed up the wall on either side of the door.

The walls of the lobby were papered with big, colorful posters of famous Greek landmarks and statues, interspersed with comical photographs with crude captions, prints of big-eyed puppies and kittens tumbling out of ribboned baskets, and old calendars showing porcelain-skinned Japanese women set against backdrops of flowering cherry trees and snow-capped mountains. In the midst of this eclectic collection, the obligatory photograph of the President of Rumura stared sternly down from its place of honor above the reception desk.

The owner of the Acropolis, Constantine Sotiropoulos, was a short, round, middle-aged man with sagging cheeks, heavily lidded eyes, and wisps of greasy black hair plastered across his bald skull. His shirt strained against his back and arms as he leaned heavily on his elbows on the reception desk, sleepily watching a soccer game on the flickering screen of a black-and-white television set. A cassette tape of Greek dance music played in the background, piped through a loudspeaker hung from the ceiling above the door.

"*Kali spera*," said Thor as they walked in.

Sotiropoulos looked up with a broad smile and responded with a rapid-fire burst of Greek.

Thor began to answer and then faltered. "Sorry," he said, "I am afraid that I only know a few words."

"But your accent is excellent," said Sotiropoulos. "Your tongue was made to speak the language of the gods. Never mind. What may I have the pleasure to do for you?"

Carol spoke up. "I called yesterday for a reservation—Carol Simmons."

"Yes, of course, Mrs. Simmons. You are most welcome. A room for two?"

"No, two separate rooms," said Carol quickly.

"And I have no reservation," said Thor apologetically.

"No matter," sighed Sotiropoulos, "we are not full. To be truthful, we are nearly empty. In the old days, before independence, at this time of the year every room was full. People came for the weekends from Kobani, and for holidays they came from everywhere to see our beautiful mountains. But now...well, now you may have your choice. I have two adjoining rooms in the west wing, very nice, and very private."

"That's not necessary," said Carol. "Just something quiet, far from the bar please."

Sotiropoulos slapped two heavy, old-fashioned iron keys on the desk in front of him.

"For Mrs. Carol Simmons, number twenty five. Our best room, at the back of the hotel, at the end of the hall with a nice veranda. Very quiet. With a shower and a bath." He consulted the card Thor had filled out. "And for Mr. Thor Nilssen, number twenty eight, on the other side of the hall." He smacked a bell on the counter. A skinny boy of about sixteen sat up on a sofa where he had been lounging out of sight and pulled himself listlessly to his feet. He picked up the two bags and shuffled off across the lobby, toward a pair of double doors leading out to an enclosed garden.

"My son, Nico," grumbled Sotiropoulos. "If only he moved a little more slowly he would go backwards." He turned back to Thor and Carol with a gap-toothed smile. "Dinner is from seven o'clock until ten o'clock. Tonight we have a splendid mousakka, such as only my Elena can make. You must come early. The dining room will be full tonight, and anything that is left, I will finish it all myself. Also, I am pleased to invite you to take a complimentary aperitif before dinner at the bar or in the garden."

Carol and Thor followed Nico outside to a small courtyard, where a few white molded plastic tables and chairs were set under a curving grape arbor. At one end was a small fountain, featuring a curly-haired cherub pouring water from an upended urn into a seashell. At the other end a set of glass doors opened onto a room with a long, wooden bar.

Carol glanced into the barroom. "Look," she pointed. "Isn't that Greg Allen?"

"Yes, I think so," said Thor.

"I think I'll go say hello, and let him know we've arrived."

"Sure, let's go," said Thor.

Carol hesitated. "Maybe it would be better if I went alone."

"Oh, yes, I'd forgotten. He may not be so happy to see me."

"It might be better if I talked to him first, and broke the news that you're here. Give him a chance to get used to the idea."

She held out her room key. "Could you please just ask Nico to drop my bag in my room?"

"Certainly. Shall we meet later here in the garden for our 'complimentary aperatif?'"

Carol laughed at his perfect imitation of Sotiropoulos' accent.

"Give me an hour. I want to take a good long soak in that tub."

As she entered the bar, Carol saw that Greg was speaking with a big, stocky Rumuran in a military style uniform and beret. He wore a loop of gold braid across one shoulder and carried a swagger stick under one arm, indicating that he was an officer. The paunch hanging over his low-riding belt suggested that he spent most of his time behind a desk. He stood solidly in front of Greg with his feet spread apart and his arms crossed firmly in front of his thick chest. His face was set and impassive.

Carol hesitated in the doorway. Greg caught her eye over the Rumuran's shoulder and gave her a brief nod. The officer turned around to look behind him.

"Please, don't let me interrupt," said Carol. I just wanted to say hi, and let you know I've arrived." Captain Kamundu Kamanga.

"It's okay. Carol Simmons, this is, the Police Chief here in Mwatumi."

Kamanga's looked at her closely but his broad face was expressionless as they shook hands.

"I was just going to my room when I saw you in here," said Carol. "I'll leave you gentlemen to your conversation."

"We have finished," said Kamanga. "Good evening." He turned abruptly on his heel and walked smartly out the door leading to the lobby.

"Shit," said Greg. He banged his glass down on the bar.

"Is something wrong?" asked Carol.

"That useless bastard," said Greg. "I've been telling him for weeks about something that's going on right under his nose, and he won't do a damned thing about it. I used to think he was just lazy, but now I'm sure he's been bought off. It's going to be up to us, as usual."

"What is?"

Greg hesitated, then shook his head vaguely. "Never mind," he said. "By the way, have you met Captain Kamanga before?"

"I don't think so. Why?"

"The way he was staring at you, I thought maybe he recognized you from somewhere."

"I was here once about a year ago, but I don't remember meeting him. Maybe he's heard my name in connection with the Mwatumi Greengoods project. I have to admit, though, he did make me a bit uncomfortable. Doesn't he ever smile?"

"If he does, I've never seen it," said Greg. "So, you still planning to come out to the research station this weekend?"

"I'd love to, if it's still convenient."

They agreed that Greg would pick Carol up at the hotel early Saturday morning. Before Carol could think of a way to broach the subject of Thor, Greg drained his glass and tossed a crumpled bill onto the bar.

"Okay, see you Saturday," he said, already on his way out the door.

An hour later, wearing her Indian dress and a hint of makeup, Carol found Thor already at a table in the garden, studying a map of Rumura. Thor stood to hold the chair as Carol sat down. The waiter came with a Campari and soda, and took her order for a glass of white wine.

"May I say how lovely you look this evening," said Thor.

"Your English may be from Berkeley," laughed Carol, "but you must have picked up your manners somewhere else."

"American women are always the easiest to charm," said Thor. "You are so unaccustomed to the smallest gallantry that it takes no effort at all."

"Really. And which women are the hardest?"

"The French are difficult, of course, because they think even the most outrageous flattery is nothing but the simple truth.

Hungarians are also a challenge because it takes practice to kiss a woman's hand without bumping your nose. But I think the hardest are the Israelis. First you must persuade them to put down their grenade launchers."

"You've obviously given this a lot of thought," said Carol. "Have you ever thought of turning pro?"

"What makes you think I'm not already?"

Carol flushed as Thor smiled at her genially. "Don't worry," he said. "My intentions are quite honorable. I will prove it by buying you dinner tonight."

"That isn't necessary," she protested. "In fact, I was going to buy you dinner, as a 'thank you' for the lift."

"You see?" said Thor. "It's just as I was saying about American women. Never mind, we'll discuss it later. For now, perhaps you can answer one question for me? Why is that large soldier watching you so intently?"

Carol turned around quickly to see the stony face of Captain Kamanga staring at her from the bar.

"Do you know him?" asked Thor.

"I just met him a little while ago, talking with Greg Allen. He's the local police chief, Captain Kamanga."

"Clearly you made an impression on him."

"He's probably waiting for someone else," said Carol.

"No, he is definitely looking at you."

"I can't imagine why."

"Perhaps you will find out. He's coming this way."

Kamanga set a chair down next to their table and sat down stiffly without waiting for an invitation. The waiter came to take his order, but Kamanga waved him away.

"So, you have come to Mwatumi after all, Mrs. Simon," said Kamanga.

Carol choked on her wine and started coughing. Thor raised his eyebrows and patted her lightly on the back as Kamanga watched impassively.

"I'm afraid you've made a mistake, Captain," said Carol when she'd caught her breath. "My name is Simmons. Carol Simmons." She stressed the short "i" and the "s" at the end.

Kamanga brushed away her protest. "You are welcome here, but I have a message for your Mr. Singh," he said.

"Oh, no, not again," groaned Carol. She shot a despairing look at Thor. "How many times do I have to tell you people, I don't know any Mr. Singh?"

"He can go back to Nairobi," Kamanga continued, ignoring her. "There is no business here for him." He leaned forward slightly toward Carol and dropped his voice. "Tell him that Mr. Yates ignored our warnings. I hope he has better sense."

"Yates!" gasped Carol.

Kamanga rose to his feet as stiffly as he'd sat down and stood scowling down at her for a moment before striding away, slapping his swagger-stick lightly against his calf.

Thor turned to Carol. "Are you all right?"

"I really thought I was through with this nonsense," she said.

"I understand why you were upset to hear the Captain mention Mr. Singh, but now who is Mr. Yates?"

"I...don't know. I've never heard of him." Carol took another sip of her wine and looked away, fixing on her eyes the cherub in the corner.

"Would you like to tell me what's going on?" Thor asked her gently.

"I'm sorry—I really can't," said Carol.

"Don't forget, I already know about the telephone calls and the business cards. Wouldn't it make sense to tell me the rest?"

"I don't even know the rest myself," sighed Carol. "Except for that awful little man at the hotel last night. I suppose you might as well know about him, too..." She stopped just short of telling him about talking with Jonathan, or about Truman Yates.

"He should be easy enough to spot if he shows up here," said Thor after hearing the description of Juma. "So we do know at least that the telephone calls and the cards are connected. Well, it's a start."

"What do you mean, a start?"

"A clue to solving this intriguing mystery."

"Please, Thor, don't. All I want is to convince these people that whatever is going on, it has nothing to do with me. If you go around asking questions, it'll only make them even more suspicious."

"Perhaps I could spread the word that I am really the mysterious Mrs. Simon in disguise," suggested Thor. "That would put you in the clear."

"I'm sure Captain Kamanga would be very amused," said Carol. "You can tell he's got a great sense of humor. Please, just promise me you'll stay out of this."

Thor leaned forward over the table and met her eyes intently. "I will promise, but on one condition."

"Well, what is it?" asked Carol, as lightly as she could.

"Tell me why you've really come here," said Thor.

CHAPTER 10

1

As the askari swung open the heavy iron gate, Nelson Waiyala stepped through it following close behind his father, Wangeru Odege. They walked through the garden up to the front door of the biggest house that seven-year-old Nelson had ever seen. All the houses he knew were made of poles and mud daub, or of rusty red clay bricks. This one was all concrete and stone like a church, and the walls were clean and freshly painted white.

Nelson watched in awe as Odege grasped the upper jaw of a metal lion's head on the door and rapped it sharply up and down against the lower jaw. The door was opened by a woman wearing a spotless white apron over a crisp, blue checked cotton dress. Her hair was pulled tightly back under the matching headscarf. Odege told her their names, his voice sounding weak and humble in the midst of such grandeur. The woman nodded and stepped aside to let them into the front hallway. Nelson saw that, instead of hardbeaten earth, the floor was made of some kind of slippery smooth, dark stones laid down in perfect flat squares.

The maid looked down at their grimy shoes and signaled for them to stay where they were while she disappeared through another door at the end of the short hall. Nelson's curiosity battled with his apprehension. He strained to peek through the door without moving from his spot but all he could see was bright light spilling out from the room beyond.

The door opened wide and a handsome man in a western suit came out. Nelson recognized his uncle, who had visited the village a few times. On each occasion there had been a feast, as the clan had gathered to offer their greetings and make presents of food and banana beer. He knew that this uncle was not the head of the clan or any kind of chief, but his visits were a cause for celebration because he distributed money for school fees, bride prices and medical bills.

"My brother Wangeru, praised be God you have arrived safely. You are welcome in my hut." Their tribal language had no other word for a man's dwelling place.

"My brother Thadeus," replied Odege. "I praise God to find you well and prosperous."

The two men embraced lightly, according to their custom.

"Here is my son, Nelson," said Odege, resting both hands on the little boy's shoulders.

"Yes, of course," said Maleke, smiling down at him. "And do you remember me, young Nelson?"

"Yes, uncle," Nelson murmured shyly, looking at the floor and fighting the urge to slink behind his father's legs. Odege gave him a push and he took a step forward, bending his head downward to receive his uncle's blessing.

Maleke laid his hand briefly on Nelson's bowed head. "You are named after a great man, my son, and some day you will also be great."

Nelson kept his eyes on the floor, trying to look grateful and modest at the same time.

"Please, follow me," said Maleke He led them into a large room furnished with an enormous overstuffed sofa and armchairs covered in dark green velvet. Oriental carpets covered the floor and, even though it was daytime, a ceiling lamp and three tall floor lamps were all burning.

"Adrienne is out just now," said Maleke, "but I hope she will return before you leave."

"I also hope she will come, so I can thank her in person for her generosity."

"Marcel!" called Maleke, in English. "Marcel, come in here."

The nine year old boy who came to join them had light brown skin and black hair that was tightly curled but not woolly like Nelson's. He wore new blue jeans, a Michael Jackson T-shirt and a pair of bright blue and white running shoes. Nelson stared at the shoes and curled up his dirty toes in their rubber sandals as though to make them disappear.

"Marcel," said Maleke, switching from English to Rumuran. "You remember your uncle Wangeru Odege and your cousin Nelson."

Marcel walked straight up to Odege and boldly offered his hand to shake. Odege took it awkwardly because this was not the proper way for a small boy to greet a grown man.

"Marcel, please take Nelson and show him around the house. Then bring him back here and you can have some cokes."

"Comme il est sal, Papa," said Marcel, wrinkling his nose as he stared at the smaller boy.

"Taisse-toi, mon petit," scolded Maleke.

Nelson flushed beneath his dark skin. He didn't understand the French, but somehow he knew his elegant cousin had just said he was dirty.

"Go on, now," said Maleke.

Marcel reached out and grabbed Nelson good-naturedly by the arm.

"Come on. Do you speak English?" he demanded, as he led the reluctant boy from the room.

"Yes," replied Nelson, dragging his feet a bit and looking over his shoulder at his father.

"Good," said Marcel. "You're going to need it."

The boys disappeared from the room and Maleke motioned Odege to sit down. "He is very young," Odege apologized.

"He will be happy here once he gets used to it. Pretty soon you won't be able to drag him back to the village."

"He is a lucky boy to have such an uncle."

Maleke shrugged off the thanks graciously. "He has earned the chance. The whole family knows he is the best student."

Odege nodded eagerly. "You won't have to beat this boy to make him study. Maybe you will have to beat him sometimes to make him stop studying to help in the house."

"We have people to take care of the house," said Maleke. "Nelson's job is only to excel in school and bring honor and good fortune to the clan. And to his father."

The maid returned carrying a tray with a silver tea service, delicate porcelain cups and saucers, a plate of tea biscuits and two bottles of Coca-Cola. She laid the tray on the heavy wooden coffee table and poured out the tea before living the room.

Odege accepted a cup of hot tea and added three heaping spoons of sugar. He selected several biscuits and sat back, sighing contentedly. It was a son's first duty to take care of his father, and now this youngest son of his would be able to make sure he wanted for nothing when he was old. Not for the first time, he congratulated himself on his foresight in marrying into Thadeus Maleke's family. His friends had laughed at him for paying such a heavy bride price, but he had been watching Maleke and knew it would be a good investment. How loudly were those same friends laughing now, with their sons stuck in the little village school with its broken desks and no books, where they would barely learn to read and write and add up numbers?

"Then tell me," said Maleke, "how are things in the village?"

"You should come again and see for yourself," urged Odege. "Everyone asks when you will come. They are saving their best chickens to welcome you, but those birds are becoming old and tough while they wait."

"Ah, yes," said Maleke regretfully, "if only I were not so busy here."

Odege nodded sympathetically. Of course his brother-in-law had important business that kept him in the capital. But he also suspected that Maleke didn't care to come home too often with his pockets full and leave with them empty.

"How is the new plantation project going?" asked Maleke.

"Very well," Odege assured him. "The headman gave some more land, so we now have more than twenty hectares planted in Eucalyptus, and the poles are bringing a good price in the market." Odege knew that Maleke had helped steer this project, funded by the Americans, to his home district. And why not? It was as good a place for the project as any.

"Of course," continued Odege, "they will fetch an even better price when we can sell them in Rendesha."

Maleke frowned and lifted his eyebrows.

"But Rendesha is too far for the women to walk there and back in one day," sighed Odege. "They will have to stay overnight and leave the girls to tend the fields and cook the dinner. I think we will need to have a truck. Do you think the Americans will buy us a truck?" he asked hopefully.

"Who knows?" Maleke slowly sipped his cup of tea. "I suppose that's something for you to raise with the project manager."

Odege sensed that it was better to drop the subject for now. Maleke enjoyed exercising his power and influence, but didn't like to be pushed. Odege reached out and helped himself to another biscuit and started in on the family gossip.

Maleke let him go on for a few minutes and then interrupted. "That reminds me, Wangeru, I hope you have some good news for me."

"Don't you worry, brother," said Odege. "Everything is fine. I'm looking out for your interests, all right."

"So you finally have some progress to report?"

Odege looked hurt. "You know these things take time, brother. Those people can take months to handle even the simplest matter. It always helps, of course, to spread a little money around to focus their attention."

"What happened to the five thousand rimands I gave you two months ago? That can't all be gone already?"

Odege nodded sadly. "You know their tricks. They arrange it so every piece of paper has to go through so many hands, and a little money sticks to each and every one."

"For all that money I expected to see some results by now."

"You will see them very soon, brother," Odege assured him. "My contacts assure me that the papers will be ready next week."

"Your contacts are all bloody liars. You've been telling me the same thing for months now. I'm not going to tolerate this any longer. I will be in Mwatumi in two weeks' time. If you can't give me better news by then, I'll find someone else to 'look after my interests.'"

"There's no need to speak like that, brother. I've said the papers will be ready. But I will need another twenty thousand rimands to make absolutely sure."

"Twenty thousand! Don't be ridiculous. I'll give you another five thousand. But this time, give it out only after we see some results and not before."

2

Nearly six feet tall, with long blond braids wrapped like a turban around her head, Celeste Hartmann was accustomed to attracting attention. She had also read that many African men believe all white women are nymphomaniacs, particularly young women who go backpacking around Africa on their own. So she paid no attention to the wolf whistles from the group of young locals as she walked past their table and into the lobby of the Norfolk Hotel. She also did her best to ignore the frank stare of the bald, pot-bellied white man at the reception desk, although it was hard to pull her eyes away from his face, which was swollen and covered with purple bruises.

"I am Celeste Simon," she told the young woman behind the reception desk. "Do you have any message here for me?"

"Mrs. Simon? A message for you?" The receptionist seemed strangely flustered by the request. "I am sorry, can you please speak with the manager?" She disappeared hurriedly into the back office.

"What's that all about?" asked the man with the bruises.

Celeste gave a vague smile in his direction and glanced quickly away again.

"You're Dutch, aren't you?" he persisted. "Recognized the accent. You travel as much as I do, you learn to pick 'em out."

"Yes," said Celeste shortly.

"I'm American, myself. From Minneapolis. Lots of Dutch up that way."

Celeste turned away, pretending to hunt for something in her backpack. "Friendly folks, the Dutch," he remarked.

A plump man in a tight black suit emerged from the back office, looking concerned.

"Good morning, Mrs. Simon. I am Morris Ndaye, the Assistant Manager. How may I help you?"

"I am expecting to find a message from a friend," said Celeste. "I was supposed to meet him here, but I am a few days late."

Mr. Ndaye's face puckered with consternation. "I am very sorry, Mrs. Simon, but it seems there has been a misunderstanding. You understand, we did not know who you are, and we had no record of any booking for you." He explained that the staff had assumed the messages were for another guest with a similar name.

"And they call this a five-star hotel," put in the American.

"Is there something we can do for you this morning, Mr. Yates?" asked Ndaye with pointed politeness.

"Naw, don't mind me," grinned Yates.

"Where can I find this Mrs. Simmons?" asked Celeste.

"I am sorry, I understand she has left Kenya," said Ndaye.

Celeste bit her lip in frustration.

"Please accept my most sincere apologies, Mrs. Simon. Perhaps another time you can notify us in advance to hold messages for your arrival." Ndaye turned to go.

"Wait," said Celeste. "Jasper...the man I was expecting to meet here...he is also from the Netherlands. Thirty five years old, very thin, with blond hair and a small beard."

Ndaye smiled encouragingly. "Yes, I remember him. He did not stop with us, but he came several days, also asking for messages." Then his smile faded. "But I fear now he must also have gone. I have not seen him since Wednesday."

"Verdammt!" said Celeste. "I suppose he has gone back to Mwatumi alone. Do you know when is the next plane to Rumura?"

"Rumura?" Yates spoke up again. "You don't want to go there, sweetheart. Godawful place. Bunch of thugs. That's where I got this." He pointed to his face.

"Were you attacked by robbers?" Celeste couldn't help asking.

"Hell, no, honey. This was the police."

"But, what did you do?"

"Not a damn thing. It was a frame-up. They planted some stuff on me and then grabbed me at the airport." Yates could see that Celeste was skeptical. "See, I made the mistake of stumbling on something they didn't want anyone to know about, so they wanted to shut me up. I'm tellin' you, I was lucky to get out of there alive. If your boyfriend was dumb enough to go into that hellhole, I sure wouldn't follow him if I was you."

"Thank you for your advice," said Celeste coolly. Then she turned back to Ndaye. "Please, where can I ask about the flights?"

Ndaye indicated the hotel travel desk. "I believe there is one tonight, if you can get a seat."

"Look, sweetheart, you seem like a nice kid," said Yates. "In case you or your boyfriend get in trouble, here's the name of a guy at the U.S. Embassy." He took a business card out of a leather holder and scribbled Jonathan Marshall's name on the back. "He's a pain in the ass, but he was the one that got me out."

Celeste accepted the card with an air of humoring him and slipped it into the back pocket of her jeans before heading toward the travel desk.

"She's gonna thank me yet," Yates said to Ndaye. "I met a Dutch guy named Jasper when I was out in Mwatumi. Got to be the same guy. She probably doesn't know it, but her boyfriend's fishin' in some mighty dangerous waters."

3

Greg twisted the dial of the radio and cursed under his breath as the signal faded in and out.

"Bravo Zebra, two, four, six, do you read me? Over."

The voice on the other end was barely audible through the crackling static. "I'm still here, but I can barely hear you. Is that you, Greg? Over."

"Affirmative. Do you have an update? Over."

"We may have a lead on the identity of..." the static rose again.

"Bravo Zebra, two, four, six. What was that? I don't copy. Repeat, I don't copy. Do you read me? Oh, shit, forget it." Greg flipped the switch to turn the radio off. "Over and out," he sighed.

He heard footsteps behind him. Lisa came in, dressed in muddy field clothes with her binoculars and camera dangling from her neck. Greg reached out his hand and pulled her in toward him.

"Hello, lover," said Lisa. "When did you get back?"

"A few minutes ago. I was running late so I came straight here for the six o'clock contact."

"Were you able to get through?"

"Yeah, but the signal was terrible—I couldn't hear a thing. We've got to get a new radio."

"Oh, no, you don't," said Lisa. "My new tape recorder and directional microphone come first."

Greg got up and stretched. "I've got a better idea. Next donation that comes in, we buy shock absorbers for the Suzukis."

"Done," agreed Lisa.

Greg locked the door of the radio shack behind them. He laid his arm across Lisa's shoulder and she circled hers around his waist as they walked up the hill and through a small stand of trees toward their house.

"How was Mwatumi?" asked Lisa.

"So-so. I talked to the Assistant Chief about those boys we caught over near Rendesha last week. I let him talk me out of pressing charges."

"But weren't they carrying spears?"

"Yeah, but I didn't catch them with anything, and they never went anywhere near the chimp area. I think one of them was the A.C.'s nephew, so now he owes me."

"Did you see Kamanga?"

"Yeah, I tracked him down at the Acropolis bar. Big surprise, huh?"

"And?"

"And nothing. I don't know why I even bother."

"At least you tried," soothed Lisa.

The house was set in a small clearing on a promontory overlooking a deep valley. The multi-layered tapestry of the forest, in a hundred shades of green, fell abruptly away in front of it, plunging and then rising again steeply to form the first of a series of sharp ridges that reached all the way to the Zaire divide. The low, slanting sun threw the texture of the hillside into sharp relief, outlining the straight, silvery trunks of the tall trees with crystal clarity. Here and there, majestic emergents, the giants of the forest, towered above the canopy, their sculpted crowns floating on their graceful, outstretched limbs like loosely anchored emerald clouds. A pair of gleaming black ravens exchanged hoarse, croaking cries as they glided back and forth across the ravine like shadows in a twilight sky.

"I forgot to tell you," said Greg. "I ran into Carol Simmons, too. She came in while I was talking to Kamanga. He kept staring at her after I introduced them—it was kind of creepy."

"Kamanga is always kind of creepy," said Lisa. "Is she still planning to come out this weekend?"

"Yeah, so she said. And guess what—she's not alone."

"So Thor came after all?"

"That's my guess. I didn't see him, but that old gossip Sotiropoulos couldn't wait to tell me she arrived from Mwatumi with some guy." He looked at her. "You're not surprised, are you? I told you he'd come."

"And you were right, as always, my darling. You're such a shrewd judge of human nature."

The red-orange sun slipped out of sight behind the furthest ridge. Greg unlocked the door and they stepped inside. The house was a small, rectangular building made of local brick and wood. In the main room, pastel dhurri rugs were scattered across the dark wooden floorboards and an old rattan sofa faced a big fieldstone fireplace. Near the back, a heavy wooden table and chairs marked out the dining area. Along the front wall, beneath the big imported glass windows overlooking the valley, a door resting on two filing cabinets served as a desk. The walls were lined with rough shelves crammed with books and cassette tapes and with photographs of friends, family and chimpanzees.

Greg and Lisa passed through the main room into the bedroom, where Greg collapsed onto the broad platform bed. The mattress had come by truck from Nairobi, their one real luxury. Lisa sat on the edge of the bed beside him and started to unlace her boots.

"I don't think it's such a good idea to have anyone here this weekend," said Greg. "Nairobi thinks something is going to break over the next few days."

"It's too late now. I promise I'll keep them out of your way."

"Them? So you're assuming Nilssen is coming too?"

"It would be pretty rude to say no, since he's already here."

"That's just what he's counting on."

"I still don't understand what you have against him."

"It's just a feeling I've got," said Greg. "That's why I decided to check him out. I sent a telex to Bill Reynolds in New York, asking him to check back issues of the New Yorker for those articles Nilssen's supposed to have written."

"You are getting paranoid, aren't you, darling?"

"Just because you're paranoid, doesn't mean they're not after you," Greg pointed out. "I was right about Yates, wasn't I?"

"That was different," said Lisa. "This is a friend of Pat's."

"She just met him a couple of days ago," countered Greg. "She doesn't know who he really is anymore than we do."

"Fine, do whatever you think is best." Lisa stood up and pulled her T-shirt over her head. "I need a bath," she said.

Greg wrinkled his nose. "You sure do."

Lisa threw the grimy shirt at him, followed by an even riper sock. Greg threw his hands up in front of his face. "Uncle, uncle!" he cried. He levered himself up to a sitting position on the edge of the bed. "I'll go tell Fiona to bring you some hot water."

He watched as Lisa finished undressing, with the evening light throwing soft shadows on her glowing, dark skin. "On second thought, I'll fetch it myself," he said.

4

Thor crooked his arm and Carol slipped her hand through it. As they stepped out into the soft moonlight, a chorus of crickets and frogs rose up from the darkness on all sides, calling back and forth across the crisp night air.

"I don't even know why I told you all that," said Carol.

Somewhere between the mousakka and the tiny cups of strong, black coffee, Carol had found herself telling Thor about how she and Neil seemed to be drifting apart, and about the affair that she was sure Neil was having with Camilla Wong.

"It's all right," said Thor. "Women are always telling me their problems with their husbands and boyfriends."

"It must be very boring for you."

"Actually, it's a wonderful way to learn what not to do. Unfortunately I must be a slow learner, since I've been divorced twice."

"I guess we're all slow learners. And we never learn from anybody else's mistakes. When I was in school I saw lots of professors getting involved with their graduate students. I even remember thinking it was okay, since their wives obviously didn't care enough to hang on to them. Now I know it's not that you don't care—you just can't compete. She's always right there, working alongside him, looking up to him, admiring everything he does. Not to mention she's gorgeous. Or did I mention that already?"

"You might have," said Thor.

"I can't even really blame him," said Carol. "Who could resist all that?"

"You don't know for sure that he hasn't resisted."

"Then where was he at five o'clock this morning when I called?"

"I'm afraid you're asking that question of the wrong person."

"Sure, but I'm six thousand miles away from the right person, and last I checked the phone here isn't working," sighed Carol. "That's pretty much been the story of our marriage for the last five years. No wonder he's sick of it."

"Are you sorry you came?"

"I had to come—I couldn't let Margaret and the others down. I just wish I didn't have to let Neil down so often."

They walked to the far end of the lawn, where a sagging wire fence smothered with bougainvillea marked the edge of the hotel's grounds and the beginning of a rocky, brush-covered slope that climbed toward the dark wall of the Mali-Kuli ridge. They could feel the presence of the mountain like a brooding giant somewhere in the darkness beyond.

"I should turn in," said Carol at last. "I have to get up to Margaret's house early, before she goes out to the fields."

"Are you sure you don't want me to come with you?" asked Thor.

"I need some time to talk with her alone first," said Carol. "But I'll try to arrange for you to meet her and some of the other women in the afternoon. See you back here at the hotel for lunch?"

"It's a date," said Thor. They had arrived at the patio outside Carol's room. Thor waited while Carol fished out her key and opened the door. He laid one hand on her shoulder and leaned forward to brush his lips lightly across hers. "Good night," he said quietly, as she stepped inside.

Carol sat on the edge of the bed and slipped off her shoes. Her shoulder still felt warm where Thor's hand had been and her lips held a feathery, tingling memory of his fleeting kiss. Even with the door open, the room seemed stuffy and confining. She went back outside and stood looking out over the lawn where they had been walking, shivering in her bare feet on the concrete. The light spilling out from her room cast her elongated shadow across the patio. The three-quarter moon was high above the horizon now, anchoring a cascade of bright stars.

Suddenly Carol heard a rustling in the dense cypress hedge right beside her. Her heart leaped into her throat as someone came around the end of the hedge and onto the patio. She was about to scream for the first time in her life, when he stepped into the light.

"Shhh," said Jasper, holding one finger to his lips.

The scream died in her throat, but her heart was still pounding.

"What on earth are you doing here?" she demanded. "You scared me half to death."

Jasper took a step closer. "Be quiet," he said, in a low, gruff voice. "I am going to tell you about V.J. Singh."

CHAPTER 11

The light from her room cast oblique, evil-looking shadows across Jasper's bony face.

"Shall we sit down?" he suggested coolly.

Carol sank slowly into one of the rickety wicker patio chairs and Jasper pulled the other one up to sit close beside her.

Carol controlled her voice with an effort. "What's going on here?" she demanded. "What do you know about Singh?"

"I know why he is trying to make contact with you," answered Jasper.

"It's a mistake," said Carol. "He thinks—they think—I'm somebody else."

"I know," said Jasper, with smug satisfaction. "I told them so."

"You did what!?" Carol's voice rose sharply.

Jasper's finger slid up to his pursed his lips again. "Keep your voice down," he told her. "Try to act natural. Someone may be watching."

Carol felt a chill that had nothing to do with the night air.

"In fact," Jasper corrected himself, "they made the initial mistake themselves. I only confirmed their suspicion."

"Their suspicion of what?"

"That your name is Mrs. Simon and that you and I are business partners." Jasper hunched forward, leaning his elbows on his lap, bringing his face right next to hers.

"I think you'd better explain," Carol said, backing away as much as she could in her chair.

"It would be better if we went inside," said Jasper. "He stood up and strode into her room. Carol hesitated a moment and then followed him inside. He shut the door firmly and sat in the armchair, gazing distractedly around the room until she sat down on the bed facing him.

"I am not really a sociologist," he began, pausing dramatically to let that sink in. "Have you ever heard of bonobos—what some people call pygmy chimpanzees?"

Carol did not answer at first, but Jasper waited her out.

"Pat told me Lisa Othieno discovered some in the Mali-Kuli forest," she said finally.

"She did not discover them," said Jasper contemptuously. "The people here have known about them for many years. She simply made the mistake of writing an article revealing their presence here to the entire world. Bonobos are very rare. Except for the Mali-Kuli forest, they are only known to be in some areas of DRC. Because they are so rare, they are very valuable. There are people who would pay a great deal to get one."

"You mean zoos?"

"I mean spoiled, wealthy people who collect rare and endangered animals as others collect paintings or Faberge eggs. The fact that it is illegal only makes them more desirable to such people, and more expensive. Because the bonobos are the closest genetic relatives of humans, they are also sought after by medical researchers. Unfortunately, some of them will also buy the animals, with no questions asked. And for every animal that makes it to the private zoo or the laboratory, at least a dozen will probably die along the way." Jasper's eyes burned and the pitch of his voice rose as he spoke. He paused again to recover his usual cool detachment. "The Green Brigade is dedicated to stopping them."

"The what?"

"It is a small organization, based in the Netherlands. A 'non-governmental organization,' like yours. I am sure you have never heard of it. We don't seek publicity, like GreenPeace and so many others. We find we can be more effective by remaining unknown. Our aim is to stop the trade in endangered species all over the world."

"Okay," said Carol, "so you're not a sociologist and you work for this noble Dutch NGO. What does all this have to do with what's been happening to me?"

"Perhaps you are not aware, but there is a great deal of wildlife poaching here."

"In Rumura?"

"All over Africa, actually. But this region is particularly bad because there are so many small countries with borders that run through forests and mountains and are virtually unguarded. That makes it easy to confuse the trail, to capture an animal in one country, slip it across the border and export it from another country with false papers or disguised as something else. Many of these remote border areas are controlled by insurgents and rebels who use poaching to get money for weapons. Even where the governments are in control, they are hostile to one another and won't cooperate to stop the trade, and in any case the government officials themselves are usually involved. All of this, of course, makes our mission very difficult." Jasper's voice sank until it was barely audible and he locked his eyes on hers. "Difficult...and dangerous."

If he was being dramatic to impress her, Carol had to admit it was working.

"The Brigade has been receiving reports for some time of a major poaching ring operating here in Rumura," continued Jasper. "We believe there is some poaching in the Mali-Kuli forest itself, and also movement of large amounts of ivory and skins across the border with the DRC. I am here to investigate."

"How do you go about investigating something like that?" asked Carol, intrigued in spite of herself.

"We work by going 'undercover.' I arranged to come to the Mali-Kuli station, pretending to be a sociology researcher wanting to study the attitudes of local people to the forest and the wildlife. I presented myself as the student of a well-known university professor in the Netherlands, who is a supporter of my group. This gave me a base for operations and also the perfect cover for questioning the people in the villages about the forest and the wildlife. Usually it is local men who actually catch the animals and pass them to a middleman, who sells them to the final buyers. The locals get almost nothing, and the middleman makes a huge profit. So, these local people are the best source of information."

"But why should they trust you and tell you anything?"

"I don't need them to trust me. I only need them to talk too much, and that is easy. I sit in the bars, pay for some drinks and keep my ears open. There are always a few young fools who get drunk and start boasting. It was simply a matter of time. Finally, about three weeks ago I got my break. I met two young fellows who wanted to impress me. They told me they are very famous hunters. They hinted that they have important connections and they are going to make a great deal of money soon. I laughed and said I didn't believe them, just to get them angry. An angry drunkard is a careless one. Finally, one night they got very drunk and very mad, and they told me that a 'Big Man' in Kobani wants them to catch a baby bonobo for a rich buyer from Europe. They would not tell me his name, but I believe this 'Big Man' is V. J. Singh."

"Then you know who he is!" exclaimed Carol, relieved to find that at least somebody did.

"Not yet. I am sure that is not his real name. But these stupid, bragging fools will lead me to him." Jasper paused dramatically again. "Or, more precisely...they will lead him to me."

"Oh. I was hoping you were finally going to clear this whole thing up."

Jasper bridled at Carol's obvious disappointment. "As you will see, that is exactly what I am going to do."

He explained that, having established contact with the two Rumurans, he had told them in strict secrecy that he was also interested in buying a baby bonobo, hoping they would put him in touch with their 'Big Man' in Kobani. He had told them he was willing to pay five thousand dollars—much more than the real buyer was likely to have offered.

126

"So you want them to sell the baby bonobo to you instead, to save it from this other buyer?" asked Carol.

"Of course not," said Jasper impatiently. "I don't want them to capture a baby at all. When their boss—let us assume it is Singh—learns that there is another customer who is willing to pay more money, he will contact me to negotiate. And when he does, I will expose him. With luck, he may try to set up a bidding war between us, and in the process the real buyer will also be exposed."

"But wouldn't he just arrange to get two babies, one for the other guy and another one for you?"

"It is not so easy. To capture a baby bonobo, you must first kill the mother, and often the whole family, which will try to protect it. Greg Allen and his supporters would immediately make a huge outcry and force even the reluctant Rumuran authorities to make a show of investigating. That could make it harder and riskier to go after a second one. I believe Singh will consider the possibility that he can only get one animal, and he will make sure in advance to get the best possible price for it."

"But what if he gets the baby first, and then starts the bidding?"

Jasper shook his head. "The authorities might find it in the meantime, or more likely it will simply die. If Singh is a professional as I believe he is, he will make all the arrangements in advance to unload the animal immediately."

"All right," said Carol. "I guess I understand what you're trying to do. But I still don't see where I come in to all this."

"I am trying to tell you, if you would stop interrupting," snapped Jasper. "So, I had laid my trap. Then matters took a somewhat unexpected turn. At first I thought I might have made a misjudgment, but it turned out to be the best thing."

"Of course," said Carol. Jasper was so insufferably sure of himself, he reminded her of the old joke, the know-it-all who admits, 'I thought I made a mistake once, but I was wrong.'

Jasper missed the irony. "Yes, it's obvious, isn't it? My offer was so good that my contacts realized Singh must be cheating them by paying them such a small amount to catch an animal that is worth so much. They started to think how nice it would be to cut him out and get all of that money themselves—more money than these country boys could ever dream of earning, maybe in their whole lifetime. They came back and said they would deal with me directly instead of involving the 'Big Man' at all. It was perfect."

"But how is that going to help you expose Singh, if that's what you're after?" asked Carol pointedly.

"The only problem in my original plan was that Singh might stay in the background and deal with me only through his agents. I had to find a way to get to him in person, and now these two fools have given it to me. As you have already discovered, this Singh has eyes and ears everywhere. He will certainly come to know about me and my offer, but now he will also learn that his men can't be trusted. You see, he will have no choice but to contact me himself. And so, I moved on to step three of my plan."

"Is this the step that explains what all this has to do with me?"

Jasper didn't seem to hear her. "When these two young fools proposed to cut out their boss and deal directly, I acted very doubtful, as though I didn't believe they could deliver. Of course, the more I backed away the more they pursued me. They insisted, and kept dropping the price. Finally I pretended to be swayed, but said that I would have to check with my partner."

"Your partner?" asked Carol, confused again.

"Celeste Hartmann, another member of the Brigade. Our plan was that I would come ahead to set the trap, and then she would join me to help spring it. Now that they were nibbling at the bait, I called her in the Netherlands to come immediately to meet me in Nairobi."

"Nairobi," repeated Carol slowly.

"Yes. I waited in Nairobi for three days, and then finally I received a message from her. She had decided it was too dangerous," said Jasper with disgust. "I told her when she joined the Brigade that it would not be a picnic."

Carol remembered the fax that he had left on the table at the Norfolk, the one written in Dutch, signed 'Celeste.' At the time she had assumed Jasper had been stood up by a girlfriend.

"So she dropped out," prompted Carol. "What did you do then?"

"I was ready to continue alone and find some way to collect the evidence I needed on my own. But then, to my surprise, I saw my two Rumurans in Nairobi."

"You didn't expect them to be there?"

"Certainly not—I had not told them or anyone else that I was going to Kenya, but somehow they had found out. It was obvious that they were trying very hard not to be seen. I assumed at first they were following me, but I soon realized that in fact they were following someone else entirely."

Carol sighed. "Me," she said flatly.

"Exactly. Clearly they expected me to meet a woman in Nairobi, and when I met you that day on the terrace of the Norfolk hotel, they assumed it must be you."

"You met me and Pat Marshall together," Carol pointed out. "Why couldn't it have been her?"

"That is where fate took a hand in the affair," said Jasper. "Back in Rumura, I had given them the name of the woman who was my partner." Jasper looked at her ironically.

Carol closed her eyes. "Mrs. Simon," she said, tiredly.

"Paul Simon is my favorite American singer," he explained.

Carol couldn't think of a response to that.

"You see how perfectly it all unfolded," he continued. "They knew I was meeting a woman named Simon in Nairobi. They saw me waiting for her at the Norfolk Hotel, and then you arrived, with your almost identical name."

"But I kept telling them it was a mistake, and that my name isn't Simon. Why wouldn't they believe me?"

"Probably because they saw us together, not only once but many times."

"You did that on purpose," Carol suddenly realized. "You kept turning up wherever I was so it would look like we were together."

The self-satisfied look on Jasper's face was infuriating.

"And I suppose you even told them I really was this Mrs. Simon?" she accused him. "That's why that man kept insisting that he knew perfectly well who I am."

"No, not then. I wanted to learn what those two were up to, so I continued to pretend I didn't know they were there."

"And what were they up to?"

"There are two possibilities. Because I said I could not make a decision without consulting you, they may have decided that you are the one with the money and I am just another middleman. So, it may be that they think they can do even better by cutting out not only Singh, but me as well. The stupid bastards," he said mildly, with the first trace of amusement she had ever heard in his voice.

"And the other possibility?"

"That one is more interesting," he continued, his excitement showing in his eyes and in the way he clutched his bony knees tightly in his hands. "It could be that Singh has scared them back into line, and now he himself is trying to by-pass me and reach you directly."

Carol remembered Jasper's interest in Singh's card when she had shown it to him at the Norfolk.

"It seemed almost too much to hope for, until I saw that he did not give up after you failed to contact him in Nairobi, but continued to leave cards for you at the hotel in Kobani," said Jasper. "But even so I was not sure until the incident outside your hotel room last night."

"You've been spying on me?"

"It was necessary," he shrugged. "The man who confronted you is one of my two drunken Rumurans—a small-time swindler named Juma Ayala. From what he told you, it seems we have got Mr. Singh on the hook."

"There's no 'we' about it," Carol said sharply. "I think I've got the picture now. Thanks to you, all sorts of disreputable and probably dangerous people think I'm in Rumura to make an illegal purchase of an endangered baby bonobo, for a hell of a lot of money."

Jasper's eyes met hers coolly. "Believe me, it is not my choice to be working with an amateur on such a sensitive operation. But it can still work if you do exactly what I tell you."

"Forget it!" Carol exclaimed as she rose abruptly from the bed. "I'm not getting myself killed helping you out with this crazy scheme."

"Calm down—no one is going to get killed," Jasper told her dryly.

"And I'm not about to land in jail over it, either."

"I promise you, there is no chance of that."

"Really? Then I guess you might be surprised to know that this afternoon Captain Kamanga, the chief of police here in Mwatumi, called me Mrs. Simon and warned me to steer clear of your man Singh."

"Really?" exclaimed Jasper. "That is excellent! Why didn't you tell me this before?"

"What!" said Carol incredulously.

"It means I was right. The police and possibly other officials here are involved in the poaching."

"How do you figure that?"

"How else could Kamanga have heard about Mrs. Simon?" asked Jasper. "Only Singh's people think she exists."

"Maybe he's got a good intelligence network and he's trying to prevent trouble. He wanted me to tell Singh that he's on to him."

"What were his exact words?"

"I don't know," said Carol with exasperation. "Something like, I was welcome in Mwatumi but I should tell Mr. Singh to go back to Nairobi because he won't be able to do business here."

"Of course!" said Jasper triumphantly. "Kamanga is trying to keep Singh off his territory. He wants your business himself."

Carol stared at him in dismay. Despite his boorish manner, she had assumed Kamanga was doing his job—warning her that he wouldn't tolerate criminals like Singh in 'his' town. He had even made a point of warning her about Yates, whom Jonathan had said was arrested for something to do with smuggling. But she had to admit Jasper's version made just as much sense— Yates could have been trying to muscle in on Kamanga's action, just as Jasper suggested Singh was trying to do.

"I don't know what to think," she said at last.

"You will see," predicted Jasper confidently. "Kamanga will be in touch with you again with a proposition."

"Oh, no, he won't," said Carol sharply, "because I've had enough of this. You have to get in touch with your contacts immediately and tell them it was a mistake, that I have nothing to do with any of this."

"How can I do that?" demanded Jasper. "I have already told them we are partners. How can I say now that you are not who I thought you were?"

"That's not my problem, is it?" said Carol.

"But you don't have to do anything," insisted Jasper. "Only wait for Singh to contact you again, and agree to meet with him."

"Are you crazy? I'm not meeting him!"

"You don't have to go to the meeting—just set it up, and I will handle it after that."

"Agreeing to meet with him would be the same as admitting that I really am your partner. What if you're wrong, and Captain Kamanga is straight? Next thing I know we'll both be in jail. Or maybe someone will decide that I must be carrying the payoff money on me and try to rob me. You've put me in an impossible position. I'm going to have to go the authorities—like you should have done in the first place."

"Which authorities?" Jasper asked impatiently. "I have already told you, most of them are probably involved the poaching themselves."

Carol thought for a minute. "What about Thadeus Maleke?"

"What about him?."

"Isn't he sort of in charge of the Mali-Kuli forest? And I know Jonathan Marshall trusts him."

Jasper snorted, letting her know what he thought of Jonathan's opinion.

"And what about Greg and Lisa?" Carol asked suddenly. "What do they know about this?"

Jasper shook his head. "Greg has apparently learned from contacts in Europe that someone is interested in buying a baby bonobo. But he does not know about my plans."

"Why not? I'd think he'd be a good ally."

"Greg is too cautious," said Jasper scornfully, "and he always has to be in charge. I originally came out here intending to work together with him but I learned very soon that I would do better on my own. Anyway, how can I be sure he is not mixed up in this business himself?"

"You can't really believe that?"

"Several years ago, Greg Allen was instrumental in exporting three baby chimpanzees illegally from Cameroon. That is a fact. We investigated the incident very thoroughly. And his explanations are not very convincing."

That reminded Carol of Jonathan, who had told her the same story that morning.

"I should probably warn you, Jonathan Marshall is looking into this whole business. It's only a matter of time before he gets to the bottom of it and finds you there."

"What do you mean?" demanded Jasper sharply. "What does he know?"

"After the incident last night at the hotel I got worried. I told him about that, and about the phone calls and business cards. He promised to look into it for me, to try to find out who this Mr. Singh is and why he's pestering me."

"Wonderful." Jasper threw up his hands in exasperation. "And I suppose the first thing he did was tell the story to his trusted friend, Dr. Thadeus Maleke. And what has Marshall found out?"

"Not much yet, I guess," said Carol a bit uneasily. "I talked to him before I left Kobani. He had some leads, but he said he wanted to keep it low-key."

"So," said Jasper with pointed sarcasm, "Jonathan Marshall has been making discreet inquiries. We can assume then that all of Kobani has now heard about Mrs. Simon and Mr. Singh. No wonder Kamanga was onto you so quickly."

"He's not 'onto' me," Carol reminded him. "There's nothing about me for him to be 'onto'."

"This means I will have to work faster," said Jasper, ignoring her. "You really have complicated matters."

"Well, who asked you to drag me into this?" Carol demanded. "And anyway, if you'd told me what was going on in the first place, I wouldn't have had to go to Jonathan at all."

"So, now I have told you, and instead of agreeing to help me you are ready to ruin everything I have done."

"You bet I am," said Carol. "If you don't go and sort these people out immediately, I'm going straight to Jonathan, and to Kamanga and Maleke, and anybody else I can think of, and tell them the whole story."

"You would not be so stupid," said Jasper.

Carol's face gave him his answer.

"Very well," he muttered, "I will find something to tell them."

"Whatever it is, it had better leave me completely out of the picture."

"I could say you have backed out, but that I am still interested," said Jasper, thoughtfully. "But you must leave Mwatumi right away—that would make it more convincing."

"I'm not going anywhere," Carol told him firmly. "I have work to do here."

"Only for a few days," said Jasper. "By next week I will spring my trap and then you can come back."

"Thanks, but no thanks," said Carol, "You figure out some way to convince them that I'm not who they think I am, or I'll tell them so myself. If I get one more card or phone call or person calling me 'Mrs. Simon,' that's it."

Jasper looked at her coldly. "I told you I will do it. But in the meantime, you must talk to no one about this. I cannot have any more of your surprises."

"I have to tell Jonathan, so he can stop worrying and chasing down leads."

"Above all, not him!" insisted Jasper. "You have already done enough damage there. And who is this man you were walking in the garden with, this Swede?"

"He's Norwegian," said Carol stiffly, "and his name is Thor Nielssen, in case it's any of your business."

"What do you know about him? What is he doing in Mwatumi?"

"He's forty five, he's lived in California, and he's traveling around Africa writing articles. Is there anything else you'd like to know?"

"How long have you known him?"

"I met him yesterday at Jonathan and Pat Marshall's house."

"And how long have they known him?"

"Only a few days—Pat met him at the French cultural center in Kobani."

"So," Jasper nodded thoughtfully. "So."

"So, what?" demanded Carol.

"Perhaps I should not tell you, since you refuse to cooperate with me. But I cannot take the chance that you will confide in him." Jasper leaned his face close to hers again and spoke softly but intensely. "I told you this whole business started with a European who wants a baby bonobo. Now someone with a European accent has been asking for Mr. Singh, saying he wants to talk business."

"How on earth do you know that?"

"Juma Ayala told me. He wants me to know that I have competition."

"Maybe he's making it up."

"I doubt it—he would be too afraid that I would catch him out. Needless to say, this Nilssen is my prime suspect."

"Don't be ridiculous. Kobani is full of people with European accents."

"Why is it ridiculous? Because he is pleasant and charming and you are, as they say, hot for him?" suggested Jasper.

"That is very rude and none of your business," snapped Carol.

"I have told you why it is my business. Your careless pillow-talk could put me in great danger."

"I think you'd better leave, now," said Carol coldly. As she threw the patio door open, a rush of cool, crisp air came in carrying a ringing chorus of frogs and katydids. Jasper started to say something, but the look on her face stopped him. At the edge of the patio, he turned back and gave her a last dark look.

"Remember," he said, "what your Mr. Nilssen doesn't know won't hurt him—or you."

CHAPTER 12

1

The Honorable Jean-Louis Benoit and his wife Annaliese stood in the entryway of the French Embassy residence, beneath an enormous crystal chandelier, greeting their guests. Together they looked like an advertisement for an expensive French perfume. The Ambassador's hand-tailored jacket accentuated his elegant figure, and his silver hair brushed the burgundy silk cravat beneath the open collar of his shirt. Madame Benoit was poised and elegant in a form-fitting, strapless black gown and a triple strand of pearls. Pat felt underdressed and overweight.

"Bonsoir, Monsieur l'Ambassadeur," said Jonathan, grasping the Ambassador's hand. He paused almost imperceptibly to give Benoit a chance to remember his name, then added, "Jonathan Marshall."

"Of course, Jonathan, how very good it is to see you again," said Benoit in accented but perfect English. "And your lovely wife," he added.

"Pat, you've met His Excellency, Ambassador Benoit?"

"Please—Jonathan," the Ambassador protested genially. "Tonight there are no formalities. I believe you know my wife, Annaliese."

Madame Benoit's hand was as cool and perfect as a marble statue's. Pat murmured a greeting and cast around in her mind for something to say, but their hosts had already released them, turning their attention to the next couple.

"My God," murmured Pat, as they stopped at the edge of the enormous living room, "look at this crowd. How long do we have to stay?"

"For God's sake, Pat, we just got here," Jonathan whispered back crossly. "A lot of people would give their eye teeth to be invited to one of the Ambassador's parties. Just try to enjoy yourself, okay? I'll go get us some drinks." He began to work

137

his way through the crowd toward the bar at the end of the room. Halfway there he stopped to greet someone and was soon deeply engrossed in conversation.

'Great,' Pat thought to herself, 'so much for my drink.' She started to walk over to Jonathan but stopped when she saw a short, round figure making its way toward him from behind. Pat changed course, grabbed a glass of white wine from a passing waiter and picked her way across the room and escaped through the French doors onto the veranda. It was bad enough having to squeeze into a cocktail dress and high heels. She drew the line at making conversation with Andre Delacroix.

"My dear Monsieur Marshall, what a delightful surprise to find you here tonight."

Jonathan heard the voice beneath his ear and felt a hand come to rest on his shoulder. He turned and looked down into the familiar, round red face.

"And such a very fortunate coincidence," said Delacroix, his nasal voice brimming with good cheer and fellowship. "I have a small question I wish to ask you, Jonathan."

"At your service, as always, Andre," replied Jonathan, smoothly concealing his surprise. He had met Delacroix from time to time at diplomatic functions, but in the social hierarchy of Kobani's expatriate community they had never been on a first name basis. As the manager of the Rumura branch of a big French timber company, Delacroix had a reputation as a ruthless businessman and a social snob. He was particularly known to regard Americans as culturally inferior. Besides that, he was speaking English. Usually he insisted on speaking French, either out of national chauvinism or, more likely, to put the anglophones at a disadvantage.

"I have been speaking with Thadeus Maleke," continued Delacroix. "You know Thadeus, of course?"

"Of course."

"Ah, there he is in fact, by the window. Another remarkable coincidence. Excuse us, if you please," he said peremptorily to the people around them, and took Jonathan firmly by the arm and led him away.

Thadeus Maleke was surrounded by a cluster of diplomats who were listening attentively to a story he was telling. As Delacroix approached with Jonathan in tow, the group burst into genial laughter. Delacroix steered Jonathan right through the crowd to Maleke's side.

"Cher ami," said Delacroix, "look who I have discovered. Now we will have an answer, n'est-ce pas?" He pulled the handkerchief from his breast pocket and dabbed at the moisture on his forehead and neck.

"Good evening, Thadeus," said Jonathan, reaching across Delacroix to shake hands. "Is Adrienne here tonight?"

"I believe she is out in the garden," said Maleke. "We must go and find her; she would be sorry to miss meeting you."

"Of course, of course," interrupted Delacroix. "But you remember, Thadeus, what we were talking about just a moment ago."

Thadeus caught Jonathan's eye over Delacroix' head. His expression was mildly amused and faintly apologetic, as though to say, what could you do with such people?

"Really, Andre, this is not the time...and anyway, this matter is not really in Jonathan's line."

"What isn't?" asked Jonathan, curious in spite of himself.

"It is as I was telling Thadeus," answered Delacroix. "I have returned today from Mwatumi, where I was together with Monsieur Yves Monceau, from the Caisse Central, the Central Bank, in Paris. You have met him? No? A charming man. Alors, he is visiting Rumura for some few days to discuss with the government a very important project to assist the country to improve its system of roads. At the request of mon ami, Monsieur l'Ambassadeur, I accompanied him on a visit to view the situation for himself. And truly, they are terrible, these roads, particularly those which go to the west, toward the Congo. Completement impossible. After twenty kilometers from Kobani, one finds oneself among the craters of the moon.

Beyond Bola it is nothing but a few tracks scratched into the earth. And after Mwatumi, nothing at all. How can a country develop without proper roads?

"I must say I agree with Andre on this point," said Maleke. "As you know, I myself come from the western province, and I can testify that the lack of proper roads is a major constraint for economic development in my region. We are so near to the Zaire River and the markets of Kisangani, and yet we could be a thousand kilometers away. Fortunately, the French government has offered to assist us to build a good road up to the DRC border at Rendesha, where we can connect with the highway to Kisangani."

"That is good news for you," said Jonathan politely.

"Yes, indeed, it would be very good news for Rumura," put in Delacroix, mopping his brow again. "Most unfortunately, however, Monsieur Monceau has told me that France may be forced to withdraw her offer of assistance. But perhaps you have also heard the same thing?" He studied Jonathan furtively.

Jonathan had already realized where the conversation was heading. He was well aware of the proposed French project, and of the snag it had hit. But he had no intention of letting Delacroix know that he knew. He wanted to learn what the Frenchman's game was.

"I'm afraid I haven't had the opportunity of talking with Mr. Monceau," he said.

"But that is surprising, is it not?" Delacroix appealed to Maleke. "I had thought surely our friend Jonathan would know of this matter, as regrettably it is due to the Americans that the problem has arisen."

"How do you mean?" asked Jonathan.

"Why, because it is meant to be a cooperative enterprise. La France and America and Germany, working together to assist Rumura."

"A joint project, co-financed by France and the U.S.?" Jonathan frowned. "I haven't heard about anything like that."

Maleke stepped in. "Not precisely a joint project, Jonathan. Rather, an overall package to link the western parts of the country with the east. The Germans have proposed to fund the rehabilitation of the road between Kobani and Bola, the French would rehabilitate the stretch from Bola to Mwatumi, and the U.S. Agency for International Development was to extend the road to Rendesha. Now it seems that the Americans are reconsidering, and of course the French and the Germans are reluctant to carry on with their part under the circumstances."

"This is what we wish to understand from you," said Delacroix, his voice rising. "Why have the Americans changed their minds?"

"Of course, I'm not with USAID..." began Jonathan.

"But surely you must have an idea—"

"—but I think I've heard something about this," Jonathan continued, ignoring Delacroix' interruption. "From my wife, actually. She does some work occasionally for USAID. Isn't this the road that would cut through the Mali-Kuli Forest?"

Delacroix threw his plump hands in the air and turned to Maleke in a mute display of despair.

"There has been some misunderstanding on that point," Maleke said to Jonathan. "The road would follow the southern edge of the forest, and not go through it as some people have said."

"That certainly is a misunderstanding then," said Jonathan. "I see Pat over there. Let's ask her about it."

Jonathan beckoned to Pat, who was standing near the doorway swapping stories of life in Thailand with the Danish Ambassador and her husband. Seeing that Delacroix was still with him, Pat frowned and shook her head almost imperceptibly. Jonathan waved again, insisting. Reluctantly, Pat excused herself and crossed the room to join them.

"Pat, you remember what we were talking about the other night, that business with the road to Rendesha," said Jonathan. "Didn't you say you'd seen some kind of report on it?"

"I know USAID brought in a consultant to do an environmental assessment of the proposal," said Pat. "He stayed with Greg and Lisa for a few days at the research station. I haven't seen the report myself, but I heard he came out against the proposed route because it would cut through the reserve."

"Ah," said Maleke, "I believe I understand the source of the confusion." He explained that, while the border of the Mali-Kuli Reserve did technically extend slightly south of the proposed route, there was no longer any actual forest there, due to heavy logging and fire damage over the years. "We have already set in motion the process of re-aligning the southern boundary of the reserve to exclude that area," he concluded.

"But if that's true, why was the USAID consultant so concerned about it?" asked Pat.

"It was the usual thing," said Maleke, his well-modulated voice taking on an unaccustomed edge. "He is from one of your American conservation organizations which seem to have appointed themselves the world's guardians. They are determined to ensure that no inch of any park or reserve everywhere in Africa is ever touched, regardless of the impacts on the country's economy or the local people."

"It is the insult," declared Delacroix warmly. "How should a person from Washington or New York tell Thadeus Maleke, who is himself a Doctor of Philosophy in Forestry, where there is a forest to protect and where there is not one? For that matter, I myself know a little something about our forests, n'est-ce pas? One can only wonder how it is that this consultant did not find it necessary to interview me at all."

"In fact, he does not seem to have carried out any independent assessment," said Maleke. "He had clearly made up his mind before he even arrived in Rumura. And then he spent a few days at the Mali-Kuli research station, where his biases were simply reinforced by Greg Allen."

"Obviously this isn't my field," said Jonathan, "but I don't understand how there can be confusion about whether or not this is a forest. Either it's full of trees or it isn't."

Maleke explained that it was not just a question of the presence or absence of trees, but of the quality of the forest ecosystem—the diversity of trees and other species—and of the prospects for restoring it to its original condition. Some people, including Greg Allen and apparently the USAID consultant, believed that the forest in that area was still viable and could recover on its own if protected and left to regenerate. But Maleke was convinced the damage was too extensive and it would be too expensive to restore, if such a thing could even be done. The money and manpower could be better spent instead on protecting and managing the intact, healthy forest in the remainder of the reserve.

"Indeed our road would be very beneficial for this purpose!" added Delacroix warmly.

"How is that?" demanded Pat, instinctively suspicious of Delacroix. Catching the warning glance Maleke shot toward him, she also suspected the "our" was a slip.

"It would make it much easier for my men to carry out their patrols," said Maleke. "Now they have to go everywhere by foot. With a good road around the southern perimeter of the reserve, they could use vehicles and motorcycles and cover a great deal more ground. It would also open up the possibility of tourism. The view of the Mali-Kuli volcano is quite spectacular from the southern edge of the reserve. And of course it would make an enormous improvement in the lives of the people in the area. For example, the women of that cooperative in Mwatumi that your friend Mrs. Simmons is supporting. It would open up new markets for their produce."

"So you see, mon ami, you must assist us," Delacroix said to Jonathan.

"I'm the Political Officer at the Embassy," Jonathan reminded him, "Even if all this is true, I don't see that it's a political issue."

"But it is, precisely, a political issue!" exclaimed Delacroix. "France has invested large sums in the feasibility studies and surveys for our part of this road, and now...? Is all this money to

143

go to waste? Monsieur Monceau has informed me that my government is protesting this matter to the Americans fortement."

"I haven't heard anything about it...officially," said Jonathan. He was gratified to see Delacroix turn even redder.

"I imagine the French would prefer to see the matter resolved quietly, without official protests," said Maleke, quelling Delacroix with another look. "Ambassador Benoit mentioned it to me, I think with the intention that I pass it on to your Embassy informally. That is really the only reason that I agreed to trouble you with it."

"I'll have a word with Jean-Louis about it," promised Jonathan.

Delacroix squeezed his plump hands together as though to stop from rubbing them with satisfaction. At that point, the conversation was interrupted as the Ambassador tapped a silver fork against a crystal wineglass, signaling the start of the speech-making part of the evening. The guest of honor, a visiting Parliamentarian from Paris, launched into a long discourse about French politics, as guests surreptitiously refilled their glasses and wondered how soon they could slip out without attracting attention.

As they waited for the driver to bring the car around, Pat yawned and checked her watch, not for the first time that evening.

"Almost twelve," she said. "You promised we'd get away before this."

"Sorry," said Jonathan, "it took awhile to get Jean-Louis alone."

Pat noticed that Jonathan now considered himself on a first-name basis with the Ambassador.

"Did you ask him about this road business?"

"I mentioned it."

"Well? What did he say?"

"Not much. He didn't really seem all that interested."

"So it's not a major diplomatic incident in the making?"

"Apparently not."

Pat looked curiously at Jonathan. He seemed to be lost in thought.

"What?" she asked him.

"Hmmm?"

"What are you thinking about?"

"Oh," he shrugged, "nothing."

"Come on, Jonathan. Give."

"Well," he said, slowly. "I was just wondering. If the French government isn't particularly concerned about our pulling out of this road, why do you suppose that little goon Delacroix is so worked up about it?"

2

It was well past dark when the old Peugot shuddered to a stop on the outskirts of Mwatumi and Juma and David climbed slowly out. David slammed his door and gave the car a kick.

"When is Muna going to get rid of this junkheap?" he demanded.

"You're lucky she let us use it at all," Juma reminded him.

David only scowled in response.

"Anyway," Juma reminded him, "next time you drive into Mwatumi it will be in your own Land Cruiser. And I'll be right behind in my Mercedes."

David gave a gleeful snort of laughter and stepped around the car. He unzipped his fly and relieved his aching bladder in a high, streaming arc into the roadside ditch. When he had finished, he gave a satisfied grunt and went back to join Juma.

"Are you hungry?" asked David. "We can go first to my place and get something to eat."

"Sure," said Juma.

David led the way up the hill, past dimly lit huts and flickering fires, until they came to the small but solid two-room brick and mud house where David lived with his mother and his brother and four sisters. David led Juma straight in through the low doorway without bothering to announce their arrival.

Margaret Waiyala sat at a small wooden table against the far wall with the two older girls, picking stones out of a panful of lentils. The younger ones perched on low stools near the embers of the small warming fire, talking quietly over an open schoolbook. They looked up, startled, when David and Juma entered, and jumped off their stools and ran over to their mother. They squatted on their heels against the wall, peering out over their bony knees.

"I've brought Juma for dinner," David said by way of greeting.

"You are welcome," Margaret replied, in a voice that suggested just the opposite.

David sniffed the air. "Fish stew," he said. "We'll have some of that."

"It's finished," said Margaret curtly.

"What, you didn't save any for me?" David demanded.

"It's almost ten o'clock," shrugged Margaret. "We didn't know you would still be coming home for dinner today."

"So what have you greedy women left for us?"

"There's nothing," she answered. "Only some ugali for breakfast tomorrow."

"Warm it up and we'll eat it with pili-pili," commanded David. "We'll get something better down at the bar later on." He turned his back on her and tore some tiny bananas from a stalk propped in the corner. He handed several to Juma and motioned him to sit down on the stool nearest the warmth of the fire. Juma sat and lit a cigarette.

Margaret nodded at her eldest daughter. Faith gave her brother a dark look and got sullenly to her feet. She collected a few sticks from a small pile in the corner and began to stir the fire under the iron grate back to life. Her sister Hope poured a bit of water into the black pot that contained the cornmeal porridge and placed it on top of the grate to heat.

146

David settled on the stool next to Juma's and accepted a cigarette. "After all," he said in an offhand manner, "a man can't eat hamburgers and steak all the time, like we did in Nairobi. All that rich food and beer and whiskey we had. I'm glad we didn't stay in Nairobi any longer—I probably would have made myself sick."

Juma took deep drags on his cigarette and stared at the little girls hunched against the wall while Hope spooned small portions of ugali onto two plastic plates and spooned some bright red chili sauce onto each. She handed them to Faith, who passed them to David without a word. David gave one to Juma and they began eating the hot mush gingerly with their fingers.

"So," David said to Juma nonchalantly as they ate, "which of my sisters do you like the best?"

Juma saw that David was not looking at him, but at his oldest sister. Faith glared back at David, then turned away. Juma felt Margaret's eyes on him like a cold wind. He shrugged and finished the last of his *ugali*.

"Let's go," he said shortly, placing the plate on the hard beaten dirt floor as he stood up from the stool.

David stood up too and glanced at his mother. She met his eyes with a stony stare. He decided not to risk asking for beer money, in case she refused and shamed him in front of Juma. Instead he laughed roughly and clapped Juma on the shoulder and started toward the doorway.

"You're right," David called loudly as they left. "Soon we'll have enough money to get any wife you want. I guess then we'll be looking for some fancy meat from Kobani or Nairobi, not stringy country stuff like this."

CHAPTER 13

1

Carol stepped out into the cool, gray morning and started walking along the road, past the lean-to shops and kiosks. At the butcher shop in the center of town, she turned right onto a steep, narrow, dirt road that tapered off to a footpath as it twisted upward through a maze of huts and vegetable gardens and scattered trash heaps. A pungent haze of blue woodsmoke drifted above the thatched roofs and mingled with the low-lying mist. Rounding a sharp bend she came on a group of young girls gathered around a standpipe, chattering and laughing as they took turns pumping the handle and filling buckets and jugs with water. They stared shyly and murmured soft greetings as she walked by.

Margaret's family compound was set off by a row of bushy leucena trees surrounding the dirt yard. Margaret had planted them a few years before, as a demonstration project when she had served as a community organizer for a project run by the Methodist Church. The idea was to harvest the nitrogen-rich leaves to mulch the gardens and feed to the livestock, but most of the donated seedlings had died of neglect or been eaten by goats. Only Margaret's trees had survived because no one else had bothered to follow her example of protecting them with chicken wire.

Carol stood at the edge of the yard and clapped her hands twice to announce her arrival. "Hodi!" she called.

"Karibu," came Margaret's voice from inside the small two-room mud and wattle house in the middle of the yard.

Carol paused for a moment in the doorway to let her eyes adjust to the dim light. Margaret was sitting at a table in the middle of the main room, re-tying a tight braid in the hair of her youngest daughter, seven-year-old Patience. Nine-year-old Grace fidgeted impatiently beside her. The girls were dressed in

148

their school uniforms, a green jumper over a bright yellow blouse, with plastic sandals on their feet. Their older sisters, Hope and Faith, were cleaning up the morning teacups, tossing the dregs into the small open fire in a corner of the room. At fourteen and sixteen they were finished with school and had jobs picking tea at a big government estate a few kilometers away.

"Carol!" cried Margaret. "It is you? You are welcome!" She dropped the braid and rushed over to seize Carol's hands in hers. She was a short, quick woman, with sunken breasts and a slight stoop that made her look much older than her thirty five years. She had a classic Bantu figure—round and very full from the waist down, with a slender and delicate face and upper body. Her close-cropped hair started far up on her smooth, bare forehead, like a woolly skullcap. She wore a brightly patterned kanga cloth as a wrap-around skirt over a faded, striped cotton dress.

Margaret stepped backwards, still holding Carol's hands, pulling her into the smoky room. "You remember my girls?" she challenged.

"Of course I do," said Carol, naming them in order. They each gave a little curtsey as they stepped up shyly to shake hands.

"You see my Patience?" said Margaret proudly, gathering her youngest to her side. "In school already."

"That's wonderful," said Carol. "But where is your little boy?"

"Nelson is gone yesterday," said Margaret brusquely. "He stops with his uncle, for going to school in Kobani." Her face was sad and proud at the same time. "I am happy," she said, softly. "School in Kobani is good, yes."

"But he's just a baby."

"That one is now already one big boy," said Margaret. "I send him to Kobani so he can grow like his uncle. Not like his father, and not like his brother." Her voice took on a bitter edge. "Is no good for any boy in the village. Here he can grow to be a no-good man."

149

Carol had met David briefly on her previous visit, and she couldn't help but agree with Margaret on the direction he seemed to be heading. With few jobs and little land to go around, many of the young men from villages like Mwatumi eventually drifted off to bigger towns looking for work. Of those who stayed, a lucky few landed low-paying government jobs or found casual labor on the tea estates, while others cut trees or made charcoal illegally in the forest reserve. They sold the charcoal and timber for next to nothing to middlemen who trucked it to Kobani and resold it for a huge profit. There was a lot of work to do in Mwatumi, but not for a self-respecting man. From time to time they would clear a new patch of land in the forest, chopping down and burning off the bushes and trees. But tending the crops and the livestock, collecting firewood and water, grinding the maize, bringing the produce to market, and cooking and caring for the house and the children was all women's work. That left the men with nothing but time on their hands and plenty of cheap banana beer to drink.

"This girl is too smart. Most smart from all my children," said Margaret, stroking the corn-rowed head. "I say to Nelson when he go, you be good boy and make your uncle happy, so maybe next year he can take Patience in Kobani also."

Patience escaped from her mother's caresses and ran into the bedroom. She returned with a battered exercise book clutched in her arms.

"Aieh, off you go," said Margaret.

Patience and Grace raced each other out the door. Faith placed steaming cups of sweet, milky tea on the table and then she and Hope said goodbye and left as well. Margaret and Carol sat down, facing each other across the table.

This was the moment that Carol had been dreading ever since the meeting that day at the Schooley Foundation. For almost a week she had been struggling over what to say to Margaret. It was only fair to tell her straight out about the accusations being made against her. But she knew that Margaret would be hurt and offended, however much she tried to reassure her that she had complete faith that the suspicions were totally groundless.

Before Carol could say anything, Margaret fixed her with a mischievous look. "I show you something," she said, and started to roll her sleeve up to the shoulder.

Carol leaned over and looked carefully where Margaret was pointing on the inside of her upper arm.

"Here, you touch." Margaret took Carol's hand and placed the fingertips on her skin. Carol felt a fan of small ridges, like matchsticks under the skin.

"Norplant!" she exclaimed. "Where did you get these?"

"I get from clinic in Bola, "said Margaret proudly. "Last month, I go there with Faith."

"That's wonderful. What made you decide to get birth control?"

Margaret spoke slowly, searching for the words to explain. "My Nelson have now seven years. Since he is born I get two more babies, but they die very soon. Then it is some months back, I think again I will get a baby. And I am not so happy. I think maybe I do not want one more baby now. Then I see it is a mistake and there is no baby, and I think, now I am happy because I do not get a baby. Better I go to the clinic and then I can be happy all the time."

"And Faith?"

"I say to Faith, you are big girl and you can choose if you come with me or you stay, but if you get a baby you can keep him. You don't give him for me to keep and you go to dance at night with your boyfriend or go to find a job in Kobani. So, she come and get also."

"That's great. I was a bit worried," teased Carol. "I thought you might be aiming to complete the set. You know: Faith, Hope, Grace, Patience, Charity, Chastity and Prudence."

Margaret tapped her arm with her finger. "For me, here is 'prudence.'" She laughed heartily at her own joke.

"But how does your husband feel about it?" Carol knew that African men often refused to let their wives practice birth control.

Margaret shrugged. "That one have a new woman now. If he want more sons she can make for him, isn't it? I am finish."

"How do you mean, finished? You're not getting a divorce are you?"

"In Mwatumi we do not know 'divorce,'" said Margaret. "I tell him, Odege, you come or you go, to me is the same. But then I stop to give him any money, so he go."

"Can you do that?" asked Carol, impressed. Like most rural African women, Margaret was very self-sufficient and independent in most ways, but traditionally a Rumuran wife had to hand any money she earned over to her husband.

"I tell him if he fight with me, I make big trouble for him with my brother," shrugged Margaret. "And never mind, now Odege have so much money. I think his new woman, she must be very rich," she added complacently.

"You mean, he's not getting it from you?" exclaimed Carol with evident relief.

Margaret looked at her strangely. "Carol, maybe you tell me now why you come and visit me today. When you are here in July, you say you come again only after one year. You don't come here from America only to say hello."

Carol blushed. From Margaret's knowing face she realized she might as well just come out with it. When she told her about Father Loretto's accusations, Margaret hardly seemed surprised.

"So now even in America they think I steal money," she sighed. "I don't know why this priest tell so many lies about me."

"The only evidence he had to offer was that your husband suddenly seemed to have a lot of money to spread around," explained Carol. "He said everybody in town knows it can only be coming from the co-op."

"Odege don't say from where he get this money," sniffed Margaret, "He make a big secret so everybody can think now he

152

make some good business. But that one, he never make business in his life. Always if he have money it is only because he get from a woman. Now it is not me, so it must be it is the other one."

"So you don't actually know for sure where he's getting it?" asked Carol.

Margaret shrugged again, as though the matter held no interest for her at all. She got to her feet and re-wrapped the kanga around her middle. "You come with me now," she said with great dignity. "I get you the account books, so you can see if the money has gone. Tomorrow you come to the community center. We have a meeting of the cooperative, and you will ask my sisters, is Margaret Waiyala a thief?"

2

The white Toyota pulled up to the back door of the decaying apartment building. The white concrete walls had peeled and faded to a dirty ivory gray, stained with black, sooty streaks beneath the windows and ledges. The ten-story building was meant to provide subsidized housing for civil servants, but many of the official residents had long ago moved to private houses in a better part of town and rented out the apartments to others at three or four times the amount they paid.

Thadeus Maleke stepped out and shut the back door of the car without a word. The driver needed no instructions. He drove a few blocks away into a side street, where he parked the car and reclined the seat, covering his face with a newspaper to block out the late morning sun.

Inside the dim lobby, Maleke ignored the elevator with its doors gaping half open and went directly to the pungent, dark stairwell. On the fourth floor he knocked on one of the peeling wooden doors. He heard footsteps and saw the shadow of an eye behind the peephole. With the sound of a turning lock and a sliding bolt, the door swung open.

Maleke walked past Muna into the apartment and sank into the deep sofa that took up most of the far wall of the cramped living room. Muna closed and bolted the door and crossed the room to unlock a tall cabinet. Still without speaking, she removed a bottle of Johnny Walker Red and poured a generous portion into a glass, topping it off with a spray from a seltzer bottle. She could feel Maleke's eyes on her, devouring her languid grace. Usually this pleased her, but today it made her uncomfortable and she moved back and forth as brusquely as she could. She handed him the glass and sat primly on the arm of the sofa.

"Are you having one?" he asked.

Muna shook her head. Maleke shrugged and lifted the glass slightly towards her before raising it to his lips and draining half of it. Leaning back against the sofa, he closed his eyes and savored the scotch sliding smoothly down his throat and spreading through his stomach.

He opened his eyes. "What's the matter?"

"Nothing. Why?"

"You're perched there like a flycatcher, ready to take off at any moment. Are you expecting someone?"

"No, of course not."

"Then come here and relax." He lifted his arm for her to nestle under. Through a closed door at the end of the room came a thin, quavering voice. "Mama!"

Maleke looked at Muna.

"Maamaa!" the child called again.

"Excuse me," said Muna. She stood up and went into the next room, pulling the door closed behind her. Maleke finished off the rest of the whiskey.

Muna came back a few minutes later. She sat down on the edge of an armchair facing Maleke, twisting her fingers nervously.

"Why is the child here?" demanded Maleke.

"My mother brought her this morning. She's ill—she must go to the doctor."

154

"Let your mother take her."

"She can't manage it on her own."

"Why, is it so serious?"

"I don't know. When my mother took her to the clinic in the village, the Sister said Clarisse must come to the hospital for a test. She wrote it all down on a paper, but my mother can't read it."

"She can give the paper to the doctor to read."

"Clarisse is frightened. She needs me with her," Muna said quietly but firmly.

Maleke met her eyes for a moment, then held his empty glass out toward her. She refilled it and gave it back to him without a word.

"Why didn't you call and tell me not to come?" said Maleke.

"We went to the doctor first thing so I could be back on time, but there were so many waiting that the Sister told us to go and come back in the afternoon. I tried to reach you just now when we returned, but you weren't at the office."

"I was with the Minister."

"Again?" demanded Muna indignantly. "Can't he do anything these days without consulting with you first? You should be the Minister, not him."

Maleke chuckled and lifted his arm again, beckoning her to sit beside him. "All right, woman, you don't need to flatter me."

Muna nestled beside him, tucking her feet beneath her and resting her head on his chest. "Clarisse knows she's to stay in the bedroom," she said. "She won't come out."

He inhaled deeply, taking in the fragrance of jasmine that rose from her hair. Her warmth and the lightness of her body pressed against his stirred him. He ran his finger lightly up and down the silky curve where her blouse stretched across her breast. "And your mother?"

"She's at the market. I've told her not to come back here before one."

"It's almost twelve now," he pointed out. "You haven't left much time."

155

She slipped her slender hand between the buttons of his shirt. "Then let's not waste any more of it," she said.

Maleke leaned back and enjoyed her exploring fingers for a moment, stroking her neck as her hand drifted across his chest and downward. When it slipped beneath his belt, he reluctantly took hold of her arm.

"Later," he said. "First tell me what's happening with Ayala."

Muna sighed and straightened up, brushing the hair away from her face and putting her feet back on the floor.

"Juma and David have gone to Mwatumi, following the American woman," she told him.

"And the other? The Dutch?" asked Maleke.

"He went too, but later, in another car. David was watching at the hotel."

"So she went alone?"

"No, there was another mzungu that David didn't know. They went to together in his car."

"A private car or a hired one? Did it have diplomatic tags?"

"David didn't notice."

Maleke snorted. "A fool like that, and he dreams about being a big gangster. All right, what else?"

Muna hesitated. She didn't know what other informants Maleke might have and what they might have told him. "It seems someone else may be interested," she said at last.

"Oh?"

"There was a telephone call yesterday at the office. A European, I think, from his voice, but not English or French. He was looking for Singh."

"Is that right?" said Maleke.

"He wanted to meet Singh at the Ankara at five o'clock. David and Juma waited outside. He came by taxi, a half hour late."

"And then?" Maleke was watching her closely.

"Nothing," said Muna, uncomfortably. "He waited in the lobby for an hour, and then he left."

Maleke looked thoughtful. "Two new mystery men," he mused. "Did that young ass David happen to notice if the one who came to the Ankara was the same as the one who went to Mwatumi with the American woman?"

"He said he wasn't sure."

"Wasn't sure!" exclaimed Maleke. "What is he, blind as well as being an idiot? Can't he tell one mzungu from another? Did they have the same color hair? The same color eyes? Were they the same height? Fat, thin, old, young? What?"

Muna shook her head sympathetically. She didn't mind letting David take the heat, and it might help her find out what Maleke knew and didn't know.

"Who knows?" she said. "David said the man who left the hotel with her wore a hat, and it was too dark in the Ankara to see the other one properly. As you said, he's an idiot."

"You didn't get a look at these men yourself, did you?"

Muna felt her heart quicken. She glanced at his face, but it gave her nothing to go by. She willed her body to relax and forced herself to meet Maleke's eyes frankly. "How could I?" she asked lightly. "I wasn't there."

Maleke straightened up and removed his arm from behind her head. "The Ankara man will telephone again to find out why Singh didn't meet him. With Ayala gone, you'll be the one talking to him. Tell him Mr. Singh apologizes that he couldn't make the appointment yesterday due to sudden, urgent business. Set up another meeting, and this time go yourself and get a good look. Maybe you'll recognize him. And we'll describe him to Samuel and learn whether he's gone to Mwatumi."

Muna nodded and rose to make him another drink and one for herself as well, taking her time to collect herself before facing him again. She felt the whiskey hit her stomach, which was churning with the knowledge of the risk she was taking. If Maleke discovered what she was up to, she could lose a lot more than this apartment. She also felt a touch of remorse—she knew his affection for her was real. But she wasn't foolish enough to believe it would protect her.

CHAPTER 14

1

The sun was blazing by the time Carol followed the winding path back down the hill toward town, but she didn't mind the heat. Her relief at having the talk with Margaret off her chest made everything seem bright and lovely. The huts and gardens seemed solid and friendly against the backdrop of red earth and cloudless blue sky. Even the littered stream bed seemed cheerful with the sun glinting off the broken glass.

As she passed the butcher store again, a young boy in a faded Rolling Stones T-shirt stepped out, carrying a steer's head wrapped in burlap, casually holding it by one horn. He tied the head to a rack on the back of a bicycle. Half a dozen limp chickens were already hanging by their feet from the handlebars. Someone was going to have a party, probably for a wedding or a funeral. Carol stopped at a stall to buy some mangoes and a pineapple and a handful of tiny, sweet bananas from an old woman with a toothless smile. Immediately a small crowd began to gather, jostling to offer her bangles and bead necklaces and rough wooden carvings of animals. One boy held up a clear plastic bag filled with small, bright green sticks that looked like cut-up green beans. Carol leaned forward for a closer look and recoiled when she saw that it was packed with live grasshoppers. The crowd laughed good-naturedly and pantomimed eating the grasshoppers, smacking their lips with pleasure.

Back at the Acropolis, she found a young Rumuran in a worn ranger's uniform waiting for her. He handed her an envelope, which she was relieved to see was address to "Mrs. Simmons." Inside was a note from the Chief Warden of the Mali-Kuli reserve, inviting her to meet him at his Headquarters that afternoon, and afterwards to visit a site in the reserve where there were ancient cave paintings.

"Dr. Maleke must have told him I'm here," said Carol. "I suppose I should go. How would I get there?"

Since the ranger didn't speak English, Elena Sotiropoulos translated.

"He has come with a vehicle," she said.

Carol glanced out at the parking lot and saw a dusty Suzuki jeep with the Forest Department's logo on the door.

"He says you must go right away, because it will take almost two hours to reach there," continued Elena.

"That's all right," said Carol. "Let me just drop my things and find Thor. Could you possibly make us some sandwiches to take along?"

"Mr. Nilssen has gone out," said Elena.

"He was supposed to meet me back here at about twelve," said Carol, checking her watch. It was almost twelve thirty. "Could you please tell the driver that I'd like to wait for Mr. Nilssen? I'm sure he'd like to come along."

The driver looked worried but went back to wait in the car. Carol changed into jeans and collected her camera and sat in the lobby to wait.

From time to time over the next hour, the driver came back inside to look at her, obviously anxious to go. Finally, he approached Elena diffidently.

"He says it is not possible to wait longer," Elena told Carol. "The Chief Warden is expecting you, and there will not be time to bring you back before dark."

"All right, let's go," said Carol, not concealing her annoyance. "When Thor comes, please tell him where I've gone, and that I waited for him as long as I could. I'll see him when I get back."

She picked up her camera bag and jacket and followed the driver out to the car.

•

2

Lisa kept her eyes glued to Samuel's bony brown ankles, which were almost level with her chin. She concentrated on visualizing strings connecting the toes of her hiking boots to the backs of his muddy sneakers. Every time he took a step upward, the string pulled her foot up, first one foot then the other, step by step, effortlessly. The trick was never to look up, to see how much farther you had to go, but to keep your eyes on the ground and concentrate on one step at a time, thinking about something else and imagining you were almost at the top.

When she had first come to the Mali-Kuli five years ago, Lisa had not even been able to reach the top of Kigeni Ridge, only a few hundred yards from their camp, without stopping to rest. Now she crossed Kigeni twice a day without getting out of breath. Her legs were as hard as a dancer's legs, with muscles that popped out when she flexed them. But climbing to the crest of Kimafiri Ridge, the highest point in the reserve aside from the summit of the Mali-Kuli volcano itself, was still a challenge.

It was particularly hard to keep up with her field assistant, Samuel Liumba, as he led the way up the slippery, muddy path that wove through the groves of tree ferns and between the trunks of the giant trees. Somehow, his torn, oversized sneakers never seemed to slip or slide the way her hiking boots did, despite their high-tech, waffled soles specially designed to grip on any surface. He never had to grab at branches or vines to keep from falling or use his hands to pull himself up over a rocky outcrop. Like all the local staff he climbed like a mountain goat, gliding up the steep mountainside. But even Samuel was sweating from the climb: the sharp, acrid smell filled her nostrils, adding one more discomfort to the stifling heat, the dead weight of the backpack on her shoulders and the constant buzz of insects around her ears and eyes. Of course, she probably didn't smell all that great herself...

160

When they finally reached the top, Lisa collapsed onto a fallen log and groaned out loud as she reached for her water bottle, not caring that Samuel was standing there grinning at her.

"What on earth could have made China group decide to cross Kimafiri?" complained Lisa. She took a long drink from the water bottle and held it out to Samuel. He took a small sip, more from politeness than thirst, then handed the bottle back to her and stripped his damp T-shirt over his head, revealing a tightly muscled chest and shoulders. Lisa glanced at him and then quickly away again, not wanting him to mistake her interest. She only wished she could remove her own sticky, clinging shirt and let the soft breeze cool her skin. Usually she did her fieldwork alone, often sitting in the observation blinds completely naked. But these days Greg insisted that she take Samuel along for protection, at least until things quieted down.

From this vantage point, they had an unobstructed, breathtaking view of the entire reserve. They looked down upon a carpet of densely packed crowns of giant trees, broken by occasional bare rock outcrops and yellow-green gaps where treefalls had opened up patches of sunlight on the forest floor. Five miles to the south, the sharp cone of the volcano rose abruptly out of the hazy green jungle, solitary and majestic, dwarfing the other peaks. The jagged edge of the crater emerged from the silver halo of clouds hovering around it, like an island in a sea of mist.

Using a crude ladder made of boards nailed to the trunk, Lisa and Samuel climbed up to the observation blind perched fifty feet up on a branch of a mvule tree. Settling as comfortably as they could on the rough bench inside, they began to comb the hillsides with their binoculars, searching for the telltale rustling of vegetation and fleeting black shadows.

"There," said Samuel, "ten o'clock." He pointed with one hand, still holding the binoculars to his eyes with the other.

Lisa shifted her gaze and soon saw what he had spotted—a slight swaying at the edge of a thicket of tall bamboo's surrounding a small clearing about a hundred yards downhill from them. After what seemed like an hour, a single dark figure emerged slowly from the protective cover of the bamboos and stood upright, looking around cautiously before sitting down just inside the clearing. With its long, slender arms and legs, it looked very much like a small person wearing an ape costume.

"It's Cheetah," said Lisa, recognizing the grizzled face of the old matriarch of China group.

Samuel nodded. "The others are coming."

One by one, other bonobos followed her out into the clearing and began to feed on the clumps of wild celery and young bamboo. Samuel checked them off in his notebook as Lisa softly called out their names.

"There's Chester and Chauncey. And Chichi with Chala on her back. Look how big he's gotten—he won't be riding around on mama for much longer. And Cheech and Chong, together as usual. And who's that young female?"

Samuel picked up his binoculars again and studied the bonobo's face. "Maybe Fanny," he ventured.

"I think you're right," said Lisa. "It makes sense—it was about time for her to leave Fiesta group. But who would have thought she'd wind up all the way over here?"

"Look at Charlie," said Samuel. "I think his leg has something wrong."

They both watched carefully as Cheetah's four year old son went up to his mother and begged food from her. He seemed to have a slight limp in his gait.

"It's his right leg," said Lisa. "But I don't see any blood or swelling and he's not picking at it. I think it's okay, but we'll have to keep an eye on him. The year before, two bonobos had developed gangrene from wire snares that had sliced deep into their ankles and cut off the circulation. They had managed to save one by darting it and amputating the foot, but the other had died.

"I still don't see Chelsea," said Lisa. "I'm really starting to get worried." The eight-year old female had been heavily pregnant the last time they saw her, six weeks earlier.

"There she is!" exclaimed Samuel, as another bonobo ambled leisurely into the clearing. "She has got her baby."

The infant was barely visible as a tiny lump pressed close against its mother's belly. The others immediately crowded around to greet them, plucking gently at the baby's silky fur with sensitive fingers. Chelsea sat calmly in their midst like a Madonna before the Magi. The baby turned its face and gazed out at them with huge, black eyes, its mouth clasped firmly onto a long, pink nipple.

"I'd say it's about a month old," said Lisa. "Okay, Samuel, you saw it first so you get to name it. What's it going to be?"

Samuel grinned wickedly. "How about Changuma?"

"Absolutely not!," snapped Lisa. "How sick can you get?"

"Only a joke," he apologized sheepishly.

"Well it's not funny, okay?"

'Changuma' meant 'food' in Ruahya. Many local people considered bonobo meat a delicacy, along with chimpanzee and gorilla.

"I think, maybe we can call him Chuyu," said Samuel.

"Chuyu," repeated Lisa. "That's nice. What does it mean?"

"It is the name of my sister's new boy, also born last month," said Samuel. "They can be spirit brothers."

"What if it turns out to be a female?" teased Lisa.

"Only the bodies are male and female," answered Samuel. "The spirits are all one."

The troop gradually lost interest in the baby and wandered away to resume feeding and then to groom each other and play chasing games. Samuel and Lisa watched, making notes on what they ate and who interacted with whom. After about an hour the bonobos began to filter out of the clearing and back into the forest, with old Cheetah leading the way.

"That's it," said Lisa. "Let's go see if we can find Delta group. Samuel? What is it?"

Samuel had stood up and was scanning the horizon off toward the south, sniffing the air like a bird dog. "Fire," he said, pointing toward the southeast. "There, past the river."

Lisa followed his finger with her binoculars and made out a wispy plume of white smoke rising lazily against the hazy blue-green background.

"Shit!" she said, "Not again."

3

Cheeya Ethungu hobbled up to Andre Delacroix as the Frenchman stepped out of his dusty black Mercedes in front of the Acropolis hotel. Delacroix scowled and muttered a few sharp words and brushed past him without a glance, walking briskly into the hotel. Ethungu stood for a moment, scratching his grizzled white hair with a long, wrinkled finger, and then followed Delacroix inside. He crossed the empty lobby and hurried through a doorway into a short, dark hallway that smelled of mildew and stale urine. Ethungu paused a moment, took a deep breath and pushed open the door labeled "Men."

"Get inside," snapped Delacroix.

The room was lit by a single bare bulb hanging from a socket over the rust-stained sink. A small, cracked window high on the wall provided ventilation.

"Idiot!" sputtered Delacroix. "What is it you were thinking about, to come up to me in that way? How many times must I tell you, nobody is to see us together?"

"Nobody see me," answered Ethungu sullenly. "Is nobody there."

"And if someone came from the hotel suddenly? Henh? You did not think about that, n'est ce pas? Next time you do as I say. Now what is it you want? Quickly, this place is like a sewer." Delacroix wrinkled his nose with disgust.

"Aieh, the job is finish," said Ethungu.

"I know," said Delacroix impatiently. "The good Father Loretto ran away naked into the night, with the whole of the village after him, and he is gone from Rumura for good. What of it? You have been paid."

"The money is finish," said Ethungu.

"Certainly," said Delacroix sourly. "I have no doubt you drank it away in two days. But that is nothing to me. I do not pay twice for the same work."

"You give other work," suggested Ethungu. "I do what you say." He licked his lips and pulled them back in a malevolent-looking grin, displaying a few forlorn remaining teeth.

Delacroix looked at the old drunkard thoughtfully, reflecting on how deceiving appearances could be, and on how fortunate it was that he himself was able to see beyond them. While the idea of framing the priest with an accusation of adultery had been his own, he had left the details of execution to Ethungu, who had proven himself surprisingly capable. In any case, it was undoubtedly safer to have Ethungu in one's pocket than otherwise, and the expense of keeping him on was minimal. Fortunately, his tastes ran to the potent local brew rather than expensive imported spirits.

"Very well," said Delacroix. "Perhaps there is something more that you can do for me." He pulled a thick handful of bills out of his pocket and counted out a few in front of Ethungu's eyes.

"Aieh..." said Ethungu, reaching for them eagerly.

Delacroix released the bills and watched the old man fold them lovingly and push them deep into the pocket of his shabby trousers. "Now listen closely," he said.

4

Jonathan Marshall stormed past his secretary and into his office, slamming the door behind him. He flung himself into the tall leather chair behind the desk, still steaming from his latest meeting with the Ambassador. You'd think someone that stupid, naive and clueless would have to be a political appointee, some redneck businessman who'd gotten the post for raising millions for the President's election campaign. But Brian McCallister was career foreign service, so what was his excuse?

The real problem, Jonathan reflected, was not that the man was an idiot, but that he was too stupid and too arrogant to know that he didn't know. This was McCallister's first assignment in Africa, following an unremarkable career in Asia and South America. His first and his last. He'd been sent to the backwater of Kobani to retire—in disgrace, rumor had it, for some unidentified indiscretion in Buenos Aires. But instead of keeping his head down and his mouth shut, he insisted on butting in and second-guessing people who had spent years on the continent.

The phone on the desk jangled, breaking into Jonathan's thoughts. It was his private line. He glanced at his watch and saw that it was almost six o'clock—probably Pat wondering where he was. He had promised to get home early today, not having reckoned on an "emergency" meeting with McCallister. He sighed and stretched out his hand to punch the "conference" button on the phone.

"Marshall," he said.

"Good afternoon, Mr. Marshall." A woman's voice rose out of the speaker into the room. It was young, African, melodious and unfamiliar.

"Good afternoon. Can I help you?"

"I am calling for Mr. Singh," she said.

Jonathan sat up abruptly and grabbed the receiver, covering the mouthpiece for a moment to collect himself.

"Mr. Singh?" he asked finally in a puzzled tone. "I don't believe I know him."

"Mr. Singh extends his sincere apologies for missing your engagement yesterday," recited the woman. "He was unavoidably detained on business."

"I'm afraid there must be some mistake," said Jonathan. "By the way, how did you get my private number?"

166

"Please do not worry, Mr. Marshall. I understand your caution, but I can assure you that it is not at all necessary. You can rely on our discretion, absolutely."

"Look, I've told you—I don't know what you're talking about." Jonathan was pointedly patient. "If you like, you can put Mr. Singh on the line and I'll tell him the same thing."

"You were at the Ankara Hotel yesterday afternoon." It was not a question.

Jonathan grimaced. He had been recognized. But by whom?

"Yes, as a matter of fact I was," he said with carefully measured asperity. "I was trying to meet up with an old friend of mine who was passing through town. But I'm afraid I don't see what business that might be of yours, or of Mr. Singh's, whoever he is."

"Mr. Singh has asked me to arrange another appointment with you, perhaps for this evening if it is convenient? He looks forward to meeting with you and also your associate."

"My associate?"

"The European gentleman who called yesterday."

Jonathan felt a quick stab of relief. So they had fallen for the fake accent after all. He would have felt very foolish if Singh had caught him out in that little ruse. But now he had the upper hand because it would keep Singh guessing: who was this European caller? Were he and Jonathan working together, or was it possible that Jonathan had just shown up at the Ankara by coincidence? While Jonathan had no clear plan yet, the important thing was that he knew something the other guy didn't.

"Tell you what, Miss. Why don't you put Mr Singh on the line? I'm sure we can sort this thing out in a jiffy."

"I am too sorry, sir. It is not possible at this moment."

"Well, then, have him call me back when it is possible," retorted Jonathan. "Now, if you'll excuse me, it's late and I've got to be going."

167

He replaced the receiver firmly and leaned back in his chair. It had been foolish to go to the Ankara in person—he wasn't exactly unknown in Kobani. But there was no point in dwelling on it—Singh knew who he was, and that was that. The question was what to do next. He could continue to play coy and let Singh and his people make the next move. Or he could take the offensive. Maybe it was time for Herr Mahlergeblinsky, or whatever he decided to call himself, to call Singh again, demanding to know why he had missed their appointment.

At the other end of the line, Muna smiled as she laid the telephone receiver slowly into its cradle. She had met Jonathan Marshall briefly at an Embassy party more than a year ago, and thought she'd recognized him in the doorway of the Ankara last night. Now she knew she was right. And she didn't believe he had gone there to meet a friend—people like Marshall didn't have friends who stayed at a place like the Ankara. The question was, now what? She had known he would be cautious, but she hadn't expected him to cut her off so abruptly. Maybe he had gotten cold feet and wanted to back out. Or maybe it was just a tactic to put her, that was to say Singh, off balance. If so, Jonathan Marshall was in for a surprise. Two could play that game.

CHAPTER 15

1

Andre Delacroix sank into the deep rattan chair with a sigh and eased off his shoes, prying each heel off with the toe of the other foot.   Whenever he performed this small ritual, he remembered doing the same thing as a young boy. His mother would smack him on the back of the head, scolding that he was going to ruin his only good pair of shoes. The handmade Italian shoes he wore now cost more than his father used to earn in a year. He looked back on those days without nostalgia. Being rich was much better than being poor. And here in Rumura, he had found, it was easy to be rich. One only had to keep one's eyes and ears open, and learn one's way around.

His Congolese houseboy, Bonaventure, appeared at his elbow, holding out a Campari and soda on a silver tray. Delacroix took it absently, focusing his attention on the sun sliding down the sky toward the line of slender cypress trees that marked the end of his property. In between lay two hundred yards of sculpted lawn and garden, painstakingly maintained with scythes and shears by a crew of three gardeners.   The flower beds glowed in the early evening light, with not a wayward stem left unpruned or a single faded blossom unplucked. It had taken six years and four head gardeners to reach this standard of perfection. His greatest pride was the plush carpet of soft, short grass. He liked to boast that one could practice putting on any part of his lawn. Not that he actually played golf, that silly British obsession.

The tranquillity was broken by an outburst of furious barking as a car pulled up outside the front gate. Recognizing the white Toyota, the *askari* swung the gate open and stood stiffly to attention, saluting as the car passed through and started up the long driveway. The three huge Alsatians loped alongside and milled around the car when it stopped in front of the house.

Agi Kiss

The driver stepped out cautiously, keeping a wary eye on the dogs as he reached for the handle of the rear door. He stood still as they sniffed intently at his ankles and crotch, running him through a security check of their own. "Go on, you bastards" he muttered at them under his breath. "Get away." He was rescued by Bonaventure, who waded in among the dogs, pushing them away with the soles of his feet.

The driver opened the back door and Thadeus Maleke stepped out, buttoning his jacket.

"Bonsoir, Monsieur le Directeur," said Bonaventure. "He is waiting for you on the veranda. You permit me to show you?"

"I know where to find him. Just bring me a scotch and water, no ice."

Maleke followed the flagstone path around the side of the house and trotted up the stone steps leading to the veranda. He could see the smooth, round top of Delacroix' head above the back of one of the chairs.

"Ah, Dr. Maleke, bienvenu." Delacroix extended his plump hand without rising. He motioned toward a chair beside him and continued, in French still heavily flavored with a Provencal accent. "Bonaventure is bringing your drink?"

Maleke sat down and Delacroix turned his attention back to the view in front of him. "Thank you for agreeing to stop by," said Delacroix. "I always try to be home at this time of the day, to enjoy the sunset properly. It is so nourishing for the soul, n'est-ce pas?"

Bonaventure materialized silently behind them and Maleke took the double scotch off the tray. "You said the matter was urgent," he said, in perfect Parisian French.

Delacroix held up a hand. "A moment," he said. They watched in silence as the fiery red-orange ball slipped behind the trees. In a matter of minutes the twilight descended around them.

"There is no sunset like the African sunset," said Delacroix. "It is worth living here only for that." He raised his glass in a toast to the horizon, then drained it and placed it on the low table between them.

Hidden spotlights flooded the garden, positioned to create a dramatic play of light and shadow. On the veranda, a row of electric lanterns came on overhead.

Delacroix turned to Maleke, suddenly all business. "Your meeting with McCallister," he said abruptly. "What was the outcome?"

"He agreed to request the USAID Director to arrange for another ecologist to be sent out to carry out a second assessment."

Delacroix pursed his lips. "That may not be enough. You know the USAID man as well as I do—he likes to regard himself as above politics, and ignoring the Ambassador is one of his favorite ways of showing it."

"I told McCallister confidentially that my government views the matter very seriously. He indicated he was prepared to press the point in Washington if necessary."

Delacroix nodded in approval. "You are learning, mon ami. Ambassador McCallister likes nothing better than to believe he is privy to sensitive, inside information. He is probably drafting the classified memorandum to the Secretary of State at this moment. How soon can we expect this ecologist?"

Maleke shrugged. "Perhaps next month. He should come before the rains begin."

Delacroix clicked his tongue thoughtfully. "Next month? It may not be enough time..."

"Enough time for what?" interrupted Maleke. His voice carried a warning.

Delacroix smiled coyly and put up his hands in mock deference. "Nothing to concern you, Monsieur le Directeur. In fact, I did not speak."

He leaned forward in his chair toward Maleke, his expression serious again. "Thanks to the recent convenient turn of events, we can expect no further trouble from Father Loretto. Kamanga is a greedy nuisance, but he can be easily managed.

171

The problem now is those two at the research camp. They have the whole of God's creation crawling with guards and informers. A man cannot piss on a tree in that forest these days without finding himself in court."

"They are becoming troublesome," agreed Maleke. "But then, they may not be there much longer."

"Oh?"

"Yes. I regret to say that we have reason to suspect Dr. Greg Allen may be up to his old tricks. You are familiar with his history?"

"Apparently I am not." Delacroix leaned further forward.

"Allen is known to have been involved in the past in smuggling chimpanzees to America," said Maleke.

"Is it possible?" exclaimed Delacroix delightedly.

"I have it on good authority from colleagues in Cameroon," said Maleke. "I have asked them to send me the details. In the meantime, he is under surveillance."

Delacroix clucked his tongue. "One can never tell about people, can one? But, this in Cameroon is ancient history, no? He has been in Rumura for many years."

"It is his activities in Rumura that concern me," said Maleke. "The inquiry to Cameroon is only for background, to learn about his modus operandi."

"So, you believe he is likely to repeat his offenses here in Rumura? But then you must take action!" Delacroix looked at Maleke appraisingly, but the Rumuran's handsome face was impassive.

"We are following the situation closely," said Maleke.

"One cannot be too careful, mon vieux."

"I think you can trust me to do my job," replied Maleke.

"I have no doubt of it, mon ami," said Delacroix placatingly. "Ah, here is Bonaventure, just when we need him."

There was a pause as Bonaventure unobtrusively replaced their empty glasses with fresh drinks. When he had gone, Delacroix gave a long, relaxed sigh. "Such a delightful, tranquil evening. Tell me, all is well with your family?"

Maleke murmured assent.

"I heard that your brother-in-law came to see you today? I hope there is nothing wrong?"

"He brought my nephew, who will be staying with us." Maleke concealed his annoyance. One of his staff must have been spying for Delacroix.

"I hope he also brought good news for you? Regarding your ventures in the west?"

"Not yet," said Maleke shortly.

Delacroix shook his head disapprovingly. "You must move more quickly, Thadeus, or you will lose your chance. My contacts in the Land Office tell me the interest is growing. Already someone has bought two plots just next to the reserve, on the eastern side. A prime location."

"Who?" demanded Maleke.

"Nobody, a local man, certainly just an intermediary for the real buyer."

"And who is that?"

Delacroix smiled. "I am flattered by your confidence, mon ami, but it is not true that I know everything. Evidently the buyer wishes to remain anonymous. But you can rely upon it that he is somebody with contacts and access, or how would he know exactly where to buy, henh? Also, it seems the owner signed over the land for next to nothing, so that may tell you something about your competition. You had better watch your step—there is only so much that I can do to help you."

Maleke nodded. "I understand."

"Good. And now, in the same spirit, it is I who must ask for your help."

Maleke took a deep draught of his drink and waited.

"I have just returned from Mwatumi, where I was summoned by my foreman. It seems there has been a small misunderstanding. I know I can rely upon you to sort it out. Perhaps you are already aware of the matter?"

"My men were only doing their duty," said Maleke shortly.

"Ah, so you have heard. But surely it is not their duty to interfere with an honest businessman's affairs?" Delacroix fixed him with a reproachful look.

"It is, when the logs have been cut illegally."

"As I thought, it is only that you have been misinformed," Delacroix said warmly. "I assure you, the logs are all of legal species and sizes."

"According to my Chief Warden, they were taken from Kiritoro Ridge."

Delacroix clucked. "Thadeus, you and I both know very well that Kiritoro Ridge is several kilometers from my concession area. It is absolutely not possible that my crew could make such an error."

Maleke studied his glass. "I was prepared to regard it as simply an error, but if you insist that it was not..."

"This is not a matter for joking, Maleke," said Delacroix sharply. "It is you who is making the error if you believe I will tolerate such intimidation. A very great error."

Maleke rose slowly and strolled to the edge of the veranda, where he stood looking out across the spotlit garden. "What is the point of this charade, Andre?" he asked mildly. "There are only the two of us here, so we can be frank. We both know the logs couldn't have come from your concession—you have no trees of that size left. You've been poaching trees from all over the reserve for years. Every now and again we manage to catch you at it. Why not pay the fine and have done with it? We can arrange it quietly, without formalities."

"Yes, you would like that," snorted Delacroix. "Is the money short at the end of the month? No matter, we can always squeeze some more from Delacroix. But I have sad news for you, mon vieux. You have gone to the well too many times. This little game has grown tiresome. You will release my men and my logs immediately, and put a stop to this ridiculous harassment once and for all. As a beginning, you can get rid of that shameless extortionist you call a Chief Warden."

Maleke turned to face him. "In view of our friendship, I have been very tolerant, Andre. But this time you've gone too far. Kiritoro ridge is in the heart of the reserve, and you must have cleared out half the mature hardwoods in one go."

"It seems you did not understand me, mon vieux," said Delacroix. "Let me repeat myself more clearly. The trees came from within my area, not Kiritoro. Your Warden is mistaken or a liar, and that is an end to it."   •

Maleke met his eyes directly. "The matter can be resolved very simply," he said. "When exactly were the logs cut?"

"Over the past few days. Why?"

"Tomorrow, we'll go to Mwatumi together. If you can show me the fresh stumps where those logs were cut inside your concession within the past week, I'll release them and dismiss the warden on the spot, and I'll buy you dinner at the Acropolis for good measure. If not, we will go with the warden to Kiritoro Ridge. If he shows me the stumps to match the logs, I'll arrest you on the spot and you can spend the weekend in prison with your men. Then on Monday, the Minister will begin the process of revoking your concession and your license."

Delacroix crossed his legs tidily and pressed the tips of his fingers together in a thoughtful pose. There was a faint smile on his lips but his eyes were hard. "Alors, mon vieux, in view of our friendship as you say, I had hoped for the more positive approach. But if it comes to this, the matter can be resolved even more simply. Come, we will go inside and telephone the Minister at home. Perhaps you were not aware that I have his private number? He was kind enough to provide it, as we so frequently have matters of mutual interest to discuss, in private. There will be no need to explain the present situation to him, as I can assure you he is already well aware of it. In fact, he is waiting for me to advise him of the outcome of our little meeting tonight. He will be disappointed to hear that we have been unable to come to an agreement. And then we will put the question to him: does he wish to revoke my license, or does he prefer rather to revoke your Directorship? So, shall we go?"

Delacroix made no move to get up and Maleke didn't answer.

"I felt sure you would wish to reconsider," said Delacroix. "Perhaps you should sleep on it, and we can speak again in the morning. Come, one final drink before you go. One for the road, as our American friends would say."

He rang for Bonaventure. When the drinks arrived, Delacroix raised his glass in another toast. "To you, Thadeus, and to this beautiful country that has given us all so much and, God willing, will give us so much more."

Maleke ignored the toast but drained the glass.

Delacroix chuckled and then stifled a yawn as he rose to his feet. "Come, mon ami, I will accompany you to your car."

As they followed the shadowy footpath around the house, Delacroix laid a hand gravely on Maleke's shoulder. "If you will permit me, mon ami, I must express my most sincere sympathies. Although, if you don't mind my saying so, it was bound to happen sooner or later. It is true that French women are more open-minded than many, but regrettably they are not so compliant as your lovely African ladies."

"What are you talking about?" demanded Maleke.

"But surely...forgive me, I understood that Adrienne has left you."

"Where on earth did you hear such rubbish?"

"It is not true, then? I am very happy to hear it. But perhaps you should take this as a warning, henh?"

Something in his voice made Maleke look at him suspiciously. "A warning of what?" he asked.

"To be sure, as a Frenchman, I myself would never begrudge you your lovely mistress. But if Adrienne did somehow come to learn of it...well, one can never predict how the ladies will react, can one? Vive la difference, as we like to say. Particularly where—please do not take offense, mon ami—how shall I say it...well, only that it can sometimes be a problem if the lady brings the money to the marriage. They can become so possessive, n'est-ce pas? Always ready to listen to any kind of evil gossip that someone might decide to put into their ears. And next thing the man knows, he is high and dry. No, taking one thing and another, one cannot be too careful..."

When they reached the car, Delacroix held the back door open for Maleke to climb in. Then he stood and waved genially after the car as it pulled away.

2

Jonathan collected his drink from the bar and carried it over to a table by the window. He had taken to stopping in at the Intercontinental's "happy hour" most days to unwind before going home. The crowd was too young for him to blend in, but he liked to sit on the sidelines and watch the young women, dressed to tease in their miniskirts and tight jeans, striking poses to show their assets off to the best effect. Sometimes he caught them watching him out of the corners of their eyes, appraising him and, he liked to think, liking what they saw. The boisterous scene relaxed and energized him at the same time, and helped release the stress and frustrations of the job.

He had waited at his desk another half-hour, but the phone hadn't rung again. Clearly, Singh was following the same tactics he was, playing it cool, biding his time, letting his adversary stew in his own juices. Jonathan admitted to himself that part of him relished the battle, locking horns with a worthy opponent. It was the same thing that made him a good Political Officer—most of his job consisted of holding his own in the midst of the maneuvering and the mind games. The secret was patience, making the other guy blink first.

"Mr. Marshall?"

The woman who stood in front of his chair looked astonishingly out of place, completely cloaked in a long black garment that fell in a loose spiral from her shoulders to the floor. He could barely make out a pair of large, dark eyes behind the filmy red shawl that veiled her face. The only part of her visible were her hands, one holding the edges of the shawl together and the other lightly clasping a small black leather handbag. The skin was the color of coffee with just a touch of rich cream, and the fingers were very long and narrow, ending in carefully manicured long nails painted a deep, dark red.

"That's right," said Jonathan. Not surprisingly, he noticed a number of people staring curiously in their direction.

"Mr. Singh will be pleased to meet with you now."

Jonathan lifted his glass and sipped it casually. "And you are?"

"I am his personal assistant, Miss Bitanga," said Muna. "We spoke today on the telephone."

Jonathan looked at her more closely, trying to make out her features, but she backed up slightly and drew the shawl further even lower over her face. "Mr. Singh felt that it would be best to meet you in person. He does not like to conduct business over the telephone."

"Is that right? And how did he know where to find me?"

"I believe you come here almost every day at this time."

"I see," said Jonathan, concealing his dismay. He hadn't realized his habits were so well known. "As I explained to you before, I have no idea what it is Mr. Sing wants from me, but I suppose I could just as well tell that to him myself, couldn't I?"

"Yes, thank you."

"So, where is he?" Jonathan glanced around the bar but didn't see any likely candidates.

"Mr. Singh is upstairs in the lounge, waiting for you."

"All right, let's go." Jonathan slipped a few bills under his glass and followed her out of the bar and across the lobby and up a spiral staircase to the second floor.

Singh was much younger than Jonathan expected, and certainly less imposing. He had a large, round head wrapped in a white turban, and his wide forehead was punctuated by a pair of high-set, wispy eyebrows. A pair of thick, black rimmed glasses did nothing to lend authority to his smooth, babyish face. The most impressive thing about him was the large, hard-sided black briefcase that lay on the coffee table in front of him.

Muna sat on the edge of the leather sofa beside him, her hands folded demurely in her lap. Jonathan took an armchair on the other side of the table and leaned back, crossing his legs casually.

Singh looked nervous. His feet shifted back and forth and his forehead was shiny with sweat although the room was cool. He cleared his throat several times before speaking.

"So, Mr. Jonathan Marshall." He spoke slowly and precisely, in a nasal, sing-song voice. "We are both busy men, so let us not waste our time. What is it I can do for you?"

Jonathan looked at him blankly. "Excuse me, Mr. Singh, but I understood it was you who wanted to see me."

Singh's eyes darted to Muna and then quickly back to Jonathan. "You wished to contact me the other day, isn't it? I am sorry, I was unavoidably detained from our rendezvous at the Ankara Hotel. I trust I did not cause you any great inconvenience?" His stilted, self-consciously formal speech was familiar to Jonathan—East African Asian seasoned with a second-rate British boarding school education.

"As I tried to explain to Miss Bitanga over the phone, I did go to the Ankara yesterday—to meet an old friend. I certainly hadn't made any appointment to meet you there. I'm afraid you must have me mixed up with someone else."

Singh took the disclaimer in stride. "Perhaps," he suggested, "it was someone else who set the appointment for you?"

"You mean my secretary?" Jonathan shook his head gravely. "No, I'm sure she would have consulted me. In any case, I'm not in the habit of conducting business at the Ankara."

"Not your secretary, Mr. Marshall. Your associate. The European gentleman."

"Oh, yes, the mysterious European. Miss Bitanga mentioned him too. Sorry, I can't think who you could mean. What was this fellow's name?"

Jonathan kept his gaze fixed firmly on Singh, but from the corner of his eye he thought he caught a slight movement of the woman's draped figure: a faint shake of the head, the suggestion of a shrug. The Indian cleared his throat again. "Perhaps that is not important for the moment, Mr. Marshall."

"Whatever you say, Mr. Singh," said Jonathan. "This is your show, after all."

Singh compressed his lips and shifted his feet. Jonathan settled deeper into the armchair and rearranged his legs, resting one ankle on the other knee. His expression was patiently bored.

"Incidentally, Mr. Singh," Jonathan remarked lightly, "I couldn't help noticing that you don't wear a beard."

"A beard? Oh, yes, yes indeed. You are most observant." Singh didn't seem very pleased about it. "In fact, my family is quite progressive. Even my father does not wear a beard."

"Really?" said Jonathan. "How things change. In my day the Sikh community in Nairobi seemed to be a pretty conservative lot overall."

"In Nairobi?" Singh's thin brows came together, creasing his smooth forehead.

"You are from Nairobi, aren't you?" Jonathan reached into his pocket and pulled out his wallet. Opening it slowly, he extracted the business card he had gotten from Carol and tossed it casually on top of the briefcase.

Singh glanced at the card and smiled with obvious relief. His voice took on a more confident tone.

"Well, well, Mr. Marshall, perhaps now we can be getting somewhere."

"Can we? And just where is that, exactly?"

"At the least, I presume we can drop this tiresome pretense that you have never heard of me, isn't it?"

"Oh, I didn't say I'd never heard of you," Jonathan said mildly. "I only said I didn't arrange to meet with you."

Singh looked uncertain again. "But the person who gave you that card..."

"A friend," said Jonathan.

Singh bobbled his head from side to side in agreement. "A business associate."

"A friend."

Singh furrowed his brows again in concentration, as though picking his way through a mental obstacle course.

"There are not so many people who are in possession of that card," he said carefully.

"I'll bet."

The words hung in the air as Singh sat back on the sofa, determined to wait Jonathan out, trying to force him to take the initiative. But Jonathan's diplomatic training was more than a match for him. The silence stretched until finally the Indian broke it.

"We are both businessmen, Mr. Marshall, so let us talk business. I assume you are in the position to speak for your partners?"

"I'm here to listen to what you have to say," answered Jonathan. He turned to Muna, who still sat erect and silent on the edge of her chair. "Either of you," he added.

Muna raised her head and looked at him straight on for the first time. She had a striking face, and Jonathan felt sure that he had seen it somewhere before.

"So," said Singh hastily, with a touch of triumph in his voice. "So, in fact you are interested in doing business."

"Could be," murmured Jonathan.

Singh eyes fell to the table and then jerked quickly up again. "I beg your pardon?" he said to Jonathan, weakly.

"I said, 'could be,'" Jonathan repeated, his voice barely above a whisper. Then he continued in a normal tone, "Is there some reason you want me to speak louder?"

Singh cast yet another covert, anxious look in Muna's direction. "I...I am a bit hard of hearing," he confessed. "When you dropped your voice just now, I could not catch what you said..."

His voice drifted off. In the silence that followed, there was an audible click from the briefcase on the table. Singh's eyes widened behind his glasses and he stared hard at a point somewhere above Jonathan's head. Muna closed her eyes.

"Right," said Jonathan briskly, rising to his feet. "I think we've had about enough of this charade." He ignored the Indian and spoke directly to Muna. "Someone has been trying very hard to get in touch with this friend of mine, and we are very interested in talking with that person. I don't know who your pal here is, but I know damn well who he isn't. You can tell the real Mr. Singh, if that's his real name, to get in touch when he's ready to meet me in person. Meanwhile, it seems you've run out of tape, so there's really no point in our continuing this conversation."

Jonathan turned and walked leisurely away from them and back down the spiral staircase.

As soon as he was out of sight, Muna grabbed the briefcase and removed a cassette from the small, portable tape recorder inside.

"I don't know what happened," said Ravi anxiously. "It is a sixty minute tape."

"A cheap sixty minute tape," snapped Muna, throwing it back into the briefcase. "It got jammed and the machine turned itself off."

Ravi picked up the tape and examined it closely, as though searching for the flaw in the workmanship.

"Not that it matters," said Muna, "You didn't fool him for a minute."

"I thought I carried it off fairly well," protested Ravi.

"Well, you didn't" she replied crossly. "Some international gangster. You were as nervous as a cat and looked about as cold-blooded as a puff pastry. I knew I should have handled this myself."

"Well, that is very nice, I should say," said Ravi, stiffly. "I shall certainly keep this in mind the next time you come to me for help with one of your ridiculous schemes. Another time you can simply leave me out of it, thank you all the same."

"Believe me, I will," said Muna, starting toward the staircase.

Ravi stood up and called after her, "You still owe me one thousand rimands, you know."

Muna stopped and looked back at him.   "For that performance? So you do have balls, don't you? Where were they when you needed them?"

"One thousand more," he repeated stubbornly. "That was the deal. Or should I ask your sweetie for it?" he suggested with an insinuating sneer.

Muna came swiftly back across the room, advancing on Ravi with such cold fury that he took an involuntary step backward.

"Listen, you little turd," she hissed at him. "You'd better forget the whole thing if you know what's good for you. And you'd better hope Maleke never hears anything about this from anybody. Because if he does, I'm going to assume it was you and I'll tear your beady little eyes out."

"I was only joking, don't get so excited." Ravi straightened his glasses and cleared his throat. "You know I wouldn't do that to you. What do I have to do with him, anyway? As for the money, just forget it. We will consider it a favor, between friends."

Muna looked at him fixedly for a moment.   "Between friends," she said, and turned back toward the stairs.

CHAPTER 16

1

There were many places to get a drink in Mwatumi, from the upscale bar at the Acropolis Hotel with its imported whiskey, to the small clearings high up in the mountains where men squatted around wooden vats sipping banana beer through long, flexible reeds while their wives cooked their suppers. Somewhere in between was the Cock and Bull, located in the center of town just off the main road. It was owned by Sanjit Dawari, a refugee of Idi Amin's expulsion of the Asians from Uganda in 1978. The name of Dawari's establishment had been suggested by a wise-cracking "overlander" student tourist from Liverpool. Dawari, who dreamed of owning a pub in England some day, had missed the joke but liked the name because it sounded British.

A half dozen small iron tables with matching chairs filled the narrow yard in front of the bar. They had once been painted white but years of rain and stacking had left them faded and scarred with rusty gouges. A rough wooden bench against the wall provided additional seating for latecomers.

The sun had just set over the mountains and the air was getting crisp when David Wangeru took a seat at one of the old iron tables. He was the only customer.

"Hey, Joseph," he called to the lounging waiter. Joseph glanced up from cleaning his fingernails with a matchstick, sighed and sauntered over.

"Bring me a Green Mountain," said David.

Joseph raised one eyebrow disdainfully. Green Mountain was export quality beer, brewed in Kobani, and it cost thirty rimands a bottle. "You got the money?" he asked skeptically.

"I'm waiting for Juma. He'll pay when he gets here."

"Then you'll get your Green Mountain when he gets here," said Joseph.

"Come on, Joseph, you know he's good for it."

Joseph just sniffed. "You want anything now or not?" he asked.

"Yeah, okay, bring me some waragi," David said sullenly.

Joseph stood waiting.

"What's the matter now?" demanded David. "You think I can't even afford your crummy banana beer?" David slammed a coin down flat on the table. "There, satisfied?"

Joseph picked up the coin without a word and headed toward the bar, slinging his towel over his shoulder.

David muttered fiercely under his breath. 'I'll remember this,' he thought to himself vengefully. Later, when he was rolling in money, sitting night after night at the best table, buying liquor and roasted meat for the girls and for all of his friends...just let that little shit Joseph come then and see what he got. 'I'll laugh right in his face. Go ahead, pal, I'll tell him. Have a swallow of waragi—it's on me.'

By seven o'clock other customers began to drift in, sitting around the tables exchanging news and amiable insults. David ignored them and kept to himself, nursing his cloudy, dark brew and his injuries.

The bus from Kobani arrived at the main intersection in Mwatumi just after seven o'clock. Wangeru Odege headed straight for the Cock and Bull, but found that the tables were all occupied. He had nearly resigned himself to a spot on the bench along the wall when he spotted David, half dozing in solitary splendor at a table, with one foot resting on an empty chair. Odege pushed his way through the crowd and yanked the chair out from under his son's foot.

David jerked awake with a start. His expression darkened in annoyance when he saw who it was. His father took no notice but snapped his fingers to summon the waiter.

"Who invited you?" asked David curtly.

"Show some respect." said the old man. "If I couldn't do better than that," he went on, pointing to the almost empty glass of waragi, "I sure as hell wouldn't go mouthing off to my betters. Not if I wanted them to buy me a real drink."

"My betters!" scoffed David, but he didn't protest when Odege sat down. A beer was a beer.

Odege turned to Joseph. "Two Green Mountains," he said, grandly. "Long ones." He pulled a crumpled bill out of his pocket and tossed it casually on the table. "And hurry up, we're thirsty."

Joseph took the bill with a shrug and headed off slowly. Odege settled back into his chair and looked smug.

Unlike most people, David didn't believe that Margaret was the source of Odege's largesse. He was pretty sure he knew his mother better than that. "What did you do?" he demanded. "Take Nelson to Kobani and sell him?"

Odege smiled benevolently, to show that he was above responding to such small-minded sallies. He leaned forward and said confidentially, "A little gift from your uncle," said Ogebe. "A down-payment, you could say."

"A down-payment for what?"

"Never you mind," said his father. "It's business, nothing to do with you."

David snorted. "Business," he said scornfully. "You expect me to believe that? Why would he be doing business with an old fool like you? I'll bet you stole it from him."

"Didn't I tell you show some respect?" scowled Odege. "Look out I don't whip you."

"I'd like to see you try," muttered David. But he fell silent as Joseph returned with the coveted, tall green bottles. The bitter liquid slid smoothly down his throat.

David downed half the bottle in a few gulps and wiped his mouth with the back of his arm. Meanwhile, Odege sipped daintily, showing that store-bought beer was no big thing to him.

"Aieh," he mused, "My brother-in-law and me, we understand each other. Remember that, boy—when you need to count on somebody, stick with the family. Family's got to help each other out."

"Huh. What could you do to help him?" David's voice was still scornful, but he could not hide his curiosity.

Odege wagged a dirty forefinger at him. "Eh, eh," he chided. "That's the other thing you got to remember. No wagging jaws. That's how businessmen get rich—by keeping their business to themselves."

"Yeah, what would you know about businessmen, or about getting rich?" David goaded him.

Odege merely frowned wisely and took another slow sip from his bottle. He regarded his son sadly. "Sometimes I think it's too bad we didn't send you to school in town. But then, you never was a smart one, like your brother."

David wavered between the satisfaction of a withering retort and the possibility that Odege might be willing to spring for at least one more beer if he let him keep talking. You were supposed to look up to the old men, the elders, full of the wisdom of their years. But all the old men he knew in this backwater village were stupid and uneducated like his father. Marrying Margaret Waiyala, with her family connections, was the only smart thing the old fool had ever done. He must have had to borrow from his whole family to come up with the bride price.

Not that David had much respect for his mother. She was only a woman after all, even if she could read and write and had once held a cash job, working for that mzungu who wanted everybody to plant trees all over the place and who had insisted on paying the salary directly to her instead of to her husband, as was proper. It didn't matter, of course—she had to hand it over to Odege later anyway. But David knew his mother always kept a bit of the money she earned hidden away for emergencies and for occasional little luxuries for him and his brother and sisters. She'd taught his sisters to do the same thing. Odege had never caught on—another reason for David's contempt.

"So, here you are," continued Odege, shaking his head gloomily. "Wasting your time, hanging around, trying to bum enough waragi to get good and drunk. A disgrace to the family, that's what. Good thing I'll have Nelson to take care of me in my old age."

David lost the battle with his temper. "Yeah? Well let me tell you something. I'm not just 'hanging around.' I'm waiting for my business associate. We've got plans to make. Something that's going to get us more money in one day than you'll ever see in your whole life."

"Your business associate?" Odege mimicked him. You mean that Pygmy you hang out with?"

"Juma's not a Pygmy," bristled David.

"Of course he's a Pygmy," sneered Odege, "His father was a pygmy, and that makes him one too. Everybody knows it. You just got to look at him."

"You'd better shut up old man, if you know what's good for you. Someday Juma's going to run this whole town and you'll all come begging to him for favors. And to me too."

"When dogs piss beer," sneered Odege. "That's when I'll ask that pygmy for anything. Except maybe to take a bath so he doesn't stink up the place. Am I right?" Odege turned around to appeal to a non-existent audience, and found Joseph at his elbow.

"Ready for another one?" Joseph asked, in a tone that bordered on courteous.

David glowered at his father. "He's just going," he said.

"Hah," said Odege, "don't worry. I'm not sticking around if that monkey is coming. But I'm not going anywhere till I finish this." He held the bottle up to the fading light and took another sip.

David shrugged and looked away from him, down the road. He saw two small figures walking from the direction of the mountains. They slowed down as they neared the bar, approaching hesitantly, their eyes fastened on their bare feet. They stopped at the entrance to the yard, a few feet from David's table.

Their filthy shirts hung by strands from their bony shoulders and their thin, scabby legs protruded from shredded, baggy trousers. Neither was over four and a half feet tall. Beneath the grime their skin was a yellowish brown. One was an old man, his head covered with an uneven mat of white, woolly hair. The whites of his eyes were stained brown and the joints of his hands were swollen with arthritis. The other was a boy in his late teens. They both hunched their shoulders as though trying to shrink from sight. With their oversized, square heads and knobby limbs, they looked like a pair of pitifully thin children. They stood, silent but defiant, ignoring the hostile stares. Over his shoulder the boy carried a bulky sack which looked like old burlap but was actually a fine mesh of tightly woven vines.

Odege followed David's gaze and saw the two Pygmies by the door.

"Speaking of monkeys, look at those two," he said. "You suppose they think they're going to get served here?"

A murmur rose from the tables as people began to notice the intruders. Joseph looked around uncertainly, then walked up to the two small men.

"What do you want?" he demanded. "No ba'shyamba here." He used the local derogatory term, meaning 'children of the forest,' meant to imply that the Pygmies were more like monkeys than humans.

The old man reached inside his dirty shirt and pulled out a small leather pouch hung on a thong around his neck. He carefully extracted a few small coins and held them out toward Joseph.

"Pomba," he said simply, using the general word for alcohol of any kind.

Joseph glanced at the coins and then at the crowd which was still watching intently.

"Not enough," he snapped. "Go on, get going."

The boy loosened the neck of the woven bag. He reached inside and pulled out a small, golden brown forest duiker and held it up the neck. The little antelope's slender legs dangled limply in the air. Its huge dark eyes were wide open and staring.

Joseph pinched one of the haunches to check whether the meat was fresh. He nodded and took the animal. As an afterthought, he held his hand out casually, holding it there until the old man dropped the coins into it.

"Wait here," he said, and disappeared with the duiker into the bar. The two Pygmies stood impassively, looking at nothing. After a moment, Joseph appeared again with two glass jars filled with a clear liquid. He handed one to each of them.

"Now get lost," he said. The Pygmies sniffed at the liquid and then retreated noiselessly, clutching the jars carefully as they withdrew to the doorway of a building across the road. There they squatted on their heels and began to drink in hasty gulps. The patrons of the bar lost interest and turned back to their drinks and conversations.

Odege held his bottle vertically to drain the last of the beer. He banged the empty bottle down on the table and wiped his mouth again with the back of his hand.

"Did you see that?" he demanded loudly. "What's it coming to, huh? Those monkeys get a little money from somewhere, and bang! Next thing you know, they walk in like they own the place, and get served just like you or me. I'd kick them out on their skinny little asses. Joseph! Hey, you, Joseph!"

"What?" asked the waiter sullenly.

"What was that you gave them? You run out of waragi?"

Joseph shrugged. "It's just cheap gin," he said. "This way they'll come back here next time. I can use the meat."

"Yeah, you made a good deal," said David. "That's a lot of good stew for two jars of gin. Stupid ba'shyamba don't know what anything's worth."

"Shouldn't give them real booze," complained Odege. "They'll be dead drunk in no time."

Cheeya Ethungu had been sitting against the wall with a group of his age-mates. He picked up his glass and a stool and carried it over to join David and Odege. He sat down and rested his elbows comfortably on the table.

"They'll be drunk on their asses for two days," he agreed. "And then they'll be back for more."

Odege warmed to his theme. "What would our fathers say, eh Ethungu?" he demanded. "In the old days, the ba'shyamba stayed in the forest where they belonged. They didn't wear clothes and put on airs and come around bothering decent people. If we caught 'em stealing from our fields we killed 'em, just like the bushpigs. Now they put you in jail if you kill one." He shook his head at the wonder of it.

"It's the mzungus," said Ethungu, bitterly. "They give the ba'shyamba ideas. Make them think they're good as we are. You remember that crazy mzungu, that American who came around here last year? He hired Ndoke to help him find some pygmies—said he wanted to 'interview' them! Can you believe it?"

"He paid Ndoke money to find pygmies?" David was envious. "All you got to do is go out to the logging camp or to the mission in Murani. You find as many as you want."

"He didn't want those," said Ethungu. "He wanted to talk to the real ba'shyamba, ones who still live in the forest like monkeys."

"Hunh!" said Odege. "Those ones nobody can find. Especially Ndoke. What does he know?"

"Nothing," snickered Ethungu. "But he told this stupid mzungu he knew where to find them. Even said he could talk their gibberish! Took him around in circles for five days, up and down the hills so many times he didn't know where he was anymore. They never got more than five kilometers from Mwatumi. At night Ndoke sneaked out and built some little huts out of sticks and leaves, then he'd take the mzungu there and tell him that's where the pygmies slept last night but they left already!"

The three men roared with laughter.

"So they never found any ba'shyamba at home," crowed Odege.

"Nope, not one. What a deal. I wish I'd thought of it."

"You mean the mzungu paid Ndoke anyway? Even though he never found the pygmies?"

191

"Sure. Ndoke said they got real chummy out there, wandering around in the forest. You know what the guy told him? He said the Americans want to buy the forest and give it to the ba'shyamba."

"Buy the forest?" Odege asked sharply. "Who are they supposed to buy it from?"

Ethungu shrugged. "Who knows?" he said. "The government, I guess. Why, what's it to you?" He looked at Odege craftily.

Odege just shook his head, chuckling. "Buy the forest," he said. "Give it to the monkeys. I never heard such rubbish. Leave it to the mzungus, right?"

"You said it." The three men shared a moment of comfortable silence, reflecting on the unfathomable foolishness of white people.

"And not just the mzungus," added Odege. "What about that crazy priest, trying to set up a damn school for them. Can you believe it, sending ba'shyamba to school? That was good riddance when we got rid of him, that's for sure. That's the problem with outsiders. What business is it of theirs, anyway? They'd better leave us alone to deal with our pygmies our way."

Ethungu nodded his agreement and licked his lips. "I'll tell you one thing," he said. "If they want the bloody forest, they can have it. It's nothing but trouble. With those bloody elephants and bushpigs and monkeys coming out of there every night to eat up all our maize and bananas, and the leopards going after our goats. We should let the mzungus take the bloody thing home with them.

"Hey," laughed David, "maybe Ndoke can figure out a way to get the mzungus to pay us for it."

Odege gave him a hard look. "Forget it," he said. "If anybody gets any money out of it, it'll be some bigwigs in Kobani, right? And we'll still be stuck with the elephants and the leopards and the bloody ba'shyamba."

Ethungu's face took on a cunning look. "That's all you know," he said.

When they didn't react, he pressed on. "Doesn't seem fair. That's all Ruahya land over there, and it would be good farmland. But they tell us we can't use it, because the mzungus and the ba'shyamba and those fat-asses in Kobani want their forest. Meanwhile, which one of us has enough land to pass on to our sons?"

Odege just shrugged and looked bored, but David perked up. "You said it," he said. "What right do they have here, anyway? This is Ruahya land."

"That's right," said Ethungu. "We should go and burn the whole thing down."

"Sure, Ethungu, just like Byanaga did," Odege said sourly. "The rangers caught him clearing out a little patch to plant some bananas. They beat him silly, and he's in jail for three years. No, thanks."

"That was before," said Ethungu, impatiently. "It's different now."

"What do you mean, different?" asked David.

"You haven't heard?"

"Heard what?"

"Buy me another waragi and I'll tell you," said Ethungu.

Odege shot a sour look at the old man. "Don't pay any attention to him. He doesn't know anything."

Ethungu looked injured. "Okay, have it your way. I was trying to do you a favor because you're my age-mate, but forget it." He started to rise very slowly from the table.

David nudged his father. "Go on, buy it for him."

"I'm not wasting my money on him."

"I want to hear what he's got to say."

"He's got nothing to say," grumbled Odege. Ethungu hovered, and David nudged his father again. When Odege ignored him, David raised his arm and snapped his fingers to catch Joseph's attention. Odege grunted but didn't interfere.

When the drinks had come, Ethungu took a long, thirsty swallow and leaned across the table. "They've moved the border of the reserve," he said in a hoarse stage whisper. "Right up to

193

the top of Kikuri Ridge. The whole south end's been cut out. And it's all up for grabs—first come, first served."

"You expect us to believe that?" sneered Odege. "How come you're the only one that knows about this?"

"I got my sources," Ethungu said smugly. He placed his hands flat on the table and fixed first Odege and then David with a solemn look. "I give you my word, it's absolutely true."

"Ha! He gives you his word," Odege told David. "That's a good one. Don't listen to him. Forget it, he doesn't know what he's talking about."

Ethungu sat back and smiled broadly, displaying his few yellow teeth. "Okay," he said. "I don't know what I'm talking about. Why am I telling you about it anyway? I don't need the whole village running out there and staking claims."

"How do you mean, staking claims?" David persisted.

"You burn off a patch, you put in a few bananas and a couple rows of maize, maybe build a little shack, and it's yours."

"Only thing that's yours is a jail cell for three years," said Odege.

"You see me in jail?" challenged Ethungu.

"You've gone and done it already?" asked David.

"Sure did," Ethungu boasted loudly. "Cleared out more than four hectares last week. Got my wife and kids putting in the bananas and maize right now."

"Shut up, you old fool," Odege whispered fiercely, as several people nearby turned to look. "Somebody's going to hear you."

"What do you care? You don't believe me anyway, right?"

"I'm just telling you for your own good," said Odege. "Makes no difference to me if Kamanga comes and puts you away."

Ethungu laughed out loud. "Kamanga!" he said. "Kamanga's wife is digging the plot right next to mine!"

He drained his glass and banged it down on the table. "I paid for my waragi," he said, getting to his feet. "What do I care

if you believe me?" Still chuckling, he picked up his stool and
drifted off toward another table.

"Good riddance," said Odege.

"Why would he make something like that up?" David said
to Odege doubtfully. "I think he knows what he's talking about.
But why didn't my uncle tell you about this, if you're supposed
to be in so big with him?"

"That old fool Ethungu got it all wrong," said Odege.

"Sure, and you know better," said David.

Odege was stung. "Of course I know. I'm just not dumb
enough to go around blabbing to everybody, like some people."
He looked pointedly first over one shoulder and then the other.
He leaned across the table and lowered his voice.

"I'll tell you, but only because you're my own son. I better
not catch you mouthing off to anybody or I'll break your neck."

"Mouthing off about what?" demanded David impatiently.

Odege lowered his voice even further, so that David had to
put his ear up close his father's mouth to hear him.

"The boundary isn't changed yet, but it's going to be soon.
But when it is, the land isn't going to just anybody who's cleared
it. Ethungu and anybody who listens to him are going to get
booted off when the rightful owners come to claim those plots.
And they won't get a cent for any of their bananas or crops or
shacks, either."

"What do you mean, the rightful owners?"

"Well, let's just say, we'll soon see who's really got the
connections around here," said Odege smugly.

"This is what you were talking about, isn't it?" asked David
excitedly. "That business with my uncle?"

Odege held up his hand. "That's all I'm saying," he said.
"Next thing I know, you'll be spreading it all over town, or
spilling your guts to that little half-breed."

"No I won't," protested David.

"Talking about the monkey, here he comes now," said
Odege looking over David's shoulder. "Listen, you don't say a

thing about what I told you to him or to anyone else, you hear me?"

"All right, take it easy. Why should I tell anyone?"

"Tell anyone what?" asked Juma, coming up to them.

"Hunh, time to go," said Odege, rising unsteadily to his feet. "It's starting to smell like monkeys around here." He picked up his satchel and shuffled away.

"What was that all about?" asked Juma, taking the chair that Odege had abandoned.

"Nothing," said David. "He's drunk, as usual. Where have you been?"

Juma ignored the question. "We've got more important things to talk about."

"Like what?"

"Reijksen says she's ready to make a deal, but she wants to meet Singh," said Juma. "He's meeting us here tonight to set it up."

2

The overloaded pickup was going too fast down the narrow, winding mountain road. The driver struggled with the sluggish steering and stepped hard on the brakes every now and then to break the momentum before heading into a sharp turn. He drove this route at least twice a day and knew every dip and twist by heart. In the daylight there were spectacular views of the mountainside falling away almost vertically, sometimes only inches from the wheels. But now, at every turn the dim headlights petered out over a yawning chasm of darkness.

The driver concentrated on the small illuminated patch of road immediately in front of him, alert for potholes and fallen rocks that could catch a wheel or puncture a tire. The three passengers squeezed into the seat beside him had dozed off. No one noticed the two pairs of pinpoint yellow lights climbing toward them, one close behind the other, ducking in and out of sight as they rounded the hairpin turns.

Suddenly they were blinded by the glare of headlights as they rounded a blind curve at the same moment that the trailing vehicle pulled into the inside lane to overtake the one in front. The pickup driver reacted instinctively, throwing the steering wheel hard to the right. With a grating crunch the pickup crashed to a stop against the side of the mountain, nearly throwing them through the windshield.

It took an instant for the men in the pickup to realize what had happened, and another to register the relief that they were safe. Then they heard the screams and jerked their heads around to see the car in the outside lane spin out of control and go hurtling over the edge of the road. They watched in horrified fascination as the tail lights of the falling car carved parallel, sweeping red arcs through the darkness, until it struck the slope a hundred yards below. It bounced crazily up again and soared another hundred yards before crashing back to the ground and bursting into flames. Pieces of burning debris flew off in all directions like a shower of sparks, and scattered across the black mountainside like a reflection of the starry sky overhead.

The four men climbed out of the pickup cab and stood solemnly at the edge of the road, watching the fires burn and listening to the eerie silence. There was nothing to do but report the accident when they got to town. They put their shoulders to the truck and wrestled it back onto the road. Amazingly, the engine was still running and nothing was broken except the right fender, the windshield and one headlight. They pulled off the fender, brushed the glass off the seat and resumed their interrupted journey.

CHAPTER 17

1

David nudged Juma and pointed with his chin. "Look over there," he said. "Isn't that the guy Mrs. Simon came to Mwatumi with?"

Unaware of their scrutiny, Thor turned in to the yard of the Cock and Bull, easing his way through the tightly packed tables. Most of the patrons were men dressed in sweat-stained, second-hand clothes. The few women in sight were very young or doing their best to look that way, in short skirts and spiked heels and scooped blouses that squeezed their breasts together and slid down to reveal their smooth shoulders. One girl leaning alone against the wall caught Thor's eye and smiled boldly. He returned the smile but shook his head and looked away, peering into the crowd on the faint hope of spotting an empty table. A boombox over the door filled the air with loud, tinny Zairean music.

A neatly dressed, middle aged Indian stepped out and extended his hand. "You are most welcome to the Cock and Bull, sir," he said with a sing-song accent. "I am Sanjit Dawari, the proprietor. You are looking for a table?"

"Yes I am, but I seem to be out of luck. You are doing very good business tonight."

Before Thor knew it, Dawari had rousted a group of four young men from their table and was holding one of the vacated chairs out for him. The men glanced at Thor without hostility as they left.

"I don't want to take their table," Thor protested.

"There is no problem," Dawari assured him. "You see, they have already joined other friends. In any case, they have purchased nothing for more than one hour. This is a business establishment, not a sitting room. Please, sit down, sir. We are honored to serve you."

He signaled for Joseph to clear the table and take Thor's order.

"Can you recommend a good local beer?" asked Thor.

"A Green Mountain, right away," Dawari told Joseph. "A long one, and make certain it is cold. And a plate of *nyama choma*. Roasted goat meat," he explained to Thor. "A specialty of the house. Very good to eat with the beer. If you do not like it, you will not pay for it. Shall I remove the other chairs or leave them?"

"Please leave one," said Thor. "I expect a friend will be joining me shortly."

Dawari moved two of the chairs aside and tilted the last one forward so its back rested against the edge of the table.

"Leave it in this position if you are not looking for company," he advised, with a glance toward the pouting girl by the wall.

The beer and the meat came quickly. Thor poured half the bottle into the tall glass, rested his ankle on his knee and leaned back in his chair. He tapped his fingers to the beat of the music as he gazed benevolently out over the crowd.

"I checked at the hotel," said Juma. "His name is Nilssen. Norwegian passport."

"How does he fit in?" asked David.

"I don't know yet," said Juma. "Reijksen won't tell me anything, but I get the idea he doesn't like him much."

"Maybe he's just Mrs. Simon's boyfriend," suggested David.

Juma shook his head. "They're in separate rooms. I think he works for her too. Maybe he's a new guy who's trying to squeeze Reijksen out."

"You think he's here to spy on Reijksen?"

"Sitting right out in the open like that? He must want Reijksen to see him—maybe to let him know he knows about our meeting."

"You think we should go somewhere else?" asked David.

Juma frowned thoughtfully. "No, if Reijksen wants to change the meeting he'll get word to us. Meanwhile, let's see what Nilssen's up to. You see he kept one of the chairs. I wonder who he's waiting for."

"Probably Mrs. Simon," said David.

"Jesus, Mary and Joseph!" said Juma with a sudden intake of breath. "What the hell is he doing here?"

As he leaned forward to pour the rest of the beer into his glass, Thor sensed someone beside him. He turned and saw Greg Allen standing there with his feet planted firmly apart and his muscular arms crossed stiffly in front of him. Thor had the uneasy feeling that he had been standing there for some time.

"Sotiropoulos told me where to find you," said Greg.

"Good evening. If you're looking for Carol, I'm afraid she hasn't come back yet. She left a message that she was going to the reserve headquarters to meet the Chief Warden."

"I've got a question for you," said Greg.

"Would you like to sit down? It's a bit noisy," said Thor.

Greg remained standing but leaned closer to him. "Why is it that there's no record of anyone named Thor Nilssen who's ever had an article in the New Yorker. Or in any other magazine in the past five years, for that matter."

"Is that right?" asked Thor mildly.

"That's right. I asked a friend of mine in New York to check."

"But why would you do that? Do I really strike you as such a suspicious character? Or do you have a reason for being particularly...cautious?"

"Never mind my reasons," growled Greg. "Are you going to tell me who the hell you are and what you're doing here? Or am I going to kick your ass back to Oslo?"

Thor reached over and set the empty chair carefully on the ground. "Why don't you sit down and have a beer," he said. "We have a lot to talk about."

2

Walking into the gloomy lounge of the Kobani Club was like stepping back into the 1930's. The new generation of diplomats who had taken over the club since independence had done their best to modernize it, adding a swimming pool and a jogging track and, more recently, rowing machines and video games. But the ghosts of the British colonial officers who had built the clubhouse, and gotten drunk, played billiards and flirted in it, still possessed the lounge, from the creaking wooden floorboards to the high, water-stained ceiling. A very few lingered in a more corporeal form, a handful of old men and women sunk deep in the worn velvet armchairs, sipping gin and reminding each other of how much better everything had worked in Africa before the sun had set on the Empire.

Pat and Jonathan hurried through the lobby and into the dining room, where they found Phil and Melissa Drayton already waiting at a table.

"Sorry we're late," said Pat, as the two couples exchanged pecks on the cheek and handshakes. "The kids were being impossible."

"No problem, we started without y'all," said Phil, holding up a half-finished whiskey and soda. Phil Drayton, Director of the United States Information Service office in Rumura, had the thick neck and beefy build of a college football player who had started relaxing into fat as soon as he graduated. His bland, good-natured face was perpetually sunburned and his thinning, white-blond hair was still cut in the style he had worn when he was twelve. Melissa was short and wiry, with thick, wavy black hair in long bangs in front and gathered into a loose ponytail at her neck. With her black eyes and deeply bronzed skin she looked Jewish or Hispanic—anything but the southern belle from an old aristocratic Louisiana family that she was.

"You yanks just don't know how to handle young'uns," teased Melissa, caricaturing her own accent. "Y'all should do like we do with our'n. Fill 'em full of corn pone an' moonshine, take 'em to the woodshed for a good whuppin', and pack 'em off to the back forty."

"It's certainly worth a try," sighed Pat. "I don't know why I ever agreed to have teenagers."

The waiter passed around menus and Jonathan and Phil fell into a friendly argument about the pennant prospects of their respective Major League teams while Pat and Melissa caught up on the local scene.

"I didn't see you at the Benoit's shindig last night," said Melissa, falling back into her usual soft, honeyed drawl.

"I guess we missed each other in the crowd," said Pat. "What a crush."

"Ain't it the truth," said Melissa, rolling her eyes dramatically. "I never even laid eyes on the guest of honor."

"Me neither," laughed Pat. "We got shanghaied by Andre Delacroix right after we arrived, and I spent the rest of the evening trying to make myself scarce in case he came around again. I wonder whether Jonathan managed to meet him."

She turned to ask Jonathan, but he was staring past her to the bar at the end of the room. She followed his gaze and saw a young, strikingly pretty African woman sitting on a high stool. She wore a low-cut black dress that ended high up on her crossed thighs. One slender hand held a cigarette and the other rested lightly on her knee, displaying very long, slender fingers tapering to deep red fingernails.

Pat tightened her lips and turned quickly back, picking up the conversation as though she hadn't noticed anything. Melissa glanced over at the bar and saw the problem.

"You know her, Jonathan?" she asked.

"Huh? Know who?"

"That girl sittin' at the bar, Sugar. The one with the red talons and the itty bitty dress."

"Hmmm? Oh, her? I don't know. I might have seen her somewhere, but I can't place her. Why, who is she?"

"Her name's Muna something or other," said Melissa. "She works at the travel agency down on Marungo street. You know, belongs to that Indian fellah, what's his name, Patel."

"Maybe that's where I've seen her."

"I wonder who she's waitin' for," purred Melissa. "Could be any number of fellahs, I reckon."

"Now Melissa, honey, I don't suppose it's any business of yours," said Phil.

"Hush up, Phil," said Melissa. "I hear she's got that round-headed Patel boy, Ravi, wrapped around her finger. And there's poor old Ian Campbell fallen for her like a ton of bricks, too. Meanwhile, there she is with a little girl by one man and set up in an apartment by a government bigshot. You know the one, Phil. Good lookin' man—real sharp dresser. Somethin' to do with trees. And him with that pretty French wife at home.

"You don't mean Thadeus Maleke," asked Jonathan sharply.

"That's the one," said Melissa. "I hear tell his wife's gotten wind of his goings on—he'd better look out or the next thing he hears'll be the door slammin' as her money walks out that door."

Phil laughed and covered his wife's small hand with his. "That's enough now, honey. I declare," he said to Jonathan and Pat, "Everybody thinks all of us in USIS are really CIA, but this here's the spy in our family."

"Melissa, how on earth do you know all these things?" asked Pat.

"Just the same as back in Baton Rouge, Sugar. Just sittin' and gossipin' with the servants. Kobani's nothin' but a small town full of big mouths." Melissa sat back and took a delicate sip of her drink with an air of a job well done.

Pat was still watching Jonathan, wondering why Melissa's revelation had gotten such a rise out of him. Before she could say anything, a waiter came up to Jonathan and leaned down to speak quietly into his ear.

Jonathan put down his drink and pushed his chair back. "Excuse me," he said. "I've got a phone call. Order the chicken curry for me, will you, Pat?"

"It's probably the embassy," said Pat as he followed the waiter away. "Jonathan is duty officer this weekend."

When Jonathan returned a few minutes later he didn't sit down but stood gripping the back of his chair with his hands.

"What's wrong?" asked Pat, alarmed at the look on his face.

"That was Thadeus Maleke," he said, his eyes fixed on hers. "He's just gotten word from his people at the Mali-Kuli Reserve that there's been an accident somewhere near Mwatumi. A car went over a cliff in the mountains."

"Oh no, how terrible."

Jonathan spoke slowly, selecting his words carefully. "The car fell hundreds of yards before it crashed and caught fire. The police won't be able to reach the scene until morning."

"But why did he call you, Jonathan?" asked Phil. "Do they think there might be some Americans involved?"

Jonathan's mouth tightened as he continued to hold Pat's eyes. "Thadeus thought we should know. There were a few witnesses who saw the car just before it went over. One of them thought there might have been a white woman in the passenger seat."

CHAPTER 18

1

"Pat. Pat, wake up."

Pat cracked opened her eyes to find Jonathan sitting beside her on the bed, gently shaking her shoulder. They had both stayed up very late trying to get a phone call through to the Acropolis Hotel, but with no luck. She'd finally fallen asleep in her clothes.

"Hunh? What is it?" she asked sleepily. Then her eyes popped fully open and she sat upright with her heart racing. "Have you heard something? Is she okay?"

"No, nothing definite yet. But Thadeus Maleke is downstairs."

"What on earth does he want?"

"He's been talking to his people in Mwatumi by radio."

Pat rushed downstairs to find Maleke waiting in the living room, neat and courteous as always.

"I know you are concerned about your friend, Carol Simmons, so I radioed my Chief Warden to go to the accident site straight away and report to me as soon as he learned anything about the occupants of the car."

Seeing the look on his face, Pat sat slowly down on the sofa. Jonathan stood behind her and put his hands on her shoulders.

"The police have found one body that was thrown clear of the vehicle before it hit the ground. The police wouldn't tell him anything, but one of the bystanders said he was fairly sure it was a white woman."

. "Oh, my God...," whispered Pat.

"Take it easy, Pat, there's no reason to assume that it's Carol," Jonathan told her brusquely.

"No...of course not, it could be anyone..." Pat's throat tightened and cut off her voice.

205

"Did your man manage to get any kind of description?" Jonathan asked Maleke.

"Unfortunately, the body had already been removed when he arrived, and as I said, the authorities at the site weren't willing to talk to him. I'm afraid our police can be very secretive at times. We were able to get the registration number of the car, however, and I'm having it traced."

"Jonathan, we've got to go out there," said Pat urgently. "I'm sure they'll talk to you."

"Let's not jump the gun here," said Jonathan. "We should at least wait until we hear something on the car registration. Meanwhile, I've got to call around to the other Embassies and alert them in case they've got anyone in the area."

"I'll inform you immediately when I know anything more," promised Maleke. "It shouldn't be long."

Jonathan showed him out and came back to the living room, where Pat was still on the sofa, looking dazed and disheveled.

"It just can't be Carol," said Pat. "For one thing, she would know better than to be out on those roads after dark."

"Of course she would," agreed Jonathan. "The odds are the Warden's information was wrong, and it was just some poor local coming home late from the market. Come on, there's nothing we can do for now. Let's go get you a bath and some coffee."

2

The swaying bus squealed to a stop in front of the Post Office, spewing thick clouds of putrid black smoke from the exhaust pipe as the driver revved the engine to keep it from stalling. The exiting passengers pushed open the doors and jostled to grab their parcels as the tout tossed them down from the roof of the bus. When the way was clear, Tabitha Akello eased gingerly down the steep steps, followed by her sons, aged five and seven, each clutching a bundle wrapped in large square of cloth knotted at the top to form a handle. Her twelve-year-old daughter, Salome, paused at the top of the steps to hand the baby she was carrying down to her mother. The driver reached out and put his hand on her buttocks and gave her a half goose, half shove, laughing as she jumped out quickly and shot him a sullen look over her shoulder. The tout tossed down a battered suitcase wrapped with twine, then hopped back inside and banged his hand on the side of the bus. It pulled away with a choking roar and another billow of black smoke.

Tabitha hitched the sleeping baby onto her back in a cloth sling, then straightened up and twisted a handkerchief into a tight ring, which she put on her head. She rested the suitcase on top of it, shifting it to balance the weight. Without a word, the children placed their own bundles on top of their heads. The family crossed the dusty street and began to walk slowly, single file up the road into the hills.

Outside Margaret Waiyala's house, they put their bundles down and stood at the gate, looking around uncertainly. Hope came to the door carrying a market basket.

"Mama!" cried Hope, "look who's come!"

Margaret appeared in the doorway, wiping her hands on her dress. She peered out into the yard, shading her eyes against the bright sunlight.

"Praise God, it's Tabitha," she cried, rushing forward to wrap her arms tightly around her youngest sister, as the children looked on with dull eyes.

"And you've brought the children. What's the matter, little ones, don't you know your Auntie Margaret? And these are your cousins, Faith and Hope. Salome, you remember me, don't you?"

"Yes, Auntie," the girl said shyly, as she stood and let herself be kissed.

Margaret kissed each of the boys by turn. "I've never seen them—they were born after Tabitha left Mwatumi," Margaret explained to Faith and Hope. "And who is this? I didn't know you've had another, Tabitha!" She reached out and touched the

207

cheek of the baby, who gazed at her solemnly from the safety of his mother's back. "If I'd known, I would have sent a present. Well, never mind. What a surprise to see you."

"Oh, Margaret..." Tabitha began, her lips and voice starting to tremble.

"No, don't tell me yet," Margaret broke in firmly. "First you will all come in and have something to eat. Then the children can go and sleep—look at them, they're almost asleep already on their feet, poor things. And then we'll have tea and you can tell me everything."

"Should we stay, Mama?" asked Faith.

"No, you two go on. I'll take care of everything and you can visit with Tabitha when you come home. Bring some extra firewood when you come—we're going to have a feast tonight to welcome Tabitha home."

Margaret picked up the suitcase, took Tabitha by the arm and herded her toward the house. The children followed behind with their bundles.

An hour later, when the exhausted children had been fed and put to sleep on straw mats in the bedroom, Margaret and Tabitha settled on the front stoop, each holding an enamel cup full of steaming, milky tea.

"Now you tell me," said Margaret, "What has happened?"

Tabitha's voice shook and the tears began immediately to pour down her cheeks. "I am so ashamed...It's all gone."

"What is gone?" demanded Margaret. "Get hold of yourself and tell me so I can make sense of it."

"The house...the land...Jacob...we have nothing left but the clothes we're wearing."

"What do you mean? Did the house burn down? And where can the land go?"

"He sold it. He sold everything, and then he took all the money and ran off. He left us with nothing...nothing." Her voice rose in a wail and she dug her nails into her cheeks.

"Who, Jacob?"

"Yes, Jacob, who else? May God curse him wherever he lays his head in some whore's lap. I swear he would have sold the children if that vulture would have bought them."

Margaret stared at her, confused. "Which vulture?"

Tabitha sobbed into her hands. After a while, Margaret pulled her hands away from her face and held the cup of tea to her lips, pressing gently but firmly until Tabitha took a few sips. The swallowing calmed her enough to speak again.

"A man came to the door," she croaked. "He said the house was his, the farm was his. Jacob sold it to him and we had to leave. He gave us only two days to get ready."

"But how could he do that?"

"He showed me a paper...he said it was all legal."

"It can't be legal?" protested Margaret. "You can't buy or sell land, like a cow or a chicken. It belongs to the whole clan."

"That's what I said," said Tabitha. "I told him: 'I don't care about your paper. Go and use it in the toilet. This is my land—get off it before I push you off at the end of a pitchfork!'"

"Of course you did!" exclaimed Margaret, grateful for the flash of anger in Tabitha's eyes. She hardly recognized her spirited little sister in this moaning, miserable woman.

"But he came back with a policeman," continued Tabitha. "The policeman said the paper was true. He said the land doesn't belong to the clan anymore. They broke it up into little pieces and gave each man one piece."

"But who? Who could do this?"

"I don't know," said Tabitha wearily, "somebody."

"It can't be. He was tricking you, and the policeman was with him."

Tabitha shook her head. "I went to see Jacob's Uncle Sese," she said. He's one of the clan elders, and he said it was true. He said this is the modern way—everybody owns his own land, and he can sell it if he wants to. He can sell it to anybody—it doesn't even have to be someone from the clan."

"I've never heard of such a thing," exclaimed Margaret. "What strange ways they have out east. Didn't I tell you not to go there? You should have listened to me and stayed here in Mwatumi. There were so many men who wanted to marry you here. Why did you have to go off with that Jacob, just because he drove a big lorry and wore shiny shoes?"

Tabitha continued as though she had not heard. "I asked Uncle Sese to let us stay with him, but he said he has also sold his land. He's taking his whole family to live in Kobani. I had to sell everything—my goats and my chickens and even my hoe—just to buy bus fare for us to come to Mwatumi. Where else could I go?"

"You were right to come here," said Margaret, putting an arm around her sister's shoulders and drawing her close. "This is your home. It's a sinful thing that Jacob and his people have done. How will they face their ancestors, after they've sold the land where their bones are buried? Who can understand these easterners?"

Tabitha wiped her eyes and nose with the back of her hand and drew her feet up more tightly under her skirt.

"Do you think it can happen here, too?" she asked tentatively, her eyes furrowed with worry.

"Don't talk nonsense," said Margaret.

"But I heard two women talking on the bus. One said she has a cousin working in Kobani, cooking for a foreigner. This cousin heard her boss talking one night over dinner with his friends, about buying land around here and in Rendesha. They were laughing and laughing about how they were going to buy the land so cheap and make so much money."

"That's ridiculous," said Margaret, firmly. "Who could imagine such a thing? You know as well as I do, for us the land belongs to the family. Every son has his share from the day he's born. So how can any one sell it?"

"That's true, isn't it?" Tabitha brightened. "I suppose it must be a different custom in the east."

"Isn't that why I warned you not to marry outside the clan?" Margaret reminded her. "How can you trust them if you don't know their customs? If you stay with your own people you don't suddenly wake up one morning and find yourself without a penny or a pot and never even knowing what happened to you."

"But what can I do about it now? I don't know if Jacob will ever come back."

"There's nothing to be done about that," said Margaret brusquely. "If he's gone, he's gone and there's an end to it. You'd better hope he never does come back, because if he does it will only mean he's spent all the money and he's expecting you to support him. You just forget about him and his whole filthy tribe. Tomorrow, after you're rested, we'll go to the elders and they'll give a plot for you and the children."

"Are you sure they will, Margaret? What will I do if they don't? I'm sure you don't have enough to take us all in?"

"Of course they will. Aren't they your uncles? Don't you worry. Now that you have come home, you are a member of this family again."

Tabitha sighed and sank her head gratefully into Margaret's ample lap. Soon she was asleep. Margaret gently removed her sister's headscarf and laid her hand on the tightly braided hair as she gazed out across the tidy garden and over the distant green hills.

3

Carol was pouring a second cup of strong, black coffee when Thor arrived for breakfast. A heavy mist had settled during the night, leaving the courtyard gray and damp. "I must say I'm very happy to see you this morning," said Thor, slipping into the chair opposite her.

"Why is that?" asked Carol coolly, as she filled the rest of the cup with hot milk and stirred in two spoonfuls of sugar.

"That's not coffee," Thor observed. "It's a milkshake."

"This is how I like it," said Carol. "Sorry if it offends you." She studiously spread marmalade on a piece of toast, giving it her full attention.

"Costa and Elena and I were worried when you were so late returning last night," said Thor.

Carol shrugged. "It took longer than I thought to get to the caves and back. Besides, I got a very late start." She took a bite of the toast, still avoiding his eyes.

Thor picked up the coffeepot and poured out a cup for himself as Costa Sotiropoulos arrived with another plate of toast and fruit. The Greek glanced at Carol's face and gave Thor a commiserating look before withdrawing.

"I'm afraid I owe you an apology," Thor said to Carol. "I completely forgot that we were going to have lunch together."

"I figured that was what happened."

"I left a message at the desk to let you know I was at the Cock and Bull last evening. I was hoping you would join me."

"I didn't feel like going out—I was too tired. I just went to bed."

"I was afraid it was because you were upset with me."

"That too."

"And you still are. I'm sorry."

They sat together in silence for a while, nibbling toast and papaya and sipping coffee.

"You'll be surprised to hear who I saw yesterday," said Thor at last. "Jasper Reijksen."

"Why should I be surprised? Doesn't he live in Mwatumi?"

"Yes, but the surprise is who he was with. I'm sure from your description it must be that small Rumuran man who came to your hotel room in Kobani. They were at the Cock and Bull together with a third man, a young African. They were talking very intensely."

Carol continued to eat her breakfast, as Thor looked at her closely. "But this doesn't surprise you either," he observed. "You already knew?"

"I've told you, I'm not interested in hearing anything about that business," said Carol.

"I thought you should know at least that he's here," said Thor.

212

"All right, so I know. Now can we drop it?"

Even knowing that Carol was upset with him over the missed lunch, Thor was taken aback by her vehemence. "Tell me what's wrong, Carol," he urged. "Has something happened?"

"There's nothing wrong—I'm just not interested," said Carol. While walking back from Margaret's yesterday morning, she had decided to tell Thor about her confrontation with Jasper despite his warnings. Now she wasn't so sure. Why was he so persistent about it, anyway? "By the way, I'm going to a co-op meeting at the community center this morning. Margaret said you're welcome to come with me if you'd like."

"And what do you say?" asked Thor.

"It's okay with me."

"I was hoping for a more enthusiastic endorsement," said Thor.

"It's up to you," answered Carol.

Thor laid his hand lightly on hers. "I really am sorry about yesterday. It was very rude of me."

"Yes, it was," agreed Carol.

Thor thought he sensed signs of thawing. "There are two things I learned from my ex-wives," he said. "The first was how to admit when I'm wrong. The other was never to try to talk a woman out of a bad mood."

"Too bad you didn't learn that women hate being told we're in a bad mood, when in fact we're legitimately hurt and angry," said Carol, pulling her hand away. "It's very condescending."

"I'm sorry," groaned Thor. "You can see now why I keep getting divorced. I think I need a little help here." He pushed his napkin toward Carol and laid his pen on top of it. "Why don't you write down the right thing for me to say, and I'll say it and we can be friends again."

Carol hesitated, then picked up the pen with the trace of a smile.

When she had finished writing, Thor picked up the napkin. "I was a stupid jerk and it will never happen again," he recited. "Dinner tonight is on me." He laughed and crumpled up the napkin. "I'm not sure I can promise never to be a stupid jerk again, but I commit myself to the dinner with pleasure. Although not tonight, since we'll be at the Mali-Kuli research station."

"Oh, that's right." Carol suddenly looked concerned. "But have you forgotten you're not invited? Greg seemed pretty adamant about that."

"I meant to tell you," said Thor. "I happened to meet him last night and we've sorted everything out. He said I'm welcome to come."

"But he wouldn't say two words to you before. What did you say to him?"

"We just talked. I can be a very charming fellow, you know." He flashed her a lounge lizard smile.

"I know, and your modesty is your most endearing quality," said Carol. "But somehow, I didn't think Greg would fall for it."

"I think he has a great deal on his mind," said Thor thoughtfully.

"Such as?"

"I don't know exactly, but for some reason he's very suspicious of anyone who shows a great deal of interest in the forest or the pygmy chimpanzees. Fortunately, I was able to convince him that I'm nothing but a carefree dilettante."

"I'm sure you had him eating out of your hand," said Carol.

"Like a puppy," said Thor. "But I'm still determined to find out what it is that has him so worked up. I smell a story there somewhere."

At ten o'clock, Thor and Carol drove the short, bumpy distance from the hotel to the Mwatumi Community Center, a small, rectangular concrete building with a corrugated tin roof and a wooden door that sagged heavily on its hinges. The dense canopy of a tall mango tree laid a cool, dark carpet over the yard in front of the building, where thirty women were waiting, dressed in their best brightly colored kinangas and head scarves. They chatted amiably as they nursed their babies and cracked roasted squash seeds between their teeth. A flock of unusually clean toddlers squatted nearby playing with twigs and stones under the watchful eyes of their older sisters.

As the car pulled up the women rose to their feet and began to ululate, swaying back and forth with their arms raised exuberantly over their heads like celebrants at an evangelical revival. The children ran and crowded behind them, peeking out from behind their skirts. When Carol and Thor stepped out, the women began to clap and cheer and started to sing a greeting song.

As they stood a bit self-consciously by the car, Thor muttered to Carol that he didn't think he had ever felt so thoroughly welcomed in his life.

Carol and Thor joined in the applause when the singing stopped. The children emerged and stood in a row, staring openly at the visitors, then nudged one another eagerly as Thor lifted three cases of bright green, orange and brown bottles out of the car. He held up a bottle, smiling. The bolder ones smiled back but no one broke ranks.

Margaret stepped forward. "Karibu," she beamed, "you are welcome. God has brought you."

Carol introduced Thor and Margaret. Unlike most village women, Margaret was accustomed to dealing with western men through her work with the Methodists. She held Thor's hand in a strong clasp.

"You are welcome, Mr. Thor. Please excuse that we can not make more good reception for you. We know only yesterday you will come and no time to make ready. Carol is our sister and we do not prepare for her like a guest."

"Please, don't go to any trouble on my account," protested Thor. "You must think of me in the same way, not as a guest but as a brother."

Margaret chuckled. "Our brothers do not come to our meetings," she said. "If you are not a guest, you must also be our sister." She repeated this to the other women in Ruahya, evoking a wave of shy giggles and nodding. The giggles turned

215

to shrieks of laughter as Thor solemnly pulled a large, white handkerchief from his pocket and tied it over his head in imitation of their headscarves. He looked perfectly serious and perfectly ridiculous at the same time. The ice broken, the women clustered around, presenting a sea of hard-skinned hands for shaking.

Still wearing his handkerchief, Thor knelt and began passing the soft drinks out to the children. One of the older girls took charge of distribution, imperiously assigning two or three youngsters to share each bottle. In the classic mold of the self-appointed dictator, she granted herself exclusive rights to one bottle. When the first two cases had been handed out, Thor stood up to signal that the rest was for the adults. Those children still waiting their turns immediately scrambled and shoved to join the small clusters around each bottle. The high, clear voices began to rise as the levels of the precious liquid fell.

Inside, the community center consisted of a single, musty room with whitewashed concrete block walls and a floor of the same hard packed earth as the yard outside. Three small windows covered with strong wire mesh were set high up on each wall to provide ventilation and light.

Margaret led Carol and Thor past several rows of rough wooden benches to the front, where four chairs faced the room from behind a rickety table. She sat them down in two of the chairs as the other women slowly settled onto the benches. A large woman in a brightly patterned green and red kinanga and rubber sandals came up to the table. Margaret introduced her as the Cooperative's vice-president, who would lead the meeting today so that she could translate for them.

The buzz of conversation slowly died and the meeting came to order. It began with an elaborate welcome to the guests, filled with flowery expressions of appreciation for the long distances they had traveled and the interest they showed in the affairs of the Cooperative. Speaking slowly to give Margaret time to translate, the speaker thanked Carol for her help and reminded the group that it was Carol who had provided the loan that enabled them to the buy seeds, tools and fertilizer to establish their vegetable plot. She thanked Carol for taking time from her important work and busy schedule to visit their small village and learn about their problems so that she could continue to help them and guide them in the future. Carol felt Thor's amusement as she tried not to squirm with embarrassment under the stream of compliments.

Then it was her turn to enjoy his discomfiture when the vice-president turned her attention to Thor, introducing him as a famous journalist who had heard of their cooperative and had come all the way from Norway in Europe to learn more about it and to write about their achievements in the European newspapers. When she asked him to say a few words about his views on women's enterprises and development in Africa, a murmur of approval rose from the group, swelling into enthusiastic applause. Carol joined in. "Good luck," she whispered, smiling wickedly.

After a few modest protestations, Thor rose to his feet and cleared his throat. He thanked them for the honor of being allowed to attend their meeting. Carol expected him to finish with a few general words of encouragement but, much to her surprise, he launched into a fluent speech on the theme of women farmers as the backbone of development in Africa. He went on for about ten minutes, talking about other women's groups he had come across in his travels.

"You are the roots and the strength and the nourishment of this plant called Africa," Thor concluded. "But, while everyone knows that the roots are the most important part of the plant, usually they are invisible. We know that they must be there but we do not see them. It is the same with outsiders like myself, as we watch this plant called Africa struggling to grow. We know that the "grass roots" must be there, but until now we have not seen them clearly. Of course, one can never see clearly from a comfortable office in Washington or Oslo, and not even from a hotel room in Kobani. We must visit the muddy field and put our hands into the soil to learn how the plant grows. It is my privilege today to do that here with you in Mwatumi. And so, I can only say to all of you, *ashahe ma yechuklai*."

As he sat down, the room shook with the din of stamping feet and ululation.

"Not bad," Carol whispered. "When did you learn to say 'thanks for the hospitality' in Ruahya?"

"Yesterday, while I was supposed to be meeting you for lunch," he whispered back.

The chairwoman banged her empty Coke bottle on the table and called the meeting to order. Carol was struck by the blend of good humor and seriousness of purpose as the women got down to business. They were mothers and daughters, aunts and nieces, cousins, sisters and sisters-in-law, but at the same time they were business partners. Few in the group had finished more than a few years of primary school and many could not write much more than their own names, but when it came to handling money they had been educated in a hard school. Walking miles to the market every week with a headload of firewood or vegetables weighing a hundred pounds or more, these "market mamas" knew the value of money. They understood what it was to borrow and pay back with interest and how to invest now for a payoff later. Their chief aim in life was to provide food for their children, and education to give them a chance to get ahead.

Carol had already explained to Thor how the cooperative worked. The women each contributed one day of labor a week in the communal vegetable plot, and each got an equal share of the harvest to use or sell however she wanted. Each member then returned a part of her earnings to the cooperative's general fund. Part of the fund was used to pay off the WCA loan and the rest was distributed to the members as a dividend or used to make major purchases like fertilizer and a storage shed.

"Already last season we get more than eight thousand rimands," Margaret was explaining. "Now we talk what we do with this money." She was clearly torn between her responsibilities to the guests and her eagerness to join in the debate. Finally, when some of the women began to stand up and

218

shout across the room to one another, she abandoned her role as translator to join in the general melee. While unable to understand the details, Carol and Thor could see that the group was splitting into two sides, for and against some proposition.

Finally, the Vice President seemed to recall that she was supposed to be chairing the meeting. With a lot of shouting and bottle banging she managed to restore order and started calling on the women to speak in turn. They leaned forward on the benches and waved their hands vigorously in the air in their eagerness to be called upon.

Margaret also remembered her responsibilities and turned back to Carol and Thor. "Some of these women, they say they need this money now, for school fees and medicines," she explained, shaking her head with dismay. "But we must use for investment." She pronounced the word with relish.

"What do you have in mind?" asked Thor.

Margaret's face lit up with enthusiasm. "We must save money enough to buy a pick-up. Then we can take so many vegetables to market too quick. We can make good business."

"Do you really have enough to buy a pick-up truck?" Carol asked with surprise.

"Now we do not have. But we start now with little and each season we have more and little more. So at last when the road is ready our pick-up is also ready."

"Which road is that?" asked Thor.

"The road from the Americans. Everybody talk about this. It is a big road, with tarmac so we can use even in the rains. It can pass from Mwatumi through the forest into Rendesha, and then it will go even into Congo. Then we can sell so many vegetables for all the big mines in Congo. But it can be just the same like now with the big trees in the forest. The one who cut the logs, they work too much and the money they get is too little. But the big man who have the truck to take the logs away to the market, he is the one to get so much money. So we also can get a truck, or soon there will be coming a big man to take our vegetables away to Congo, and the money will be for him instead."

Before they could ask anything else, Margaret turned her attention back to the group, which was ready to take a vote. There was a show of hands, with one old woman carefully recording the numbers for and against in an old diary in which the Co-op recorded its minutes. Several of the women counted along with her, but everyone waited patiently for her to announce the official result before breaking into another excited discussion.

When the meeting finished, Margaret took Thor outside to photograph the eager children while Carol interviewed some of the members who spoke some English or Swahili. They all assured her that it was quite impossible that either Margaret or any of the other officers was stealing money from the cooperative. They explained that three members had to go together in person to withdraw any money from the bank account, and any member had the right to see the bankbook at any time. By their readiness with the answers, Carol suspected that Margaret had briefed them in advance on what she was going to ask, but they sounded confident and sincere and, if anything, politely indignant that anyone could suspect Margaret of such a thing. Some admitted they had heard the rumors that had reached Father Loretto, but claimed they were being spread by a few women who had been expelled from the cooperative for laziness and were jealous of its success.

Afterwards, Margaret led Carol and Thor out of town to see the cooperative's vegetable plots. She had vigorously denied that they had cleared land inside the forest reserve. As she had told Carol, not only was that illegal, but it was pointless—the monkeys and bushpigs would eat up everything if they tried plant in the forest.

"How did the vote come out?" Carol asked Margaret as they walked.

Looking pleased, Margaret told her the group had agreed the money should be saved. Those who needed money urgently could borrow from the general fund, but must pay it back by the beginning of the next planting season or risk losing membership privileges.

"How long do you think it will take to save enough to buy a pick-up truck?" asked Carol.

"It will take long, maybe three years," answered Margaret.

"I'm very impressed that your group is able to set such long-term goals and have the patience to achieve them," said Thor.

"This pick-up is not so sure yet," said Margaret. "Some of my sisters, they say we can't keep this money so long without spending. And they do not believe yet the Americans will build this road. They have too many sweet promises from the government before, and always there is nothing coming. They will believe this road only when they are walking on it already."

"Then how can you be so sure about it?" asked Carol.

Margaret dropped her voice, although there didn't seem to be anyone around to overhear. "It is my brother in Kobani," she confided. "He tell me, because now the priest is gone, they can build this road."

4

The call came in on Police Commissioner Gideon Bashega's private line. "It's about time you reported back in," he grumbled, leaning back in his desk chair. "I've had everyone from the Foreign Minister to the American Ambassador calling, and I've had nothing to tell them."

"Sorry, sir, there's been problems with the phone lines." Captain Kamanga's gravely voice came through over a background of static. "I was at the accident site all morning. We've had the devil of a time keeping people away from it."

"I know—Thadeus Maleke was in here an hour ago, complaining that you refused to give his men access," said Bashega. "I assured him I'd look into the matter immediately."

"But, sir, I thought—"

"Nonsense. Quite right to keep them out of it. What business is it of theirs? The crash wasn't inside the reserve was it?"

"No, sir."

"All right, then. You leave those bloody rangers out of it. I'll handle Maleke. Let's have your report."

"Yes, sir. There's nothing much left of the car, except that number plate you already know about."

"We're tracing the registration. Go on."

"Two victims confirmed," continued Kamanga. "The driver burned up inside—nothing left of him to identify, either. The passenger got thrown clear before it burned. It's a white woman, like the witness said. Maybe about twenty or thirty years old, but it's hard to tell anymore."

"She's dead, then?"

"Aieh, she's dead all right."

"Where's the body?"

"At the clinic in Mwatumi. I put a man on the door."

"Do we know who she was?"

Kamanga hesitated. "Not exactly, sir."

"What do you mean, not exactly?" demanded Bashega. "Did she have identification on her or didn't she?"

"There is something, but it's not exactly identification."

"Don't give me riddles, man. What did you find?"

"Anyone there with you, sir?"

Bashega sat forward slowly and rested his elbows on the desk. "I'm alone," he said cautiously.

"And this is a secure line?"

"Of course it's secure. Now what is it?"

"There's no passport or anything, but I found a card in her pocket."

"So who was she?" snapped Bashega.

"Not her card, sir. It's from Truman Yates."

"Yates!" exclaimed Bashega. "Bloody hell." He took off his glasses and laid them on the table beside him as he rubbed his eyes. "Who else knows about this?" he asked after a moment.

"Nobody, sir. I found the card myself and removed it immediately. It's with me now."

"Good. Let's keep it that way, at least until we find out who this mzungu was and what she was up to. There's a doctor in Mwatumi, isn't there, a British volunteer? Has he examined the body yet?"

"No, sir. I decided to wait and talk to you first. I reckoned she's not going anywhere."

"Good. I'll send someone out from Kobani this morning to write the death certificate. Meanwhile, no one sees her unless I say so. I'm not having a balls-up now."

"No, sir."

"You did a good job, Kamanga—I won't forget it," said Bashega. "Truman Yates," he mused. "That's a name I wasn't expecting to hear again. I was a bloody fool for letting Marshall talk me into letting him go."

"What's that, sir?"

"Heh?" Bashega hadn't realized he'd spoken aloud.

"Who's this Marshall, then, sir?"

"That jackass, Jonathan Marshall, at the American Embassy. He said Yates was a friend of the Ambassador's and he wanted to impress his boss by getting the man off. He swore he'd see to it Yates didn't give us any more trouble."

"Might be that's not the real reason this Marshall was keen to get Yates sprung," said Kamanga. "Looks to me like they're working together."

"Why, what do you know about it?" demanded Bashega.

"This card I found on the deceased, sir." said Kamanga. "It's got Jonathan Marshall's name written on the back."

CHAPTER 19

1

Greg pulled out of the Acropolis' parking lot and turned onto the main road, heading west. "Okay," he said over the roar of the old Suzuki's diesel engine. "Lisa wants me to take you on the scenic tour before we go up to the station. Here, I've sketched out a map so you can see where we're going."

He grabbed a piece of paper from the dashboard and held it out to Carol, who sat next to him in the front seat. Thor leaned forward from the back seat to look over her shoulder. The map showed Mali-Kuli Forest Reserve as a truncated triangle, about forty miles along the north-south axis, ten miles wide at the top and about twenty at the base.

"The terrain is really steep, lots of deep gorges and high ridges," said Greg. He reached out and put his finger on the map, keeping one eye on the road. "The highest point is the Mali-Kuli volcano, here, just west of the center." He traced their route, which would take them around the southeastern edge of the reserve. "It's a bad road, but there's an outlook point where you get a spectacular view out over the reserve and the volcano. After that we'll turn around and enter the reserve at the main gate, here, and get onto an even worse road. That'll take us over Kigeni ridge, where we pick up a really awful road. That should get us to the research station right about dinner time."

"Great!" said Carol. Thor added his agreement from the back.

They drove through the outskirts of Mwatumi, passing in front of small, clay-brick houses and shacks made of mud packed onto wattle-pole frames. Leaving the village behind, they entered into a narrow, winding green valley whose steep sides were lined from bottom to top with earthen bunds and long grass strips tracing the contours of the slope, like the parallel ripples of sand left on a beach by receding waves. In between the lines were rows of pole beans, feathery cassava and blue-green eucalyptus trees. Here and there, clusters of round, thatched-roofed huts perched precariously on the slope, nestled among dense banana groves.

"These hillsides are way too steep for planting," said Greg. "Sometimes people have to hold onto the tree stumps with one hand while they're hoeing with the other. Even with all those bunds, the soil erosion is terrible."

The road began to climb the face of a steep hill, snaking back and forth and doubling back on itself so they could look down over the dizzyingly steep edge and see where they had just been. The air coming in through the windows grew noticeably cooler, and the tidy farm plots began to give way to scrubby brush and scattered outcroppings of bare rock. The jeep bucked and bounced as Greg steered it over half-buried rocks and across deep erosion gullies. Every now and then it bottomed out with a thud that sounded even more painful than it felt. After one particularly solid landing, there was an involuntary yelp from the back seat.

"You okay back there?" Greg called.

"Don't worry about me," answered Thor. "By the way, is this the bad road, the worse road or the really awful road?"

"This is just the bad one," said Greg. "You ain't seen nothin', yet."

After an hour of twisting and climbing they reached the top, where they stopped and got out of the car at a flat patch of loose gravel beside a crumbling concrete foundation. Greg told them it was an old observation post set up by the Germans around the turn of the century. "The British took it over during World War I and used it as a communications station for awhile. Then the colonial government used it occasionally until independence, and it really hasn't been touched since. But the locals still call it the German fort."

He led them past the foundations to look out over a steep, heavily forested hillside which formed one side of a narrow, V-shaped valley over a thousand feet deep. The land rose sharply up again on the other side into a ridge that was slightly higher than the one they were standing on. Off to the left, a stream emerged from the thick mesh of trees and cascaded down a series of rocky outcrops, forming small, glittering waterfalls all the way to the valley floor. There the trees gave way to dense, yellow-green thickets of bamboo and tall grasses and the stream emptied into a bright green patch of papyrus-filled marshland.

Suddenly there was a sound of muted clapping and two huge green birds with long heads and flashes of red on their wings broke out of the forest below them and crossed to the other side of the valley, flapping their wings in perfect unison.

"Emerald hornbills," Greg told them. "'The local name for them is the 'wings of the forest.' They're kind of a national symbol because this is the only place in the world where they exist. There are probably only about a hundred pairs left. They used to get poached a lot for their feathers, but nowadays the main problem is there just isn't enough forest left to support a much larger population."

To the north and west the land rose in successively higher waves, giving way to tall, jagged peaks. Like a giant in a fairy tale, the gray-green cone of the volcano loomed over them, its summit hidden in a wreath of silvery clouds.

Greg squatted on his heels and nibbled on a blade of grass. "Pretty spectacular, isn't it?" he said. "This is the area we were talking about the other night. The road they want to build would go right along the top of that ridge."

Thor pointed to a spot where the blanket of green was interrupted by a few dark gashes. "Are those landslides?" he asked.

"No, they're burns," frowned Greg. "We've been having a lot of trouble lately with people coming in and clearing patches for planting. The whole western half of Rumura used to be one huge forest. The Mali-Kuli Reserve is all that's left, and they keep nibbling away at it. And the way the population keeps growing, the situation isn't going to improve anytime soon. The average family around here has at least six or seven kids, and everyone's got to get some land. But sacrificing the last tiny patch of indigenous forest isn't going to help. Like I said, it's really too steep to plant for more than a couple of years. Without the tree roots to hold it, the soil washes away by the ton every time it rains. Besides, without the forest to hold the water, all the springs and streams coming off these mountains would dry up."

"Maybe this is the area the Schooley Foundation is worried about," Carol realized suddenly. "But it's not Mwatumi Greengoods' fault. Their plots are nowhere near here."

"The burned area still seems small," said Thor.

"Yeah, so far," answered Greg. "Up to now, it's just been a couple of people sneaking in from time to time, and we've been able to chase them out before they did too much damage. But it's been getting a lot worse recently. And I think I know why." Greg told them about the rumor that was going around Mwatumi that this part of the forest had been degazetted—excised from the reserve—and opened up for settlement.

"I don't know where they get that idea," he said. "The reserve is too small as it is—the last thing we're going to do is let them carve off a big chunk like this. Just like there's no way we're letting them build that road through here to Rendesha."

"But people in Mwatumi need that road," said Carol. "We were just hearing about it from the women at the Greengoods co-op."

"What for?" scoffed Greg. "To sell their tomatoes in the DRC? That's just a load of bull the timber companies are spreading around to drum up political support. Congo is full of farmers—why would they want to buy vegetables from Mwatumi? And if the idea is to link Kobani with the DRC, the road could just as easily go south, around the reserve. The only thing a road through here is going to do is make it easier for those bastards to smuggle logs out."

Carol glanced at Thor and saw that he was as startled as she was by Greg's sudden passion.

"This is a critical part of the reserve," continued Greg. "It's used by several troops of chimpanzees and bonobos, especially in the dry season. And the Pygmies get a lot of their food and medicines from some tree species that only grow here, and some of their sacred caves are behind those waterfalls. But those crooks in Kobani don't care about any of that—everybody just wants a piece of the action." He lapsed into a brooding silence.

"It's so beautiful," said Carol after awhile, gazing across the tranquil scene. "It would be such a shame if it were destroyed."

They stood for a few more minutes, admiring the view and enjoying the sunshine and the breeze singing around their ears.

"Come on," said Greg at last. "We'd better get going."

Descending along the narrow, winding road was even scarier than going up, as the Suzuki seemed to hover on the brink of disaster at every sharp turn. Carol found herself pressing her feet against the floor and bracing her hands on the dashboard, willing the old jeep to slow down and to keep its grip on the road. She also fastened her seat belt.

"I wouldn't do that," Greg grinned at her. "If it looks like we're going over the edge, you want to be able to get out as fast as you can."

"What about me?" called Thor from the back seat.

"Oh, you'd be a goner for sure," said Greg cheerfully. "But don't worry, I had the brakes checked last year sometime. Or was it the year before?"

"Thanks a lot," said Carol, trying to laugh through the tightness in her chest and throat. By the time they reached the bottom her legs and shoulders were sore from the strain and she felt a bit sick.

At the bottom of the hill they rejoined the main road heading north and continued past the turn-off to Mwatumi. Soon they began to climb steadily again through a roller coaster of rises and dips, the jeep's engine whining in protest all the way up each steep grade and racing down the other side. As they came around a sharp bend, the forest suddenly appeared in front of them like a barricade. They turned and followed the edge for a few miles, with the dark wall of trees on the left and the sunny, cultivated fields on the right. Then Greg slowed down and turned off on a small dirt road that led into the reserve.

The entrance was marked by a green metal sign with the words 'Mali-Kuli National Forest Reserve' across the top in white paint. In the lower left corner was the silhouette of a hornbill, the symbol of the Rumura Forest Department, and in the lower right the logo of the Mali-Kuli research project. Behind the sign was a long metal bar that could be lowered across the road as a gate, but it was propped in the raised position, leaving the way clear. To the left of the gate was a small, wooden hut with a barred window and a corrugated tin roof. Greg slowed down to look inside as they passed the hut.

"Damn it," he said. "No one there. They're supposed to man this gate seven days a week, twenty-four hours a day. But the guards keep taking the weekend off. I guess I'll have to report it. Again."

Passing under the gate, they entered into the cool, dark shade of the forest. They drove between tall, straight tree trunks draped with strangler figs, and an undergrowth of scattered saplings interspersed with the feathery crowns of prehistoric-looking tree ferns. The sun barely penetrated to the ground through the thick filter of leaves, except in small clearings where a tree had fallen, creating a light gap. Carol half expected to see fairies flitting back and forth across these sunlit patches along with the butterflies and birds.

"Look at that!" exclaimed Thor suddenly, pointing at the road ahead.

Greg stopped the jeep but left the engine running.

"What is it?" asked Carol.

"Wait a minute, you'll see them," said Greg.

A moment later the huge gray bulk of an elephant emerged slowly out of the forest, onto the road about fifty feet in front of them. It was followed by two other smaller ones.

"Three of them!" said Carol.

"Four," said Thor. "Three females and a baby. You can just see its trunk peeking out sometimes from underneath this one that's closest to us."

"It's so tiny!"

"Only for an elephant," Thor pointed out. "If it were a dog you'd say it was enormous."

The elephants stopped in the road, facing the jeep.

"Uh oh," said Greg. "I'm not sure they're planning to get out of our way any time soon."

As he spoke, the largest one shook her head, flapping her ears menacingly.

"She looks mad," said Carol nervously.

"She's just a bit spooked because of the baby," said Greg. "If we sit here quietly she'll probably calm down."

The elephants stayed in the road for about ten minutes before ambling back off into the forest. Greg waited until they had disappeared before putting the jeep back in gear and moving cautiously forward. "We've got about twenty five left in the reserve," he said, as they picked up speed again. "Used to be a lot more, but most of them got poached out. They seem to be coming back a bit now, thanks to us and the ivory ban."

Suddenly a band of men slipped out of the forest and into the road in front of them. Carol counted six of them, dressed in shabby jungle fatigues, olive-green military-style berets and knee-high black rubber boots. Five carried long, thick-handled spears. The sixth, a tall, solid man who was clearly the leader of the group, had a rifle slung over his shoulder. A jagged scar cut across his shiny, black cheek and pulled up one side of his lip, revealing two large white teeth with a wide gap in between.

Carol felt a quick flash of fear, thinking that they might be guerrillas or renegade soldiers from Rwanda or Congo. But she relaxed when she recognized the Mali-Kuli logo on the T-shirts they wore under their open shirts.

Greg stopped the car and stepped out as the men came awkwardly to attention. The leader faced Greg with his eyes front and his chin held high. He brought his right hand stiffly to his forehead and raised his right knee almost up to his waist. He stood poised for an instant with elbow·and knee cocked, then snapped both the arm and the leg smartly downward so that he stood ramrod straight, one hand holding the rifle upright and the other pressed flat against his leg. Greg returned the salute matter-of-factly and stepped forward to shake hands with each of the men in turn.

He talked with them for several minutes as Carol and Thor watched from the car. From time to time the man with the rifle pointed off in one direction or another as Greg nodded or shook his head and scratched absently at his beard. Finally, Greg pulled his wallet out of his pocket and counted out a handful of bills, which the man folded carefully into the pocket of his shirt. After a final round of handshakes and another exchange of salutes, the men headed back off into the forest in loose formation behind their leader. Greg returned to the car.

"Friends of yours?" asked Thor.

"One of our ranger patrols," answered Greg as he started up the engine and eased the jeep back into motion. "We've got five of them deployed in the Reserve right now."

"They work for you?"

"Not directly," said Greg, speaking over his shoulder to Thor. "Officially, of course, they work for the Forest Department. But we top up their salaries and give them training and supplies and equipment. Otherwise they'd never be able to go out on patrol. The Forest Department can't even afford to give them uniforms. They were going around barefoot until we bought those boots."

Carol asked what the money was for.

"There's a trial coming up the day after tomorrow. A truck driver they caught last week with a load of monkeys. The magistrate's going to let him off scott-free unless the sergeant can get there to testify, so I gave him the bus fare."

"What was the truck driver doing with the monkeys?" asked Carol.

231

"Probably taking them to one of the timber camps," Greg answered. He explained that the timber companies usually didn't provide meat for their workers, leaving them to forage for themselves illegally in the forest. The trucks that carried the logs out of the forest were also notorious for taking poached game out for sale in the villages. "It's this day-to-day meat trade that's the big problem nowadays," he said. "We've done pretty well getting rid of most of the poaching for the international trade, like the elephants and leopards and apes."

Carol hoped he might say something about the bonobos, perhaps even revealing that he already knew about Jasper's scheme, relieving her of the responsibility of deciding whether to tell him. But he drove on in silence.

"It looked like a well-disciplined group," said Thor.

"Yeah, it's a good bunch now," agreed Greg. "Hand-picked. We had to make the Forest Department get rid of a lot of rangers when we first came in. They were used to getting bought off by the local poachers, and even poaching themselves, and some weren't willing to change their ways. We told Maleke they had to go if we were going to provide any support. He didn't like it much, but he finally went along with it, and I think he'd have to admit it's worked out pretty well. But even with these guys you've got to keep up the pressure, or they start slacking off. Like, just now—I asked who was supposed to be on the gate today. Turns out it's a cousin of the sergeant's, so I read him the riot act. Told him to make sure the guy's at his post next time I come through or I'll have him sacked."

Greg stopped the jeep again and pointed through the windshield, up toward the crowns of the trees on the left side of the road. Carol and Thor craned through the windows to look. At first they could only see the heavy swaying of some leafy branches, then they managed to make out a few black shapes against the green. Finally, one of the shapes leaped gracefully across twenty feet of open air to a tree on the other side of the road, its arms and legs stretched forward to catch hold of the branch, and the long tail arching behind like the tail of a kite.

One after another, five more followed in its wake and disappeared into the trees.

"Black mangabeys," said Greg. "We've got a good population of them."

Eventually they came to a fork, where Greg bore left onto a heavily overgrown trail barely wide enough to squeeze through. They could no longer see the sky at all through the canopy of the trees. The path grew steeper as they tore through branches that scraped the jeep on both sides with a sound like chalk being pulled the wrong way over a blackboard, and it sloped so that they tilted precariously to one side.

"The 'worse road,' I believe?" said Thor.

"Right. It's an old logging road." Greg raised his voice to be heard over the rasping whine of the straining engine. "There used to be a lot of them criss-crossing the reserve, but they're mostly overgrown like this now. The logging companies found it didn't pay to keep them up, since the valuable trees that are left are so widely scattered around the forest. Now the logs get sawed into boards right on the spot and carried out of the forest to the roads on peoples' heads. Trucks come by to pick them up and transport them to Kobani or across the border. It's a lot slower this way, but the companies seem to be determined to keep going until they've cut out every last hardwood tree in the forest."

After fifteen more bone-jarring minutes, they rounded the top of the ridge, only to find it was the shoulder of an even higher ridge. Greg stopped the car again, and Carol and Thor looked out the window at the sheer, rocky wall that stretched for more than a hundred feet above them.

"The truly awful road?" guessed Thor.

"We're not going to drive up that, are we?" asked Carol doubtfully.

Greg grinned and gunned the engine. "Would you rather get out and walk?" he asked.

"Sounds like a pretty good idea to me," said Carol.

"What do you say we give it a try, first," said Greg.

He eased the jeep forward around a sharp bend to the back side of the cliff. There they suddenly found themselves on a smoothly graded, broad dirt track, sprinkled with a layer of loose gravel and neatly edged with drainage culverts.

"Surprise!" said Greg. "We built this ourselves. Pretty nice driveway, huh?"

The jeep rolled easily up the final, steep grade and came to a stop in front of a long, one-story building made of crude reddish brown bricks and a corrugated tin roof. They climbed out of the car, stretching their sore legs and shoulders.

"I guess Lisa isn't back yet," said Greg, glancing around. "Her car's not here."

They were at one end of a small clearing on top of a narrow ridge. At the other end were four smaller brick buildings set in a semicircle. A footpath led away from them, through a dense hedge and past a small stand of trees. On a point at the far end of the path they could see a tidy, wooden A-frame house.

Carol and Thor picked up their bags and followed Thor to the long building. "These are our student and guest quarters," he said, opening the door and motioning them to go inside.

They entered a narrow, whitewashed room that stretched the length of the building. A row of large, screened windows on one side had handmade curtains with a pattern of green bamboo's on white. The near end of the room contained a large wooden table with eight mismatched wooden chairs. At the far end, a worn sofa and two armchairs were set around a coffee table. The wall in between was covered by a bookshelf half filled with dusty books and stacks of magazines and scientific journals. A few large, framed photographs of animals and forest scenes hung from nails pounded into the walls. Overhead, a row of compact fluorescent light bulbs were suspended from the ceiling, connected by a wire to a switch beside the front door.

"Very nice," said Carol, looking around. "You have electricity here?"

"Solar powered," said Greg proudly. "The panels are on the roof. We have a diesel generator for emergencies, but we hardly ever use it."

On the wall opposite the windows were five wooden doors, painted dark green. The two at the far end were open.

"We've got students using three of the rooms right now," said Greg. "You can have those two at the end."

"Is one of these Jasper Reijksen's?" asked Carol.

"Yeah, but I didn't see his car either. He must have decided to stay in Mwatumi tonight."

Greg suggested they drop their bags in the rooms and go up to the main house. The bedrooms were tiny, almost filled by a roughly finished wooden bunk bed, a small armoire and a desk and chair. The pleasantly musty smell reminded Carol of summer camp.

As they followed the footpath toward the A-frame house, Greg pointed out the other buildings—the staff quarters, a bath house, a shed for tools and equipment, a covered well with a pump and concrete water tank, and a radio shack with a tall antenna on the roof. A partially covered kitchen area was built on to the rear of the house, with an open fireplace, a small iron woodstove and a kerosene-powered refrigerator humming in one corner.

"And down that path is our outhouse," said Greg. "It's worth a trip by itself—the greatest view of any latrine in Africa. Probably in the world."

The main house was made of cypress planks stained and varnished to a deep gold, with a pair of large plate-glass windows on either side of the front door offering a breath-taking view out over the forest. Except for the shiny solar panels on the roof and the enormous, drooping leaves of a Monestera vine growing up one side, it looked like a chalet tucked away in the Swiss Alps.

Inside, the sloping walls were of the same glowing cypress, and the sunlight streaming in through the windows painted bright rectangles on the dark wood floor and the dhurri rugs. Most of the house was a single open space furnished as combined living room, dining room and study, with a ladder in the back leading to a loft under the peaked roof. The walls on either side of main room were lined with tall shelves containing a compact stereo system, stacks of books and a few African carvings and other knickknacks. The dining corner was occupied by a round table and chairs made of dark brown wood with a reddish heart. The top of the table was strewn with sheets of drawing paper covered with sketches of leaves and flowers, along with the wilting models. Beneath each of the picture windows on either side of the front door was a large desk made of a door resting on twin filing cabinets. On the wall beside one of the desks was a bulletin board covered with snapshots of chimpanzees in various poses, like a family portrait gallery. Carol walked over to take a closer look.

"Oh baby oh baby oh baby!" exclaimed Greg behind her, in a loud, rasping voice.

Carol spun around, startled. To her surprise, she saw that Greg was actually off to her right, unpacking some groceries into a small pantry that opened off the main room. Behind her, suspended from the ceiling above the other desk, was a cage occupied by an African Gray parrot.

"Thor, look at this!?" exclaimed Carol.

"That's Rasputin," said Greg. "He's Lisa's bird. He can't stand me. Tries to take a chunk out of me every time I get near the cage. Actually, he hates men in general. Loves women, though."

Rasputin edged over on his perch toward Carol, fluffed up his soft, silvery-gray neck feathers and cocked his head to peer at her with one bright, oddly human-looking eye.

"Oh baby oh baby oh baby," he repeated, sounding exactly like Greg with a sore throat. He leaned closer toward her and wrapped one leathery black foot around the bars of his cage, as though frustrated that it was coming between them. "Ooh, la la," he cried, in a sharply nasal French accent, and then switched into a breathy, Zsazsa Gabor voice. "Dahlink!" he shrieked excitedly, spreading his brilliant red tail feathers, "Dahlink!" He bobbed his head gravely up and down, as though he'd weighed all the factors and come to an important decision. "Let's boogie," he suggested lasciviously in a deep, grating voice, and then topped it all off with a loud wolf whistle.

"Sounds like you have an admirer," laughed Thor.

"Yeah, he's giving you all his pick-up lines in one go," said Greg.

"Just my luck," said Carol. "A real charmer, but he really is too short for me."

The door opened and Lisa came in. She greeted them warmly. "I was hoping you'd arrive in time to visit the bonobos today. China group is close by, just up on Kigeni ridge. There's no telling how far away they might be by tomorrow. Are you coming with us, Greg?"

"No, you go on ahead. I've got stuff to do here. Is Samuel around?"

"I left him with the group," said Lisa. "We've been with them since morning. I just came back to see if you'd arrived."

Lisa sent Carol and Thor back to the guesthouse to put on loose pants and long sleeved shirts. "If you didn't bring boots, we have some extras you can try on," she said. "We wouldn't want you stepping on any snakes in those sandals. Whatever would I tell Pat?"

CHAPTER 20

1

Jasper lowered his binoculars and looked impatiently at his watch. The hillside overlooking the Acropolis was covered with nettles, and teeming with ants and beetles determined to crawl up his legs and down the back of his neck. He swiped impatiently at the gnats buzzing around his ears and cursed the lazy workman who had already managed to waste over an hour replacing a simple light socket. He wondered where Sotiropoulos was—didn't he supervise his people at all?

Finally the workman climbed down from his ladder, gathered his tools together and ambled off into the hotel. Jasper forced himself to wait ten more minutes to make sure he wasn't going to return, then picked up his camera bag and backpack and started cautiously down the hill, staying within the cover of the trees as long as possible. When he reached the hotel, he went quickly to the veranda of room 23 and pulled out a pair of keys he had gotten from Sotiropoulos' son last night in exchange for a few grams of marijuana. The lock clicked open and he slipped inside, closing the door quickly behind him.

He went to the window and pulled the curtains closed before dumping the contents of the backpack out onto the bed. There was a heavy-duty cordless electric hammer-drill and a box of masonry drill bits, a set of compact earphones, a retractable tape measure, a small dustpan and brush and two light bulbs. Next he unzipped the camera bag and removed a compact video camera fitted with an adapter over the lens, a six foot long coiled black cable, a two-hour video cassette and a pocket tape recorder with a tiny remote microphone.

Using the second key to open the adjoining door into Carol's room, Jasper used the tape measure to gauge the thickness of the wall between the two rooms. It was a solid wall, nearly five inches of concrete. Going back to the bed, he fitted a long, half inch diameter masonry bit into the drill, securing it firmly with the drill key. He pulled the armchair over to the wall near the adjoining door and climbed up onto it with the drill in hand. Selecting a spot a few inches below the ceiling, he gripped the drill tightly, pressed the bit firmly against the wall and put his finger on the trigger. The drill whirred into life, carving out a shallow depression as a thin trail of cement dust began to stream down. He stiffened his arms and pressed harder, putting his weight behind the drill. He could feel its hammering action as it chewed slowly into the cement. Ten minutes later, he finally broke through the wall. He climbed down from the chair, massaging his aching shoulder and arm. He used the dustpan and brush to sweep up the cement dust and tossed it out the window.

Going back to the bed, he picked up the coiled black cable. One side ended in a convex glass lens and the other side in a screw fitting. Inside were thousands of the hair-thin glass filaments called optical fibers. He measured off five inches from the lens end. Stepping back onto the chair, he began to ease the cable, lens end first, into the hole in the wall, stopping at the five inch mark. He stepped back into Carol's room to examine his handiwork from that side. The lens was flush with the wall and visible only as a dull gray spot against the white paint near the ceiling. Neither Carol nor her visitors were likely to spot it— unless they were suspicious and actually looking for something. But that was a chance he had to take.

Returning to the other room, Jasper screwed the free end of the fiber optic cable into the adapter on the front of the video camera and put his eye up to the viewfinder. Through the special wide-angle lens he could see almost all of Carol's room, although it was too dark to make out much more than the outlines of the furniture. He laid the camera on the back of the armchair and switched it on. Then he put the small tape recorder on the desk and switched it on, too.

Back in Carol's room again, Jasper secured the tiny remote microphone under the night table with a piece of double-sided adhesive tape, and replaced the 40-watt lightbulbs in the lamps with the 75-watt bulbs he had brought along. Then he began pacing up and down and across the room, counting aloud in a conversational tone of voice.

When he played back the video and audio tapes, he was pleased with the results of his trial run. The microphone had picked up his voice from every point of Carol's room, and his features were plainly recognizable on the video whenever he faced the camera. Satisfied, he eased the cable out of the wall and packed up all the tools and equipment. It would have been easier to leave the cable in place instead of having to thread it back through the hole again later, but it was too risky; the maid might come in to clean, or the Sotiropoulos kid might get curious and sneak in to see what he was up to. He would just have to find a way to return tomorrow in time to set it all up again.

2

Pat and Jonathan were finishing a late lunch when the houseboy showed Thadeus Maleke onto the veranda. Looking at his somber face, Pat felt her stomach sink and her hand sought Jonathan's across the table.

Maleke politely declined to join them, and came directly to the point. "We have traced the registration of the vehicle. I'm sorry to say, it's not good news. It belonged to the car-hire agency at the Intercontinental hotel. It was hired out yesterday afternoon."

"Yesterday afternoon!" exclaimed Pat. "But then it couldn't have been Carol—she left Kobani on Thursday, didn't she?" She appealed to Jonathan.

"That's certainly what she told me she was going to do," confirmed Jonathan. "I spoke with her around lunch time, and she said she wanted to leave as soon as possible to get to Mwatumi before dark."

"That is curious," said Maleke, thoughtfully. "I wish very much for the sake of your friend that you are right, but perhaps there was a change of plan. You see..." as his voice trailed off, he pulled a small piece of paper from the breast pocket of his jacket and held it out to Jonathan.

"What's this?" asked Jonathan.

"It is the receipt from the car hire agency. It is your friend's name on the receipt."

"But, that doesn't make sense!" Pat protested shrilly. "I'm sure she would have called us Thursday night if she was still in Kobani. They must have mixed up her receipt with someone else's who left on Friday."

"I'm sorry, but that's not possible," said Maleke quietly. "The manager told me they have only hired out one car in the past three days."

"Hold on a minute," Jonathan broke in, examining the paper closely. "Look here, Pat—this name isn't Carol Simmons. It's made out to a Mrs. C. Simon."

Pat looked at him uncertainly, wanting to believe but not able to. "Are you saying there's another woman, with almost exactly the same name, who just happened to come to Rumura and drive out west this weekend?"

"It's not impossible," said Jonathan awkwardly. "The name 'Simon' isn't all that uncommon. And why would Carol have misspelled her own name on the form? Besides, if I know Carol, she would have used 'Ms.' instead of 'Mrs.'"

Pat took the receipt from him with a faint flickering of hope, which was soon snuffed out. "Jonathan, can't you see this isn't a woman's handwriting? The clerk must have filled it out himself, and he just misspelled the name. And you know people here always call grown women "Mrs.," whether they're married or not. She probably just didn't bother to correct him. I'm afraid it must be Carol." Her voice choked on Carol's name.

"I'm not jumping any conclusions," Jonathan insisted stubbornly. "I'll admit it would be a remarkable coincidence, but it could still be someone else."

Pat looked at him with a mixture of exasperation and tenderness, knowing he was pretending to be hopeful for her sake. She took a deep breath and turned back to Maleke. "Thank you for coming to tell us," she said. Jonathan got up and stood next to her, and she turned and buried her face against his chest and began to sob quietly. He put his arm around her, drawing her in to him.

"I am very sorry to be the bearer of this tragic news," said Maleke.

"Thank you, Thadeus," said Jonathan. "But I'm still going to wait for a positive identification."

"Of course," said Maleke. "I understand the body has been taken to Mwatumi. I plan to go out there myself in the morning. I'll send a radio message to you through my office as soon as I know anything more. Again, I am very sorry."

After Maleke had left, Jonathan stood for a moment, stroking Pat's shaking shoulders. "Listen to me, Pat," he said. "I'm serious. I don't think it's Carol." Something in his voice made her look up at him.

"I know you'll find this hard to believe," he continued. "But it seems there really is a Mrs. Simon here in Rumura."

"You mean you've actually met her?"

"Not exactly." Jonathan sighed. He pulled his chair around the table and sat down next to her. "I know I should have told you about this before..."

By the time he had finished telling her about the mysterious business cards, his attempt to meet Mr. Singh at the Ankara hotel and the apparent botched blackmail attempt at the Intercontinental, Pat was furious. "I can't believe this! How could you not tell me?"

"Pat, I'm sorry. But I thought Carol would have told you about the cards and the phone calls if she wanted to. And I guess I was a bit embarrassed about all this cloak-and-dagger stuff I've been trying to pull off. I thought I'd wait until I turned up something."

"You could've at least said something last night, after we heard about the accident. I've been going nuts worrying about Carol."

"But until Thadeus mentioned Mrs. Simon just now, there wasn't any reason to think the accident had anything to do with this other business," Jonathan pointed out.

"But then why didn't you say something right away, instead of all this stupid hinting around about how common the name Simon is?"

Jonathan hesitated. "To tell you the truth, I was watching Thadeus. I've been wondering whether he knows anything about this 'Mrs. Simon,' and the people who've been trying to contact her. I guess I thought he might give himself away somehow."

"Give himself away?" asked Pat. "What do you mean? I thought you liked him."

"I do like him. And I've always trusted him. As a matter of fact, until yesterday I'd been planning to talk to him and see if he could help sort this thing out, since I didn't seem to be getting very far."

"Until yesterday? When he came to tell us about the accident?"

"No, before that, when we saw that girl at the club. The more I looked at her the more I was sure I recognized her from somewhere. She has very distinctive hands—very long, narrow fingers, with bright red nails."

"I can't say I noticed her fingers," said Pat dryly.

"I'm sure it was the same woman as the one at the Intercon last night," said Jonathan, ignoring the jibe. "I haven't figured out how it all fits together, but I'm sure she's linked into this somehow."

"And since Melissa told you she's Maleke's girl friend, now you wonder if he's involved somehow too," said Pat.

"Exactly. I just wish I could figure out what the hell is going on.

"All I know is, I've got to find out if Carol's okay," said Pat. "And I'm not going to wait for Maleke to tell me—I want to drive out to Mwatumi myself first thing in the morning."

"I'll go to Mwatumi," said Jonathan. "You should stay here, in case there's any news." Pat started to argue, but then realized that Jonathan wanted to protect her from having to view the body, just in case. She nodded and gave him an understanding squeeze.

They stood up and started to go back inside the house, with Jonathan's arm resting lightly across Pat's shoulders.

In the doorway, Pat stopped suddenly. "So, what do you think, Jonathan? Does Thadeus know there really is a Mrs. C. Simon, who's not Carol Simmons?"

"He didn't give that impression, did he?" said Jonathan.

"No, he didn't. But you know something, sweetheart? Just in case he was also watching you—you certainly did."

3

With every ragged breath, Carol felt as though her lungs would burst. The blood pounded a deafening beat in her ears and there was a sharp, stabbing pain in her side like a knife twisting between her ribs. Her legs seemed to be encased in blocks of cement.

"You can make it, Carol—you're almost there!" called Thor encouragingly from somewhere above. She looked up but couldn't see him through the trees.

They had been hiking for nearly two hours, following a twisting, nearly vertical path strewn with roots and boulders and rotting logs that Carol was sure must be teeming with poisonous snakes and huge insects. She concentrated on taking the next step and then the next one, and tried not to think about how far away Thor's voice sounded. It was cool and misty and very quiet except for the distant echo of a pair of birds, calling back and forth to one another in a syncopated duet.

She stopped for another breather, steadying herself with one hand on the smooth trunk of a sapling. Her leg muscles were twitching so violently she could hardly stay on her feet.

"Where are you?" she called.

"We're at the top," Thor answered. "Just a few more steps."

With a burst of determination Carol forced herself upward again, toward the sound of his voice. She half-walked and half-crawled up the last steep, muddy stretch, grabbing onto branches to keep from sliding back down. The path disappeared in a tangle of vines dangling from a rocky overhang. She reached up blindly to grab the vines, and felt Thor's strong, warm hand close over hers. He pulled her up and over the ledge so suddenly that she collapsed in an undignified heap at his feet.

"Thanks a lot," she gasped, "but that's not exactly the grand entrance I was trying for."

Thor smiled and squatted on his heels beside her, holding out a bottle of water. Carol was gratified to see that his face was red, too, and he was still breathing hard.

"Quite a climb," he said.

"Whew," agreed Carol, taking a long swallow of water. "I wasn't sure I was going to make it. I was thinking of letting you two get out of sight and then turning around and waiting for you back at the car. I was going to say I'd twisted my ankle or something."

"But now that you're here, you're glad you kept going."

"I don't know yet. I'll tell you once I know if my legs will ever move again."

Thor stood up and reached his hand down to her. "Come on, let's try," he said.

Carol let him pull her to her feet and then went dramatically limp. He caught her with an arm around her waist and held her for a moment, giving her a squeeze and a smile before letting her go.

"Come along, you two, the view is over on this side," called Lisa from the other side of the small clearing.

Carol and Thor went to stand beside her. They found themselves looking down into a dizzying drop of more than three hundred yards, into a huge basin lined with an unbroken green carpet of the forest canopy. Looking across the reserve from the old fort yesterday, they had seen the forest from the outside. Now they were deep in its heart, surrounded by its sounds and damp shadows.

"Have you ever seen anything so beautiful?" asked Carol.

"What color is the forest?" responded Thor.

Lisa glanced at him with a curious smile.

"What is that, some kind of riddle?" asked Carol.

"In a way. I see you know it, Lisa."

"Sure, but I'm surprised you do," said Lisa. "Where did you hear it?"

"Someone said it to me the other day."

"I don't get it," said Carol.

"It's what people say around here, when you ask them a question there's no simple answer to," explained Lisa. "The idea is that if you look at the forest from far away, it looks like a blanket of solid green. When you get a little closer, you see there are actually lots of different shades of green. And if you get right inside it like we are now, you see it's also black and white and brown and yellow and red...Between the tree trunks and the flowers and the birds and frogs and insects, you can see every color in the world in the forest."

"And so, the closer you look at something, the more complicated it becomes," Thor concluded.

"And now you can see why the people here call this '*mali kuli,*' meaning 'the deep, dark place'," said Lisa. "In the places where the forest is thickest, the sunlight doesn't reach the ground at all. We have to use a torch to write our notes."

Lisa grasped the heavy pair of binoculars hanging around her neck and panned from left to right, slowly scanning the hillside on the other side of the valley. Then she trained the binoculars down onto the plunging slope below them.

"Come on, chaps, where are you?" she murmured, her voice just audible above the rustling of the trees and the buzzing of the cicadas.

"Yesterday they were on the far side of Kimafiri Ridge," said Lisa, pointing to the steep wall rising up about half a mile ahead of them. "I'm glad they came back so we don't have to go all the way over there to find them."

"You and me both," remarked Carol, with feeling. "What was it you were saying in the car, about this being the most *accessible* group?"

Lisa laughed sympathetically. "The hike does rather take it out of you at first, doesn't it? But it's worth it. Greg and I have been working with China group and a couple of the others, trying to get them habituated to people so we can eventually let small groups of tourists come in to see them, the way they're doing with gorillas in Rwanda and the DRC and Uganda. We started with China group because it's close to home and it's also a nice, big group with some cute youngsters. And Cheetah, the old leader, is rather easy-going. She doesn't seem to mind having people around. She even let Diana bring her new baby out yesterday, where Samuel and I could see it—ah hah!" she interrupted herself suddenly. "There they are."

Lisa pointed toward a huge fig tree about a hundred yards down the slope. She started to hand her binoculars to Thor, who was standing next to her, but he had already reached under his jacket and pulled out a very compact, expensive-looking pair of binoculars nestled in a self-contained carrying case.

"What are those?" asked Lisa. "May I see them?"

Thor handed them to her. "They're the new Leitz model."

"Wow!" she exclaimed, looking through the slender glasses. "These are brilliant. Really powerful, and the optics are incredible." After awhile she passed them somewhat reluctantly to Carol.

Through the binoculars the vegetation on the far side of the valley leaped into sharp, clear focus. Carol could see the individual leaves on the trees and felt like she could reach out and touch them with her hand.

"You must be a serious birdwatcher," said Lisa.

"Yes, a bit," Thor confessed, sounding embarrassed. Lisa and Carol both looked at him curiously.

Carol handed the small binoculars back to Thor and accepted Lisa's big ones. They both tried to pick out the tree Lisa was pointing out to them.

"The one with two big forks and a dead branch on the left side?" asked Thor.

"That's the one. You can see all the birds moving around up in the leaves. There are a couple of small monkeys, too. They're all feeding on the figs."

"I haven't even found the tree yet," complained Carol.

"Let me show you," said Thor. He stepped around behind her and rested his arm lightly on her shoulder to point over it. The fine blond hairs on his forearm tickled her cheek, and she could feel his breath warm on her neck. His hand rested on the small of her back to steady her. When she shifted backwards to get a better footing, she felt his fingers pressing gently in response.

"Do you see the monkeys?" asked Thor.

"Now I do. They look like the ones Greg showed us yesterday," said Carol.

"Black mangabeys," said Lisa. "You probably can't see them from here, but the bonobos are on the ground below, feeding on the figs that have dropped. Ready to go?"

"Sure," said Carol, with as much enthusiasm as her she could muster while flexing her sore muscles. It didn't take a genius to figure out that if they went down the slope a hundred yards, they would eventually have to climb back up that same hundred yards.

Lisa led the way down a narrow path so overgrown that they had to bend at the waist to duck beneath the branches criss-crossing overhead. Within minutes Carol felt completely lost, hemmed in by tree trunks and drooping vines, and unable to see more than a few feet in any direction.

After about five minutes, which felt more like twenty, they came upon a young African sitting on a stump about fifty feet from the fig tree. He had a pair of binoculars around his neck and a small spiral notebook in his hand. Lisa introduced him as her field assistant, Samuel Liumba.

"They are there," said Samuel in a low voice.

"Where?" breathed Carol. She felt the tension of excitement mixed with some apprehension. Her breathing suddenly seemed like the loudest sound in the forest.

"They went back into the trees when they heard you coming," said Samuel. "They are acting nervous today."

"Look at the fallen log just in front of the tree trunk," whispered Lisa. "There are two sitting in the underbrush at the end of it. It's dark, so you might have to wait until they move."

Carol strained her eyes, trying to make out black shapes in the shadows. Then one of the shadows got up and ambled on four long legs out onto the log. The bonobo sat down gracefully in a small patch of sun and looked straight out toward them, like an actor taking up his position in the spotlight. He nibbled delicately on a small, round fruit that he raised to his mouth with one hand, keeping his eyes fixed thoughtfully on the interlopers.

"That's Chauncey," said Lisa softly. "He's about six years old. He's quite a clown, and very curious. He's usually the first one to come out in the open when there are new people around."

"Does he know we're here?" asked Carol.

"Of course. He's watching us just as much as we're watching him."

Chauncey finished the fig that he was eating and stood up again, balancing effortlessly on the narrow log. He scratched his side lazily with one hand, examined his fingernails and then swung himself down onto the ground in a single fluid motion. He began to rummage in the loose litter, seemingly absorbed in his search for more fruit, but Carol had the distinct impression that he was still watching them out of the corner of his eye.

"Here come some more." Thor's voice was soft in Carol's ear.

More bonobos took shape at the edges of the shadows. Carol could feel their watchful eyes on her.

"They're always a bit shy at first with new people," said Lisa.

She eased herself downward into a sitting position and Thor and Carol followed her example, trying to make as little noise as possible. The ground was cool and damp and smelled pleasantly moldy, like wild mushrooms. Carol glanced down and saw a few enormous black ants on the ground near her feet. She quickly tucked the legs of her pants into the tops of her boots.

Slowly the bonobos came out into the open, stopping to pick figs up off the ground and glancing up casually from time to time as though to check whether the visitors were still there. Lisa murmured their names as they appeared: Cheetah, Chester, Cheech and Chong, Charley, Chobe...Three of them jumped up onto the fallen log and sat in a row eating their figs, like spectators on a · bench munching on popcorn and patiently waiting for the show to begin.

Lisa spoke in a low whisper, pointing out the differences between bonobos and regular chimpanzees: the longer arms and legs, the narrower shoulders, the smaller heads and the highly mobile, expressive faces. "Altogether, much more like human beings," she said.

"It's funny, but to me they kind of look Japanese," said Carol.

"Many people say that," said Lisa. "I think it's because of that long, shiny black hair on top of their heads, parted straight down the middle."

"Oh, look, doesn't that one have a baby?" said Carol.

"That's Diana, with Chuyu. He's the newborn I was telling you about," said Lisa. "Diana moved here from Delta group two years ago," explained Lisa. "Female bonobos leave their natal group and join another when they become sexually mature. It helps prevent inbreeding. Look, there's Chichi with her baby Chala. He's almost a year old now."

Chichi came ambling out along the log with big-headed, skinny-armed Chala straddling her back like a wizened jockey. Ignoring the others, she walked straight up to Chester, the biggest male, who was holding several figs in one hand. She stood in front of him, rocking slowly back and forth and gazing earnestly into his face. At first, Chester ignored her, popping another fig into his mouth, but as she continued to rock he finally got to his feet and took a step toward her. She turned around, presenting her rump, and he calmly mounted her, one hand resting on her back while the other still clutched his figs. He dislodged Chala, who tumbled off over his mother's shoulder with a sharp squeal of protest. Chester rubbed himself briefly against Chichi, then dismounted and put another fig into his mouth. When Chichi turned around and faced him, he made no objection as she reached out and plucked a fig out of his hand.

"Did you see that?" exclaimed Carol. "Did they just mate?"

"No, they didn't actually copulate," said Lisa. "Just a bit of genital rubbing. They do it all the time."

"It looked to me like she exchanged a quickie for a fig," observed Thor. "I guess it really is the world's oldest profession."

"This time she was doing it to beg for food, but bonobos often rub and copulate just as a way of greeting each other. It can be any combination—a male and a female, two males, two females, even a mother and child. It's more of a social activity than a sexual one. It reduces tension and helps them get along with one another. Bonobos are much more peaceful than other chimpanzees."

"Make love, not war," suggested Thor.

"The hippies of the monkey world," agreed Carol.

The gathering did have the air of an orgy, as the bonobos alternated between devouring the juicy figs and copulating with one another, seemingly at random. They usually coupled face to face, gazing into each others' eyes as the female reclined on her back and wrapped her legs around the male's torso as he lay on top of her. Sometimes they would touch each other's faces with unmistakable tenderness. It looked much more like lovemaking than mating, and Carol began to feel uncomfortably like a voyeur. She was also very conscious of Thor sitting beside her. From the way he kept clearing his throat, she guessed he was feeling the same way—as though they had accidentally wound up at a blue movie on their first date.

"Oh, look," said Carol. "That little one's coming towards us."

Chala had decided to abandon his playmates and investigate the strangers. He edged his way towards them tentatively, like a shy toddler, ready to turn and bolt at any moment. The other youngsters stopped playing and watched him with interest. A few times he seemed to lose his nerve and retreated a few steps, once so quickly that he stumbled and turned a somersault. But finally he was only a few yards away, directly in front of Carol.

Chichi suddenly seemed to notice what her wayward son was doing, and she gave a sharp, coughing yip. She ran forward a few steps, chattering and hooting, and then stopped, clearly expecting Chala to come running back. Instead he froze in place, crouching down slightly with his eyes fixed on Carol.

Chichi took a few more stiff-legged steps towards them, flanked by Chester and Chauncey, the two largest males. She rocked and pulled her lips backwards, displaying long, white teeth in a nervous grin as she hooted again. Chester bounced up and down a few times, his head lowered slightly so that he was looking at them from under his heavy brows.

"What should I do?" whispered Carol urgently.

"It's okay, just sit still," Lisa whispered back, "And don't stare into their eyes. That's a sign of aggression."

Carol tried to make her breathing as shallow as possible and fixed her eyes on the ground in front of her, not wanting to even seem to be looking into anyone's eyes.

Chala started to sidle towards Carol again, a few steps at a time, until finally he was only a few inches away from her feet.

There he stopped again and sat on his haunches. Carol could not resist glancing at the comical little face peering up at her. As the baby's wide black eyes met hers, he cocked his head to one side and raised his tiny, leathery black hand up to scratch his chin, as though mystified as to what kind of peculiar animal this could be. Carol held her breath and bit her lip, trying hard not to laugh.

Suddenly Chala picked up a stick from the ground and stood straight up on his skinny legs. He started to hoot and to jump up and down, thrashing the stick from side to side like a pint-sized King Kong. The laugh that Carol had been struggling so hard to hold in finally bubbled over and burst out. Chala leaped straight upwards and twisted around in midair. He hit the ground running, his hands and feet scrambling for a purchase on the ground as he scampered back to the safety of his mother's belly. She wrapped her arms around him protectively.

"I'm sorry," whispered Carol. "I couldn't help it—he was so funny."

"Don't worry," Lisa reassured her. "You just gave him a little scare, that's all."

Chichi checked Chala over briefly, and then began eating again, as though she'd already forgotten the whole incident. The others also calmed down and went back to eating and playing.

"It's just as well if you did scare him a bit," said Lisa. "I'm afraid Chala's becoming too bold. We'd rather the bonobos don't get comfortable with coming quite that close to people."

"Are you afraid someone will get bitten?" asked Carol.

"No, that's very unlikely. But the bonobos could pick up pneumonia or other diseases from people. And it could make them more vulnerable to poachers if they completely lose their fear of people."

"Also, some of your tourists might not like it if a bonobo came up and tried to engage in a bit of friendly genital rubbing in order to get acquainted," Thor pointed out.

Suddenly, the peaceful scene was shattered by a burst of shouting on the ridge above them, followed by the sound of something crashing through the trees. A dog yelped sharply and began barking furiously. The bonobos raced into the shelter of the trees, hooting and screaming.

"What's that?" exclaimed Carol.

"It sounds like Samuel," Lisa shouted back over her shoulder, already scrambling up the path toward the noise. Thor followed close behind her, leaving Carol to struggle after them.

By the time she reached them, the commotion had stopped. Thor and Lisa and Samuel were standing in a semi-circle looking at a very small, very old-looking man in tattered clothing, whom Samuel held in a tight grip. The old man looked confused as he peered up at them through rheumy, blood-shot eyes. A slim wooden-handled spear lay on the ground in front of him.

"Didn't I hear you say you wanted to see a pygmy, Carol?" said Lisa.

Lisa burst into the house and found Greg dozing in the armchair, the latest issue of the Journal of Primate Ecology open on his lap.

"Come with me," she said. "We've got something to show you."

He followed her quickly back up the path to the parking area in front of the guesthouse, where Carol, Thor and Samuel were standing next to Lisa's Suzuki. Samuel was holding the old Pygmy firmly by the arm. The old man's head hung limply on his thin neck as though he were half-asleep. He glanced up briefly at their approach, looked at them dully and let his head drop heavily again.

"What've you got there, Samuel?" asked Greg.

As Samuel let go of his arm, the old man sank slowly down to squat on his heels, still staring at the ground.

"Samuel caught him on Kigeni Ridge, spying on us while we were visiting China group," said Lisa. "There were at least five or six of them and a couple of dogs, but the others got away."

Greg stood over the old man, who swayed slightly as though he was having trouble keeping his balance.

"I think he is very drunk," said Samuel.

"He must be, if you were able to catch him," said Greg. "Nobody catches a Pygmy in the forest."

Lisa reached in through the window of the jeep and pulled out a rough wooden spear with a long, steel tip.

"He had this with him," she said, handing it to Greg.

Greg took the spear and looked it over for a moment, testing the edge with his finger. Then he plunged it, tip down, into the ground next to him.

"Does he understand Ruahya?" he asked Samuel.

"Maybe only a little. He is not from here. Maybe from Congo."

"Ask him where the others went," said Greg.

Samuel spoke a few sharp words in Ruahya. The old man shifted his heels slightly but said nothing.

Samuel repeated the question, then looked at Greg and shrugged.

"He can understand but he does not wish to answer."

Greg frowned and went down on one knee next to the old man and Samuel squatted on his heels on the other side. Even in this position they both loomed over the Pygmy.

"Tell him I know what they're up to," Greg said slowly. "I know they're after a baby bonobo."

Samuel repeated the message in Ruahya. The old man gave Greg a sullen look, then dropped his eyes again.

"Tell him he's in big trouble. I can put him in prison for a long time. Maybe for the rest of his life."

As Samuel translated Greg's words, the old man's slack lower jaw trembled slightly.

"Ask him if he wants me to let him go," said Greg.

The old man blinked and rubbed his cheek against his bony shoulder. He looked off to the side and spoke a few words in a soft, raspy voice.

"He say, yes, he want to go," said Samuel.

"Tell him I want to know who's paying him to get the bonobo," said Greg. "I'll let him go if he tells me."

255

The old man stayed silent for a moment, staring at the same spot on the ground beside him. Then he spoke again, so softly they could barely hear him.

"He say, a man from the village," reported Samuel.

"Which village?" asked Greg impatiently. "Which man?"

Samuel repeated the question in the same tone of voice. The old man's face stiffened. He muttered one word and hunched his shoulders up around his ears.

"He say he don't know."

Greg sighed and stood up. "Let's give him some time to sober up and think about it," he said. "Lock him up in the tool shed for now."

Samuel took hold of the old man's arm and pulled him roughly to his feet. He half led and half dragged him toward one of the small brick buildings as the four of them watched.

"That poor old man," said Carol.

"Don't worry," said Greg. "He'll be okay in there. I just want to scare him a little."

"He looks scared to death already."

"Not scared enough to talk, apparently."

"But maybe he really doesn't know," protested Carol.

"Look," said Greg, "he knew what he was getting himself into. Everybody knows the rules around here. Any traps or snares we find get confiscated. Any dog running loose in the reserve gets shot. And anyone we catch carrying a spear inside the reserve gets arrested. We've got to enforce those rules or there will be no control at all."

"But shouldn't you turn him over to the Warden, instead of locking him up in your tool shed?" asked Carol.

"Believe me, he's a lot better off here," said Greg. "If I turned him over to the Forest Department they'd beat him up."

"But how long are you going to keep him locked up?"

"Not long," said Greg. "Just overnight."

"Do you think by then he'll tell you what you want to know?" asked Thor.

"Probably not," said Greg. "But it'll keep him out of trouble for awhile. And it might make the rest of them think twice about going after a bonobo, at least as long as I've got the old man. He's probably the father or grandfather of that bunch Lisa and Samuel saw. I imagine they've been watching this whole show pretty carefully."

"You mean watching us right now?" asked Carol, looking around quickly as if she expected to see dozens of pairs of eyes peering down at them from every tree.

"Sure, they're out there somewhere, watching to see what happens. It's taken me a long time to prove to these people that I mean business. If I just let the old guy go, they'll lose all respect for me."

Lisa spoke up for the first time. "I know it seems harsh, Carol, but it's necessary. We try to be fair—we have a sort of unspoken agreement with the Pygmies. We don't interfere with their hunting as long as it's only for themselves, for subsistence. We even look the other way when they sometimes take game and sell it in the villages, so long as they stick to the common species like duikers and porcupines. But we have to draw the line at the primates and the other protected species. And we certainly can't let them get involved in commercial poaching. That's how they lost most of the elephants and leopards from this forest."

"Not to mention the gorillas," added Greg.

"I didn't know there were gorillas here," said Carol.

"We believe there must have been mountain gorillas in the Mali-Kuli at one time," said Lisa. "They're in almost identical forests just north of here, in the Virungas volcanoes range and in the Impenetrable Forest in Uganda. There are only about six hundred mountain gorillas left in the world, and they're all in those two areas. They could easily be wiped out by an epidemic, or in a war. Since this seems to be perfect habitat for them, we're thinking of trying to reintroduce them here as a protective measure. We've discussed the idea at some international conservation meetings, and there's a lot of interest in it. It could be a very important project."

"But nobody's going to give us any gorillas unless they know they'll be safe here," said Greg. "We haven't lost a single bonobo or chimpanzee to poachers or chimpsnatchers since we started working here four years ago. And we sure as hell aren't going to start now," he added, frowning grimly in the direction of the tool shed.

CHAPTER 21

1

Tabitha Akello sighed and shifted her legs, which were stretched straight out on the ground in front of her, in the proper way for a woman. She glanced at Margaret, who was sitting straight-backed and motionless beside her, hands folded in her lap and eyes fixed straight ahead. They had been sitting for over an hour outside the hut where Assistant Chief Elkannan Mojio, their mother's half brother and head of the clan, had called a meeting of the elders to discuss Tabitha's case. Margaret's husband, Wangeru Odege, was inside as well, even though he was not yet a member of the council. They could see the glow of the fire and hear the soft rise and fall of the men's voices through the window. Tabitha shivered again and pulled her thin cotton shawl tighter around her.

Just after seven o'clock the door of the hut opened and the five men emerged. Odege, as the most junior, placed Mojio's three-legged stool beside the door. Mojio sat down facing the women while the other four men settled on a reed mat beside him.

"Greetings, my daughter," said Mojio, looking at Margaret.

"Greetings, Uncle," replied Margaret. "May God grant you peace and give you many children and cattle."

Tabitha didn't say anything. Margaret had warned her not to speak unless she was asked.

"We have discussed your petition on behalf of this woman who was your sister," continued Mojio.

Margaret's heart sank. She knew Mojio's words meant he was rejecting Tabitha as a member of the family. But desperation lent her the courage to press the issue by pretending not to understand. "Thank you, Uncle," she replied carefully. "Your daughters are grateful that you concern yourself with our small problems."

"This woman has not behaved as a daughter of the clan," said Mojio. "She has brought shame and disgrace on us."

"She has suffered greatly, Uncle," said Margaret. "And her children have been left in hardship."

Children were the wealth and the future of a family, and Margaret hoped to focus Mojio's attention on them instead of their mother.

Mojio was not moved. "She brought this misfortune on herself, when she went away with a man who was not her husband."

"But they were married, Uncle," Margaret said quickly. "In a church in his village."

"There was no marriage!" roared Mojio. "Her father did not give permission, and the man paid no bride price."

According to tradition, the bride price compensated a girl's father for the loss of a valuable worker from his household. A man who took a woman away without paying for her was not a husband but a thief.

"But the children, Uncle—"

"The children must go back to their father," said Mojio sternly. "They belong to his family, not ours."

Margaret flushed and bit her tongue. It was true that in the Ruahya tradition children were the property of their father, but in the end it was still the mother who was left to support and care for them if the father left for greener pastures. But she knew that arguing with Mojio wouldn't help her sister's cause. And she still had some hope, because the elders had spent so long discussing the matter. It was possible Mojio was only setting out the situation clearly so Tabitha would be properly grateful when he finally agreed to help. She glanced out of the corner of her eye at her sister, silently willing her not to argue.

"By going with a man who paid no bride price, this woman forfeited any share in the clan's wealth or land," continued Mojio. "She cannot return now and claim any rights to it. However..." Margaret and Tabitha both held their breaths as he paused.

"However," Mojio continued, still speaking to Margaret, "your husband Wangeru Odege has generously offered to take her under his wing."

Margaret was stunned. She had pleaded with Odege to support Tabitha's case with the elders, but she hadn't expected this. Her first thought was that the old goat's intention was to take Tabitha not so much under his wing as into his bed. But she knew her husband well enough to feel sure that he wouldn't take on the responsibility of supporting another man's children just for the chance to sleep with one more pretty young woman. Besides, while it might be the custom in some tribes, marrying sisters wasn't an accepted practice among the Ruahya. Their saying was that a man who did that was asking for trouble because his wives would surely join forces against him.

She also knew better than to believe Odege was doing this to please her. So, whatever his reason, she was sure it must have some sort of benefit to him. Maybe the elders had pressured him to make the offer as a face-saving way out of a sticky family situation. Or maybe he believed that Tabitha's husband would eventually come to reclaim her, and might then pay the long-overdue bride price to him, since her father was dead. But whatever the reasons, at least it meant that Tabitha could stay and the elders would allocate her and her family some land.

But Mojio's next words seemed to crush that hope. "As Odege has agreed to take Tabitha in," he said, "he will also provide her with some of his land."

"But the land we have can hardly feed us," objected Margaret. "It can't feed five more mouths as well."

"Then you'll have to give her some of the land from your ladies' vegetable garden," said Odege smugly. He had always been furious about the cooperative garden, which took up so much of Margaret's time and earned nothing for him.

"But that land isn't mine to give," said Margaret. "It belongs to the Cooperative."

"Unless you want your sister to starve, you'll just have to persuade the others to give some of it up," said Odege.

Margaret appealed to Mojio, who had allocated the land to the Cooperative in the first place. "Uncle, you know the Cooperative is a good thing that will earn money and prestige for the whole village. It pays the school fees for your nieces and nephews."

Mojio placed his hands one on top of the other on the knobby head of his walking stick, spat on the ground and looked skyward. Everyone fell silent as he pondered the question.

"There is one other alternative," he said at last. "I will allocate a piece of land in the forest to Odege, and he will let Tabitha clear it and use it."

"But Uncle, that land belongs to the government," said Margaret. "Tabitha will be arrested if she clears it."

"Silence!" thundered Mojio. "Do you dare to question my decision? Do you think I don't know what I'm doing? The forest is Ruahya land, that our enemies in Kobani have tried to take from us. But we have fought them, and at last we have won. The government has given the land south of the Likari River back to us, and we can do what we want with it. So, Odege, you may claim five hectares of good land between the old English road and the river. Tabitha will clear it and build a hut there to live in. On half of the land she will grow what she needs to feed herself and her children, on the other half she will grow for you whatever you tell her to. Do you accept this arrangement?"

"I accept it," said Odege, looking pleased.

"Tabitha," said Mojio sternly, addressing her directly for the first time. "Do you understand that you are permitted to occupy and dig this land only by the good grace of Odege, and that you must obey him?"

"I understand," said Tabitha, meaning that she understood that she and the children would have a roof over their heads and food in their stomachs. Anything else, she would worry about later.

"And you know that you may plant trees or tea only for Odege's use and not for your own, and the hut you build may

262

only be of mud and thatch, not of wood or with an iron roof," continued Mojio.

"Yes, Uncle," said Tabitha. All of this was Ruahya tradition that she knew very well.

"Are we agreed?" Mojio asked the other three elders.

They murmured their assent immediately, and Margaret realized that this arrangement had been agreed beforehand. The whole procedure from the moment the men had emerged from the hut had been only for show.

Mojio dismissed the council and Margaret and Tabitha went back to Margaret's house. Tabitha hugged the anxious children and told them buoyantly that everything was going to be fine. They were going to have a brand new farm and a good, dry house. And next year, after she had sold the extra harvest, they would be able go to school again.

"And will you be married again, Mama?"

Tabitha laughed and ruffled her oldest son's hair. "Such questions you ask your Mama," she scolded him. "Maybe I will and maybe I won't. But don't you worry about an old woman like me. What you boys must do is find a good, rich husband for your sister."

"Yes, Mama," the little boy said solemnly. He made up his mind to start his search the very next day.

2

The small clearing just inside the Mali-Kuli Reserve was quiet except for the buzzing of a cicada high up in the treetops. Juma flicked another cigarette butt against the trunk of a giant fig tree. David watched it bounce off and lie smoldering among the dry leaves. When a thin wisp of smoke began to rise from the spot, he got up from the stump he was sitting on and crushed the butt out with his foot.

"Where the devil are they?" demanded Juma. "What time is it anyway?"

David looked up at the sky, judging. "Six, maybe."

"They should've been here hours ago," said Juma.

"Maybe something happened."

"Something happened all right. They got drunk and forgot about the whole thing."

"They'll get here," said David. "The *ba'shyamba* don't know anything about time."

"The bloody little bastards don't know anything about anything," said Juma. "And neither do you, if you're crazy enough to count on them."

"What else could I do?"

"That's your problem," said Juma. "That's the deal, remember? I line up the buyer, and you get the merchandise."

David didn't answer.

"So?" goaded Juma. "The buyer's waiting. The money's waiting. I'm waiting. Where's the merchandise, partner?"

"We just got to wait," said David sullenly.

"You're going to wait a long time," said Juma. "You saw them squatting there, sucking it down last night. That gin'll knock those monkeys flat on their skinny little asses. They'll be whooping it up for days."

"Joseph shouldn't have given them real booze," complained David miserably. "He should've just given them *waragi*."

"They'll be out of it for days," repeated Juma. "Well, I got news for you, *partner*. We don't have days. We've only got till tomorrow night."

Suddenly a Pygmy boy materialized silently out of the shadows, dressed in rags and carrying a short spear. It was Boku, the teen-aged grandson of the old man they were waiting for.

"See, Juma, I told you they'd come," said David triumphantly.

Juma looked the ragged boy over disdainfully. "Who the devil is this kid?" he demanded.

"Where's your grandfather?" David asked Boku.

264

"There," the boy said, gesturing off toward the forest. "In cage."

"Kid can't even talk Ruahya," said Juma scornfully.

"He's not from around here," explained David. "He came with his grandfather from Congo. But it's okay, he can understand me."

He turned back to Boku. "What do you mean, he's in a cage? What kind of cage?"

"Bricks cage, in forest." Boku grimaced and spit on the ground. "*Mzungu*."

"What's he talking about now?" demanded Juma.

"Sounds like the old man's got himself caught by those *mzungus* at the research camp," said David. "I told him to watch out for them."

"*Mzungu* bad," agreed Boku, looking worried. "He maybe kill Baba?"

"No, don't worry, he won't hurt him," said David.

Juma turned on the boy with vicious impatience. "Forget that—where's my ape?"

Boku took a frightened step backward and looked toward David.

"Where's the baby?" repeated David, anxiously. "Did you get it?"

Boku shook his head. "No baby," he said.

"I knew it!" exploded Juma. "Stupid, good for nothing little bastards."

"You go get it right now," said David firmly to the boy. "We need it tonight."

Boku planted his feet firmly on the ground and stared down at the tip of his spear. "No baby," he said again.

"What are you waiting for, more money?" demanded David. "I already gave your grandfather money yesterday. No more until we get the baby, understand?"

"You get Baba," said Boku.

"What?" exclaimed Juma.

265

Boku looked at from one to the other, then tried again to explain, struggling to find the Ruahya words.

"*Mzungu* have Baba. You come, get Baba out cage. We catch baby after." He smiled confidently.

"You hear that, David?" said Juma. "He thinks we're going to go right up there to the research camp and set his bloody Baba loose. What do you say to that?"

David bit his lip, thinking hard. "Sure, Boku" he said lightly. "We'll get him out of there. No problem. But first you get us the baby."

Boku frowned and shook his head stubbornly. "Get Baba now," he insisted.

Juma glowered at Boku and took a step toward him. "Where's the money we gave you?" he snarled.

The boy clutched his spear more tightly in his hands and stared at Juma wordlessly. "You spent it already, right? Drank it all away last night, didn't you? Now you owe us that ape, so get moving."

Boku narrowed his eyes. "Get Baba," he said once again.

Juma raised his hand to slap the boy across the face. "I'll give you Baba," he said.

Boku ducked, easily evading the slap. He raised his spear slightly, bringing David and Juma up short. Then he said something short and harsh in his own language melted away back into the forest.

The echoing silence he left behind him was broken by Juma's derisive laugh. "Well, well, well. You're up the creek now, aren't you?"

"What are we going to do?" asked David.

"Don't ask me," said Juma. "That's your job, remember?"

David just looked at him miserably.

Juma gave a pained sigh. "It's not like I even need you in on this job, right? I already did all the hard parts, anyway—thinking it out, contacting the buyer, setting up the whole deal. I was giving you a break—letting you prove you're ready for the big time. But I guess you don't have the balls for it. All right, go on back home and tell Mama it looks like she's got herself another girl to marry off. I'll get the bloody ape myself."

"No, come on, wait, Juma," said David desperately. "I can do it."

Juma shook his head. "I didn't go to all this trouble and put my neck on the line just to let the whole deal fall apart now because of you."

"I swear I'll take care of it," insisted David. "What you want to go tromping around in the forest for? You're a city man now."

Juma seemed to waver.

"We don't even have to go fifty-fifty on the money this time. You decide how to split it."

Juma grunted and stared off into space. "Okay," he said at last. "I'm giving you one more chance. You get it by first thing tomorrow morning, and I mean early. That's so I still have time to do it myself if you screw up again."

"I won't let you down, I promise," said David.

"Yeah, fine. Meet me up at the shed by the old church by nine tomorrow. And don't bother showing up if you don't have it."

When Juma had left, David stood alone in the clearing, surrounded by the rustling leaves and buzzing cicadas. His anger grew as he thought about how close he had come to blowing everything, not only this deal but his whole promising future partnership with Juma. All thanks to those bloody drunken *ba'shyamba*, and those bloody *mzungus*. He would get back at them later somehow. But meanwhile, he had a bigger problem. The realization settled on him like a heavy weight—somehow, he had to find and catch a baby bonobo by nine o'clock tomorrow morning. And he didn't have the slightest idea how he was going to do it.

3

Andre Delacroix stepped out of the elevator on the top floor of the Intercontinental Hotel. Two shapely young women came around the corner and hurried past him on stiletto heels, slipping inside just as the door started to close. The aggressive scent of their cheap cologne raked his nostrils as they passed. He glanced briefly after them and then followed the lingering trail of scent down the hallway. Brass placards on the doors on either side bore the names of African birds—the Ibis Suite, the Flamingo Suite, the Bateleur Suite. He went straight to the last door on the right, the Turaco Suite, and knocked four times in quick succession.

"Come."

Gideon Bashega sat on a plush sofa in the middle of the sitting room with his bare feet stretched out in front of him. A red silk robe was knotted loosely around his waist, revealing his smooth, naked chest and round belly. Delacroix was glad to see that he was at least wearing his trousers under the robe.

"Commissioner," said Delacroix respectfully, which was always something of a struggle under the circumstances. He wished Bashega would find some place other than this tawdry love nest, provided courtesy of the hotel management, for his private meetings. He smoothed the sleeve of his dinner jacket and pointedly avoided looking at the open door leading into the bedroom with its bedful of tangled sheets.

"Make yourself a drink," said Bashega, casually motioning with his own glass toward a trolley in the corner of the room.

"Thank you," said Delacroix. Finding nothing to his taste, he selected a bottle at random and poured out half a glass to be polite.

"Sit down," said Bashega, waving Delacroix toward an adjacent armchair. He sighed luxuriously and recrossed his ankles. "You should have come earlier. I had an extra one for you."

Delacroix stood where he was and smiled vaguely, managing an expression of polite amusement and cool disapproval at the same time. He was not a prude about sex—he was French, after all—but he did believe in decorum. A man could have two girls at a time, or a dozen as far as he was concerned, and swing from the rafters with them. But he should put on his shirt and tidy up before entertaining a business associate.

"You will excuse me, *Monsieur le Commissioneur*. I have a dinner engagement at the club this evening..."

Bashega looked at Delacroix out of the tops of his eyes, over the gold rims of his glasses. Delacroix stopped talking and sat down, taking a tiny sip from his glass. He regretted to find it was bourbon.

"Jonathan Marshall," said Bashega abruptly. "What do you know about him?"

Delacroix was disconcerted. "Marshall? He is with the American Embassy, *n'est-ce pas?*"

"What else?"

Delacroix shrugged. "I know him only slightly. Arrogant and a bit stupid, like the rest of them."

"I think you underestimate him," said Bashega.

"So?" said Delacroix cautiously.

"He is working with Yates."

"Now you truly puzzle me, *mon vieux,*" said Delacroix. "Did you not tell me yourself, Yates is gone?"

"He's gone from Rumura, yes. But not out of the picture, apparently."

"But how? And what is the connection with Jonathan Marshall?"

"I called you here to answer questions, not to ask them," said Bashega.

Delacroix' face grew red and he sat forward, setting his glass sharply down on the coffee table. "It is not possible, *mon ami,*" he declared. "You summon me and pepper me with questions, offering no explanations. If you wish to interrogate me, let us go

269

together to the prison where you can do it properly. But if at all we are to work together, we must be frank with one another."

"Calm down, Andre," Bashega admonished him mildly, with a faint schoolmaster's smile. "There is no question of an interrogation. And I have every intention of telling you what I know as well." He described the car crash and the discovery of Truman Yates' card, with Jonathan's name written on the back, in the victim's pocket.

"We know what Yates was doing in Mwatumi, poking around in our business, perhaps in league with this mysterious Mr. Singh we've heard about," Bashega continued. "So I removed him from the scene before he could cause any more trouble. It was Marshall who persuaded me to release him, after suitable warnings not to set foot in Rumura again. But instead of being grateful to God for his good fortune, only a few days later Yates sends this woman to Mwatumi—presumably to take up where he left off, if she had not suffered the misfortune of going over that cliff. But that's only the beginning."

Bashega proceeded to lay out the long string of people and events that seemed to him to be weaving itself into a net closing in on their operations in Mwatumi. According to the car hire agency, the crash victim was a "Mrs. Celeste Simon," whom they had already been expecting, thanks to his own network of informers. But then there was Carol Simmons, a friend of Marshall's, who was clearly associated with Jasper Reijksen and who also happened to arrive in Rumura and go to Mwatumi at this particular time. He noted that neither she nor Marshall was forthcoming about the real reason for her visit. Until now, Bashega had naturally assumed she was the woman his informers had been warned him about. "As we may assume it was not part of the plan for the one called Celeste Simon to be killed, this matter of the similar names is clearly a clumsy attempt to spread confusion," he said.

Then there was Thor Nilssen, who had dined with Carol Simmons at the Marshall's home and then accompanied her to Mwatumi the next day. According to his passport and visa forms he was a Norwegian journalist, but Bashega revealed that he was not registered with the Norwegian embassy and they claimed to know nothing about him. Naturally, Bashega had alerted Kamanga to keep an eye on Simmons and Nilssen. And sure enough, Kamanga reported, the day after he arrived in Mwatumi, Nilssen met with Juma Ayala, the small-time crook who was claiming to be working for this Mr. Singh they'd been trying to unveil. And meanwhile, the woman called Carol Simmons was visiting the mother of Ayala's sidekick, David Wangeru.

"Clearly it cannot be a coincidence that all of these *mzungus* are flocking to Mwatumi exactly at this time," concluded Bashega. "Yates and Marshall must know more than we believed. We must act quickly or the whole deal could go sour."

Delacroix had been growing increasingly impatient as Bashega talked. "I agree with you absolutely, *mon vieux*. But I fail to see why you bring all of this to me. I know nothing of any of these people, and I see no reason why I should concern myself with them. It is understood, *n'est-ce pas*, that my role is to arrange matters on the receiving end? The Rumura side of the operation is purely your affair."

Bashega stiffened and narrowed his eyes dangerously, but Delacroix seemed not to notice.

"In a business relationship, each partner is expected to do his part," continued Delacroix haughtily. "I think you will agree that I have done my part admirably, maintaining the channels open in South Africa and Europe. But how is it with yours? Already it was I who was forced to take action to rid us of that troublesome priest. And now again you seem to be at a loss to deal with a handful of amateurs in your own garden."

"I am perfectly capable of sorting them out," said Bashega angrily.

"Then, with respect, *Monsieur le Commissioneur*, I will leave you to do so. I have enough to occupy me. But one word of advice, *mon vieux*. I would keep a close eye on Dr. Maleke."

"What about him?"

"He shows signs of becoming difficult. I was forced to speak with him quite sternly yesterday about having my men arrested in the Mali-Kuli forest."

"I thought you had an arrangement," said Bashega.

"It is possible he is receiving pressure from the outside, or perhaps he is becoming greedy. I understand he has troubles at home and it may be that he will be needing money. And I do not need to remind you, Maleke and Marshall appear to be particularly friendly, so perhaps you should consider his place in this spider's web you have been describing. In any case, it would be just as well to ensure Maleke is not in a position to interfere over the next few days."

Bashega nodded briefly, the schoolmaster's eyes glinting inscrutably behind the round glasses.

Delacroix stood up and smoothed his sleeves again. "Speaking of interfering, *Monsieur le Commissioneur*," he said. "I am entertaining my countryman, Monsieur Monceau, from the *Caisse Central* tonight. I have heard he is a sociable man, who particularly enjoys the company of compliant ladies, and even more so those who are perhaps initially not so compliant. I believe I do not need to remind you that it is in everybody's interest that he not encounter any unpleasantness from the authorities during his visit?"

"This is the one you want to build your road, isn't it?" said Bashega. "Do you really believe that road will make logging in the Mali Kuli forest profitable again?"

"It is not what I believe that is important, *mon vieux,* but what my Board of Directors believes. It is not in my interest, or in yours, for the company to shut down the Rumura operation, as they have indicated they are considering doing. Fortunately, I have been able to persuade them this road is precisely what is needed to put us back into the black. And of course they are pleased that I am arranging for it to be built at no cost to the company. Once the *Caisse Central* and the other donors have approved the project, there will be the matter of the surveying, the design, the contracting, the construction...I estimate it will take three years at the least, perhaps longer."

"And in the meantime you carry on, not caring in the least whether you are making money or losing money on your logs?"

Delacroix cocked his head to one side and chuckled warmly. "I assure you, *mon vieux*, I will be making money in any case. It is a lesson I learned long ago: no one will never live to die a rich man, if he looks at the forest and sees only the trees."

CHAPTER 22

1

Thor tapped lightly on the door of Carol's room. She opened it, wrapped in a short *kanga* and carrying a towel and a toiletry bag.

"I see you've slipped into something more comfortable," he smiled.

Carol glanced down at her bare legs and hugged the towel to herself self-consciously. "I was just going up to the house to take a bath before dinner," she said.

"May I come in for a moment? I need to talk to you."

"Sounds serious," said Carol. She had meant it to sound light-hearted, but when he didn't answer she stepped aside to let him into the room. He leaned against the edge of the desk and waited while she cleared some clothes off the bed and sat down. The room was so small that they were only a few feet apart. She crossed her legs, pulling the kanga down over her knees, and looked at him expectantly.

"I've been wanting to say this for awhile," he said, "but somehow I couldn't find the right moment. I was planning to tell you last night, but then I didn't see you. And then this morning you were so annoyed with me that I didn't want to risk it."

"Risk what?" asked Carol, although she thought she knew. What she didn't know was how she felt about it. She had already admitted to herself that she was attracted to him, and that it was a nice feeling, but she wasn't a teenager or even a carefree twenty-year-old any more. She was a married woman of thirty-three. She felt her heart hammering and wondered whether he could hear it.

"I'm afraid I haven't been completely honest with you," said Thor. "About the reason I came to Mwatumi with you."

274

"So it wasn't because you wanted to write a gripping story about the Mwatumi Greengoods Cooperative?"

"No. And it also wasn't just to enjoy your company, although of course that's been a very nice bonus." He smiled at her again, in a way that left her even more confused. Was he getting ready to make a pass at her, or apologizing for not making one?

"Meeting you at the Marshall's was an unexpected bit of good luck. I was planning to come to Mwatumi anyway, but this way I was able to pretend I was just tagging along with you. It was a good cover."

"Now I really don't understand," said Carol. "Are you telling me you're some kind of spy?"

"No, I'm a writer, just as I told you, but I'm after a different sort of story. Let me start from the beginning. I came to Rumura about three weeks ago, following a lead for a story I've been working on, about how government and anti-government forces in Africa are both financing their wars through smuggling gold and diamonds. A few days after I arrived in Kobani, I met an American named Truman Yates at the bar in the Intercontinental. He dropped a few hints, bragging about breaking into a big smuggling operation based here in Mwatumi, one that involved some very high level people. I didn't really believe him at the time, but then a week ago I learned he had been arrested on a trumped-up drug charge and deported, and I decided it might be worth investigating after all. But I was worried that someone might have seen me talking with Yates and might become suspicious if I came out here for no reason."

"And then I came along and solved your problem."

"Yes, I'm afraid that's right. I didn't think it could do any harm. I convinced myself that I could poke around without attracting much attention, while playing the part of the dilettante boyfriend. But immediately after we arrived here, I realized I might be wrong. You remember Captain Kamanga?"

"How could I forget? He was horrible. And he thought I was this 'Mrs. Simon' and that I was here to meet Mr. Singh."

"He also told you not to ignore the warnings, like Yates did."

"That's right," remembered Carol. "And you pretended you'd never heard of Yates."

"When Kamanga assumed you did know Yates, I realized I might be inadvertently putting you in danger," continued Thor. "And then, when you hadn't come back by dinner time yesterday evening, I became worried. I was frankly very relieved to see you in one piece this morning. It forced me to realize that I couldn't continue like this—it simply wasn't fair to you. So, I decided to come clean with you, and also to let you know I'm stopping my investigations until after you've left Mwatumi."

When he had finished, there was a long silence. Carol stared at her lap as though mesmerized by the sight of her own fingers twisting the strap of her toiletry bag. After a while Thor went and sat on the bed beside her.

"I'm very sorry, Carol," he said. "I should have told you all of this right from the start. You have every right to be furious with me."

Carol looked up at him slowly. "You're not the only one around here who hasn't been completely honest. I've also heard of Truman Yates before."

Thor smiled and took her hand. "I know. You're a terrible liar. But it doesn't matter. This is supposed to be my confession."

And because he didn't press her to tell him anything, she found herself telling him everything.

2

A noisy crowd of scruffy young *mzungus* had taken over most of the tables at the Cock and Bull. David went to the back where Joseph was serving *waragi* to a small cluster of regulars who watched them resentfully.

276

"Overlanders," said Joseph contemptuously, indicating a battered, canvas-covered truck parked on the other side of the street. These low-budget travelers were notoriously bad tippers.

"Americans?" said David, listening.

Joseph shrugged. "Australians, I think. Just look at them. They probably haven't had a bath since they left Johannesburg. And you can't even tell the girls from the boys."

"Sure you can," said David. "Just look for the boobs bouncing around under their T-shirts."

Joseph and the others laughed loudly. One of the overlander girls looked over at them and smiled, oblivious to the insult. This made them laugh even louder and they called out a few rude comments in Ruahya. The girl's smile turned uncertain, and she looked away uncomfortably.

She was startled to find herself looking directly into the slack, grinning face of a very skinny, very black teenager who had sidled up beside her. He wore a stained, ragged T-shirt and filthy shorts, and had a dirty bag slung over one shoulder. His arms and hands were covered with scaly patches of psoriasis, crusted and scabbed from scratching. Everyone in Mwatumi called him Mjuju, "lizard" because of his skin. His eyes were heavy-lidded and seemed somehow vacant.

"Derek..." she said to the tall sunburned boy sitting next to her. "This bloke's staring at me."

"Huh?" said Derek, turning. "Christ, would you look at him. What d'you reckon he wants?"

"I don't know. He won't say anything, he just stares."

Derek swung around to confront the boy, taking another swig of his beer. He flicked his head to swing a curtain of dirty blond hair out of his eyes. "Get along, now, mate. You're botherin' the lady."

Mjuju said nothing but kept grinning at them in his slow-witted way.

"D'you hear me, mate?" Derek demanded. "I said, push off."

Mjuju slipped the bag from his shoulder and opened the top. He thrust his arm inside and fumbled around, and pulled out a tiny, squirming animal which he held out toward the girl.

"Oh!" she exclaimed. "Look out, now, you'll drop him." she took the little creature from him and cradled it in her hands. Mjuju grinned even wider.

"Give us a look, Cindy."

She held it out for the others to see. The animal was about four inches long and covered with a pale yellowish downy fluff. It had dark spots in rows down its back and head, and rings around its whip-like tail. Its small, pointed ears were pressed flat against its head and its pink mouth opened to reveal tiny, needle-like white teeth. It made soft mewing sounds as it squirmed and struggled against her fingers.

"I think it's a kitten," suggested someone.

"Naw, can't be a cat," said another. "Look how pointy its head is."

"Look at the spots. Maybe it's a baby leopard or something."

"Too small for a leopard."

"Well of course it's small, you dimwit—it's a baby, isn't it?"

"What d'you think it is, Trevor? You're the one's got all the animal books."

Trevor reached across the table and Cindy reluctantly handed the little animal over. He placed it on the table, where it sprawled on its belly, mewing and working its stubby legs as it tried to gain a purchase on the smooth wood.

"I think it's a genet," said Trevor.

"A what?"

"A genet. Like a cross between a cat and a weasel. Remember, we saw one at the camp that night in Malawi."

"The poor little thing's frightened," said Cindy. She picked it up and held it in both hands against her chest. Eventually it stopped struggling and quieted down, burying its head in her cupped hands. She could feel the tiny nose damp against her fingers. It took a fold of her skin into its mouth and began sucking.

"Isn't he sweet," she cooed.

"You buy," said Mjuju, nodding vigorously.

"Hey, he wants to sell it to you, Cindy," laughed Derek. "He's spotted you for a soft touch right quick."

"D'you think I should?"

"What are you, daft?" demanded Derek.

"I think he'd make a brilliant pet," Cindy said defiantly.

"They'd never let you take him back to Australia," said Trevor. "Anyway, he'll probably die. You can see he's too young to be away from his mother."

Cindy looked down at the tiny, warm bundle breathing softly in her hands. "The poor little dear. Where did he come from?" she asked Mjuju. "Where's his mother?"

"You buy," he repeated, still grinning. "How much?"

Cindy looked around at her friends uncertainly.

"Come on, Cindy," said Derek, a bit more kindly. "It's fair dinkum, what Trevor says—you can't keep him. Now give him back to the kid, will you?"

"Well, I think it's bloody awful," said Cindy. "Just leaving him to die."

"It's no good you worrying about it, is it? There's nothing you can do."

"Maybe there's a veterinary or somebody here in town I could take him to," said Cindy.

"We haven't got the time," said Derek impatiently. "You know we're off first thing in the morning. Besides it's probably illegal to buy it anyway. You want to get arrested?"

He reached over to take the baby genet out of Cindy's hands. She put up a token resistance, then reluctantly yielded it up. The little animal began mewing again.

"Here," said Derek, holding it out to the Mjuju.

"You no buy?" Mjuju's grin faded.

"Too right, mate. We no buy. Now take it and get the hell out of here. Go on, scram."

Joseph had been watching the interaction neutrally, not planning to interfere unless he had to. You could never tell. Sometimes people bought Mjuju's animals. Then again, once when he had tried to sell a baby monkey to an American couple, the man had made a big scene, saying he was confiscating the monkey and yelling for the police to come and arrest him. The poor kid had gotten so scared he hadn't come around again for weeks.

"Okay, that's enough," he told Mjuju. "They're not interested. Get going."

Mjuju scowled and took the genet kitten from Derek, thrusting it roughly into the bag. It squealed a weak protest.

"Hey, be careful," cried Cindy. "You're hurting him. Derek, tell him to be careful."

"Forget it, Cindy. It's nothing to do with you."

Mjuju slung the bag over his shoulder and slouched away to try his luck at the Acropolis Hotel. If he couldn't sell the baby genet to a tourist there, at least he knew the gardener would give him a few hundred rimands for the skin of the mother, which was also in the bottom of his bag.

As he rounded the corner onto the main street, Mjuju felt a hand on his arm.

"Hey, hold up," said David. "I want to talk to you." Mjuju stopped and looked at him uncertainly.

"Where'd you get that thing?" asked David, indicating the bag.

Mjuju's face darkened with suspicion and he jerked his arm away. "Never mind," said David quickly. "You want a cigarette?"

Mjuju nodded eagerly. David pulled two crumpled cigarettes from his shirt pocket and held them up tantalizingly. He led the way over to a narrow alley behind the post office. Mjuju followed close behind, his eyes on the cigarettes.

David leaned casually against the wall and put one cigarette into his mouth, handing the other to Mjuju. He lit them both and took a deep, satisfying drag on his. Mjuju started back toward the street.

"Wait a minute, where you going?" said David. "Come on back here, I want to ask you something."

Mjuju stopped and looked backward over his shoulder.

David beckoned to him. "Come on," he said, encouragingly. "It's okay."

Mjuju grinned nervously and stayed where he was.

"I'm not going to hurt you, you dimwit," David said impatiently. "I gave you that cigarette, didn't I? Look, you want to make some money or not?"

Mjuju edged closer, gripping the bag over his shoulder tightly.

"You've got more of those somewhere, right? More animals?"

The boy didn't answer. David couldn't tell whether he was being stupid or stubborn.

"Come on, I see you around with them all the time. Monkeys and birds and lizards and things. You catch them in the forest, right?

Mjuju nodded slowly.

David smiled to himself. Why hadn't he thought of this before? "What about apes? You know, *ba'shyamba kipu*," he said, using the local term for bonobos, which meant 'little children of the forest.' It was a reflection of the villagers' disdainful view of the Pygmies, whom they also called *ba'shyamba*, implying that there was no difference between the two.

Mjuju's eyes narrowed, thinking of the *mzungus* who lived in the forest. They didn't like him catching and selling animals. At first they had tried to make him stop, telling his father they would report him to the police, but his father had just beaten him for causing trouble and then forgotten about it. He tried to steer clear of them, but sometimes they caught him hunting in the forest. If he had a monkey, they always took it away and never paid a cent. And they always warned him never to touch the apes. They told him the apes were protected by powerful *mzungu* magic, and if he ever killed or caught one he would go to prison for the rest of his life. He knew about prison—a tiny, black room with no windows, where they locked you up and beat you, and no one ever saw you again. He had often dreamed about it, waking up in the middle of the night, thrashing and crying out with fear. Then he would run out of the hut and sleep the rest of the night outside in the open, ignoring his mother's shouts to come back inside.

Mjuju shook his head vigorously. "No good," he said.

"Sure it's good," urged David. "I'll pay you a lot of money for a baby *ba'shyamba kipu*." He leaned forward and lowered his voice conspiratorially. "Five hundred rimands—how about that?"

Mjuju just blinked and frowned. He had no idea what that meant—he could barely count to twenty. His mother had taught him a simple rule for bargaining with the tourists. First he asked how much they would pay, and rejected the first offer immediately. When they made a second offer, he pretended to think it over and rejected that too, and then he accepted the third offer, whatever it was.

"All right, a thousand rimands," said David impatiently.

Mjuju paused and then shook his head again.

"Aieh!" exclaimed David. "What do you want? All right, two thousand rimands, and I'll throw in a pack of cigarettes."

He was relieved to see the boy's slack face light up.

"That's right, a whole pack, all for yourself," David repeated.

Mjuju knotted his eyebrows fiercely as he struggled to think. He guessed it must be a lot of money, which would make his mother happy. And his mouth watered at the idea of a whole pack of cigarettes just for himself. But he was still gripped by his fear of the *mzungus* and his terror of their prison.

"I get you monkey," he suggested hopefully.

"I don't want a monkey," snapped David. "You get me a *ba'shyamba kipu*. A baby one."

Regretfully, Mjuju started to shake his head again. Then, slowly, an idea started to take shape in his mind. He squeezed his eyes shut and stood very still in the effort to think hard. Finally, he opened his eyes and gave David his widest, snaggletoothed grin.

David grinned back. "So, we got a deal?" he said.

3

It was well past midnight when Jonathan turned the television and VCR off. He glanced over at Pat, sound asleep on the sofa, and wondered whether to wake her up to go to bed. He had just decided to leave her to sleep when he heard a tentative knock on the front door.

"Good evening, sir, I am sorry, sir," said the night guard. "It is a young woman who want to see you. I tell her go and come back tomorrow, but she cannot go." He dropped his voice and flashed a conspiratorial grin. "She say I tell you she is woman from the hotel."

"Where is she?" asked Jonathan, frowning past him.

"I leave her at the gate, sir."

"Well, let's have a look at her."

Jonathan followed him down the dark driveway to the front gate. Muna Rabukoko stood in the harsh wash of the floodlight, dressed in tight jeans and a baggy sweater and a dark shawl pulled low over her head like a monk's hood. When she saw Jonathan coming she stepped up to the iron gate and pushed the shawl back so he could see her face.

"Are you here alone?" asked Jonathan.

"Yes. I have to talk with you—privately." Her voice was low and urgent.

"All right, let her in," said Jonathan.

The guard opened the gate cautiously, as though expecting to be rushed at any moment by the woman's knife-wielding accomplices. As soon as Muna was inside, Jonathan turned without a word and led the way back to the house. He let her precede him through the front door and closed the door to the den before motioning her into the dining room.

"Sit down," said Jonathan, pulling out a chair for himself. Muna sat across the table from him, looking nervous but determined. The shawl had slipped down to her shoulders, revealing shining, smooth hair pulled tightly back into a bun at the base of her neck. One strand had escaped and lay loose and wavy across her forehead.

"You remember me?" she asked.

"I'm not likely to forget, am I? It's not every day someone tries to blackmail me."

Muna frowned delicately as though Jonathan had spoken an obscenity that she was pretending not to notice.

"So, what's the news from Mr. Singh?" he asked.

"I did not come from Singh," replied Muna.

"That's too bad," said Jonathan. "I told you I'm not interested in talking with anyone but him."

"I have some important information for you. You will be very interested."

"I doubt it," said Jonathan. "But go ahead, I'm listening."

Muna shook her head. "I would be taking a very great risk to tell you."

"You came all the way out here at this time of night, just to tell me you've got some information that you're not going to give me?"

"I...I would like to tell you," stammered Muna. "But...you understand...the risk..."

"You're obviously no better at this than you are at blackmail," snapped Jonathan. "Let's cut to the chase. You've got this information, but you're not going to give it to me for nothing, right? Well, young lady, you've miscalculated badly again. Once and for all, tell Mr. Singh to either get in touch with me by tomorrow or forget the whole thing. That is, if you actually do work for him, which I'm beginning to doubt."

"My information concerns Mr. Singh, and also your friend, the American woman, Mrs. Simon," Muna said hastily.

"What about her?"

Muna hesitated. "I know who has been trying to contact her, and also why. And I know that she may be in very great danger." Her large dark eyes met Jonathan's searchingly.

Jonathan returned her gaze sternly. "If you have information that an American citizen is in danger, you'd damn well better tell me right now. Otherwise, you'll be an accomplice and fully responsible if anything should happen to her. You should be thinking about staying out of prison right now, not about money."

"But I am not asking for money," protested Muna.

"What do you want, then?"

Muna took a deep breath. "A scholarship," she blurted. "To America."

Jonathan whistled softly. "You've got to be kidding."

Muna gripped the edge of the table with her long, red-tipped fingers. "I want to continue my studies in business management," she explained earnestly. "And if I tell you this information, I must leave Rumura. It will not be safe for me. So I can tell you only if you promise that I can go to America, with my daughter."

Jonathan looked at her thoughtfully. "I have to admit, it's different," he said.

"So you will help me?"

"I suppose I could talk to some of my colleagues, find out what scholarship programs we've got, get you the application forms..."

"No, that is not enough," exclaimed Muna. "It is always the same ones who win those scholarships, the ones who have relatives and friends who are important people in the government. You must arrange this for me. You could use your influence—"

"I'm afraid it doesn't work that way," said Jonathan. "If you want a scholarship you'll have to compete for it along with

285

everyone else. All I can promise is that your application will be considered fairly."

Muna scowled. "So you will not help me, and so I cannot help you." She stood up from the table and gathered the shawl back over her head.

"I promise anything you tell me will be in complete confidence," said Jonathan. "No one would know it came from you."

"Singh would know immediately," said Muna scornfully. "Who else could it be?" She started for the door.

"Hold on a minute," said Jonathan, standing up to block her exit. "Now I've got something to tell you. You've got the wrong person. This friend of mine you're talking about isn't the Mrs. Simon that Singh is after. Her name is Carol Simmons, and whatever this is all about, I promise you it doesn't have anything to do with her."

Muna didn't answer but stood waiting for him to get out of her way.

"You don't believe me? Well, here's something else you might not know. The real Mrs. Simon is dead. She was killed out near Mwatumi last night."

Muna was clearly caught off guard. "Dead? Killed?" she exclaimed. "No, I don't believe you."

"Ask Thadeus Maleke," said Jonathan, watching her closely.

Muna looked at him aghast. She clutched her shawl reflexively around her throat. "Maleke..." she said weakly.

"He seems to know all about it," said Jonathan.

"No—" said Muna. She gave him one more distraught look and pushed past him into the hallway and out of the house.

Jonathan watched her run down the driveway and out the gate, then turned back into the house. Pat was standing in the doorway of the den.

"What was that about?" she asked.

"Just thought I'd stir the pot a bit," grinned Jonathan. "You never know what might come floating up from the bottom."

CHAPTER 23

1

Mjuju squatted in the doorway of David's sleeping hut, listening to his deep, rattling snores. David was curled up on a mat on the floor near the cold fire, tightly wrapped in a gray woolen blanket. Only the top of his head was showing, his hair dusted with dirt and flakes of gray ash. Overhead, the thatched roof rustled with insects.

Mjuju sneezed loudly at the stale woodsmoke, blew out his nostrils, one after the other onto the dirt floor of the hut and gave a soft whistle between his teeth. When David didn't stir, Mjuju edged over and squatted again next to him. He put out a cautious hand and touched David tentatively on the shoulder, then tapped him harder. Finally he took his shoulder in his hand and gave it a sharp shake. David groaned and drew himself up tighter in the blanket.

"Go away," said David hoarsely. "I'm sleeping."

Mjuju shook his shoulder again.

"I said, get out of here—leave me alone!"

Mjuju scraped a small handful of dirt from the floor and held his had above David's face, letting the dirt slip through his fingers.

"Bloody hell!" sputtered David, jerking his head up and rubbing his face. He opened his eyes and saw Mjuju.

"Oh, it's you," he said thickly. "I thought it was one of my sisters."

Mjuju grinned at him.

David sat up slowly, pulling the blanket tighter around him in the damp, cold air. "Those useless women never put enough wood on the fire," he complained. "Look at this, it's stone cold. Well, what do you want?"

Mjuju scooted a couple of steps backwards toward the door. "*Ba'shyamba kipu*," he said. "I bring."

287

David's eyes popped fully open. "What, you got it already?"

Mjuju nodded eagerly and straightened up as he reached the doorway, holding the door drape partly open.

"What are you doing bring it here? I told you where to meet me."

"I bring," repeated Mjuju insistently. "Come look." He slipped outside.

David groaned and pushed the blanket away. He struggled to his feet, groggy from sleep and the first bite of a wicked hangover. He stood for a moment to let his head stop reeling and followed Mjuju outside.

The first faint light of dawn cast a feeble, ghostly shadow of the large mango tree across the yard. Mjuju was waiting beneath the tree, next to a large, battered cardboard box tied closed with a criss-cross of dirty twine.

"All right, open it up. Let's see it," whispered David hoarsely.

Mjuju frowned and laid his hand protectively on the top of the box. "He go out," he said, also whispering. "Too fast."

"I've got to have a look at it," said David. "How do I know there's even anything inside?"

Mjuju gave the box a sharp kick with the side of his foot. There was a brief shuffling and thumping inside the box, and a muffled squeal.

"Shhhh!" hissed David. "Cut it out, you idiot. You want to wake everybody up?"

"He inside," said Mjuju.

"Well, I've still got to see it," said David. "That could be anything in there. Open up the box—I'll make sure it doesn't get out."

Mjuju reluctantly fumbled with the knot in the semi-darkness and carefully lifted the edge of one flap of the box by about an inch. A small, leathery black hand shot through the crack, groping toward the open air. Mjuju smacked the hand and it fell back as another, sharper shriek and more thumping came from inside the box.

"He go out," warned Mjuju again, slamming the flap firmly closed again.

"Move aside," said David. He lifted the flap again and put his eye close to the opening, trying to peer inside.

"I can't see a thing," complained David. "It's too dark in there."

He pulled a box of matches out of his pocket and lit one and held it up to the gap and peered inside again. This time he could make out a furry dark figure, about two feet long, huddled against the back wall of the box. The flame reflected back in two large black eyes and caught two rows of sharp white teeth.

"Yow!" David yelped as the match burned down to his fingers. He threw it onto the ground and then hurriedly slammed down the flap on the wiry black arm that shot out again, this time all the way up to the elbow. "Okay," he said, straightening up. "Tie it back up again."

Mjuju hurriedly pulled the twine back over the top of the box and tied it down tightly.

"Now take it away and bring it to the big mvule tree near the church road at seven o'clock, like I said," said David.

Mjuju shook his head vigorously and held out his hand, palm up. "I bring," he said. "You pay now."

"Forget it," said David. "Where am I supposed to hide it around here, so no one sees it?"

"You pay now," Mjuju repeated insistently.

"I'll pay when I'm good and ready," growled David. "Who asked you to come here in the middle of the night? You do what I said or the deal's off."

Mjuju glowered at him sullenly.

"Hurry up," said David. "It's getting light already." He turned and stalked back into the hut. Mjuju looked balefully after him, and then at the box. The thumping resumed again from inside, along with the sound of scratching and some faint whimpers. Finally Mjuju grasped the string at the top and started to half carry, half drag the box out of the compound.

2

Carol awoke slowly, to a pale, gray light filtering through the curtains. Just outside the window a bird was tuning up his song, a lilting, lyrical phrase repeated over and over again. She gradually became aware of the cold wall against her back, and the warmth of Thor's body pressed up against her in the narrow bed. She opened her eyes and found herself looking at the back of his neck, so close that the hair on his nape fluttered in her breath. He was breathing deeply and slowly. The intimate sound of the air passing back and forth through his nostrils filled her with tenderness.

Carol closed her eyes again and asked herself what she was doing there. She retraced their steps after they had said goodnight to Greg and Lisa and headed back toward their rooms, pausing to gaze silently at the enormous disk of the moon. It seemed to be hanging at eye level on the far side of the ravine, just out of reach, the contours of its craters and peaks etched against the silvery gold background.

They had drifted down the path, picking their way through the inky darkness under a breathtaking dome of stars. They talked quietly, walking side by side, close but not quite touching. The air felt charged with electricity, sending sparks crackling up the nerves of her arm when it accidentally brushed against his.

And then, on the doorway, they had come together in an embrace that seemed as natural as it was inevitable, flowing into one another's arms like partners in a ballet. Their kisses began softly and then grew fiercer as their bodies began to respond to one another. His tongue parted her lips and slipped between her teeth. She closed her teeth gently over it and felt his sharp intake of breath as his arms tightened around her. His fingertips traced circles across her shoulder blades and down her back as he began to press against her, hesitantly at first and then more and more insistently. She returned the pressure, the skin of her belly tightening against him.

He had pulled back, just for a moment, to look into her eyes. "Are you sure you want this?" he asked her softly.

She hadn't answered, afraid the sound of her own voice would cut through the fog in her head, forcing her to remember that she should be saying no. She guided his hand to her breast and let her galloping heart speak for her.

Lying beside him now in the chilly morning air, she remembered the initial urgency, the exploration, the laughing, the moaning, finally the slow drifting away into sleep together. Remembering made her want him again, but she couldn't bring herself to wake him up. She brushed her fingertips lightly across his shoulders and neck and down his spine. His back arched lazily but his steady breathing continued. She let her hand slide forward, along his side and onto the smooth skin of his belly and the line of soft hair below his navel. His arm shifted slightly and his hand closed over hers.

"You're awake," she murmured.

"I am now," he answered, his voice gruff with sleep.

"I'm sorry, did I wake you up?"

"Yes, lucky me," he said. He rolled over and slipped his arms around her, crushing her breasts against his chest. She slipped her leg over his.

"Hold that thought," he murmured, and stretched one hand out behind him toward the night table beside the bed. He groped around until he found the box of condoms and removed one from its wrapper, rolling it on with one quick, smooth motion.

"Seems like you've had a lot of practice doing that," remarked Carol.

"Sure," he said. "I practiced for hours when I was a boy. Just in case. No one wants to look like an amateur."

"Don't worry," said Carol. "You look very professional."

"Hmmm. I'm not sure I really like that, either."

"Okay then, what do you want me to say you are?"

"Let's see..." he said, "How about virile...masterful...wonderful...fantastic..." He punctuated each word with a kiss at the base of her neck, sending ripples of goosebumps radiating in all directions across her skin.

"You Vikings certainly have a way with words, don't you?"

"The gift of gab," he answered. "But we also know when to stop talking." He lowered his mouth over hers and pulled her gently on top of him.

A little while later, Carol was dozing with her head on Thor's shoulder when they heard a car pull up outside and someone came into the guesthouse, and started moving around noisily in the room next to them.

"Oh, no, that must be Jasper," whispered Carol. "I think I left the door to my room open. Now he'll know I'm in here with you."

"Why does it matter if he knows?"

"Because he accused me of having the hots for you. I'd hate to give him the satisfaction of knowing he was right."

"Was he making a pass at you?"

"Good God, no. He made it clear he dislikes me as much as I dislike him. He was trying to convince me you were a crook and warning me not to fall for your smooth lines and manly charm. Obviously I didn't listen to him."

"Perhaps you should have," said Thor.

"What's that supposed to mean?" demanded Carol.

"Maybe Reijksen is right and I am a crook. After all, how much do you really know about me?"

"Now you're teasing me," smiled Carol, snuggling her way under his arm. "Anyway, I could tell Jasper was ready to say anything to get me to help him with his scheme. He's a total liar."

"Carol, do you know the riddle about the native at the crossroads?" asked Thor, twisting his fingers thoughtfully around the hair at the base of her neck.

"Hmmm? Tell me."

"Let's say you find yourself on an island. You are walking around, admiring the scenery..." Thor's two fingers began strolling around randomly on Carol's belly to demonstrate.

292

"Then it is getting late and you realize you are lost. Suddenly, you arrive at a fork in the road." The fingers froze in place near her navel, and his hand seemed to be looking around in confusion.

"You have heard of this fork, and you know that one road will take you to a beautiful village, where it is safe and all your friends are waiting for you." The fingers trooped up toward Carol's head and came to rest for a moment in the hollow of her neck before going back to the imaginary fork at her navel.

"But if you take the wrong road, you will fall into a treacherous swamp filled with dangerous crocodiles that will eat you up." The fingers started down in the other direction.

"Hey, thanks a lot!" laughed Carol, batting at his hand.

"Unfortunately, you don't know which road is which. But there is a native standing there, and he knows the right way to go. Now, it happens that on this island there are only two tribes of natives. One tribe always tells the truth and the other always lies. Unfortunately, it is impossible to tell the difference between them. So, what question can you ask this native, to be sure you will end up in the village and not in the swamp?

"'What road do you tell people to take to go to the village?'" answered Carol promptly. "That way, if he's the kind that always tells the truth, he'll tell me the truth now. If he always lies, he'll have to lie to me about what he tells all the other people that he lies to, so the two negatives make a positive."

"You've heard it before," Thor accused her. "Why did you let me go through the whole story?"

"I liked the way you told it," smiled Carol.

"Thank you."

"But why?" asked Carol. "What's the point?"

"The point is that the solution to the conundrum only works because you know that the native is either a complete liar or completely truthful. In real life this isn't so, and the riddles are much harder to solve."

3

Pat poured out a cup of strong, black coffee and handed it to Jonathan. "I wish you'd take Charles, or one of the Embassy drivers," she said.

"We've been through this," said Jonathan impatiently. "It's better if I go on my own."

Pat sighed and gave up. "At least have some breakfast before you go. You've got time—it's not even light out yet."

"I'll stop for something in Bola if I'm hungry," said Jonathan. He drained the cup and slung his bag over his shoulder. "Would you please stop fussing? I'll be fine." He gave her a quick kiss on the cheek and stepped out into the early morning darkness.

The light spilling out from the kitchen door threw his shadow long and thin in front of him. The crisp, still air magnified the sound of his footsteps crunching across the gravel driveway. The cook's rooster challenged him truculently from the top of the garden wall.

"Same to you," said Jonathan, slamming the car door behind him. The engine roared into life and gravel flew out from under his tires as he pulled away, with a wave to Pat's silhouette in the doorway. He waited impatiently at the gate with the car idling while the sleepy guard fumbled with the lock.

Out on the road, Jonathan gunned the engine and sped down the middle of the empty road. He felt vaguely guilty, thinking he should be more worried about Carol. But by now he had convinced himself she couldn't have been the victim of the car crash. With that burden lifted, he was free to relish the intriguing mystery of Mrs. Simon and Mr. Singh. The sky ahead was lightening like a door swinging open in front of him. He was the hunter, setting off into the dawn in pursuit of an unknown and elusive prey.

By the time Jonathan reached Bola, the sun was well up in the sky. He stopped briefly at the run-down hotel for more coffee and a greasy omelet that he regretted as soon as he'd finished eating it. About five kilometers past the turn-off toward Mwatumi, the road was blocked by a rusty metal strip studded with wicked, upward-pointing spikes. Two policemen were leaning casually against a car they had pulled over, talking to the driver through the open window. It was a battered green Datsun with a smashed right fender, that Jonathan remembered seeing parked in front of the hotel in Bola as he'd gone in for breakfast.

Jonathan slowed down to maneuver around the roadblock, raising his hand in casual acknowledgment to the policemen. Cars with diplomatic plates weren't expected to stop at these roadblocks, whose main purpose seemed to be to extort money from traders and *matatu* drivers. To his surprise and annoyance, however, one of the policemen stepped forward and waved him down. Muttering a curse, he pulled over and stopped the car.

"Good morning, officer," said Jonathan with cold politeness. "Is there a problem?"

The policeman walked slowly up to the car. "You are coming from Kobani?" he asked, glancing into the back seat.

"That's right. I'm with the American Embassy. This is an Embassy car," said Jonathan pointedly.

"Aieh," the policeman grunted and looked over his shoulder as the green Datsun drove by. Jonathan followed his glance in the rearview mirror and saw the second policeman talking into a 2-way radio.

"Is there a problem?" asked Jonathan again.

"Routine check, sir," said the policeman. "Please turn off the engine." He walked around the car, pausing to peer the rear window into the luggage compartment.

Jonathan fought his impatience as the policeman walked slowly all the way around the car again, this time apparently studying the tires. He wondered whether the fellow was working up the nerve to demand a bribe.

The second policeman finished talking on his radio and came up to the car. The two of them approached Jonathan's window together.

295

'Here it comes,' Jonathan thought to himself. 'I suppose they'll claim I was speeding, or I had my turn signal on or something.'

"It is fine, sir. You may go," said the first policeman.

Jonathan concealed his surprise. He still wondered why he had been stopped in the first place, but he wasn't about to press the point.

"You will find a diversion ahead, sir," the policeman said as Jonathan turned the key. "The road is being repaired."

"Thanks, I'll look out for it," said Jonathan shortly as he pulled back out onto the road.

True to the policeman's word, about five kilometers later Jonathan came upon a line of rocks stretched across the road. A crudely lettered wooden sign propped against one rock read 'Diversion.' An arrow pointed toward the right, where a rough dirt track led off into the densely packed plots of banana and maize. Jonathan soon lost sight of the main road, but kept track of his direction by watching the position of the sun. After driving northward for more than a kilometer without seeing another sign or any chance to turn westward again, he began to think he must have missed it. He decided to give it one more kilometer and then turn around.

Rounding a sharp bend, Jonathan suddenly let out a shout and slammed on the brakes. The heavy Land Cruiser skidded and fishtailed and screeched to a stop just before smashing into the green Datsun, which was stopped sideways in the middle of the narrow road, blocking it completely. Jonathan was thrown forward sharply against his seatbelt and then back against the seat.

As soon as the Pajero stopped, two men suddenly emerged from a thick grove of banana trees and ran toward it. One was a tall, thickly built man with a heavy black stubble of beard covering the bottom half of his face and his broad throat. The other was small and bony, with a grayish tint to his clean-shaven hollow cheeks. In their worn, dusty clothes and broken-down shoes they looked like a pair of local farmers, except for the mirrored aviator-style sunglasses covering their eyes.

The bearded man reached the car first and thrust a beefy arm through the open window, holding a heavy revolver up to Jonathan's face.

"Jesus Christ," breathed Jonathan. His stomach churned as he looked down the dark barrel.

"Come out!" the man shouted, gesturing with the pistol. His teeth were large and yellow, and they all slanted to the right like old books jammed into a shelf that was too low for them to stand upright.

"Okay, don't get excited," said Jonathan, holding his hands up where they could be seen. He remembered the instructions of the Embassy security coordinator in case of a carjacking: stay calm, avoid eye contact, obey orders and announce what you're going to do before making any moves. "I'm getting out now. I'm going to unlock the door and open it."

The man stepped back to let Jonathan get out, keeping the gun trained on him. The other one stood a few yards away, leaning on a *panga* with a long, rusted steel blade. His right hand, wrapped around the wooden handle of the *panga*, was missing two fingers.

"Go ahead and take the car," said Jonathan, holding his hands up at shoulder level. "I won't give you any trouble."

"You lie down," ordered the bearded man, pointing to the ground in front of him.

"My wallet's in my back pocket," said Jonathan. "Just let me get it out."

"Down!" shouted the man, pointing to the ground again.

Jonathan swallowed hard and lay slowly face down on the ground with his head resting on his forearms. His heart was hammering painfully against his chest. He closed his eyes tightly, expecting at any moment to feel the bullet ripping through his spine between his shoulderblades.

Instead, the smaller man leaned down and grabbed his arms, pulling them behind his back and tying the wrists together with

297

scratchy twine. Jonathan felt his wallet being pulled out of his pocket. Then his head was yanked up by the hair and a cloth was tied tightly over his eyes. Another was stuffed into his mouth as a gag. The two men grabbed him by the shoulders and pulled him roughly to his feet.

They exchanged some words that Jonathan didn't understand, but he sensed that the bearded man was giving orders and the other was acknowledging them. He stumbled over his feet as they half led and half dragged him over to the Datsun and pushed him into the back seat. He hit his head sharply on the door handle on the far side. They bent his legs to force his feet inside and slammed the door. A moment later Jonathan heard his own car start up and drive away. Then the front door of the Datsun opened and closed. By the way the springs sagged, Jonathan assumed it was the heavy, bearded man who had gotten in. The engine sputtered to life and the car jerked forward.

They traveled for what seemed an eternity on a winding, bumpy road. Jonathan was bounced up and down and back and forth on the seat and hit his head on the door several more times before finally slipping down into the footwell. The smell of exhaust made him nauseous, but he couldn't vomit because of the gag in his mouth. He forced himself to breathe slowly through his nose and fight down the panic. He told himself it was a good sign that they hadn't killed him immediately. They probably just wanted to drop him somewhere far from the road so he couldn't report the theft for a long time. That was what had happened to the German Attaché who'd been car-jacked last year. He'd wound up walking a few miles barefoot and in his underwear to reach the nearest town, but he hadn't been hurt. Everyone said the organized gangs were only interested in grabbing cars, not in creating unnecessary trouble for themselves by killing people. And this was clearly a well-organized gang, with the fake policemen at the roadblock using their two-way radios to alert their accomplices.

The car finally stopped and the back door opened. Someone grabbed Jonathan's ankles and pulled him out to a point where he could put his feet on the ground and struggle into a standing position. A big hand grabbed him roughly by the neck and maneuvered him across a stretch of ankle-high grass and through a low doorway into a hut that smelled of woodsmoke and cowdung. He was pushed down into a chair with his numb arms pressing against the hard, wooden back.

Someone pulled the gag out of his mouth. He gratefully took a huge gulp of air and leaned forward and vomited onto the ground between his feet. After he'd stopped heaving he leaned back weakly. A moment later, he felt the edge of a tin cup against his lips and water started dribbling down his chin. He opened his mouth and drank some of the gritty water. He was almost glad he couldn't see what he was drinking.

"Where am I?" he asked in a hoarse whisper.

"You wait," growled the bearded man's voice.

Footsteps retreated across the dirt floor and a door slammed. Then there was nothing but darkness and the sound of his own breathing.

.

4

Kamundu Kamanga grunted as he eased himself out from behind the wheel of his jeep. He was wearing his full uniform, complete with shoulder braid and epaulets, although the effect was somewhat marred by the growing sweat stains at his armpits. He put his hat firmly on his head, tucked in the shirttail that always worked itself loose, slipped his swaggerstick smartly under his arm and started up the path toward the main house.

"To what do we owe the honor, Captain?" asked Greg, standing aside to let Kamanga enter. Kamanga recoiled instinctively as Rasputin flung himself furiously against the bars of his cage, shrieking and gnashing his powerful bill uselessly on the wire. He recovered himself with a scowl at the bird and moved a few steps away.

"Will you have some coffee, Captain?" asked Lisa. "We were just finishing breakfast." Thor and Carol murmured greetings from the table.

"No, thank you." said Kamanga. He set his shoulders stiffly and cleared his throat. "I must request you to come in to Mwatumi with me, Dr. Allen."

"What, now? It's Sunday. Whatever it is, can't it wait til tomorrow?"

"I regret the inconvenience, but it is urgent. If you will come with me now, please."

"Could you please tell us what this is about, Captain?" asked Lisa.

"I am not at liberty to say."

"Let me get this straight, Captain," said Greg. "Am I under arrest?"

"No." said Kamanga, clearing his throat again. "But I must insist that you accompany me."

Greg hesitated, glancing at Lisa, who returned his look blankly.

"How long is this going to take?" asked Greg. "I've got a lot to do today."

"Not long."

The words hung in the silence of the room as Greg considered.

"All right, I'll come," he said. "I've got to find out what this big mystery's all about. Mind if I take my own car?"

"I have said already, you are not under arrest."

"All right. Let me just finish my coffee." Greg sat back down at the table and drank the rest of his coffee unhurriedly, as Kamanga stood tapping his swagger stick impatiently against the side of his leg.

When he had finished, he kissed Lisa quickly on the cheek. "Don't worry, honey. I'll be back soon," he said.

After the two of them had gone, Lisa started collecting the breakfast dishes together, clattering them loudly as she stacked them.

"Here, let me help you with those, Lisa," said Carol. "Is everything okay?"

"Yes, of course. Kamanga's always doing things like this. He'd love to pin something on us, but he can't, so he just harasses us whenever he has a chance. Greg will probably get all the way down there and find out it's about paying his bar tab, or something like that. Or maybe it's about that Pygmy Greg locked up in the tool shed. Someone might have decided to report it—we know Kamanga has got spies on our staff. Anyway, we should let the old man out now. Greg was going to do it this morning."

When they arrived at the toolshed, it was empty and the door was sagging open.

"It looks like the lock was broken," said Thor, holding it out for Lisa's inspection.

"It seems his boys beat us to it," said Lisa. "Never mind, I'm sure he's learned his lesson. They hate being confined more than anything."

Lisa headed back to the house and Carol and Thor decided to go for a birdwalk.

"I wonder what all that was about," remarked Carol they headed out along a path into the forest. "Lisa was definitely more upset than she was letting on."

"Would you say she was angry, or frightened?" asked Thor.

"More frightened, I'd say."

"I think so too. My guess is she's either worried Kamanga is onto something they're trying to hide, or she's afraid he's trying to get Greg out of the way."

"Now I'm really worried," said Carol. "Maybe I should have told Greg about what Jasper was up to, after all. Jasper made it sound like some very big people could be involved in this poaching business. Maybe by not telling him, I've put Greg in danger."

"On the other hand, it could be that Greg is involved in it himself, as Jasper suggested. Maybe he and Kamanga are partners, and he was just putting on a good show for us."

"Do you really believe that?"

"It's not impossible," said Thor.

"But then why would Lisa be so upset?"

"Maybe she doesn't know what Greg is up to. Or maybe she does know and she's also only pretending for our sakes."

"Well, I don't believe it," Carol said firmly. "You saw how Lisa knows every single bonobo by name. And you've seen the pictures all over the walls in their house. The bonobos are like their family."

"You can never know, when it comes to money," said Thor. "But let's assume for now that Greg and Lisa really are completely innocent. Maybe the real villain here is Jasper. It could be that he really is trying to buy a baby bonobo, and he's trying to use you as some kind of cover."

"You really do have a devious, suspicious mind, don't you, Thor?" Carol smiled to show she was joking, but her voice was troubled.

"It is a devious, suspicious and complicated world we live in," said Thor. "It's a road with many turnings, and things are often not what they seem." He stopped and turned to face her in the cool shadows of the forest path. "And then there is me."

"What do you mean?"

"How can you be sure that I'm not somehow mixed up in all this? Maybe I'm even the big cheese behind the whole plot."

"The mysterious European buyer, right? Don't think it hasn't been suggested."

"I thought that might be what Jasper was trying to warn you about. And?" Thor sought her eyes with his and she met them.

"Well...I have to trust someone, don't I?" sighed Carol, with the trace of a smile.

"Yes, you have to trust someone." Thor drew her toward him. His kiss was gentle but firm, and left a lingering warmth on her lips.

"That's for letting it be me," he said.

CHAPTER 24

1

Following the winding path back up from the scenic outhouse, Carol turned a bend and nearly ran into Jasper Reijksen.

"You startled me!" she exclaimed. "Go ahead, it's free."

"I was looking for you," said Jasper. "So, you slept with him after all."

"I don't see that's any business of yours," said Carol.

"It's only amusing that you're so predictable," said Jasper. "And I suppose you've also told him and Allen everything I told, despite promising not to."

"I didn't promise anything of the kind, and you know it."

"Did you tell them?" Jasper's eyes locked onto hers like the beam of a searchlight.

"You're the one that made the promise," she reminded him. "You were supposed to get your people off my back."

"That nonsense," shrugged Jasper. "You don't have to worry. They won't bother you anymore."

"What did you tell them?"

"What does it matter? You're out of it, that's all."

"I want to know."

"Just what we agreed—that it was all a mistake and you are not the buyer."

"I don't believe you," snapped Carol. "You said it yourself—if you told them that, they'd know you were lying from the beginning."

Jasper scowled. "If you must know, I told them you backed out. You decided it was too risky to do business here just now. It's the perfect solution—it takes you out of the picture, while allowing me to keep my credibility."

Carol stared at him. "Perfect?" she exclaimed. "How stupid do you think they are? If I really were the buyer and I'd given

304

up on the deal, why would I stick around? Why not just turn around and go home?"

Jasper shrugged again. "Who knows?" he said.

"I'll tell you why. Because I haven't really given up on it at all. I've just decided to cut a better deal with someone else. Isn't that what they're going to think?."

"Maybe. It's not important."

"Greg Allen might think it's important," said Carol.

"So you did tell him?" scowled Jasper.

"No, but now I wish I had. For all I know he's in big trouble thanks to me. I'm afraid maybe your people think I've decided to make a deal with him instead of them."

"Why, what makes you say that?" asked Jasper.

"I suppose you don't know that Captain Kamanga came here this morning and took Greg away with him?"

"Is that right?" Jasper's reaction was impossible to read.

"Yes, that's right. And Lisa is very worried about it."

"Why should she be worried, if he hasn't done anything wrong?"

"Maybe because it means Kamanga knows they know what he's up to, and he's decided he has to get Greg out of the way."

"You're letting your imagination run away with you," said Jasper. He leaned back against a tree and folded his arms thoughtfully. "No, I think Greg and Kamanga have gone to meet with their other partners, to decide what to do about this very upsetting news that their buyer has backed out."

"That's ridiculous," said Carol. "Greg is not a poacher."

"Have you asked him about the chimpanzees in Cameroon?"

"No, because I don't believe a word of that, either."

"But it is a fact," insisted Jasper. "I told you, I know the man who was the head of the World Wildlife Fund in Yaounde when it happened, in 1983. Three young chimpanzees sent to America illegally, and nobody seems to know where they ended up. There is no question Greg was behind it. Ask him. He can't deny it, because he knows there is proof."

Before Carol could answer, they heard the grating roar of a laboring engine. It cut off with a sputtering cough and a car door slammed.

"Greg? Is that you?" called Lisa's.

Carol brushed by Jasper and continued quickly up the path. Jasper followed close behind. When they reached the house they found Greg already inside with Lisa and Thor. His face was grim.

Greg looked around at the curious faces, pausing when he came to Jasper's. "I guess I should tell you—he wanted me to identify a body."

"A dead body?" exclaimed Carol, realizing immediately how foolish she sounded.

Greg didn't seem to notice. He shifted his gaze from Jasper to Lisa. "A woman who'd been in a car crash," he continued. "She was really smashed up. It was pretty bad."

Lisa walked over and set next to him on the sofa and laid her hand his arm.

"Was it someone you knew?" asked Carol.

"It was hard to tell at first, but yeah. It's kind of weird, though..."

Suddenly, Rasputin began shrieking and hurling himself from one side of his cage to the other.

"Jesus, what's the matter with that damned bird?" said Greg. "Can't you get him to shut up, Lisa?"

"There must be someone outside," said Lisa.

Greg stomped over to the door and flung it open, revealing Samuel Liumba. "God, you'd think it was Jack the Ripper the way that bird's carrying on," snorted Greg. "What's up, Samuel?"

Samuel stepped inside, looking a bit sheepish. "I saw you returned, so I stopped to see if everything is okay," he said.

"Nothing to worry about," said Greg. "You know Kamanga. He just likes to hassle me every chance he gets. But thanks for your concern."

"I am glad for that," said Samuel.

"Aren't you going out to the field, Samuel?" said Lisa.

"I am going just now," he answered.

"Okay, keep an eye out for those Pygmies in case they come back," said Greg. He shut the door and returned to the sofa, shooting a dirty look at Rasputin as he went past the cage. "I'm telling you, Lisa, that bird is nuts."

"He's only looking out for us," said Lisa. "Never mind that, tell us about this woman. Who was she?"

"You remember Celeste Hartmann? That Dutch student who stayed with us for a few months last year, collecting data for her Masters degree?"

"Celeste!"

"I was as surprised as you are, but it was her, all right."

"But Greg, she left more than a year ago. Why would she come back, without telling us?" asked Lisa.

"Beats me." He turned to Jasper. "Maybe you know Celeste, Jasper? She was from Breuningen University too—one of Professor Heidelmann's students, just like you."

"Yes, I know her." Jasper's voice was tight and his face was even paler than usual.

"Any idea what she could have been doing here?"

Carol shifted slightly and Jasper glanced toward her. She caught and held his eyes, raising her eyebrows slightly and compressing her lips. There was no mistaking her expression—'You tell them, or I will.'

Jasper looked away. "She might have been coming to see me," he said.

"To see you?" exclaimed Lisa, with genuine concern. "Oh, no, Jasper, I'm sorry—was she your girlfriend?"

"No, just someone I knew," answered Jasper stiffly.

"It's a long way to come just to see someone you know," observed Greg. "And how come you didn't tell us she was coming?"

"Why should I tell you?"

"We are in charge of this research station, after all. Don't you think it's common courtesy to let us know if someone's coming?"

"She wasn't going to stay here," said Jasper.

"Even so," said Greg. "We have to keep track of these things. The government seems to feel we're responsible for every *mzungu* who shows up here."

"I saw no reason to tell you," repeated Jasper. "And in any case, I didn't think she was coming. We talked about, but then she sent me word she had decided against it."

"But she came after all," said Lisa. "Why do you suppose she changed her mind?"

"I really have no idea," said Jasper. "And now it appears we will never know."

Something about his matter-of-fact tone was finally more than Carol could take.

"That's not quite the whole story, is it Jasper?" she said.

Greg and Lisa turned to her in surprise.

"What are you talking about, Carol?" asked Greg.

"I'll let Jasper tell you about it," said Carol.

Jasper glowered at her as all eyes turned to him.

"There is nothing to tell," said Jasper. "She wanted to come and help me in my work, but then she decided she was too busy. I don't know why she came after all. I'm very sorry she was in this accident but it has nothing to do with me."

"And just what work was she going to help you out with, Jasper?" asked Greg. His voice was dangerously quiet.

Jasper took a matchstick from his pocket and slipped it into the other corner of his mouth. "Nothing in particular," he said casually. "It doesn't matter anymore."

"That's okay, Reijksen. You don't have to tell me. I already know."

Jasper's eyes remained fixed on Greg's and his expression didn't change.

"He thinks I'm bluffing," announced Greg. "Okay, how about this for a bluff, shithead? Celeste was coming to help you snatch a baby bonobo."

"Greg!" Lisa was aghast. "You can't be serious!"

"Oh, I'm serious all right," said Greg. He got to his feet and stood in front of Jasper's chair. "All the time he's been here, pretending to be doing research, what Jasper's really been doing is setting up a poaching deal with a couple of young punks in Mwatumi. Shit, man, did you really think you could just sail in here and pull something over on me? I've been here more than five years now—I've got informers all over the place. We got word from our contacts in Europe that someone was coming after a bonobo. I've had a line on you from the day you got here."

"Greg, why didn't you tell me about this?" demanded Lisa angrily. "We should have turned him in."

"It was better if you didn't know, honey," said Greg. "You might have accidentally letting it slip that we were on to him. I wanted to give him time to really nail his own ass to the wall, not to mention leading me to whoever it is he's working with in Kobani."

"But what if he'd succeeded in getting a bonobo? It was too risky."

"Come on, Lisa, give me some credit, will you?" said Greg impatiently. "I had it all under control."

"That is where you are wrong," sneered Jasper. "You have nothing under control. In fact, you have it all wrong."

"Is that right?" Greg stood up and crossed his arms, glowering.

Jasper walked over to stand eye to eye with him. "I am not here to steal a bonobo, you fool. I have been doing my best to stop one from being stolen, right under your nose."

"You're going to have to do better than that," said Greg.

"It is the truth," said Jasper. "Carol will tell you."

Once again, they all turned to her in surprise.

"What in the world is he talking about, Carol?" asked Lisa.

"Jasper did tell me he was trying to stop some kind of plot to steal a baby bonobo," admitted Carol. "He said some men in Mwatumi had told him they were being paid to get one. He pretended to be representing someone else who wanted to buy a bonobo, so he could expose the poachers."

"And you believed him?" demanded Greg.

"I honestly didn't know what to believe," said Carol uncomfortably. "I guess it sounded possible."

"But why would he tell you of all people about it in the first place?" wondered Lisa. "I thought you two hardly knew each other."

"Unfortunately, she became involved by accident," said Jasper. He explained how the men had mistaken Carol for his buyer when Celeste had failed to turn up in Nairobi. "I had to tell her what was going on so she wouldn't be frightened."

"You mean, so I wouldn't blow it for you," put in Carol.

"So, you see, it is not what you thought," said Jasper. "Maybe next time you will be more careful before jumping to conclusions and accusing people."

"You're not off the hook yet, pal," said Greg. "I'm not sure I buy any of this. But let's say for now you're telling the truth. Why the hell didn't you come to me if you had information about a planned poaching?"

"Come to you?" Jasper answered scornfully. "What would you do? Write a report? File a complaint? This needed strong action, someone who was not afraid of rocking the boat."

"What's that supposed to mean?" demanded Greg.

"It means that I expect to hook some very big fish here. Maybe some of the people you have become so cozy with in your five long years in Rumura."

"Listen here, you phony Dutch bastard—" sputtered Greg.

"Relax, Greg," said Jasper condescendingly. "I understand that you have to stay on the good side of crooks like Kamanga and Maleke if you want to remain here. But I don't have that problem. I am free to step on any toes that I need to. And I intend to crush every set of guilty toes I can find."

"So you just went off on your own, blundering around in the dark, hoping you might stumble onto something."

"And I did, didn't I?" said Jasper. "That's what you are really upset about, isn't it? That I discovered this plot that you knew nothing about?"

"There's nothing that goes on around here I don't know about," said Greg. "Like I told you, we already knew someone was after a bonobo. And my people and I were handling it just fine until you showed up and pulled this dumb stunt of posing as a buyer—and that's still assuming you really were just posing. Aside from messing up my investigations, you've gone and handed us to Maleke on a silver platter. He's been trying for years to get something on me, and now here's someone from my research station going around telling everybody in town he's ready to buy a bonobo. We'll be lucky if we don't all get kicked out this time. Or maybe even killed, like poor Celeste."

"It's not my fault the stupid girl crashed her car," snapped Jasper. "And I don't have to stay and listen to this kind of nonsense." He stormed out of the house, slamming the door with such force that the windows rattled and Rasputin squawked an angry protest from his cage.

"Stupid bastard," muttered Greg. "Good riddance." He sat back down on the sofa and accepted a mug of coffee from Lisa. "So, Carol," he said after a moment. "Mind telling me just how long you've known what Jasper was up to?"

"I'm not sure I really know even now," said Carol, uncomfortably.

"But when did he tell you about this ridiculous "sting" operation?"

"Thursday night, at the hotel in Mwatumi."

"I don't suppose it occurred to you that Lisa and I might be interested to hear about it?"

"The whole thing just sounded so absurd, I didn't know whether to take it seriously. And then he told me he was calling it off, anyway. But I was going to tell you about it today, as soon as you got back."

311

"That's true," put in Thor. "Carol told me she regretted she hadn't yet told you."

"So you knew about it too, did you? Just how do you figure in?" asked Greg.

"He doesn't," said Carol quickly. "I just told him about it because I got worried when it seemed like these people had followed me to Mwatumi." She told Greg and Lisa the trail of events, beginning with the phone call at the Norfolk hotel in Nairobi and ending with her refusal to cooperate with Jasper.

"And when you got to Mwatumi, Kamanga thought you were this 'Mrs. Simon' too?"

"That's right. And he told me to warn Mr. Singh to stay away from Mwatumi. He said something about someone named Yates, who had ignored "their" warnings. I had no idea who that was or what it was about, but it certainly sounded like a threat."

"But you knew who Yates was," Greg said to Thor.

"Only that I met him briefly in Kobani, and he seemed to know about some sort of criminal activity going on in Mwatumi, maybe involving some highly placed people in government. It sounded like a promising story. Do you know any more about this Yates, Greg?"

"Never mind what I know about," said Greg. He held up his coffee cup and Lisa silently refilled it. He took a few deep swallows and then put the mug firmly down on the coffee table.

"I don't buy it," he said shortly.

"I beg your pardon?"

"I said, I don't buy it, Carol."

"But that's really how it happened. I know it's a weird story, but—"

"Oh, yeah, it's weird all right, but that's not it. What I don't buy is that the only reason you didn't tell me or Lisa any of this before was because Jasper said he was calling the whole thing off."

Carol hesitated, and then met his gaze levelly. "All right," she said. "There was another reason. Jasper asked me not to tell

312

you about it, because you might be involved in this poaching business."

"Shit!" exploded Greg. "And you believed him?"

"No, of course not. Not really. But—well, at the same time I couldn't be positive about it, could I? I guess I thought I should just wait and see if I could figure things out for myself."

"I'm very disappointed, Carol," said Lisa. "You thought you could trust Jasper more than us?"

"No, that is, I didn't know what to think. And it wasn't just Jasper."

"What wasn't?"

"He wasn't the only one who suggested you might somehow be involved in poaching."

"Who else?" demanded Greg.

"I happened to meet Dr. Maleke at the Intercontinental..."

"Maleke! I knew it!" Greg kicked the coffee table, knocking the mug off onto the floor where it shattered and splashed coffee in all directions. "What the hell did he tell you?"

She told him about the Cameroon chimpanzees. "And then Jonathan told me he'd heard about it too."

Greg brought shook his head with disgust. "Shit, didn't I tell you, Lisa? It's Maleke who's been spreading that old story around again. And morons like Jonathan Marshall are swallowing it hook, line and sinker. These guys all think Maleke's the greatest thing since sliced bread, with his Oxford English and his tailored suits. The ultimate suave, cultivated, bullshitting African with all the right lines rolling off his tongue, and meanwhile he's as rotten as they come. He's got them all completely bamboozled."

"The dudu in the mango," said Lisa.

"Jasper told me you couldn't deny it, because there's proof," said Carol.

"Of course I don't deny it. I mean, I did arrange to have three young chimpanzees sent to the U.S. from Cameroon back in 1983. They were confiscated from poachers and very sick, practically dead. One of them had its arm caught in a snare and gangrene was starting to set in. There was no one in Cameroon qualified to treat them. I sent them to a primate research center, where the vets saved their lives. And they're still alive today, by the way, even though that one lost the arm. There's no question it was the right thing to do."

"But why did Maleke and Jasper both make it sound like some kind of a crime?"

Greg just groaned and waved his hand wearily.

"It was a complicated situation," said Lisa. "The Cameroon authorities didn't want to let them go—they said that they could care for the chimps themselves. What they were really after was a bribe, but Greg didn't have the money or the time to deal with that. So he had to get the chimps out without any of the right paperwork. The people Greg wouldn't pay off decided to make a big case out of it, accusing him of smuggling them out for his own profit."

"God, it was a mess," said Greg. "And that isn't even the whole story. See, it was more than just people being pissed off because I wouldn't grease their palms. We'd just published some articles about how some of the authorities in several west African countries were in cahoots with a big European safari hunting outfit, getting kickbacks for giving them exclusive hunting rights in places where there wasn't supposed to be any hunting, and letting them take species that were supposed to be protected. They wanted to discredit me and my organization, so they hyped up this story about the chimpanzees. I don't know about Jasper, but I'm sure Maleke knows all about it."

"And now we're afraid he might be trying to do the same thing here, to force us out of the Mali-Kuli forest," said Lisa. "He's made it clear he wants us out, but so far we've managed to avoid giving him an excuse."

"Until now, thanks to Jasper," said Greg.

"Dr. Maleke told me he you were beginning to act like you owned the forest and everything in it," said Carol bluntly.

"Yeah, they always trot out the old "arrogant *mzungu*" line when it suits them," said Greg. "But it's just an excuse to use when they want to get rid of you for some other reason."

"What other reason?" asked Thor. "Is it the same sort of thing as you were describing in Cameroon?"

"He's not saying, but I'm pretty sure it's because of this road," said Greg. "I told you about it yesterday—the one that would cut right through prime forest area in the southern part of the reserve. Maleke wants that road real bad, and we've been throwing a monkey wrench in his plans." He described how they had persuaded the environmental assessment consultant to advise USAID against funding the road. "Now it looks like Maleke has managed to convince those idiots at USAID to do the assessment over again. And of course he's afraid we'll exercise the same kind of 'undue influence' the second time around."

"Which of course we will," added Lisa. "But we expect to get a lot of resistance, and not just from Thadeus Maleke. There's a lot of land speculation going on, with some very big people claiming or buying up land all along the route they think the road will take. They're getting it for next to nothing, and as soon as the road goes in it will be worth a hundred times what it is now. Maleke's brother-in-law is one of the ones going around trying to file claims. And meanwhile, there's Maleke himself making plans to degazette that part of the reserve the minute he's got the titles to the land."

"And he's creating rumors you're involved in poaching to get you out of the way?" said Thor.

"That's how we read it," said Greg. "I just wish people weren't so gullible and ready to believe this kind of crap."

"People like me, you mean," said Carol.

"I was thinking of Jonathan Marshall. The U.S. Embassy is supposed to be looking out for the interests of American citizens, and instead he's helping these scumbags kick us out and destroy the forest."

"That's not fair," objected Carol. "You can't expect Jonathan to assume you're right and Dr. Maleke is wrong. He

315

told me he has to deal with a lot of American crooks and conmen who come over here trying to take advantage of people."

"Thanks a lot," said Greg.

"Sorry—I didn't mean it like that. But Jonathan said Maleke told him he was investigating reports from his people in the field that people at the research station were poaching apes."

"And that's where our friend Reijksen comes in," said Greg. "I still can't believe he could be so stupid."

"But foolish as his scheme was, Jasper was trying to expose a real buyer," Thor pointed out. "Do you have any idea yet who that is?"

"I'll tell you what I think—Reijksen cooked this whole thing up himself—there never was a real buyer at all," said Greg.

"But he told me it all started when some local men said they'd been hired by someone to steal a chimp," said Carol.

"Of course he told you that—he probably figured you wouldn't cooperate with him otherwise."

"I didn't cooperate with him anyway," protested Carol.

"Yeah, okay," said Greg. "But I'll bet you'd have been a lot quicker to blow his cover if you knew he dreamed the whole thing up himself, instead of trying to stop an existing plot."

"I suppose so."

"This whole thing smelled pretty fishy to us all along, anyway," said Greg. "First of all, the buyer being a European. These days it's a lot more likely to be an Arab, or maybe a Latin American drug baron. And anyway, if someone wanted to get his hands on a baby ape, he wouldn't have to go to all the trouble and expense of hiring someone to catch it specially. Unfortunately, you can find hundreds of the poor little buggers tied up outside huts all over central Africa, dying left and right. People kill the mother for food, and they bring the baby back for their kids to play with, or they take it into the capital and try to find some expat who'll buy it. Bonobos are harder to find than regular chimps, but you can find them easily enough in the DRC. But people like Reijksen wouldn't know that, since they just sit around in Europe being righteous and sanctimonious, and never bother getting out to find out what's going on in the real world. You can't believe how much trouble these well-meaning types cause us sometimes."

"Well-meaning types. I guess that includes me," said Carol.

"I just hope you're right, that he's called it off."

"I'm afraid he hasn't," said Carol. "He only told me he was going to, to keep me quiet." She told him Jasper had told the people he was dealing with that "Mrs. Simon" had backed out of the deal, and about her worry that they might think she had really just decided to switch her business to him. "That's when I really got worried about Captain Kamanga coming to get you this morning. I was very relieved when you came back so soon."

"You thought they might have decided to get me out of the way? Like poor Celeste?"

"But that was an accident, wasn't it?" asked Carol, horrified at the suggestion.

"A pretty convenient accident, don't you think?"

"But it wouldn't make sense for them to eliminate her if they thought she was the buyer." said Thor.

"True, but what if they'd somehow figured out exactly who she was—a stupid do-gooder *mzungu* who was trying to play a fast one on them and put a stop to their business? Some people around here might not take so kindly to that sort of thing."

"I wish you hadn't told Kamanga who she was," said Lisa. "It might make him think this whole business is somehow connected to us."

"I didn't tell him," said Greg. "I didn't like the way he was looking at me when he showed me the body. It made me think he was up to something, so I pretended not to recognize her."

"I wonder whether Jasper also thinks it could have been something more than an accident," said Lisa. "He must be afraid they'll come after him, too."

"Serve the stupid bastard right," said Greg. "Someone should put a scare into him so he and his "Green Brigade" buddies don't ever try a dumb stunt like this again. There's nothing more dangerous than a bunch of amateurs meddling where they don't belong. Isn't that right, Nilssen?"

"I'm sure you're right, Greg," said Thor.

CHAPTER 25

1

Samuel Liumba reached Bola just before noon and drove his motorscooter into the dirty yard behind the Mountain View hotel. On the seat behind him, the Pygmy boy, Boku, held his waist in a death-like grip, frozen with the thrill and terror of the fast ride.

"All right, we're here. Let go of me you bloody little fool," said Samuel. He indicated a patch of dense bushes and trees at the far end of the yard. "Go and wait in there. Make sure no one sees you."

Samuel locked the scooter and entered the hotel through the back door, beating the dust off his clothes. He made straight for a small, dark room behind the stairs. He had been worried about being late, so he was relieved to find he was the first to arrive. He unwrapped a stick of chewing gum and popped it into his mouth, and sat down on the sagging sofa to wait.

Thadeus Maleke arrived about ten minutes later. He sat down in a mildewed armchair opposite Samuel.

"Congratulations on your new nephew," Maleke said in Ruahya, using the word for a boy born to a man's sister. In Ruahya tradition this was a very close kinship tie, almost the same as the man's own son. "May God grant him long life and many children."

"Thank you, sir," said Samuel. "We hope you'll come to the christening to give him your blessing."

"It will be my pleasure," said Maleke, as a matter of form. Samuel's sister was Maleke's distant cousin, through marriage on his father's side. That placed the new baby on the fringes of his extended family. He would be expected to send a gift but not to come from Kobani to attend the ceremony.

"How is little Nelson?" asked Samuel.

"Settling in," said Maleke. "He's a bit homesick and he misses his mother and sisters, but he'll get over it. He's excited about starting his new school."

"He'll be a credit to you," said Samuel.

"I'm sure he will. What's the news from Mali-Kuli?"

"The American woman showed up at the station yesterday, together with a man named Nilssen. I think Lisa said he's from Norway. The two of them went out with Lisa this morning to see China group, but so far there hasn't been anything suspicious."

"Then Jonathan Marshall was right," Maleke said thoughtfully. "Carol Simmons wasn't the one killed in the car crash on Friday night."

"No, but they know who it was."

"How do you know?"

"Kamanga came to collect Greg early this morning, while the others were out with the bonobos. When Greg came back I could see from his face that something was up, so I followed him to the house and tried to listen at the door. I heard him tell the others that Kamanga had taken him to Mwatumi to look at the woman's body. He said it wasn't easy, because she was so smashed up, but he was able to identify her."

"And who did he say she was?" asked Maleke impatiently.

"I don't know. I couldn't hear very well so I tried to get closer, and then that bloody parrot of Lisa's spotted me and started kicking up a row, so I had to go."

Maleke made a disgusted noise that made Samuel wince.

"I'm sorry, sir," said Samuel. "I would have tried again, but I had to come here to meet you. But I'm sure I can find out tonight who she was."

"I already know who she was, or at least what she called herself on the car hire papers," said Maleke. "It was Mrs. Simon who went over that cliff." Samuel stared at him, bewildered. "But—I thought the American woman was Mrs. Simon."

"Apparently not."

"But didn't Muna tell you Reijksen himself said she was the one?" said Samuel.

"Yes. So the question is, what kind of game are they all playing here? That's why it's so unfortunate that you didn't hear the rest of what Greg had to say. Was Reijksen there, by the way?"

"Yes, he was with them in the house when Greg arrived. But before I left the station I saw him storming out, like they'd had some kind of argument."

"Interesting. By the way, I've heard a rumor the crash might not have been an accident—that the car could have been forced off the road deliberately."

"That's what one of the witnesses has been saying, but most people think he's just trying to make the story more interesting," said Samuel.

"Still, if they've heard the rumor, some of them might be getting cold feet," said Maleke. "Maybe that's what the argument was about. How did Greg behave when Kamanga came to get him this morning? Did he act frightened or worried? Or did he seem to know what it was about?"

"He was just mad. You know, demanding to know if he was under arrest, and like that. Of course, it could all have been just an act for me and the rest of the staff. He's always making such a big point of how much he hates Kamanga. You have to wonder if there's something else behind it."

"What's behind it is that they're both poaching on the same turf," said Maleke confidently. "What I don't know yet is whether they're partners or competitors. All right, then. See what you can find out tonight. I want to know how these people all fit together."

"There's something else before you go, sir," said Samuel. He told Maleke about the old Pygmy that he and Lisa had caught following China group. "Someone wanted him and his boys to snatch a baby bonobo all right. Greg tried to get him to say who it was, but he was so drunk he could hardly talk. Greg finally locked him in the toolshed. He said the others wouldn't dare take a bonobo as long as we had the old man."

"Is he still in there?"

"No, I took him to my sister's place this morning, while everyone was gone. I broke the lock to make it look like his people helped him escape. I thought I could get some more out of him after he sobered up. But all I've been able to get so far is a description of the two men who sent them after the bonobo."

"Juma Ayala and David?" asked Maleke.

"That's what it sounds like it."

"Well, no surprise there," sighed Maleke. "Do you think the old man knows anything more?"

"No, but his grandson might," said Samuel, sounding pleased with himself.

"What grandson?"

"Right after I left the research station to come here, this *Bashy'amba* boy stopped me in the road. He'd been keeping watch and he saw me take the old man away. I brought him with me if you want to talk to him. I told him I couldn't let the old man go without your say-so."

"All right—let's hear what the fellow has to say for himself."

They went out into the yard and Samuel summoned the apprehensive Boku out of the bushes. The boy seemed anxious to talk, but all he could tell them was that they were supposed to deliver the baby bonobo to Juma and David that morning, and that they had been promised five hundred *rimands* for it. His voice grew dejected as he recalled the fortune that had slipped through their fingers. As Greg had anticipated, with their grandfather held captive by the *mzungus,* Boku and his cousins hadn't dared go after the bonobo.

"You let Babu go," insisted Boku with a show of bravado. "We go home now. We leave *bashy'amba kipu.* No take no baby no more."

Maleke looked at him thoughtfully and was about to answer, when a breeze came up and stirred the leaves and his eye caught the glint of sunlight on metal deep inside the bushes.

"Go and have a look what that is," he told Samuel.

Samuel pushed his way through tangled undergrowth. "It's a car," he called back, in surprise when he reached the spot. "A good one!"

Maleke went in after him, pushing Boku along ahead with a hand firmly on the boy's neck. They found Samuel clearing a loose pile of leafy branches away from a late model silver Land Cruiser with orange stripes on the side.

"It hasn't been here long," said Maleke, looking at the freshly broken branches. Seeing that the license plates were missing, he stepped up to the car and looked closely at the corner of the windshield, where the registration number was etched into the glass.

"Bloody hell," he muttered to himself, and laid his hand on the hood. It was still warm.

"I know this car," he announced. He started to say more, but stopped himself and turned to Boku sternly. "Did you see who brought this here?"

Boku looked quickly down at the ground and shook his head vigorously.

"You'd better tell me the truth if you want us to let your grandfather go," warned Maleke.

Boku wrapped his arms around his narrow shoulders and toed the ground in an agony of indecision.

"Come on, boy," said Maleke impatiently. "What are you afraid of?"

"Police," whispered Boku miserably.

"It's all right," said Samuel. "We're not going to turn you over to the police. We just want to know who brought the car here."

"Police," said Boku again. "Bad men."

"You bloody idiot, answer the question," exclaimed Samuel, grabbing the boy's shoulder and shaking him.

"Wait," said Maleke, pulling Samuel's hand away. "I think he's trying to tell us." He spoke to Boku gently. "Don't be afraid, boy. No one's going to hurt you. Just tell us what they looked like."

Boku looked into Maleke's face anxiously and seemed to find reassurance there. Hesitantly, he described the two men who had driven the car into the bushes and left it there.

"All right, that's enough," said Maleke. "I know who they are." He turned to Samuel. "I'm off to Mwatumi to see Kamanga. Take the boy back to your sister's place and let the old man go. And I have a thousand rimands for anyone who can find me the owner of this stolen car. If you learn anything, leave word here at the hotel. I'll stop on my way back."

Samuel looked at him curiously. "A thousand rimands? All right, I'll pass the word around. Anything else, sir?"

"Yes, stop by the Reserve Headquarters and tell Chief Warden Butaagi to stand by on the radio. I have a feeling tonight could be the night."

2

David cursed as the front wheel of the rickety pushcart dropped into a deep rut and it came to an abrupt halt, nearly jerking his arms out of their sockets. The big cardboard box catapulted forward and toppled off the cart onto the ground. He cursed again and strained backwards, maneuvering the wheel free. He laid down the handlebars and wiped his sweating face with his shirt tail, then half lifted and half shoved the box back onto the cart. The stink coming from it was so bad it took his breath away.

It would have been much easier to tell Mjuju to take the thing up to the old church himself. But then Juma would have known where he had gotten it, and Mjuju would have known who wanted it. If there was one thing David had learned from Juma, it was the value of being the middleman.

He had his answer ready for when Juma asked him where the bonobo had come from. "Juma, my friend," he would say, "you have your contacts and I have mine. Isn't that why we are partners?" And he would give a little shrug and the hint of a smile and say no more.

Thinking about that cheered him for a moment, but then he looked up and caught sight of the sun high in the sky. This was taking much longer than he had expected. He was following an old path up the back side of the hill, away from the village. It was a long and tortuous route, but it kept him out of reach of prying eyes. No one used this path any more, since the big fire three months before.

The official report had called it a fire of unknown origin, but the people of Mwatumi knew better. For them it was the hand of a just God, taking revenge for the light-skinned baby that had been born to old Ethungu's daughter. The old man himself had pointed the finger at the priest, despite the shame, so no one could doubt that it was true. The girl Emily had stood trembling before the stony-faced elders and confessed that the priest had led her into sin and threatened her soul with eternal damnation if she breathed a word of it to anyone.

The elders had given her ten strokes of the cane and sent her home to repent. And that night the fire had erupted out of nowhere and raged through the church and the rectory like a force of hell, engulfing them in minutes. Father Loretto had been awakened by the heat and the crash of the church's metal roof collapsing. He had jumped naked out of the window, one step ahead of the flames, and come running into town wrapped in nothing but a filthy, threadbare towel he found in the stream bed. The next day he was gone from Mwatumi for good, lucky to escape with his life.

David reached the clearing at the top of the hill and pushed the cart past the charred chimney stump of the church, already blanketed with delicate green vines. About twenty yards away a small brick hut with a corrugated iron roof was still standing, although the brick was crumbling and the roof was pocked with holes where it had rusted through. It had once been the storage shed. Now it stood vigil beside the ruins like a decrepit, solitary mourner.

The pile of cigarette butts littering the ground around the doorway of the hut testified that Juma had been waiting for a long time.

"Phew," he said, waving his hand crossly in front of his face as David stopped the cart in front of him. "What a stink."

"Oh, I don't know," said David triumphantly. "It smells like money to me."

"So you got it after all? How about that. I was sure you were going to come up with another lame excuse." Juma squatted down in front of the box and rapped it sharply with his knuckles. "Hey, are you sure there's anything inside?"

"He's probably just asleep."

"So, who did you get it from?" asked Juma casually.

"Just a guy I know," stammered David. He shifted uncomfortably as Juma looked at him closely.

"Just a guy you know," repeated Juma. "All right then, what did you pay for it?"

"Two thousand rimands."

"Two thousand, eh? That's a lot."

"It was short notice," David pointed out. "You have to pay more if you want something in a hurry. I had to pay him half in advance," he added.

"Where'd you get that kind of money?"

David would have liked to shrug casually, as though a thousand rimands were nothing to him, not even worth talking about. Unfortunately, he couldn't do that.

"The truth is, I was a bit short so I had to borrow it from someone," he said. "I need an advance so I can pay the guy back. He needs the money back right away."

"You mean you stole the money from your mother, and you're worried about putting it back before she notices it's gone."

David scowled and spat on the ground.

"Don't worry. After tonight you can pay it back ten times over," said Juma. "Now let's have a look at this thing."

"Don't open the box," warned David. "He might get out."

"I'll make sure he doesn't. I want to get a look at him, to make sure you didn't get gypped." He started to pull the box off the pushcart. "Come on, give me a hand here."

Reluctantly, David helped him lift the box off the cart. Juma picked at the knot until the string fell away. He raised one flap of the box cautiously and tried to peer inside.

"I can't see anything," he said, opening the flap wider.

For a long moment, Juma looked down into the box at the dark, inert figure huddled at the bottom.

"Bloody hell," he said softly.

David looked anxiously from Juma to the miserable little creature and back to Juma again.

"Shit!" The word exploded from Juma with such fury that David jumped backward and cowered against the wall.

"You idiot!" shouted Juma. "You bloody, good-for-nothing idiot! I should've known you'd screw it up again!"

3

"Wake up, Mr. Marshall."

The voice was oddly pleasant and low-key, like a train conductor advising a napping passenger that his stop was coming up.

Jonathan jerked awake and a flood of sensations washed over him. His arms and hands were dead numb, his neck was stiff and aching, his stomach was queasy from the heat and the smell of smoking kerosene, and he desperately needed to urinate. He was still blindfolded and felt helpless and disoriented. After a moment, he remembered what had happened and the fear hit him like a body blow. Then he registered that someone had spoken his name. He tried desperately to collect his thoughts as he slowly raised his head.

"That's better." The gruff voice came from directly in front of him. Jonathan could feel the man's presence and smell the mixture of sweat and dust that came off of him.

"What do you want from me?" croaked Jonathan. His throat felt parched and felt swollen.

"We want to ask you some questions. If you answer correctly you will not be hurt. If you play games it will be bad for you. You understand?"

Jonathan nodded slowly, his head reeling with the movement.

"All right, then. Who is Mr. Singh?"

Jonathan swallowed painfully and cleared his parched throat. "I don't know," he said.

"That is the wrong answer."

The sound of the slap was like a gunshot as Jonathan's head was knocked sharply to the right with the force of the blow.

"I swear to God, I don't know who he is," gasped Jonathan. "I tried to meet him in Kobani, but it was a trick. He never showed up."

"Why are you meeting him in Mwatumi?"

"In Mwatumi?" asked Jonathan, confused. "Is that where he is?"

This time the slap came from the other side. Jonathan tasted salt and felt the dribble of blood from the corner of his mouth.

"I'm not meeting him," he protested. "That's not why I'm going to Mwatumi."

"Why then?"

"To meet a friend, a woman. We're worried about whether she's okay."

"The American?"

Jonathan hesitated. "Yes."

"She is the one who will meet Singh?"

"No! She doesn't know him either. She doesn't want anything to do with him. I swear, it's all some kind of crazy misunderstanding."

"A misunderstanding?" said the voice dryly. "And perhaps this is also a misunderstanding?"

Jonathan heard the man walk around behind the chair and felt a hand grasp the blindfold at the back of his head.

"When I remove this, look straight in front only. If you turn around to look behind, I will kill you."

The blindfold was jerked off, leaving Jonathan blinking in the dim yellow light of a kerosene lantern hanging from the thatched roof over his head. As he trained his eyes forward into the gloom, a hand extended over his shoulder and held a photograph a few inches in front of his face.

It took a moment for Jonathan to focus his eyes on the photograph. A cold shudder ran down his spine as he realized he was looking at the face of a young woman. It must have been pretty once, but now it was a mask of bruises and bloody cuts, the nose smashed and the eyes swollen shut. The skin was white and drained, throwing the swellings and cuts into sharp relief. The jaw looked unnaturally set and rigid.

"My God," whispered Jonathan, closing his eyes to shut out the gruesome sight.

"You recognize her?"

"No."

"I have warned you, Mr. Marshall," snapped the man behind him. "No games."

"I don't know who she is—I've never seen her before in my life," protested Jonathan, bracing himself for another blow.

"There is no point in lying. We know already that you knew Mrs. Simon very well. Unfortunately, she is dead now."

"Mrs. Simon!" exclaimed Jonathan. "So...it was the accident." Despite everything, he felt a flood of relief that the woman's injuries weren't the result of a brutal beating.

"Now you admit you know her?"

"No! I just heard she was killed in a car crash."

"How did you hear this?"

"From Thadeus Maleke," admitted Jonathan uneasily.

"Indeed? We thought perhaps it was from Mr. Truman Yates."

"Yates!" exclaimed Jonathan with surprise. "What's he got to do with it?"

"That is what we wish to learn from you."

"I swear to God, I don't know anything about this. And neither does Carol."

"But you admit you know Yates."

"Yes, I know him. I helped him get out of jail and leave the country."

"We know how you helped him. We want to know why."

"It's my job. The Ambassador asked me to get him out. That's all I know."

"And this man who calls himself Nilssen. Who is he?"

"My wife met him in town and brought him home for dinner. He's a Norwegian. He says he's a writer," Jonathan added uncertainly.

"You'll have to do better than that. The Norwegian Embassy knows nothing about him, and immigration has no record of anyone of that name entering the country."

Jonathan closed his eyes as the man leaned down and spoke harshly into his ear. "Enough of your lies, Mr. Marshall. We already know about your dirty group of collaborators—Yates, Mrs. Simon, Reijksen, the American woman Simmons, this man who calls himself Nilssen, and Thadeus Maleke. We want to know about Mr. Singh."

"I don't know what you're talking about," protested Jonathan. "What kind of collaborators?"

"You are only making this harder for yourself, Mr. Marshall. We will get him with or without you."

"I swear to God, I've told you everything I know."

Jonathan heard footsteps retreating and then a whispered conversation somewhere behind him. He hadn't realized there was anyone else in the room. He fought the urge to turn and look.

A few minutes later the footsteps approached again. The blindfold was pulled back down over his eyes and a hand slipped under his armpit to pull him roughly to his feet.

"All right, let's go."

"What—where are you taking me?" asked Jonathan, stumbling forward.

"One way or another, you are going to lead us to Mr. Singh," said another voice, which Jonathan recognized only too well.

CHAPTER 26

1

Elena Sotiropoulos greeted Carol and Thor after Greg dropped them off at the Acropolis. "We are finished serving lunch, but I can warm it for you again," she offered. "Goat stew, a specialty."

"Not for me, thank you," said Thor, laying his hand on his belly. "How about you, Carol?"

"I really should go to see Margaret," said Carol. "I told her I'd come by this afternoon to drop off the accounts books and say goodbye. Would you like to come along? I'm sure she'd be pleased."

"Thanks, but I'd better not. I'm afraid I must have eaten something that didn't agree with me. I think I'll go lie down for awhile."

Elena clucked her tongue sympathetically. "The stomach is bad? Don't worry, Mr. Nilssen. I have a remedy I learned from my mother in the old country. It doesn't smell so good or taste so good, but you'll see. Your stomach ache disappears, like magic." She snapped her fingers dramatically, and her black eyes gleamed with anticipation.

"I'll check in on you when I get back, to see if you survived," Carol told Thor. She gave him an encouraging pat on the arm and escaped into the hot afternoon sun, leaving him trying to talk his way out of Elena's hospitality.

When Carol arrived at Margaret's house, she was surprised to find a baby sitting on a blanket in the yard, wearing only a dirty T-shirt and chewing dreamily on a sliver of sugarcane. Two little boys squatted close by, engrossed in a game involving twigs and pebbles, under the watchful eye of Margaret's youngest daughter, Patience.

"*Hodi!*" called Carol.

The boys jumped up and ran to stand behind their cousin, staring at Carol with wide eyes. Patience smiled shyly at her and ran into the house.

A moment later, Margaret appeared in the doorway. "Carol, *karibu*. I hope you have had a good journey."

"Yes, it was very nice thanks. Who are these cute little fellows?" She squatted down and stretched her hand out to the baby, who immediately seized her finger in a tight, sticky fist.

"They are from my small sister, Tabitha. She have come back to Mwatumi to stay with us."

Carol looked around the small compound, trying to imagine how it could accommodate another family.

"Mind, he can make you dirty," warned Margaret, as the baby pulled Carol's finger into his mouth. "Come. I make tea and we talk."

A short while later, Hope and Faith arrived, dressed in identical bright red dresses made of stiff, shiny polyester with high, puffed sleeves. Their broad feet were squeezed into well-worn leather pumps and they wore small lace caps pinned to their hair. They greeted Carol politely before going into the bedroom.

"The girls come now from church," explained Margaret. "After mass they stay always to teach in Sunday school."

"And to flirt with the boys, I suppose," said Carol. "At least, that's the main reason I went to church when I was their age."

Suddenly there was a shriek and an outburst of angry exclamations from the bedroom. Faith came running out, half undressed, shouting and waving a small wooden box in the air. Hope followed after her, wailing. Margaret tried to soothe them, but she was clearly upset as well. Faith spat out a few more harsh words and stormed back into the bedroom, with Hope close behind. Margaret sat slowly back down at the table with a sigh.

"What was that all about?" asked Carol.

"My boy David," Margaret said bitterly. "For what sin God gave me this no good son?" She glared at David's photograph on the wall.

"Why, what's he done?"

"He steal all the girls' money when they are in church. Almost two thousand rimands!"

"Are you sure it was David?"

"Who else is it?" exclaimed Margaret. "It is not the first time and it is not the second time. Always Hope and Faith hide their money and always David find it and steal it. He is too bad." She shook her head and sighed heavily again.

"I'm sorry," said Carol.

"Before he was not bad like this," said Margaret wearily. "Even he was a good boy before. But now he find bad friends. They make him all the time hungry for money. That Juma, that one is very bad." Margaret paused, looking uncomfortable. "I am sorry to tell you, Carol, but maybe you don't know so good. You and your friend, it is better you leave Juma alone. Why you want to make business with that thief?"

"Me and my friend?" asked Carol, puzzled. "Who do you mean?"

"That one who come with you to our meeting. He put a cloth on his head and say he is our sister."

"Thor? What do you mean, we should leave Juma alone? Who is he, anyway?"

"Your friend, he say you know Juma," said Margaret. She told Carol that Thor had asked Joseph, the waiter at the Cock and Bull, where he could find Juma and a man from Nairobi, called Singh. "At least, he don't say Juma, but he say a very small man with voice like a woman. In Mwatumi there is only Juma who is like that. He say you talk with this man before in Kobani and now you want to talk with him again and with Singh. Then he give Joseph some little money, and he say Joseph cannot tell nobody."

Carol concealed her dismay. "But how do you hear all this?"

Margaret shrugged. "Joseph tell David, because David is friend with Juma and maybe he know where Juma can be. And David have to tell me. He like to tell me all the time about Juma." Margaret altered her voice in a rising imitation of David's. "'Juma is too smart. Juma can be too rich one day, and me also because I am partners with him. See, Mama, now even so many rich *mzungus* come to have business with Juma.'"

She took a long drink of tea to calm herself, and continued in her normal voice. "David make me always too angry with his 'Juma, Juma, Juma,'" she apologized. She laid her hand earnestly on Carol's arm. "Carol—I don't know what is this business you have. But this Juma, he is no good. It is better you leave him."

"I promise you, I don't have any kind of business with Juma or anyone else," said Carol. "Are you sure it was Thor that Joseph was talking about, and not someone else? Maybe a man called Jasper Reijksen?"

"This man tell Joseph he stay with you together at the Acropolis Hotel. That is how I know it can be your friend."

"Believe me, Margaret," said Carol. "That was no friend of mine."

2

Thadeus Maleke pulled up in front of the small, square brick building that was the Mwatumi police station. The fierce afternoon sun assaulted him as soon as he stepped out of the air-conditioned car. Despite the heat, he pulled on his suit jacket and tightened his tie before going inside.

A ceiling fan revolved slowly overhead in the small office, its loose bearings giving off a rattling sound. Captain Kamanga was asleep in his swivel chair, his feet crossed on the desk in front of him and his chin cradled on his chest. His uniform shirt gaped open, revealing thick black hair curling over the top of his yellowed undershirt. Dark sweat stains spread out from under his arms. Maleke looked at him distastefully, listening to his labored breathing.

"Kamanga!" he said sharply. "Wake up."

Kamanga started awake, nearly tipping the rickety chair over backwards. He sat up hastily, pulling his feet off the desk, and then registered who his visitor was.

"Ah, Maleke, it's you," he said, pointedly putting his feet back up.

"Aren't you on duty?" demanded Maleke. He spoke in English to lend the proper weight of official disapproval.

"I'm here, aren't I?" replied Kamanaga in Rumuran. "What can I do for you, *Doctor*?" He managed to convey disdain rather than respect with the title.

Maleke paused and reconsidered his approach. Antagonizing Kamanga wasn't going to help. He sat down in the stiff wooden chair in front of the desk and tried to make himself comfortable. "I heard there was an accident out here yesterday," he said casually, slipping into Ruahya, their common tribal language.

"Aieh," confirmed Kamanga noncommittally. "Very messy."

"A white woman involved, wasn't there?"

"Aieh. And her driver."

"Have you made an identification?"

"We're not prepared to make a public statement at this time," Kamanga said, smugly.

"I want to see the body."

"Not possible, Doctor." Kamanga stifled a yawn.

"Why, what's the problem? Why all the secrecy?"

"Official business. Can't see her unless you're a relative." Kamanga cocked an eyebrow at Maleke waggishly. "You think you might be a relative of the deceased, Doctor?"

Maleke controlled his temper with an effort. "My interest is also official. I understand the accident occurred in my jurisdiction."

"It was outside the Reserve and you've got no jurisdiction at all. I already told Chief Warden Butaagi that, and I know he must have told you. So why did you come all the way from Kobani just to hear it again?"

"I'll be frank with you," said Maleke, leaning forward confidingly. "There are people in Kobani worried that she might be a friend of theirs. I promised I would look into it for them."

"Why didn't you say so from the beginning, instead of swaggering around about your jurisdiction?" smirked Kamanga. He sat up and made a show of pulling a pad of paper from his desk drawer and poising a pen over it. "Now, who exactly are these people in Kobani who are worried?"

"I don't see why that's relevant."

"Now who's the one with the secrets? We have a case under investigation, here, Doctor. I assumed you're coming forward to give evidence."

"It's my wife, actually," said Maleke. "She has a cousin visiting from France, who was coming to see the mountains."

"And the name of this cousin?"

"What does it matter, unless I'm able to identify the body as hers?"

Kamanga smacked the pen down on the paper. "Let's not waste any more of each other's time, Maleke," he said. "We both know there's no cousin from France. You want to know whether the victim was the American woman, Carol Simmons, or the other one who calls herself Mrs. Simon. And I want to know where to find Mr. Singh. It's a fair exchange, don't you think?"

Maleke stiffened. "I'm aware of what you're up to around here, Kamanga. I'm prepared to make things very uncomfortable for you back in Kobani if necessary."

"You're in no position to make threats, Maleke," warned Kamanga. "You don't want to see that fool nephew of yours get hurt, do you?"

337

Maleke seemed taken aback. He studied Kamanga's face appraisingly for a moment and then sighed. "You're right," he said. "He is a fool."

Kamanga smiled triumphantly and pulled a thick cigar out of his desk drawer. He bit off the tip and spat it onto the ground, and took his time lighting up. He took a few strong puffs, tipping his head backward to send the blue smoke curling toward the ceiling. The air stream from the fan caught the smoke and sent it swirling downward again, spreading it across the desk.

"Why should you and I be enemies, Maleke?" Kamanga continued in a philosophical. "The two of us are age-mates after all—we were circumcised together. And we aren't so different, even now. What are we but a pair of foot soldiers, doing our best to serve our commanders faithfully, and meanwhile picking up a few scraps they drop along the way? I understand your situation perfectly. We know the Americans will pay compensation for land and crops that are taken over to build this road to Rendesha. Your Minister is set to make a fortune by grabbing up land along the route beforehand, so we can be sure the road is going in one way or another. Since there's nothing you can do about it, why shouldn't you and your family get a fair share of the profits? Why should it be always only the big men who eat?"

"A man has to take the opportunities life puts in his way," agreed Maleke cautiously.

"Exactly!" exclaimed Kamanga. "I don't mind telling you, I'm sending my wife into the forest to clear a small patch or two along the way myself. What harm is there in that? Now as for my small business here—what's the use in threatening to expose me? The Commissioner would only replace me with someone else and things would carry on just as before. You don't think anyone else in my position or yours would do any different? But the thing is to know how to go about it, my friend. How to take some of the honey without stirring up the bees too much. That nephew of yours is poking his hands into the wrong hive."

"I know," Maleke sighed again. "But when do these youngsters ever listen to good advice? I've been trying to stay out of it, hoping David might learn a lesson."

"The lesson may be a harder one than you had in mind," said Kamanga. "The boy is in way over his head. But it's not too late. Tell me where the meeting with Singh is tonight, and I'll see to it David comes to no harm. You have my word."

"As I said, Kamundu, I haven't been involved. If David and Juma are meeting Singh tonight, I don't know anything about it."

"Then why are you here?" demanded Kamanga.

"I told you, I wanted to see the body of the woman who died."

"This 'cousin' of your wife's?"

"I admit, that wasn't entirely true. But I do think I might recognize her and there are friends in Kobani who are worried. It has nothing to do with any of this."

"You heard the deal, Maleke," scowled Kamanga. "You can see her as soon as you tell me where to find Singh."

"I don't know."

"Then I you'd better get busy and find out," said Kamanga. He put his feet back up on the desk, one after the other, leaned back into his chair again and closed his eyes. After a while, Maleke left the office, pulling the door closed behind him.

A short time later, Maleke was thoughtfully sipping a beer in the empty bar at the Acropolis when he glimpsed Samuel Liumba through the window. Samuel beckoned to him urgently and then ducked out of sight. Maleke laid his money on the bar and strolled out the door into the back garden.

"I've found him," said Samuel excitedly. "The owner of the Land Cruiser."

"All right, let's go. We'll have to take your motorscooter," grumbled Maleke. "Kamanga probably has someone watching my car."

Maleke's charcoal gray suit was red with dust by the time they reached the end of the rough dirt track that wound up the mountain behind the town. They left the motorscooter there and continued on foot, through a grove of trees to the edge of a small clearing. Samuel carried a heavy iron *panga* at the ready as he led Maleke nervously through the thick underbrush. Through the branches they could see a round metal hut like a broad tin can with a pointed lid. The door was closed with a rusty metal latch held together by a sturdy new padlock.

They approached cautiously, but there didn't seem to be any guard. Samuel used the *panga* to pry the latch off the door.

Inside the windowless hut it was like an oven. There were boxes and gunnysacks scattered around the floor, and a pile of stiff animal skins that gave off a sickly sweet smell. A half dozen large wooden crates were stacked in the center. Maleke lifted the lid of one and whistled softly under his breath. It was filled with military-style automatic rifles packed in straw.

They found Jonathan slumped on the dirt floor against the back wall, drenched with sweat and still bound and blindfolded.

"My God, Thadeus, am I glad to see you!" exclaimed Jonathan, as Maleke roused him and pulled off the blindfold.

"Quiet," cautioned Maleke in a low voice. He used the *panga* to cut the twine binding Jonathan's wrists and ankles.

Samuel led the way quickly out of the hut and into the trees, while Maleke helped Jonathan stumble behind. A few hundred feet into the trees they stopped to let Jonathan rest and rub the circulation back into his cramped legs and arms.

"How did you know where to find me?" asked Jonathan.

"We started searching after we discovered your car in Bola," said Maleke. "You were lucky Samuel thought to look here."

"I knew Kamanga sometimes uses this hut to hide things before taking them across the border," said Samuel.

"It was two of his thugs who kidnapped you," explained Maleke.

"Gideon Karibani, the Police Commissioner, is the one behind this," said Jonathan. "I recognized his voice."

"Kamanga is the police chief here in Mwatumi," Maleke told him. "He must have arranged it on Bashega's orders. What did they want to know from you?"

Jonathan told him about the interrogation he'd gone through. "I kept telling them I didn't know anything, but they wouldn't believe me. Then they brought me here, saying I was going to take them to Singh whether I liked it or not. Who is this guy Singh, anyway?"

"I don't know any more than you do, Jonathan," said Maleke. "But never mind that, we have to get you out of here before they discover you've gone."

They continued through the grove back to Samuel's motorscooter, where Maleke quickly explained his plan. "Samuel will take you to a safe place along the road to Kobani, where you can wait," he told Jonathan. "I will return to the Acropolis Hotel now and find your friend Carol Simmons. As soon as it's dark she will take my car to drive back to Kobani, picking you up along the way."

"What about you?" asked Jonathan.

"I have other business here in Mwatumi. I'll use a Department car to return to Kobani in a day or two."

"But how will you get back to the Acropolis from here?"

"This is my home village. I have friends living nearby who can give me a lift. Don't worry about me. Just make sure you stay out of sight until you see the signal." Maleke pulled a leather-bound notepad and a slim, gold-plated pen from his breast pocket. "Write a note to your friend so she will believe me when I explain the situation. Include something only you would know so she can be sure it is authentic."

Jonathan scribbled a hasty note and handed the pad and pen back to Maleke. Maleke glanced at the note, which read:

Popeye: I'm okay now but I need your help. Do what Thadeus says—you can trust him. Jonathan.

"That was my nickname for Carol in the Peace Corps," explained Jonathan. "She hated it. When you talk to her, warn her about this guy Thor. I don't know who he really is, but I'm sure he's trouble." He climbed onto the seat behind Samuel. "I can't tell you how grateful I am, Thadeus," he said as Samuel revved the engine.

They shook hands and Samuel began to maneuver the motorscooter back down the track. Maleke waited until they were out of sight and then started after them, picking his way carefully among the rocks in his expensive Italian shoes.

3

Jasper glanced over his shoulder to make certain the hall was empty, unlocked the door and slipped into the room. He closed the curtains, throwing the room into a twilight darkness. Holding a small penlight in his teeth, he quickly set up the video camera and the tape recorder, connecting them both to an automatic timer. He opened the connecting door to Carol's room, where he replaced the 40 light bulbs again. He felt around under the bedside table, found the microphone he had attached there earlier, and pressed the switch to turn it on.

As he walked around the room, counting out loud to test the volume, a patch of white on the floor just inside the door caught his eye. It was an envelope, addressed to Mrs. C. Simon. He tore it open and used the penlight to read the short note inside.

Jasper folded the note and the envelope and slipped them into his pocket. "Stupid bastards," he muttered to himself with a touch of wry amusement. "So that's what they were up to. Sorry, fellows, you don't get rid of me that easily."

Returning to the adjoining room, he checked the tapes and rewound them. He smiled to himself as he disconnected the timer—he wouldn't be needing it now. Before leaving the room, he studied the note again, scratching his chin thoughtfully:

Mrs. Simon:

*Mr. Singh comes to find you here tonight at 9:30. So
he can meet with you alone, we have tell Riksen*
*Mr. Singh waits for you at Mountain View Hotel at
Bola at 9:00.*

A Friend.

He folded the note carefully in half just below the third line
and used the blade of his pocket knife to slit the paper smoothly
along the crease. Stuffing the top half back into his pocket, he
looked with satisfaction at the remaining piece:

*Mr. Singh waits for you at Mountain View Hotel at
Bola at 9:00.*

A Friend.

He opened the door cautiously, checking again to make sure
the hall was empty. Crossing the hall, he bent over and slid the
scrap of paper under Thor Nilssen's door before hurrying back to
his own room. The trap was set and there was nothing to do but
wait.

CHAPTER 27

1

Returning to the hotel, Carol found Nico Sotiropoulos leaning on his bony elbows on the reception desk as he watched a soccer game on the grainy television screen across the lobby.

"Hello," she said loudly, to get his attention.

The boy tore his eyes from the screen and looked at her distractedly, as though wondering why she was there, or why he was.

"Room twenty five, please," said Carol.

Nico straightened up listlessly and pulled a key from the row of pigeonholes on the wall behind him.

"Thanks," said Carol. "By the way, could you please tell me whether you have a Mr. Jasper Reijksen staying here?"

"Room twelve, south wing," muttered Nico, his attention already back on the game.

Carol headed for her room with a lighter heart. Not that she had seriously doubted Thor, but it still came as a relief to know that it could have been—in fact, she was sure now it must have been—Jasper that Margaret was talking about, and not Thor.

Carol knocked on Thor's door, but there was no answer. Apparently he had recovered sufficiently to go out. She rummaged in her bag for a piece of paper and a pen, scribbled a note saying she was back, and slipped it under his door.

A weak wash of late afternoon light filtered in through the window of her room. Carol tossed her briefcase onto the bed and kicked off her shoes as she went to close the curtains and switched on the bedside lamps. She was glad to see that Sotiropolous had replaced the old bulbs with new ones, that were bright enough to read by.

Carol was nearly undressed and heading for the shower when she heard a soft knocking on the door.

"Just a minute!" she called. Wrapping a short towel around herself, she opened the door with a warm, expectant smile.

"You have a telephone call at the desk," said Nico, staring at her frankly.

"Thanks—I'll be right there," said Carol. She gave him a bright smile to cover up her embarrassment, and hastily shut the door.

"Carol? It's Pat." Carol could barely hear her through the static on the line. "Thank God you're all right!"

"Hi, Pat," Carol half-shouted into the phone. "You'll have to speak up, it's a terrible connection. Of course I'm all right. Why, is something wrong?"

"We were worried sick about you when we heard about the accident. That car that went over the cliff Friday night. Didn't Jonathan tell you?"

"Jonathan?" asked Carol, surprised. "I haven't talked to him since I left Kobani. Did he try to call me?"

"We couldn't get through by phone, so he drove out to Mwatumi to check up on you. Didn't he find you at the hotel?"

"I've been out visiting Margaret Waiyala. Hang on, maybe he left a message."

At Carol's insistence, Nico checked all the pigeon holes and searched perfunctorily behind the desk, but came up with nothing.

"There's no message," said Carol. "Maybe he hasn't arrived yet."

"But he must have—he left before six this morning!. Maybe he's had an accident." Carol could hear the anxiety rising in Pat's voice.

"I'm sure you'd have heard something by now," said Carol, with a confidence she didn't entirely feel. "Someone would have reported it. He probably just had car trouble."

"I told him he should take one of the Embassy drivers, but he wouldn't listen," said Pat. "Jonathan is hopeless with cars. He can barely change a tire."

"He must have broken down and had to go get help somewhere along the road."

"I'm going to call the Embassy and get them to send someone out to look for him," said Pat. "I'd hate for him to have to spend the night in some fleabag *hoteli*."

"Good idea. Be sure to call me when he turns up," said Carol. "I'll feel better when I know for sure he's okay. I'm really sorry. I heard about the crash, but it never occurred to me you might think it was me. I could have sent you a radio message from the research station."

"As a matter of fact, we were pretty sure it wasn't you, Carol," said Pat. Her voice had suddenly become distinctly cooler.

"But then why did Jonathan want to come all the way out here to find me?"

"He thought you just might be interested to know that the name of the woman killed in the crash was Mrs. Simon."

For a moment they both listened to the crackling static. "So you know about all that," said Carol at last.

"Jonathan told me. Finally." There was no mistaking the hurt in Pat's voice.

"I guess I should have told you about it before."

"That would have been nice."

"It just seemed kind of silly—I didn't want to make a big thing of it and worry you over nothing." Carol's voice faded out. Even to her it sounded lame.

"We'll talk about it later," said Pat, briskly. "I think you'd better come back to Kobani right away. Jonathan still doesn't know what this is all about, but we're worried you could be in danger."

"You don't have to worry," said Carol. "I finally found out what's going on and everything's okay now."

There was a long burst of static. "What's that, Carol? Can you hear me?" said Pat. She seemed to be shouting but Carol could barely hear her.

"I said, 'don't worry, everything's okay'," shouted Carol. "It's too complicated to yell over the phone. I'll tell you all about it when Thor and I get back to Kobani tomorrow. Call me again when you've tracked Jonathan down, so I know he's okay. Bye."

Carol laid the receiver down and planted herself in front of Nico, purposely blocking his view of the television to make sure she had his attention.

"Did Mr. Nilssen happen to say when he's coming back?" she asked.

"He didn't say," grinned Nico knowingly. "Shall I tell him you were looking for him?"

"Yes, please," said Carol with all the dignity she could muster. She could feel Nico's smirk following her all the way across the lobby.

The door to Thor's room was open, but it was only the housemaid turning the bed down for the night. As Carol passed by on the way to her own room she saw two pieces of paper on the floor just inside the doorway. She recognized one as the note she had pushed under the door. After a brief and unequal struggle, curiosity triumphed over conscience and she picked up the second note and unfolded it gingerly. She read it and then reread it, bewilderment turning to dismay and then to anger as she realized it was Thor that Margaret had been talking about after all.

2

The overloaded Peugeot station wagon bottomed out with a painful scrape and came to a shuddering stop.

"Mwatumi!" shouted the driver unnecessarily, as the doors all popped open at once and the passengers started to pour out—far more of them than would have seemed possible.

Sharp pains shot through Muna's legs as her feet hit the ground and she felt the tingling stab of pins and needles as the blood began to trickle back into her numb arms and legs. She inhaled deeply, savoring her first breath of fresh air in over five hours. She had turned down the taxi driver's offer to ride in the front seat beside him, knowing he would have expected her to let him grope her the whole way in exchange. Instead she had squeezed into the rear seat with four other people, pressed so tightly together that they rose and fell as a single mass whenever the car hit a bump.

The afternoon was fading into dusk as Muna hurried up the road, shivering as she pulled her light cotton jacket tightly around her. She had forgotten how cold it got in the mountains when the sun went down. The tables in front of the Cock and Bull were empty and the deserted yard was dark and shadowy. It reminded her of a cemetery, with the white iron tabletops and chair legs gleaming like gravestones and bones in the pale light.

She walked around to the back, into a small dirt yard with a sagging wooden outhouse on the right and a tall rubbish heap on the left. At the far end was a row of squat, tin-roofed concrete blocks which the Cock and Bull advertised as guestrooms. Light leaked through the wooden window shutters and under the door of the last one on the right. Grimacing at the combined stench of outhouse and rubbish, Muna hurried across the yard and knocked sharply on the door.

A shadow appeared and paused behind the shutter as the occupant peeked through the window.

"What the hell are you doing here?" demanded Juma, as he threw the door open.

"Let me in, it's important," said Muna urgently. She pushed past him into the small room. It was cold and moldy, lit by a single bare bulb hanging from the ceiling and furnished with a narrow iron cot and a wormy wooden table and chair. Juma closed the door quickly behind her.

"Okay, you're in."

"Where's David?" asked Muna tensely.

"Up at the old church. Why, what's up?"

"You don't know?"

"Know what, for God's sake?"

"Mrs. Simon is dead!"

"What the hell are you talking about?"

"I think Maleke killed her."

Juma had never seen Muna like this—clenched and jittery, her voice shrill and tight. "No one's been killed," he said. "Mrs. Simon is fine. She's over at the Acropolis right now."

"That's not her, you idiot!"

"Of course it's her. Didn't I follow her here all the way from Nairobi?"

"That isn't the real Mrs. Simon. You made a mistake," snapped Muna, frustrated with the effort of trying to make him understand.

"You're bloody crazy!"

"I'm not crazy. Jonathan Marshall told me."

"Who the devil is he?"

"A friend of hers, from the American Embassy. He told me he knows all about you following her, thinking she's this Mrs. Simon, but she's not."

"Slow down, will you? You're not making any sense. Why was he telling you all this, anyway? How do you know him?"

Muna prevaricated quickly. "A friend of mine pointed him out at the Intercontinental and told me he was the one who got Yates out of prison. I thought I'd chat him up and see what I could get out of him, but then he turned around and started in on me! I'm sure he knows something."

"Sit down and pull yourself together. What did he say, exactly?"

Muna sat down on the bed and took a deep breath. "He said the woman you've been following isn't Mrs. Simon, and the real Mrs. Simon was dead. Then he said I should ask Maleke about what happened to her! He said it in a mean kind of way, you know, like a threat. How could he know that I even know Maleke?" Muna's voice trembled.

"No mystery there—everybody in Kobani knows you're shacked up with him," said Juma scornfully.

"And now Maleke is here in Mwatumi—I saw his car in the carpark at the Acropolis hotel. He didn't tell me he was coming here!"

"So he came to Mwatumi. Why shouldn't he come to Mwatumi? It's his home village isn't it?" asked Juma reasonably. "Did this Marshall say how Mrs. Simon was supposed to have been killed?"

"A car crash," said Muna. "But the way he said it, I could tell he was saying it wasn't an accident."

"Bloody hell!" exclaimed Juma softly. He flung himself into the chair, which creaked loudly under the impact.

"What is it?"

"A car went over a cliff near here on Friday," Juma said slowly. "Two people killed—an African driver and a white woman."

"You see! It's true!"

"We don't know that—it could have been anyone in that car," countered Juma.

Muna shook her head. "Marshall sounded like he knew what he was talking about."

"Maybe he was lying."

"Why would he do that?"

"How the hell do I know?" exploded Juma. He jumped to his feet and began pacing the cramped floor. Muna watched him anxiously.

When Juma spoke again he sounded more confident. "He's got to be lying, because I know for a fact that this woman we're onto is Mrs. Simon. Reijksen told me so himself, and he's the one who set up the whole deal in the first place."

"Then maybe he's the one who's lying."

"I know what I'm doing," snapped Juma. "We've been working together on this deal for more than a month now. If there was anything funny I would have found out by now."

"I'm sure that's what Reijksen thinks, too—about Mr. Singh," Muna said pointedly.

Juma glowered at her, but she stared him down and pushed her advantage. "I don't like it, Juma. I don't know how Marshall fits in, or what he knows, but I'm not taking any more chances. If there's any chance Maleke is onto us, we've got to call the whole thing off. I've got too much at stake."

"There's no need to get all worked up over nothing," said Juma reasonably. "Okay, so we don't know what this guy Marshall is up to, but there's no reason to start worrying about Maleke. He's got nothing to do with this."

Muna stared at her hands. Juma had no way of knowing that her real fear was whether Maleke might somehow have learned more than she had chosen to tell him.

"This guy Marshall probably just heard about the car crash and told you it was Mrs. Simon to see how you'd react. And he knew you're hooked up with Maleke, so he just threw that in to scare you," said Juma. "Believe me, there's nothing to worry about."

"That's easy enough for you to say, but it's gotten too risky for me. We've got to call it off."

"It's too late for that," said Juma firmly. "We've got the chimp and we're bringing it to her tonight."

"I don't care—let it go."

"You want to throw away five thousand U.S. dollars?" shouted Juma.

"Yes, if that's what it takes to stay alive," Muna returned hotly. "I've had a bad feeling about this *mzungu* from the start. How do you know he's not just setting you up?"

Juma sat down and leaned back in the chair, balancing it on its back legs. He slowly lit a cigarette, looking maddeningly pleased with himself.

"The secret in this business is always staying one step ahead of the other guy." He paused to take a few leisurely drags, blowing the smoke carelessly towards the ceiling and carefully tapping the ash off onto the floor as Muna bit her lip in exasperation.

"You don't think I was actually going to trust everything to Reijksen, do you?" continued Juma. "My plan all along was to go around him and deal with Mrs. Simon directly."

"I know that," Muna interrupted impatiently. "That's why you went to Nairobi. And I also know that when you contacted her there, she said she didn't know what you were talking about."

Juma scowled. "She knows, all right. Shut up and let me finish." He crossed his hands behind his head and the self-satisfied look returned to his face. "I've had a devil of a time getting to her without Reijksen spotting me—he stuck to her like a leech. But I guess he found out what I was up to somehow, because he warned me to lay off her. Anyway, he said now she won't deal with anyone but Singh himself. So I said I'd set it up. I let him stew for a couple of days, then today I told him Singh has agreed to meet the two of them at the Mountain View hotel in Bola tonight. That got him pretty excited—he's been trying to flush Singh out ever since he got here."

"But what's this all in aid of?" demanded Muna. "They'll go to Bola and Singh won't be there to meet them. After a while they'll get fed up and come back here."

"Stop interrupting. I haven't gotten to the best part." He told her about the note he had slipped under Carol's door. "Now it's up to her whether she tells Reijksen the truth or makes some excuse and lets him go to Bola without her."

"Good thinking," said Muna sarcastically. "This way they can both be mad when Singh doesn't show up in two places instead of one."

"Maybe Singh won't show up at her room tonight, but David and me will, with the bonobo. Once she's got her ape, why should she care about Singh anymore?"

"I suppose so...," said Muna doubtfully. She was still nervous, but Juma's confidence was reassuring. More importantly, his plan seemed to make sense. "What about the other European, the one who's been traveling with her? Who is he and how does he fit in?"

"I don't know," Juma admitted. "They're both working with her, but they don't seem to be working together. All the time I've been setting things up with Reijksen, Nilssen's been putting word out that he wants to meet with me himself. I asked Reijksen about him, but he wouldn't say anything except that I shouldn't meet with him. I think Nilssen's trying to squeeze Reijksen out."

"Do you still think it's the same man who called asking for Singh that day?" asked Muna.

"Got to be. Have you heard from him since then?"

"No."

"Right, because he's been out here. How else could he know about Singh, and where could he have gotten the phone number, except through her?"

"Maybe he'll be with her when you go to make the delivery."

"Or maybe she'll send them both off to Bola together. It's none of my business how she sorts out her boyfriends. All I care about is delivering the bonobo, getting our money and getting out. They can wait as long as they want for Singh to show up." Juma laughed appreciatively.

"What if they're not as patient as you think, or they figure out it's a trick?" asked Muna. "They might come back here too early."

Juma snapped his fingers. "You just gave me an idea. You take the car and go to Bola in case anyone shows up there. You can say you're Singh's personal assistant, and he sent you ahead to say he's been delayed but he's still coming. That way they'll stay and wait for him."

Muna stood up quickly, shaking her head. "I'm not going to be a decoy. What if they're putting together some kind of trap and I walk right into it?"

"Don't be stupid, there's not going to be any trap. And even if there was, it's Singh they'd be after, not you. All you have to do is keep them busy for an hour or so. Then you excuse

353

yourself to go to the Ladies, and just keep walking right out the back door."

"Well, if you're sure..." said Muna hesitantly.

"Of course I'm sure. There's nothing to it." Juma nodded encouragingly.

Muna stood up and smoothed her skirt. She had no intention of going anywhere near Bola, but there was no reason to tell Juma that.

"Okay," she said, holding out her hand. "Give me the car keys."

3

"Just a minute—I'm coming!"

Carol shivered on the cold tile floor as she toweled herself down hastily, thinking to herself that it never failed. There was nothing like getting into the shower to guarantee that the next sound you'd hear was a knock on the door. This time, though, she modestly pulled on her ankle-length *kitenga* before opening it.

Looking up and down the empty hallway, she nearly jumped out of her skin when the knocking suddenly started up again, coming from behind her. She spun around and was even more startled to see Thadeus Maleke at the patio door. He beckoned to her impatiently.

"Please let me in, it's very urgent," he said, when she reached the door. He was covered with red dust.

Carol hesitated. "Let me get dressed, and I'll meet you in the lobby in five minutes," she said.

"There is no time for that," insisted Maleke. "I have a message for you from Jonathan Marshall."

"Jonathan!" exclaimed Carol. "Where is he, is he all right?"

"Yes, but he needs your help." Maleke took Jonathan's note from his pocket and pressed it against the glass.

Carol read the note quickly and unbolted the door, letting Maleke slip inside. He immediately closed the door after him and drew the curtain shut.

"Popeye!" said Carol. "Jonathan's the only one who ever called me that."

"That was the intention—so you could have no doubt the note was genuine," said Maleke.

"But where is he? Pat just called—she's worried sick about him."

"He was abducted by Captain Kamanga's men, but I was able to find him and rescue him," said Maleke bluntly. Without giving her time to absorb this astonishing information, he immediately began to outline his plan.

"Wait a minute, what are you talking about?" Carol cut in sharply. "Jonathan's been *kidnapped*?" •

"He was on his way here to find you, when Kamanga's men stopped his car," explained Maleke impatiently. "Fortunately, I happened on the car hidden in some bushes, and I recognized it immediately. I was able to locate a witness who gave me a lead on where they had taken Jonathan. I've taken him to a safe place."

"But why?"

"It seems they think he has information about someone they're looking for. A man named Singh."

Carol went cold at the all-too-familiar name. "Oh, God, not again. Who the hell is this guy Singh, anyway?"

"A very dangerous criminal," answered Maleke shortly. "Please believe me, Mrs. Simmons, there really is no time to explain, and in any case you are better off not knowing anything more than is absolutely necessary. Kamanga has certainly discovered by now that Jonathan has escaped and he will be looking for him, and very likely for me as well. I have some things to attend to, but I will return as soon as it is dark, and give you my car so that you can return to Kobani. Jonathan will be waiting for you along the road."

Maleke told Carol where she would find Jonathan and how to signal him to come out of hiding. "I suggest you pack your things and be ready to leave instantly when I arrive," he said. "And you must tell no one that I have been here, or that you are leaving. It could be a matter of life or death." His tone and his manner were grave but calm, inspiring belief and confidence. She found she wanted to put herself in his hands.

"Can I at least call Pat and tell her Jonathan's all right?" she asked.

"No, I'm sorry, that's not possible. Their telephone line may be tapped," said Maleke matter-of-factly.

"What about Thor?" Carol asked suddenly. "We came here together. I can't just take off without letting him know."

Maleke frowned. "He of all people must not suspect anything is amiss," he said emphatically. "Tell him you are unwell and going to sleep early, and you will see him in the morning. Forgive me for being direct, but he does have a separate room?"

"Yes, of course he does," said Carol, realizing with annoyance that she was blushing. "But I don't understand. Why Thor 'of all people'?"

Maleke hesitated, as though deciding how much to say. "I know you will find this difficult to accept, Mrs. Simmons, but I'm afraid I must tell you that Mr. Thor Nielssen is not who he says he is."

"Who is he then?" demanded Carol.

Maleke looked at her appraisingly. "I see you do believe me," he remarked. "In fact, you are hardly even surprised. Has something happened to make you suspect him?"

It was Carol's turn to hesitate. Maleke's tone had taken on an edge of eagerness that she found disquieting. Jonathan's note said to trust him, but she remembered Jasper saying scornfully that Maleke had Jonathan eating out of his hand. She had also mistrusted Maleke instinctively at their first meeting, even before Lisa's warning about the 'dudu in the mango.' So why was she so ready now to believe his incredible story about

356

rescuing Jonathan from Captain Kamanga? And yet, if it wasn't true, why had Jonathan written the note, and why was Maleke here at all? There must be some truth in it, but not necessarily the whole truth. It reminded her of Thor's story of the native at the crossroads, and the circumstances in which he had told it, and she felt a rush of warmth and loyalty toward him.

"No, nothing," she said. "I was just asking what you know about him."

"I see," said Maleke tersely. "We don't yet know who he is, but we have established that he entered Rumura using a false passport, and he has had repeated contacts with known criminals since he has been here. It is my belief that he may be involved with Singh in some way."

"I find that very hard to believe," said Carol, but her voice lacked conviction. It was the one thing she had hoped Maleke wouldn't say, forcing her to recall her shock and dismay on reading the note she had found under Thor's door. Whatever Thor was up to, he had certainly lied to her, letting her believe he had no idea who Singh was, and certainly never letting on that he was going to meet him tonight. That didn't prove he was a poacher or anything else, and she wasn't about to betray him to Maleke here and now. But she couldn't deny the doubts gnawing at her mind, and she knew she wouldn't tell Thor about Maleke either, at least not until he had explained himself.

Maleke seemed satisfied. He told her to expect him in about two hours, and left abruptly by the back door.

4

The car threw up a cloud of dust as it pulled up in front of the tidy thorn fence around Margaret Waiyala's compound. The excited children had already run inside to fetch Margaret, and a small crowd of curious neighbors had begun to gather even before Maleke got out.

"Let's go inside," Maleke suggested to Margaret in a low voice after acknowledging their greetings. "I must talk with you privately."

Margaret took his arm and led him into the house, shooing the children back outside when they tried to follow. Maleke softened their disappointment by passing out a handful of brightly wrapped sweets before disappearing inside.

"You didn't tell us you were coming," Margaret scolded her brother. "I haven't prepared anything. Let me make some tea."

"Never mind," said Maleke, "this isn't a social call." He sat down at the table.

Margaret sank into the chair across from him and waited silently for what had to be bad news.

"Where is David?" asked Maleke.

"I haven't seen him since morning," said Margaret. "Why, what's wrong? What has he done?"

"You must tell me the truth," said Maleke sternly. "He's in danger, and it won't help to hide him from me."

"It is the truth," said Margaret. Her voice was tense and worried, but somehow resigned. "What kind of trouble is he in?"

"I didn't say trouble, I said danger. This is very serious."

"I don't know what to tell you. He disappeared right after breakfast, and he didn't tell me where he was going. He never does anymore."

"Was he with anyone?" insisted Maleke.

"No, but I suppose he's probably gone somewhere with that Juma Ayala. They were here together last night, and David was hinting about some big business they're doing together. I've warned him a thousand times to stay away from that trouble-maker, but he doesn't listen."

"Ayala is trouble, all right," agreed Maleke. "I suppose I should have come around more often, taken David in hand, forbidden him to have anything to do with him."

"It would be good if you would come more often," agreed Margaret. "Or maybe you could take David to stay in town with

358

you for awhile. He's only hungry for guidance. He needs a model to follow, and now he thinks it is Juma. But you can give him another model."

"We'll have to see about that later," said Maleke shortly. "For now, I have to find the young idiot before he's thrown into prison or gets his head blown off."

"Oh!" cried Margaret, pressing her fists to her mouth in dismay.

"No, now don't get upset, it's not as bad as all that," said Maleke, trying to calm her. "I'm just out of temper with the boy, that's all. He's gotten himself mixed up with some nonsense and I want to warn him to get out before there's trouble."

"But he could go to prison?" demanded Margaret.

"When I get through with him, he'll wish he had," said Maleke brusquely.

Margaret smiled gratefully. Her brother was a big man in Kobani, big enough to take care of David if he got himself into trouble. Of course, David would have to be punished and set firmly back on the right path, but that was family business. Prison was for truly evil men, criminals who robbed and killed people, not for misguided but decent and God-fearing boys like David.

Maleke stood up. "I'm going out now to look for David. If he should happen to come home, you must make certain he stays here. I don't care what you tell him or what you do. Hide his pants if you have to, but keep him at home tonight."

As Maleke left the house, he saw three figures standing beside his car. The crowd of neighbors were staring at them from a respectful distance. He quelled the instinct to turn around and go back inside. There was no escape in that direction. He straightened his shoulders and his tie and approached the car nonchalantly.

"Good afternoon, *Doctor*. What a surprise to see you again so soon."

"Good afternoon, Captain. The pleasure is mine." Maleke stopped as Kamanga stepped forward, casually placing himself between Maleke and the car.

"Dropping by for a little family visit? How nice." Kamanga's smile was more of a sneer.

"I had some business to discuss with my sister," said Maleke. He brushed past Kamanga to the car and put his hand on the door handle. He studiously ignored the other men flanking the car, but had recognized them immediately as two of Kamanga's henchmen, not police officers but brutish "irregulars." The neighbors had recognized them too, and were whispering uneasily amongst themselves.

"What a coincidence," remarked Kamanga. "I also have some business to discuss with your sister. I wonder, could it be the same business?"

"I doubt it," said Maleke mildly. "I don't imagine you could have any interest in the price I got for the sunflower seeds I sold for her in town last week."

"You're quite right there, Doctor. I'm not interested in your sister's sunflowers. It's her son I want." He chuckled at his own joke.

"He's not in." Maleke unlatched the car door and opened it a few inches.

"Are you sure?" Kamanga took a step closer and Maleke stopped again. "Maybe he just didn't want to see you right now. Maybe he's hiding under the blankets in his sleeping hut, or under his mother's bed."

"He's not in, and Margaret doesn't know where he is," said Maleke firmly.

"You won't mind if I ask her that myself? You never know, something might just come to her, if the question is put in the right way."

One of the henchman showed a set of yellow teeth in a cruel grin.

"Leave her alone, she doesn't know anything," repeated Maleke stiffly.

Kamanga sighed deeply and spat on the ground between their feet. "It's a funny thing, *Doctor*. I just can't get it out of my head that someone around here has to know something. And it's very frustrating for my boys. They're ready to get some answers out of somebody. Now, who's it going to be?"

Maleke looked at him distastefully. "Get in the car," he said at last. "We can't talk out here."

Kamanga signaled his men to stay where they were and went around to the other side of the car. They both climbed in and slammed the doors shut.

"All right, talk," said Kamanga.

"My sister doesn't know anything, but I managed to contact David earlier," Maleke said reluctantly. "He didn't want to talk, but I forced him to tell me. They're meeting Singh tonight."

"Where?"

"I need your word David won't come to any harm. Otherwise I won't tell you anything. I don't care what you and your goons do to me."

"Don't be so dramatic, Maleke. I don't want to hurt you or your fool nephew. Singh's the one we're after. As far as I'm concerned, David can slip away in the confusion and no one has to know he was even there."

"I have your word?"

"Isn't that what I just said?" snapped Kamanga. "Now stop testing my patience and get on with it."

"David said they're meeting Singh up at the German fort tonight," said Maleke.

"What time?"

"He didn't know. This Singh seems to be a very cautious man. He told them to get up there as soon as it's dark and wait for him. All night if need be."

"He expects them to wait for him all night? Thinks a lot of himself, doesn't he?"

Maleke shrugged. "That's what he told them. If you get up there ahead of them, while it's still light, you can set up an ambush."

Kamanga looked at him for a moment and then started to chuckle. The chuckle turned into a belly laugh. "A very good suggestion, Doctor," he wheezed. "A great idea. We'll get up there right away and set up an ambush. And then we'll wait right there for as long as it takes—all night, if need be. That's what you said, isn't it?"

"That's what Singh told them," said Maleke.

"Only I'm going to make the plan even better," said Kamanga. The laughter had gone out of his voice. "You're coming up there with us."

Maleke's face was calm. "I'd only be in the way."

"You're coming, all right," snapped Kamanaga. "And for your sake, Singh better show up. It would be too bad if we waited there all night for nothing. Then my boys would really be frustrated."

Kamanga rolled his window down and shouted at the men to get in the car. They climbed into the back seat and sat staring ahead impassively.

"Drive," said Kamanga.

CHAPTER 28

1

There were only three two-story houses in Mwatumi, and two of them belonged to Police Commissioner Gideon Karibani. One he had built for his father, and the other for his first wife and family. His town wife had never set foot inside it, just as his village wife had never been to his sprawling estate in the suburbs of Kobani. As a native son who had made good, he was expected to make a show of his wealth, just as he was expected to contribute generously to local funds drives for scholarships and funeral expenses. No one ever questioned how he had managed to afford all this on a civil servant's salary, except quietly and among highly trusted friends.

Sunk deep into a richly upholstered armchair with a tall glass of his favorite lukewarm Green Mountain beer in his hand, Captain Kamanga should have been comfortable and content, perhaps lost in a daydream of owning a house like this himself someday. Instead he was wilting under the icy glint of the gold-rimmed glasses resting on Karibani's round, schoolmaster's cheeks. A few short hours ago he had been basking in the glow of the Commissioner's grudging approval of his planning and execution of Jonathan Marshall's abduction. But now he had been forced to confess that Marshall had disappeared.

"I swear on my mother's grave, sir-there's no way he escaped by himself. I don't know how anyone could've found him so fast. Nobody saw anything—my men made sure of that."

Karibani cleared his throat impatiently.

"But he won't get far, sir, I promise you that. I've got my men watching every road and trail and cowpath out of here. We'll get him." "I'm sure you will," Karibani said. It was not a reassurance, but a warning.

"Yes, sir," declared Kamanga briskly. "But as I said, we don't even really need Marshall anymore, now that Maleke's told us where to find Singh tonight."

"Ah, yes, this supposed meeting at the German fort. You're saying you believe him?" asked Bashega acerbically.

"Of course I understand he could be lying sir," said Kamanga, wounded. "But I warned him what would happen to him if it turned out he was trying to trick me, and he's had a couple hours cooling his heels in my office to think about it. He hasn't backed down from his story yet."

"All right, check it out, but I'm still expecting you to find Marshall before he manages to contact anyone in Kobani. And the same goes for the Simmons woman and her boyfriend, and all the rest of them. It's your responsibility to make sure none of them leaves Mwatumi or communicates with Kobani until tomorrow morning."

Kamanga waited for Bashega to go on and say something about the importance of making sure nothing interfered with tonight's meeting, but as usual, his superior failed to confide in him. Through his own channels, Kamanga had long ago discovered the identity of Bashega's secretive Zairean partner, and he knew they were meeting tonight to discuss arrangements for transporting the latest load of contraband that Kamanga himself had helped to assemble. It irked him more and more that Bashega persisted in treating him as nothing but hired muscle.

"If you do make contact with Singh, bring him here to meet me," said Bashega off-handedly. "But wait until Delacroix has gone."

Kamanga acknowledged the instructions with an equally casual nod and stood up to go. He had witnessed the disrespect with which Delacroix increasingly treated the Commissioner, and had been wondering how long he was going to put up with it. If Bashega didn't want Delacroix and Singh to meet, it might be because he was in the market for a new partner. Recognizing the value of this information, he filed it away with silent satisfaction.

2

At exactly nine thirty, Juma left his hut behind the Cock and Bull and slipped quietly out of the courtyard. Sanjit Dawari's small Toyota pickup truck was waiting for him in a narrow, garbage-strewn alley a few yards away. Joseph had passed him the spare keys earlier in the day in exchange for five hundred *rimands*, along with pointers on coaxing the old truck into life and a flood of anxious warnings to bring it back before daylight, and without adding to its already extensive collection of scratches and dents. Juma had promised to cherish the truck as though it were his own child. Fortunately, Joseph had no idea how much Juma disliked children.

Juma wrestled the front seat forward as far as it would go and cranked the tired old engine until it finally caught and turned over. He drove slowly to the end of the alley and turned left onto the main road. He chose the long way around to avoid passing in front of the Cock and Bull, just in case Dawari should happen to glance out the window at the wrong moment. Soon the truck was straining and jolting up the steep, rocky track into the darkened hills, following the narrow beam of its faded headlights.

The road ended about two hundred yards from the old mission. Juma climbed out and wedged a rock behind one wheel to hold the truck in place on the steep slope. He walked the rest of the way quickly, guided by the light of a gas lantern shining through the cracks between the boards of the wooden shack behind the ruins of the church.

Juma rapped sharply on the door. "It's me," he said. "Let's go."

"Come in, but be careful," came David's voice from inside. "Don't let the bloody thing out."

"What!" Juma slipped through the door and closed it quickly behind him.

David was standing in the middle of the floor just under a large hole in the roof. He held a long stick in one hand and a limp loop of twine in the other. The cardboard box lay on its side behind him, gaping open. In the far corner, a pair of unblinking eyes reflected the yellow light of the lantern.

"What the hell!"

"I couldn't hear anything inside the box, so I opened it just a crack to take a look," said David. "The bloody thing charged out at me like a rocket."

"You let it out?" demanded Juma. "Why didn't you grab it?"

"Have you seen the teeth on that thing?" responded David in an injured tone. "I've tried to catch him, but every time I move away from here he makes a break for the hole."

"Jesus, can't I trust you to do anything?" groaned Juma. "It's bad enough we had to settle for this mangy thing in the first place. Come on, give me the bloody stick."

"I need the stick in case he jumps me," protested David. "Here, you take the rope."

"What do you want me to do with that bloody piece of string? Stay there—I'll go get another stick."

Juma slipped out the door and came back a few moments minutes later, carrying a length of rusty iron pipe. He hefted it with satisfaction. "Let's see him try to sink his teeth into this."

Juma picked up the box and started to edge toward the corner, holding the pipe out in front of him. The shining black eyes watched him closely and a low snarling sound filled the shack. When he was about five feet away, Juma put the box down and used his foot to slide it toward the wall, open end forward. Meanwhile, he waved the pipe back and forth in a menacing way and rapped it on the ground. Suddenly the huddled animal burst from the corner and shot across the floor, brushing against Juma, who leaped backward with a startled yelp. By the time he turned around it was already glaring at him from the opposite wall of the shack.

"That's showing him," crowed David.

"Shut up," hissed Juma, raising the pipe menacingly.

For an hour they tried to maneuver their quarry into the box. Finally, the frustrated Juma dropped his stick, charged straight at the startled animal, and simply threw the box over it. David dropped his stick and ran over with the twine. They quickly tied the box closed and sagged against the wall, listening to the furious scratching and shrieking from inside the box. After a while the sounds stopped.

Juma held his watch up to the lantern. "Bloody hell, it's nine thirty," he exclaimed. "It'll take at least half an hour to get back to town. Reijksen and Nilssen will probably be back from Bola already."

"It's not my fault," muttered David defensively. "I was just checking to see if it was dead."

"Shut up and put the bloody thing into the truck," said Juma. "Let's get this over with."

3

Gideon Bashega saw no reason to let Delacroix know Jonathan Marshall was temporarily at large. He had had more than enough of the little Frenchman's pained expressions and reproachful tongue-clucking, and all his other patronizing mannerisms. "They won't be causing any trouble," he answered brusquely, when Delacroix asked him what he had done about Marshall, Carol Simmons, Thor Nilssen and Thadeus Maleke.

"I have no doubt, *mon vieux*," responded Delacroix, "but you will not mind providing me with the details? Simply to set my mind at rest, *n'est-ce pas?*"

"We agreed it is for me to take care of things, this side," bristled Bashega.

"*Vraiment*," agreed Delacroix coolly. "But you will understand my excessive caution, in light of the circumstances." He pulled a folded paper from the breast pocket of his jacket and handed it to Bashega.

Bashega unfolded the paper and glanced over it quickly. "Where did you get this?" he asked.

"From my contact in the American Embassy in Nairobi," said Delacroix. "Such contacts are a necessity in our business."

"It doesn't say who it's from," frowned Bashega, studying the paper.

"Your concern is with the receiver, rather than with the sender," admonished Delacroix. "It is not the best of news to learn that one's activities have attracted the interest of the authorities."

Bashega examined the paper again. "It doesn't say that, either."

"Allow me to enlighten you," said Delacroix dryly. "This highly confidential document is addressed to the Director of the Fish and Wildlife Service of the United States of America."

"How do you know that?" demanded Bashega.

"It is my business to know, as it is my business to be familiar with their clumsy code. This letter reveals that a certain informant has taken it upon himself to advise the Director of the existence of an illegal trade in ivory and other animal products across the border of the DRC and Rumura. From the details provided, the informant appears quite knowledgeable. Furthermore, it appears that a Fish and Wildlife Service agent has already been dispatched from Washington to Rumura to investigate the matter."

"Who is it?" demanded Bashega, glaring at the paper.

"Even the Americans are not so foolish as to put such information on paper," said Delacroix. "The identity of the informant is of course also not revealed. We do, however, find here the code words by which the agent and the informant are to recognize one another when they meet here in Mwatumi."

Bashega followed his finger and saw two words circled in red. "Jonathan Marshall!" he exclaimed suddenly.

"Henh?"

"Marshall must be the American agent. That's why he was coming to Mwatumi, to meet the informant here tonight."

"Really, *mon vieux*," Delacroix snapped impatiently. "How is it possible for Marshall to be this man from Washington, when he himself lives in Kobani? No, it is that he is connected, but in another way. Have you not yourself many times said you suspect him to be an agent of the CIA?"

"Then who else?" asked Bashega. "Not the woman?"

Delacroix shook his head decidedly. "If it were so, would she have allowed herself to attract so much attention? Surely she is being used as a lure, a 'red herring' to confuse us and distract us. In the meantime, the real agent remains hidden in the background, watching and awaiting his opportunity."

Delacroix looked at Bashega expectantly, but saw no glimmer of realization dawning. "Surely you have guessed," he prompted. "Who is it that is heard of everywhere and yet is to be seen nowhere? Who but the elusive Mr. Singh? *Voila*—the mystery of Singh is solved. He is a ruse, an invention of the United States government."

Bashega appraised Delacroix thoughtfully. "It makes sense," he said slowly. "How else could he have appeared so suddenly out of nowhere, when nobody has even heard of him before?"

"*Exactement!*" exclaimed Delacroix triumphantly. "It is now so clear that we can only ask of ourselves, how is it we were so foolish not to see it long before? However, it is not yet too late. As our American friend would certainly say, the ship has not yet left the dock. According to my information, the so-called 'Mr. Singh' will indeed be here in Mwatumi tonight, to meet with his informant. It remains only for you to find him and...dispose of the matter."

Bashega observed with interest that the Frenchman's round face was red with excitement, and wondered whether he realized he was rubbing his plump hands together. "Dispose of the matter?" he echoed dryly.

"As you yourself said, *mon ami*, it is for you to remove obstacles that arise here in Rumura, while I address myself to the overseas side. I am confident you have the means at hand?"

369

"Are you telling me to kill them?"

Delacroix clucked his tongue reprovingly. "I am telling you to ensure they do not interfere any further with our business."

"As I did with Yates?" suggested Bashega.

"Really, *mon vieux*, you know that I have no interest in the details," Delacroix said stiffly. He placed his brandy snifter deliberately on the coffee table and with some difficulty extricated himself from the deep armchair. "And now, you will pardon me. Monsieur Muhwenazi will have arrived already from Congo and will be expecting me."

"Don't you mean, expecting us?" demanded Bashega.

"I will give him your apologies," said Delacroix. "You have other pressing matters to attend to."

Bashega smiled grimly to himself in the doorway as he watched Delacroix' car disappear through the gate. Based on five years of uneasy partnership with the devious Frenchman, he was inclined to suspect that the coded letter and the whole ridiculous story were nothing but Delacroix' clumsy attempt to discredit Singh, whom he clearly perceived as an intruder and a threat. Galling as it was to play into Delacroix' perceptions of himself as a dull-witted native pawn, pretending to swallow it gave Bashega the upper hand. Of course, there was always the remote possibility that the story was true, but that would be simple enough to check once Kamanga brought the man to him. Depending on his reaction to the word 'evergreen,' Singh would either become his new partner, or his next victim.

4

Greg unfolded his aching legs and stood up, stamping his feet to get the blood flowing back into them. The night covered the hill like a black woolen blanket, the moon barely visible as a dull glow behind the clouds. The only signs of life were the bats squeaking and swooping overhead and crickets serenading each other on every side. His clothes were cold and clammy from the mist that was settling into a fog. The black stocking cap kept his head warm, but his feet were freezing.

He looked at the illuminated dial of his watch. A few minutes to ten. He had been up on the hillside overlooking the Acropolis for nearly four hours. Reijksen had arrived at about six thirty and hadn't left again. Bergen had left at about seven thirty and hadn't returned yet. Otherwise there had been nothing to see, nothing to report. He sat back down on the cold, rocky ground, shifting around to find the least uncomfortable spot.

A few minutes later he checked his watch again and pulled the compact 2-way radio out of his shirt pocket. He raised the slender antenna and pressed the transmit button.

"Come in, Mick-Pick, this is Suzuki One. Come in, Mick-Pick, do you read me? Over."

"Greg? Where are you calling from?" Lisa's voice was so clear she could have been standing right next to him.

"In Mwatumi."

"But you're coming in so clear!"

"I know, can you believe it? It's this radio Bergen gave me. It weighs about six ounces and it's got a range of more than a hundred kilometers. And you should see the night-vision binoculars. You've got to hand it to these guys."

"Is anything happening?"

"Nothing except I'm freezing my ass off."

"Why don't you come home, then? I hate the idea of you up there on your own."

"I will," promised Greg. "As soon as Bergen gets back I'm going to tell him I'm calling it a night."

Suddenly he spotted a pair of dim, yellowish headlights in the blackness below, pulling into the loading area behind the hotel. "Gotta go now, honey. Don't worry. Over and out."

Greg hastily picked up the binoculars and focused them. Two men were getting out of a small white pick-up truck. He studied them carefully as they went around to the back of the truck and unloaded a large cardboard box. Trying to hold the binoculars steady with one hand, he used the other to flick the switch on the radio to the security channel.

"Come in Papa Bear. This is Allen. Do you read me, Bergen? Over."

"Allen, this is Bergen. I read you. What's up?"

"Two guys just pulled up at the Acropolis in a pickup truck and unloaded a box from the back. I'm pretty sure one of them is Juma Ayala."

"Shit!" Bergen's voice exploded from the radio. "I can't believe what an ass I've been. All right, I'm on my way back. Stay on the line and tell me what you see."

Over the radio Greg heard the sound of a car engine starting up and the squeal of tires making a sharp turn.

"They're walking towards the back of the hotel, carrying the box," he said. "They could be heading towards Carol's room, but it's hard to make out anything from up here. I'm going in closer."

"Stay out of sight, Allen," warned Bergen. "Don't do anything till I get there."

"Don't worry. I just want to get a better look." Greg switched off the radio before Bergen could protest and slipped it back inside his shirt pocket. He put the heavy binoculars inside his backpack and stashed it beneath a bush. He held onto his flashlight, but left it off as he began feeling his way through the darkness down the steep slope.

After several minutes he reached the dense cypress hedge bordering the Acropolis' back yard. He followed the hedge until he found a small gap he could peer through and get a view of Carol's patio. He pressed in closer, using his hands to spread the stiff branches as far as he could to widen the gap. The short, sharp needles caught in his cap and beard and poked into his ears, but he didn't notice them as he concentrated on trying to see into the dimly lit yard. He also didn't notice the soft pad of footsteps behind him. For one fleeting instant he did notice the explosion of pain in his head. Then he slumped face down into the prickly arms of the cypress.

CHAPTER 29

1

Finding herself reading the same paragraph of her novel for the fifth time, Carol snapped it shut with a sigh. The night seemed eerily quiet. Even the chorus of crickets and frogs seemed to be taking an intermission. She glanced at her watch again. Almost ten o'clock. Ten minutes since she had last checked, and almost three hours since darkness had fallen and Maleke was supposed to return.

She had packed quickly as soon as he'd left, meanwhile rehearsing her speech to Thor about not feeling up to dinner and wanting to turn in early. As it turned out, she didn't get a chance to use it. Thor had stopped by at about seven thirty and immediately launched into the same speech himself, almost word for word, smiling ruefully as he complained of a griping stomach. She had pretended to be sympathetic, hiding the hurt and anger of knowing that he was really on his way to meet Singh.

Carol slouched down in the armchair, propped her feet up on the bed and stared restlessly at the flaking paint on the wall across the room. She had never noticed how many cracks there were, and how much they looked like rivers on a map. As she traced them upward, her eye caught on a small, shiny spot about a foot below the ceiling.

She was standing up to take a closer look, when the silence was suddenly shattered by a sharp, staccato rapping on the patio door behind the closed curtains.

"It's about time," she exclaimed, as she hastily unbolted the door and swung it open. "Where have you been?"

Instead of Maleke, she found herself looking into the protruding eyes of the small, dark man from the garden of the Intercontinental, the one she now knew was called Juma. He was holding one side of a large, battered cardboard box. On the other side was a tall, thin young African, who seemed vaguely familiar. Before she could react and slam the door shut they had carried the reeking box inside.

"What do you think you're doing?" demanded Carol. "Get out of my room."

"You told them both to go away, yes," Juma observed with satisfaction, glancing around the room.

"What are you talking about? Told who to go away? No, don't bother, I don't want to hear it. Just get out, right now."

"We have your merchandise here, Mrs. Simon. You only pay us and we go. Five thousand U.S. dollars."

A sense of unreality swept over Carol, as if she were in a dream, or watching a scene unfolding on a movie screen. Her voice sounded strange and detached. "I don't believe this," she shouted. "How many times do I have to tell you I'm not—"

"It's all right, Carol, I will take over now." Jasper walked briskly in from the adjoining room, shutting the connecting door firmly behind him. He was cool and self-assured, completely in command. Carol sat slowly down on the bed, her initial astonishment turning to cold anger as she began to understand what Jasper had done.

Jasper turned to Juma, his eyes narrowed in annoyance. "Where is Singh?"

"In Bola, as I told you," said Juma. "He will be very cross you did not go to meet him."

"Like hell he is," said Jasper. "You didn't think I would really fall for that stupid trick, did you, Ayala?"

Juma flashed a wide, nervous grin. "Now we do not need Singh anyway," he said quickly. "The bonobo is here." He indicated the box.

"You weren't supposed to get it yet, you damned idiot," snapped Jasper. "We haven't finished negotiating the terms."

"Five thousand U.S. dollars. You give us and you take him, yes. Finished."

"As easy as that, is it? Where are the papers?"

"The papers?" Juma's grin faded slightly.

"I thought so. You have no idea what I'm talking about, do you? I don't suppose your boss has ever told you about customs stamps, or veterinary clearances, or export licenses and CITES certificates. Then let me give you a free business lesson. This animal is worthless to us without the official papers to transport it. That is all to be arranged by the seller."

Juma scowled to cover his dismay and thought quickly. "Mr. Singh will bring them to you tomorrow in Kobani. That is how we always do."

"Bullshit. The papers are part of the deal. No one would pay until they have been delivered as well. And the signatures had better be authentic. If they're forgeries, the price goes down by half."

"Mr. Singh always brings the papers after," insisted Juma. He pointedly turned away from Jasper and addressed Carol. "But maybe we can make a special case for you, because you are American. Mr. Singh has told me he wants to have more business with Americans. You give me only half the money now to show you are serious, and I can bring to Mr. Singh and give him your proposal."

Jasper cut in before Carol could speak. "We are not paying a penny until we get those papers. And tell Mr. Singh we're through dealing with go-betweens. Either he comes here himself by tomorrow, or we take our business elsewhere."

"You do not know Mr. Singh," protested Juma shaking his head gravely. "How can I go to him without some little money at least? If you give me nothing I must take the bonobo away with me now for another buyer. There is one European who wants it very much. He has called Mr. Singh many times. Give me one thousand only, and maybe I can hold it for you."

"You want a down payment? Here." Jasper pulled out his wallet and handed Juma two one hundred dollar bills. "For this much, I can buy two baby bonobos in any village in the DRC. Mr. Singh knows that as well as I do. The bonobo will stay here as security for the money."

Juma looked at the bills distastefully and started to protest again.

"No more arguments," said Jasper icily. "This is becoming tiresome. Take the money or take the animal, but get out of here before I throw you out."

Juma glowered but took the money. "Mr. Singh will be very cross," he warned darkly. "You think you are very smart, but you are very stupid."

"Out!"

Juma jerked his chin at David and stalked out the door. David hurried after him, jostling him in the doorway in his eagerness to get out.

As soon as they had gone, Jasper turned and kicked the desk chair viciously, sending it skidding across the floor.

"*Verdomme!*" he swore.

Carol stood up to confront him, her teeth and fists clenched. "Just who the hell do you think you are—" she began.

Jasper turned away with an impatient gesture.

"Don't give me that—" said Carol, stepping around in front of him again. "I demand an explanation."

Suddenly they heard the sound of scuffling outside and several loud, dull thuds, each followed by a sharp cry. A moment later a man's voice shouted something harshly and there were two sharp, explosive pops like a car backfiring.

"My God, what's that?" Carol started quickly toward the noise.

Jasper pushed past her and reached the door first. He stopped in the doorway to listen, then took a step outside. He was immediately knocked backwards into the room, barely keeping his feet as David came stumbling in, propelled by a hard push from a tall, beefy man wearing a black cloth hood over his head. He was followed by another, smaller man dressed the same way. Only their eyes and mouths were visible through jagged holes in the hoods. The big man was carrying a double-barreled shotgun. He snarled, displaying long, crooked yellow teeth slanting sharply sideways. The smaller man held a long, curved *panga* in his right hand, which was missing two fingers.

David scrambled across the room on his knees and one hand, his other arm dragging limply alongside him. He pressed himself into a corner, cradling his injured right arm against his chest. Blood streamed from his nose and cuts on his cheeks and mouth and soaked into his shirt. One eye was beginning to swell shut, while the other was wide open in shock.

"My God, what have you done to him?" Instinctively Carol rushed over and crouched in front of him. He didn't seem to see her, but kept moaning softly to himself.

Three Fingers snarled out a few harsh words in Rumuran and David fell silent.

"You come," Crooked Teeth barked in English, gesturing toward Carol with the barrel of the shotgun. Carol stood up slowly and went to stand next to Jasper, who seemed frozen in place.

"The money," continued Crooked Teeth. "You give me."

Carol looked at Jasper, half expecting to see the familiar smug, knowing expression on his face. He looked as astonished as she was.

"The money!" Crooked Teeth shouted again, waving the gun at them menacingly. Carol swallowed hard and tried to steady her voice. "Take it easy, I'll give you money," she said as calmly as she could. "See, I'm getting it..."

Moving slowly, she went over to the desk and picked up her purse. She removed her wallet, careful to keep her every move visible, and held it out to him. "There's about ten thousand rimands and three hundred dollars," she said. "That's all I've got."

He took the wallet, flipped it open and glanced inside. With one hand he dexterously lifted out the bills and stuffed them into the front pocket of his pants. Then, to her dismay, he spat out a curse, threw the wallet onto the floor and started to close in on her. She backed away from him until her back was pressed against the wall.

"The money!" he said again. "Five thousand dollar."

"So that's it," Jasper exclaimed softly. "They want the money you were supposed to pay for the bonobo. They must be Singh's men. I knew he would be watching Ayala."

Crooked Teeth's glaring eyes and the barrel of the gun shifted to him.

"Singh, yes? You work for Mr. Singh?" asked Jasper.

"You quiet!" The man turned his attention back to Carol and moved forward until his face was inches away from hers. His eyes gleamed from the shadows beneath his hood. "You give me."

Carol spread her hands, palms up. "I don't have any more," she said desperately. "See? No more. It's all a mistake." She somehow managed to dredge up a few words of Rumuran. "*Se nani*—I don't have."

Crooked Teeth took a step back, keeping the gun fixed on her chest, and barked a few words. Three Fingers nodded and grabbed Carol's purse from the desk. He dumped its contents onto the bed and rifled through them, then did the same with her briefcase. He pulled out the drawers of the desk and emptied them out onto the floor. Yanking open the door of the wardrobe, he found it was empty. Growling something under his breath, he turned and found the suitcase and struggled briefly with the latch until he realized that it was locked. He tried to slice open the side with the *panga*, but the thick canvas wouldn't give way. He stood back and pointed the *panga* at Carol and then at the suitcase.

Carol's fingers stumbled over the tiny tumblers of the lock, but she finally managed to turn it to the right combination and snap the latches open. Three Fingers shoved her aside and started to pull out her clothes and toss them in a pile on the floor, as the three of them watched. His eyes lit up briefly when he found her short wave radio, which he quickly pocketed.

Finding nothing in the suitcase, he went over to the bed and tore the covers off. Finally, he slashed the mattress a few times with the *panga*, he straightened up and shrugged.

Crooked Teeth growled something hoarsely and waved the shotgun toward Jasper. Tucking the panga under his arm, Three Fingers went over to Jasper and started searching him, running his hands up and down his legs and torso and digging into his pockets. Jasper stood stiff and resentful, but said nothing.

Carol felt a queasy knot in the pit of her stomach as Crooked Teeth spoke again and gestured toward her. She stared straight ahead and set her teeth, determined not to give them the satisfaction of seeing her recoil as Three Fingers grinned and walked over to her. He stood very close and put his hands on her waist and started moving them upward with a patting motion. When he reached her shoulders, he started back down again.

As one of his hands closed over her breast, there was a loud crash as the hallway door seemed to explode inward.

"Drop it!"

Carol felt a dizzying wave of relief as Three Fingers jumped backwards and she saw Thor braced in the doorway. Then she saw the cold, blue-black glint of the pistol in his hand.

"I said drop the gun," Thor repeated, with a quick upward jerk of the pistol. His voice was flat and hard, and the Norwegian accent had disappeared.

Crooked Teeth grabbed Jasper by the neck and pulled him in front of his body like a shield. The shotgun was now pointed at Thor. Out of the corner of her eye, Carol saw Three Fingers making a grab for her. Instinctively she threw herself to the floor and rolled quickly out of reach. As he dived after her, she lashed out with her foot and caught him under the chin, snapping his head sharply backwards. He fell back against Jasper's legs for a moment, then got up onto his hands and knees and scrambled around behind his partner.

Crooked Teeth raised the barrel of the shotgun so that it pressed against Jasper's chin. "You drop, or I can kill him," he growled.

"They kill Juma already," David spoke up weakly from his corner.

"For God's sake, Nilssen, do as he says," croaked Jasper, his face red from the pressure of the arm around his throat.

Thor kept his pistol pointed directly at the three of them as Carol slipped behind him. "If I drop my gun how do I know they won't kill you anyway?" he asked reasonably. "Or all of us?"

"Well do *something*!"

"There is no money here," Thor said calmly to Crooked Teeth. "It was a trick. Why don't you tell them, Reijksen?"

"A mistake," gasped Jasper. "Those two men came here trying to sell us a chimp, but we don't want it. We don't even know who they are."

The man spat out a few words and tightened his grip on Jasper's neck.

"They're not going to buy that, Reijksen," said Thor. "Not after the way you've been running around, saying you wanted to buy a bonobo. You'd better just tell them the truth and hope they believe you."

"All right, it was a trick." Jasper's voice was thin and weak for lack of air. "I said I'd pay five thousand for the bonobo, but I don't have it. I made them take two hundred instead."

"Nobody here has five thousand dollars," said Thor.

The two thugs looked at each other uncertainly. Jasper sounded desperate enough to be telling the truth, and their search hadn't turned up the money they had been told to collect. Of course, it could still be somewhere else in the room, or maybe in a lockbox at the front desk. On the other hand, the *mzungu* hardly seemed to care that they were choking his partner. His finger on the trigger of the pistol looked firm and steady. "We take him," Crooked Teeth said to Thor at last, prodding Jasper's chin with the shotgun barrel. "Tomorrow you bring money. Five thousand dollar. You don't bring, then we kill this one." He reflected for a moment and jerked his chin towards Carol. "We take her too."

"Take one step toward her and I'll blow both your heads off," said Thor grimly. "And I don't much care if Reijksen catches a bullet in the process."

Jasper squirmed and stared at him through bulging, bloodshot eyes. It was clear to all of them the man meant what he said. The two thugs started backing clumsily toward the door, dragging Jasper with them and trying not to trip over each other's legs. They reached the door, crowded through it and disappeared into the darkness.

After a moment, Thor lowered the pistol and went over to Carol. "How are you doing?"

"I'm okay," she said a bit shakily.

"They sent me off on a wild goose chase. Thank God I got back here in time." Thor started to embrace her, but Carol stiffened and pulled away sharply.

"Who the hell are you?" she demanded.

"Oh, right. Sorry. I'm Special Agent Peter Bergen, with the U.S. Fish and Wildlife Service, covert operations section."

Carol slipped past him and sat down on the edge of the bed, staring as he slipped the pistol into a shoulder holster under his jacket.

"I know it must come as a bit of a shock," said Peter. "I kind of got used to being Thor Nilssen myself."

Carol took a deep breath. "I want to see some ID," she said.

"We don't carry ID when we're working undercover, for obvious reasons," explained Peter. "You're just going to have to trust me for now."

Carol glared at him. "Everyone's always telling me to trust them," she said hotly. "Why the hell should I? You've been lying to me since the day we met."

"I told you, I was working undercover," said Peter, with an edge of impatience. "There isn't time to explain it all to you now. We've got to get you out of here in case those goons come back, or in case someone else decides to join the party." He reached down and picked up a crumpled blouse and tossed it into her suitcase.

"I'll do that," Carol said sharply.

Peter stood back and watched silently as she started to snatch the scattered clothes from the floor. After a moment he went over to the corner and looked down at David, whose head had fallen forward between his knees. He squatted down and lifted David's drooping head to study his swollen face. "He's alive, but he's going to need a doctor. Who is he?"

"I'm not sure," said Carol. "He just showed up with Juma..." As she started on a disjointed explanation of the events, beginning with David and Juma's arrival, her voice seemed to be coming from somewhere far away.

When she reached the part about hearing gunshots, Peter stood up abruptly. "Where's Greg Allen?" he cut in.

"I don't know," answered Carol, startled. "I haven't seen him since he dropped us off this afternoon. I suppose he went back to the research station."

"No, he was on surveillance up on the hill behind the hotel."

"Greg works for you?"

Peter shook his head impatiently. "He was just helping out. He called me by radio about a half hour ago, when I was still in Bola. Said he'd spotted something and was going down to check it out. I didn't hear anything from him after that."

As he spoke, Peter was already on his way out the door, pulling a small penlight from his pocket. From the doorway Carol watched the powerful, thin beam zig-zagging across the yard.

David groaned behind her, and she went back in and knelt next to him. His eyes were still closed, but he had lifted his head and leaned it back against the wall. His right arm was clutched tightly against his chest, with the hand pointing in the wrong direction. She was sure she had seen him somewhere before.

"Carol, give me a hand." Peter struggled through the doorway with Greg leaning heavily against him, dragging his feet as he walked.

Carol helped Peter steer Greg inside. The hair on one side of his head was matted down with blood.

382

"I'm okay," mumbled Greg. "Just let me sit down for a minute. You have some water?"

Carol went into the bathroom to fill a glass, while Peter helped Greg lower himself into the armchair.

Greg groaned and leaned back heavily. "Christ, my head is killing me."

"I'm not surprised," said Peter. "You've got a lump the size of a basketball."

Greg gulped down the water and pressed the empty glass against his forehead. "Someone must have come up from behind and whacked me. Next thing I knew, you were dragging me out of the bushes."

"You're lucky to be alive," frowned Peter. "I found Ayala out there in the grass while I was looking for you. He's dead— shot in the back. And they've grabbed Reijksen as a hostage."

"Jesus," said Greg.

"My guess is those thugs were waiting outside to rob Ayala and this one after Carol paid them for the bonobo. They must have figured it would be safer than going after Carol and Jasper themselves. Then when they didn't find the money, they came in looking for it. They probably panicked and shot Ayala while he was trying to get away."

"The bonobo!" exclaimed Greg. "Where is it?" He stood up too quickly and swayed dizzily.

"Take it easy," said Carol. "You could have a concussion."

"I'm okay. Where's the chimp?" Greg looked around and spotted the box against the wall. "Close the doors, will you? I don't want it to get out."

Greg tore the twine off the box and cautiously lifted the flaps open. "Oh, Christ, would you look at this?" He sounded sick and disgusted. "Those stupid bastards."

"Is it dead?" asked Carol.

"Not yet. But take a look."

At the bottom of the box was a small, fragile-looking black figure, curled up on its side with its long arms and legs pulled in, like a frightened child. Its fur was covered with a foul mixture of urine and feces and blood. Its eyes were shut, and its tongue protruded part way out between its leathery lips. At the base of its spine there was an ugly red gash and a large clot of blood and matted fur.

"The poor thing," exclaimed Carol. "But it doesn't look anything like the baby bonobos we saw yesterday."

"That's because it's not a baby bonobo," said Greg harshly. "It's a black mangabey monkey. Looks like they've chopped its tail off, trying to pass it off as a chimp. Hard to believe they actually thought that was going to work."

"Is there anything we can do for him?" asked Carol.

"I'll try, but he looks pretty far gone," said Greg. He lifted the limp form from the box and laid it on the floor. "Bring me a dripping wet towel, would you?"

Carol brought the towel and Greg gently pried the monkey's mouth open and squeezed a rivulet of water into it. The water dribbled out onto the floor beneath its head. Patiently, Greg squeezed again. This time the monkey's throat contracted as it swallowed a bit of the water. Finally, its mouth closed around the end of the towel and it began to suck.

"Attaboy," said Greg softly.

Carol heard another sharp groan and turned to see Peter running his hands carefully along David's limp arm, as David stared with his one open eye.

"Looks like a simple fracture, nothing serious," said Peter. "Mind if I use this?" Without waiting for her answer, he picked one of her blouses off the floor and started making it into a rough sling.

"Be my guest," said Carol.

"Where did you say Reijksen came in from?" asked Peter. "Through the back door?"

"No, from the next room, through there." Carol indicated the connecting door, which Jasper had shut firmly behind him.

Peter finished tying the sling and stepped into the adjacent room. He gave a low whistle.

"What is it?" asked Greg, looking up from the monkey.

"Reijksen's damned lucky those thugs didn't think to come in here. He's got quite a set-up."

As Greg and Carol examined the video camera and tape recorder, Peter quickly searched for and found the microphone on the underside of the night table in Carol's room.

"Looks like his idea was to get some video footage of our mysterious Mr. Singh in action, negotiating to sell you a bonobo," said Peter. "Setting up a sting like this is a pretty risky business for an amateur. I just hope he's got the sense to keep his mouth shut now. This would be a bad time to pull out his Green Brigade ID card."

"How do you know about that?" asked Carol.

"I had my office in D.C. run his name through our database," said Peter. "This thing seemed to have the Brigade's prints all over it."

"So you knew who he was and what he was up to all along?" demanded Carol.

"I never thought it would go this far. Believe me, if I'd had any idea you'd get dragged into it like this..." Without finishing the sentiment, Peter turned back to David and pulled him roughly to his feet. "Now I think it's time for some answers. What's your name, son?"

David grimaced and turned his head away.

Peter took hold of David's chin and pulled his face back around so their eyes met. "You're in big trouble, son. Your partner is dead, a *mzungu's* been kidnapped, and I'm guessing a Big Man somewhere is really pissed off at you. Believe it or not, I'm your best friend right now, because I'm the one who's going to grab that Big Man before he gets to you. But you're going to have to help me, okay? So, let's start with Mr. Singh."

David looked at him blearily through his one open eye.

"Then again, we could just take you straight to Captain Kamanga and let him ask the questions," said Peter.

David stiffened and his eye widened with fear, but he still didn't answer.

"Or maybe you'd rather talk to your uncle, Thadeus Maleke." Peter ignored the astonished stares that Carol and Greg turned on him. "Is that what you want, David?"

"David—that's it!" Carol broke in. "I knew I'd seen him before. You're Margaret Waiyala's son, aren't you? Is Dr. Maleke really Margaret's brother?"

David nodded dispiritedly.

"Fine, but who is Singh?" repeated Peter impatiently.

"Singh is nobody," said David sullenly.

Peter gave him a shake that made him yelp. "You're not helping yourself here, son."

"Is nobody called Singh," repeated David defiantly. "Is only me and Juma. We make him up." Frightened as he was, he was also clearly proud of himself.

Under Peter's prompting, David revealed that Juma had come up with the idea of telling Reijksen that they worked for a mysterious 'Big Man,' so he would take them seriously. They had chosen the name 'Singh' because most of the rich businessmen they knew of were Asians. Later, when they had decided to bypass Reijksen and go directly to 'Mrs. Simon,' they had kept up the pretense, even printing up a few dozen business cards to make it more convincing.

"I thought as much," said Peter coolly. "This whole thing didn't smell right, from the beginning. Who else knows about this? Maleke?"

David shook his head.

"Tell me the truth," warned Peter, tightening his grip painfully on David's shoulder.

"Is nobody knows," whined David. "Only Juma and me. And Muna," he added after a moment. Reluctantly, he told them his friend Muna had been in on the scheme, and that she was the one who had tracked Carol's travel itinerary, through her travel office connections. After more quizzing by Peter, he also admitted that Muna was Maleke's girlfriend.

"So Maleke does know," said Peter.

"She don't tell him nothing," insisted David. "She don't like him now and she want to leave him, only she need to have money first."

"That's what she told you, but she was probably spying on you two for Maleke all along. I happen to know he has a pretty good idea what you've been up to."

David's dismayed expression showed that this had never occurred to him.

"All right," said Peter briskly. "We're running out of time. Carol, you've got to get out of here in case someone comes back. I don't want you on the road after dark, so Greg had better drive you to Margaret's house for the night. You can head back to Kobani first thing in the morning."

"I can't do that," said Carol, irritated at Peter's autocratic manner. "I've got to go pick up Jonathan." She was gratified to see the puzzled look on Peter's face. She quickly told him about Maleke's visit to her room and Jonathan's abduction by Kamanaga and his rescue. "Dr. Maleke was supposed to come back right after dark and give me his car. I don't know what's keeping him so long," she finished a bit lamely. Hearing herself tell the story, she realized how implausible it sounded. She began to wonder whether it was just another trick she had fallen for.

"I know what's keeping him," said Peter, regaining his annoying self-assurance. "Kamanga's got him. He wants Maleke to lead him to Singh."

"How in the world do you know that?" demanded Carol.

"Simple," said Peter. "I put a bug in his car while it was parked outside the hotel this afternoon. Maleke went looking for David at his mother's house, and Kamanga waylaid him there." He frowned for a moment, thinking quickly. "All right, new plan. There's a pickup truck parked behind the hotel, with the keys inside. Carol, you take it and collect Jonathan like Maleke told you, then keep going on to Kobani. Considering everything, I guess it's better you don't stick around Mwatumi after all. Just be careful driving, and don't stop for anything or anyone. Do you have a hat?"

"Yes, why?" asked Carol, bewildered.

"Put it on, with your hair tucked underneath. With any luck, anyone seeing you in the truck will think you're a man. Greg, you drive David home in your car and then find a spot somewhere west of town just off the main road, where you can stay out of sight. Wait for me there with your radio on in case I need you."

"Why, where are you going?" asked Greg.

"Maleke promised Kamanga that Singh was going to be at the old fort tonight," said Peter. "I'm going to make sure he's not disappointed."

CHAPTER 30

1

As Carol approached the rendezvous point she had to fight the temptation to keep going, straight on to Kobani. She was nervous enough just driving the borrowed pickup, expecting any moment to find the road blocked or have the tires shot out. The idea of actually stopping along this dark, empty stretch seemed inconceivable.

But she did stop, exactly two kilometers west of Bola, at a spot where the road crossed over a dry drainage culvert. Jonathan was supposed to be hiding inside. She pulled off the road, leaned across to unlock the passenger door and hurriedly flashed the headlights twice.

The darkness pressed in on all sides, amplifying the pounding of her heart and the sputtering and coughing of the engine. She pressed the accelerator pedal gingerly to keep it racing and cursed Jonathan under her breath. She flashed the signal again, then several more times in quick succession, like Morse code. Finally, after what felt like hours, the door jerked opened and Jonathan scrambled in.

"Thank God," exclaimed Carol. She popped the clutch and stamped on the accelerator, sending the truck jerking violently back onto the road. "What took you so long?"

"You're supposed to be in Maleke's car," said Jonathan breathlessly. He was disheveled and dirty and his jaw was so swollen so she could barely understand him. "When I saw the truck I thought it was a trap. Whose truck is this, anyway?"

"It's a long story," said Carol. She did her best to fill him in and swerve around the worst of the potholes at the same time.

Jonathan listened in silence until she was finished. "I knew there was something fishy about that Nilssen guy," he said.

"Is that all you can say?" demanded Carol.

"But if he really is a U.S. agent he should have briefed the Embassy on his mission," complained Jonathan. "As it is, I've taken some very serious risks unnecessarily. I even posed as a buyer myself to get to the bottom of this."

"You what!" exclaimed Carol.

"I called the number on the card you gave me and tried to set up a meeting with Singh, pretending I wanted to do business. I had to do some pretty fancy footwork, too, since I didn't know what business he was in. Anyway, it didn't work. All I got was a young Rumuran woman pretending to be his assistant and trying to blackmail me."

"I don't believe this," fumed Carol. "You told me you couldn't get through to anyone on that number."

"What are you so mad about? I would have let you know if anything came of it."

Carol didn't bother to answer.

"The more I think about it, it's hard to believe Washington wouldn't have notified the Embassy if this guy were legit," said Jonathan. "He never did show you any ID, did he?"

"Maybe the Ambassador knows, but he didn't tell you," suggested Carol.

"I have a security clearance," said Jonathan stiffly. "Besides, McCallister's out of town and I'm in acting for him. He would have briefed me."

"Well, I think Thor, I mean Peter, was telling the truth," said Carol.

"Pat told me you had a thing for him," said Jonathan, as if that explained everything.

"That has nothing to do with it," bristled Carol. "And anyway, for your information I happen to be furious with him for tricking me and lying to me. I let him know it, too."

"I suppose you told him everything."

"What could I tell him?" demanded Carol. "You, Jasper, Peter, Greg...all of you seem to think what I don't know won't hurt me. After all, I'm just the person who's been hounded all the way from Nairobi to Mwatumi and held up at gunpoint. Why should you men bother to tell me what's going on?"

They drove on for a while in chilly silence.

"I guess we have to help him, anyway" said Carol finally. "What if Kamanga sees through it and figures out he's not Singh after all?"

"Help him how?" asked Jonathan.

"I was thinking...maybe when we reach Kobani, you could send out a few Marines from the Embassy..."

"What I'm going to do when we get to Kobani is call Washington to find out what the hell is going on," said Jonathan. "*If* it turns out this Bergen's for real, and *if* Fish and Wildlife makes a formal request for back-up, I guess we'll see what we can do."

"But that could be too late," Carol protested.

"It could be too late already," said Jonathan sourly. "If he was telling you the truth, he must be at the fort right now, trying to bluff his way through. What was Thadeus thinking about, anyway, telling Kamanga he was meeting Singh there? What did he think he was going to do when Singh didn't show up?"

"Peter said it sounded like a spur of the moment thing, to buy time and keep Kamanga away from David and Margaret," said Carol. "He must have been counting on finding a way out of it somehow later. He's sure going to be surprised when 'Singh' shows up after all."

"This could get tricky if Thadeus doesn't know what's going on."

"Peter's going to try to send him a signal to let him know it's okay and he should play along," said Carol.

"What kind of signal?"

"The only thing we could think of was the same way you let me know I should trust Maleke—he's got to work the name 'Popeye' into the conversation."

Jonathan looked at her in disbelief. "Now *that* I'd like to see," he said.

2

The broken walls of the old fort rose out of the darkness, spotlit by the moon like center stage as the curtain goes up. Peter stopped the old Renault in the overgrown gravel yard, cut the engine and the headlights, and stepped out into the starry stillness. As his eyes adjusted to the darkness he made out first the shape of another car in the shadow of the wall, and then two silhouettes in the back seat. Pointedly ignoring them, he leaned against his car in a casual pose, alert for any sound behind the ringing of the crickets and the soft rustle of the leaves.

He didn't have long to wait. A moment later the crisp crunch of boots on gravel approached him from the shadows and the powerful glare of a spotlight struck him full in the face. He fought the urge to throw up his arm to shield his eyes, shifting his gaze to one side instead to avoid looking directly into the beam. He kept his hands in his pockets and a slightly bored expression on his face.

"Mr. Singh?" growled a voice from behind the spotlight.

"That is correct," said Peter coolly, in his Thor Nilssen accent. "Would you mind shifting the light a bit, Captain? Unless you particularly wish to blind me."

The beam fell to his chest, leaving flashes of red and green dancing in front of his eyes.

Captain Kamanga took a few steps closer until they were face to face in the gray moonlight. "You are not what we expected," he observed, glancing disdainfully past Peter to the old Renault.

"You would prefer I drove a Mercedes?" asked Peter. "Only an amateur draws attention to himself."

"But you're not an Asian," objected Kamanga.

"No." Peter allowed himself a condescending smile.

"Your real name is not Singh."

"Singer," explained Peter shortly. "Erik Singer. Who is in the car?"

"A friend of yours," said Kamanaga. He beckoned toward the car and Thadeus Maleke emerged and started towards them, with his arm in the grip of a roughly dressed, stocky man with a brutish expression. As Maleke recognized Peter, his face clearly showed his surprise.

"What is he doing here?" demanded Peter angrily, before Maleke could speak. "I suppose next we'll see Popeye and Olive Oil leaping out from behind the bushes." He stressed the names as though emphasizing the absurdity.

"Who?" demanded Kamanga, taken aback.

"Never mind," muttered Peter. Meeting Maleke's eyes quickly, he had seen the flicker of understanding and caught Maleke's almost imperceptible nod. "Just get him out of here. This is meant to be a private meeting."

"You know him?" asked Kamanga.

"Of course I know him. He is Thadeus Maleke, Director of the Forest Department. I asked you what he is doing here."

"We thought maybe he is working with you," said Kamanga.

"No one is working with me," said Peter archly. "Certainly not this man. I've been using his fool nephew to make contact with your boss, that's all. I presume you are here to take me to him?" He lifted one eyebrow imperiously.

Kamanga hesitated a moment, then barked out an order and marched back to his car, lighting his way over the uneven ground with the spotlight. He held the front passenger door open. "You come with me," he said to Peter. "My man will follow with your car."

"I'll drive my own car," said Peter, sliding inside the Renault. "Lead the way." He started the engine and revved it a few times impatiently.

Kamanaga scowled but shrugged elaborately to show it was all the same to him. He got behind the wheel and his man let go of Maleke and hurried to climb in on the other side.

Peter rolled down his window and put his head out. "What about him?" he called out over the sound of the engine, indicating Maleke with a jerk of his chin.

"He can walk home," Kamanaga called back with a short laugh as he started to pull away.

As the two sets of taillights faded from view, Maleke glanced down at his already battered Italian shoes and sighed, thinking of the ten kilometers of dusty, rocky road that lay between him and Mwatumi.

Peter followed Kamanga through a tall iron gate into a spacious compound and stopped in front of the solid, two-story house. The servant who opened the door was expecting them. Without a word, he led them down a short hallway and into a richly decorated sitting room. Where Gideon Bashega sat in a deep armchair in front of a crackling fireplace. Peter recognized the school-masterish face immediately from the photographs in the briefing book. As Bashega rose to meet them, Kamanga stepped forward and leaned down to whisper in his ear. Bashega listened briefly, then nodded impatiently and waved him away.

"We meet at last, Commissioner," said Peter, as they shook hands firmly and took one another in.

"Mr. Singh, is it?" said Bashega wryly.

"He says his name is Singer," put in Kamanaga.

Bashega turned to Kamanaga as though surprised to find him still there. "You may wait outside, Captain. I will call if I need you."

Kamanaga stiffened. With a quick, resentful look, he retreated, shutting the door behind him.

Bashega motioned Peter to one of the overstuffed armchairs and offered him a drink. Peter glanced at the well-stocked sideboard and chose an expensive, single malt whiskey. Bashega nodded approvingly, poured out two doubles over ice, and handed one to Peter. He sank comfortably into the chair opposite Peter and turned his benign gaze on him.

"Singer," he mused, "Not Singh after all."

"I saw no reason to correct the error," said Peter with a faint smile.

"It is a German name?"

"My father's family is from Germany," Peter acknowledged. "I am Norwegian."

"I apologize that we could not meet sooner, Mr. Singer."

"A man in your position must be cautious," responded Peter. "I had no doubt you would arrange the contact when you were ready."

Bashega nodded, pleased. "In the meantime, I trust you have had a pleasant visit to our small village and our beautiful forest."

"Very pleasant, thank you." Peter crossed his legs, allowing a shade of impatience to creep into the gesture.

"I consider the Mali-Kuli forest to be the most beautiful in the world," continued Bashega casually. "But of course, we all believe this about our own homes. I have heard that your evergreen forests in Norway are also very beautiful."

His emphasis on the word 'evergreen' was subtle but unmistakable, as was the questioning glint in the small eyes behind the round glasses. Peter took a slow sip of his whiskey and studied the Commissioner thoughtfully.

"They stretch almost as far as the Arctic Circle," he agreed carefully.

Bashega's expression remained blandly pleasant, revealing nothing of his reaction to hearing Peter give the correct response to the code. In fact, his first reaction was disappointment and pique at learning that Delacroix had apparently been telling the truth. He had been hoping the story about 'Singh' being an American agent would prove to be a lie, partly because he had been hoping to do business with Singh. Besides, it would have vindicated the decision he had already made to drop the annoying Frenchman. Nevertheless, he had allowed for the possibility that it was true, and had made a contingency plan.

"Welcome to Mwatumi, 'Mr. Singer'," he said. "Shall I continue to use that name? Or perhaps you will give me your real name, as you already know mine?"

"Singer will do."

•

"As you like," shrugged Bashega. "Perhaps you are surprised to learn the identity of your anonymous informant? I think it is not what you were expecting."

"I try to avoid having expectations," said Peter. "That way I don't get surprised. But I would be interested to know, why all the subterfuge? As the head of law enforcement in Rumura, you could just as easily have contacted my agency officially."

"Impossible," said Bashega. "It would have required the formal clearance of several other officials, many of whom I fear have appetites that exceed their paychecks. The information could have been worth a great deal to certain people. I was forced to resort to a more roundabout channel."

"A fugitive priest in exile in Nairobi is certainly 'roundabout'," agreed Peter.

Bashega silently registered the revelation about Father Loretto with another twinge of annoyance. Once again, he was forced to admit Delacroix' instincts appeared to have been right. Since seeing the intercepted letter, he had been speculating about the identity of its author. He had settled on Truman Yates as the most likely suspect, and had been chiding himself for letting the man go so easily.

Of course, if he had been left to deal with things in his own way, the priest would be safely tucked away in Kobani prison right now, instead of sitting in Nairobi stirring up trouble. But Delacroix had insisted on taking charge of the matter himself, and for some reason had relished this absurdly elaborate scheme of framing the priest and getting him run out of the country. It was exactly the type of arrogance and amateurism that made him an intolerable liability. Besides, Delacroix' insistence on meeting Muhwenazi alone tonight had strengthened Bashega's suspicions that the Frenchman was in the process of dropping him from the partnership. It was clearly time for a preemptive strike. He allowed himself a brief reverie about teaching Delacroix a lesson the hard way, as he had just done with Jonathan Marshall, another white man who was too cheeky for his own good. But satisfying as the mental image of Delacroix' battered face might be, he had a better plan for getting rid of the man.

"You have come at an opportune time, Mr. Singer," he said, leaning forward earnestly. "I have been conducting some undercover investigations of my own for the past several months. You will be interested to know that a large consignment of ivory and leopard skins and gold will be coming in from the Congo in the next few days. My 'partners' are finalizing the details this evening, and by tomorrow I will know the time and the route the shipment will be taking. Now, here is my plan..."

3

Mwatumi was dark and silent at two o'clock in the morning, but at Margaret Waiyala's house a weak light filtered through the tightly drawn curtains. When Maleke knocked sharply on the door, the sound echoed loudly in the stillness.

"It's me, Maleke. Open the door," he said impatiently.

One of the curtains shifted slightly as someone tried to peer out. Maleke turned his face toward the window to let the light fall on it. A moment later the door scraped open.

Faith's face was pale and frightened as she stepped aside and let her uncle enter. As soon as he was inside, she closed the door and latched it.

"Is David here?" asked Maleke.

Faith pointed silently to the door to the bedroom and backed away as Maleke brushed past her. After he had gone in, she and her sisters crowded in the doorway and stood watching solemnly.

Inside the small bedroom, Margaret was sitting on a stool beside the narrow iron bed, where David was asleep under a thick woolen blanket. His face was covered with cuts and bruises and one of his eyes was swollen shut. His right arm rested on top of the blanket, roughly splinted with sticks and strips of cloth.

Margaret glanced up as Maleke entered.

"The arm is broken?" he asked, looking at David impassively from the foot of the bed.

"David wouldn't let me call the doctor to set it properly," Margaret answered in a hushed voice. "He told me to call Godfrey, because he could trust him not to talk." Godfrey Wawere was an orderly at the Red Cross clinic, and a boyhood friend of David's. "He wouldn't tell me anything else."

"When did he come here?"

"More than one hour ago. A *mzungu* brought him in a car. Someone I didn't know. A very tall man with curly yellow hair and a beard."

"Greg Allen," said Maleke, concealing his surprise.

"The *mzungu* wouldn't tell me anything either. He just looked embarrassed and said David would explain later."

Maleke walked around the bed to stand beside Margaret, looking down into David's face. "Wake him up."

Margaret hesitated. "Maybe we should let him sleep a little longer."

"I haven't walked ten kilometers in the dark just to watch the boy sleep," snapped Maleke. He leaned down and put his hand on David's shoulder and shook it firmly. David's good eye cracked open.

"Wake up, you young imbecile," said Maleke, shaking him harder.

David opened his eye the rest of the way and looked at his uncle blearily. Margaret adjusted the blanket over his chest and lifted his head to smooth the pillow.

"Stop fussing with him," ordered Maleke. "Start talking, boy. What nonsense have you been up to this time?"

Speaking painfully through his cracked and swollen lips, David stumbled through a dubious account of the events of the past few days. In his version, Reijksen had introduced him and Juma to Carol at the Cock and Bull a few days before. She had invited them to come to the hotel that night to discuss an unspecified business proposition. They had thought it peculiar, but decided it couldn't hurt to go and see what the *mzungus* wanted. By pure bad luck, just after they had arrived at her room, two huge thugs had suddenly burst in, wearing hoods and armed with automatic rifles. From the way they had set about tearing up the room, David was sure they were searching for something. He suspected gold or drugs.

"If Juma'd stayed and helped me fight, we could've taken them," David concluded. "Instead he tried to make a run for it and got himself shot, leaving me to handle both of them by myself. I was laying into one guy when the other one snuck up from behind and clobbered me over the head with something. Next thing I knew, I was back here."

The room was starkly silent as Margaret and the girls looked first at David then at Maleke.

"You're an ass, boy," said Maleke disgustedly. "You always have been. Didn't I warn you not to hang around with Ayala? I told you he was nothing but trouble."

"I told him the same," said Margaret.

"You're right, uncle," said David contritely. "I should have known what a stinking coward he'd turn out to be. I wish I'd listened to you—"

"Quiet!" snapped Maleke. "We've had enough of your big mouth. I've know all about your ridiculous little scheme from the beginning. I've been doing my best to protect you, hoping you'd come to your senses. I don't know why I bothered."

"I never asked you to butt in," David said sullenly.

"Do you have any idea what kind of trouble you're in?" demanded Maleke. "As soon as Kamanga hears what happened he's going to come after you like divine vengeance."

"Shows what you know," said David triumphantly. "The two thugs I told you about were Kamanga's men—I recognized them. So they can't make any trouble over this."

Maleke grabbed David's face in his hand and bent down so their faces were only inches away. David cringed into the pillow.

"Listen, you puppy," growled Maleke. "You have no idea who those men were. You couldn't see their faces, and as far as

399

you know you never saw them before in your life. Do you hear me?"

"But why?" whimpered David.

"Because if you let on you know who they were you might as well be signing your own death warrant. Understand? As it is, they're certainly going to try to frame you with Juma's murder."

David stared at him with dismay, but he quickly recovered some of his bravado. "Those two *mzungus* saw everything. They'll testify it wasn't me who killed him."

"They'll never get the chance," said Maleke. "Once Bashega and Kamanga get you into Kobani prison, that's the last anyone will see of you until you come out in a box." "You promised you wouldn't let him go to prison!" cried Margaret. "You said you would take care of him."

"Every time this young idiot turns around he gets himself deeper into trouble," said Maleke. "How can I do anything for him if he won't listen to me?"

"The only thing you have to do for me is get me out of Rumura," David put in. "I've wanted out of this hole for a long time anyway. I could go back to Nairobi."

"And who's going to pay for you to set yourself up in Nairobi? I'm not made of money, you ungrateful little pie-dog."

"You'll give me the money, won't you Mama?" said David defiantly.

"Me?" asked Margaret, astonished. "How do you think I have that kind of money?"

"You can take it from the co-op's bank account. Weren't you telling me just last week you've got more than ninety thousand rimands in it?"

"Nine thousand, you foolish boy, not ninety. And it isn't my money. It belongs to the cooperative. To everyone."

"Well you're just going to borrow it, aren't you? Everybody thinks you're dipping into it already anyway. It's enough for a start. I'll pay you back as soon as I get a job in Nairobi. You're not going to let me get tortured and killed in prison, are you?"

Margaret's eyes filled with tears as she looked anxiously at Maleke. "Brother, you have to help him."

"I don't have to do anything of the kind. All I've gotten from him is insolence and trouble."

"He doesn't mean it. He's only frightened and hurt. David, tell your uncle you're very sorry, and ask him to forgive you," Margaret urged insistently.

"He's the one who should be sorry, coming in here and calling me names," muttered David. "Anyway, it's his fault if I have to scratch around trying to earn a living. What has he ever done for me? Why didn't he take me to Kobani to school, like Nelson? I'm the oldest."

Suddenly they heard a heavy pounding on the door and a man's gravely voice shouting angrily for it to be opened.

"It's Kamanga," said Maleke tersely.

"What should we do, uncle?" asked Faith from the doorway.

"Let him in. Otherwise he'll only break it down."

Captain Kamanga strode in followed by two other men, this time police officers in uniform. Maleke took a step forward to place himself between Kamanga and David.

"Did you have a pleasant stroll, *Doctor*? I'm surprised to see you here already."

"I'm visiting my nephew," said Maleke. "He's been injured and he needs to rest."

"I know all about his injury," snapped Kamanga. "Get up and get dressed, boy. You're coming with us."

Behind Maleke, David shrank down under the blanket and Margaret pressed her fist silently against her mouth.

"Suppose you tell me what this is all about, Captain," said Maleke evenly. "What do you want with my nephew?"

"He's wanted for questioning about the shooting tonight. Don't pretend you don't know what I'm talking about."

"I know there's been a shooting, but David wasn't responsible. There are two witnesses who can testify to that— Mrs. Carol Simmons and Mr. Jasper Reijksen."

"Your friends have flown the coop, Doctor," scowled Kamanga. "Probably half way back to America by now. And don't be surprised if they swear on the Bible they've never met you or David before in their lives."

"They've returned to Kobani at my suggestion," said Maleke. "I'm sure you'll find them at the Intercontinental Hotel in the morning. Meanwhile, I promise to deliver my nephew to the authorities in Kobani tomorrow. He's ready to cooperate fully in your investigations after he's had a chance to rest."

"Forget it, Maleke," growled Kamanga. "Let's go, boy. Get up out of that bed unless you want me to come and get you out."

When David didn't respond, Kamanga pushed past Maleke and Margaret and flipped the blanket away, revealing David shivering in his underwear. The two officers moved forward and stood stolidly at the foot of the bed with their heavy wooden truncheons resting ready in their hands. Ignoring Margaret's cry of protest, Kamanga grabbed David by his good arm and started to drag him out of the bed.

"Stop!" said Maleke. "There's no need for that. He'll go with you if you insist. Let him get dressed."

Margaret looked at her brother in dismay, but he avoided her gaze and addressed David. "It's all right, son," he said. "I'll follow you to Kobani and make sure you're taken care of."

Maleke, Margaret and the girls followed David into the yard and watched as the two policemen pushed him into the back seat of the waiting police car. The commotion had awakened their neighbors, who watched silently from their doorways. As the car pulled away with a spray of gravel and dust, Maleke reached out and rested his arm lightly across Margaret's shivering shoulders.

"He'll be all right, I promise," he said.

Margaret nodded numbly.

"After this is over, we'll buy him a bit of land and get him a wife. I expect this business with Juma will finally put a scare in him and bring him to his senses. He'll be glad enough to put it behind him and settle down."

"You're sure he won't have to stay in prison?" implored Margaret. "You'll get him out before they hurt him any more?"

"I'll sort it out." Maleke sighed wearily as they walked slowly back toward the house. "Don't I always? But somehow I have the feeling it's going to be expensive this time."

CHAPTER 31

"They told me at the desk I might find you here," said Jonathan. He sat on the edge of the lounge chair next to Carol's, looking out of place at the poolside in his suit and polished leather shoes. The bruises on his face had turned yellowish green and a row of neat stitches closed the cut on his cheek. His forehead shone with perspiration in the blaze of the noon sun.

"Just snatching a few last hours of African sunshine, before I head back to the States tonight," said Carol. "You look awful."

"Thanks. I thought you'd want to know, Reijksen's okay. My contact at the Netherlands Embassy just called to tell me he was released early this morning near Kobani. They're putting him on the next plane back to Amsterdam."

"I'll bet he'll be glad to get out of here," said Carol.

"Actually, Jan said he's mad as hell. Wants to stay and get the guys who abducted him."

"But from what you said last night, it must be the same ones who abducted you, and that's the police themselves!" said Carol.

"Not the police officially," Jonathan corrected her. "The Police Commissioner and probably Captain Kamanga acting in their private capacity. Not that I can prove it. Anyway, it's better Reijksen doesn't know anything about that. He's already caused enough trouble. He's damned lucky Bashega decided to limit the damage and release him unharmed. I just hope this has scared some sense into him."

"I doubt it," said Carol. "You can question his methods, but you've got to admire his courage."

Jonathan raised an eyebrow. "You've sure changed your tune. I seem to remember some very unladylike language last night, about being treated like a mushroom—kept in the dark and fed on shit."

"Believe me, I'm still furious at all of you," said Carol. "You had no right to go around behind my back the way you did."

"Speaking of which, any word from Bergen?" asked Jonathan.

"Nothing," said Carol, trying not to sound as worried as she felt. "He should have gotten here by now, even if he waited until morning to leave Mwatumi. Don't you think it's time for the Embassy to get involved?"

"His home office asked us not to interfere for at least twenty four hours," said Jonathan. "It could do more harm than good, since we don't know how he decided to play things."

Carol frowned at the water, unconvinced.

"Don't worry, Carol. He's a professional. And the fact that they let Jasper go is a good sign. Bashega and his crew won't want to risk an international incident. Being an American still counts for something around here, especially if you're a U.S. government employee."

"They could always claim they didn't know who he was. Or make it look like an accident, like another car going over a cliff in the mountains."

"You're letting your imagination run away with you," said Jonathan lightly, although the same thoughts had occurred to him. "I'm sure he'll turn up soon."

As if on cue, Peter Bergen emerged from the hotel and strolled across the hot concrete towards them. He sat on the foot of Carol's lounge chair, looking dirty and tired but cheerful.

"Looks like you had a hard time of it, Marshall," said Peter. "I'm glad to see you got back safely."

Jonathan shrugged. "Just a few scratches," he said.

"Any news about Reijksen or Maleke?"

Jonathan told him about Jasper's release. "And I called Thadeus' house this morning and talked to his wife. He arrived a couple of hours ago, with his sister Margaret from Mwatumi. It seems his nephew David has been arrested on suspicion of murdering Juma Ayala. They've gone to Kobani central prison to try to see him."

"But David didn't kill Juma!" exclaimed Carol. "Peter and I can testify to that."

405

"We can't, actually. We didn't witness the shooting," Peter pointed out.

"But we know what happened. It was those two thugs who killed him and beat David up. And we can all identify them. It has to be the same two who carjacked Jonathan—the big one with bad teeth and the short one with two missing fingers."

"The Police Commissioner, Gideon Bashega, is directly involved," added Jonathan. "I recognized his voice when they were trying to interrogate me about Singh."

"I assumed as much," said Peter. "It was Bashega that Kamanga took me to see, after I convinced him I was Singh."

"So you were able to pull it off?"

"It went over okay with Kamanga," said Peter. "Bashega himself was a different story. I wasn't surprised when Kamanga took me to him—we'd already suspected he might be the top honcho in this operation, or at least one of them. The real surprise came when it turned out he already knew all about me and my operation." He told them about the secret letter from Nairobi, and Bashega's knowledge of the code words 'evergreen' and 'Arctic Circle.' "Bashega claims to be the informant who's been giving Father Loretto information to pass on to us. He's fingered a logger named Delacroix as the head of the operation. He says he's wormed his way into Delacroix' confidence and become his partner, in order to expose him."

"I'd certainly go along with the part about Delacroix. I've thought he was bad news all along. But Gideon Bashega as a good guy? I don't buy it," said Jonathan, gingerly fingering the cut under his eye.

"I'd say you're probably right," said Peter. He pulled a folded envelope out of his shirt pocket. "I found this message waiting for me at the reception desk. It seems there's a security breach at the U.S. Embassy in Nairobi. One of the local staff has been getting hold of confidential letters and telexes and leaking them to collaborators outside. Operations all over east and central Africa may have been compromised."

"I had no idea the Fish and Wildlife Service had such a big presence here," said Carol.

"That's the ironic part," said Peter. "It actually has very little to do with us. It turns out the man at the Nairobi Embassy is a member of an extremist Hutu organization based in eastern Congo, near the Rwanda border. It's one of the main groups responsible for some of the recent massacres of Tutsis in Rwanda and Burundi, just like some Tutsi extremist groups are working out of the DRC to launch attacks on Hutus. Both sides rely heavily on a supply of weapons and ammunition, most of it originating in Belgium and France and South Africa. Some of the western governments, including the U.S., have been working behind the scenes to try to stop the arms smuggling. Fish and Wildlife got dragged into it because we've been trying to track down ivory shipments coming in to the U.S. from this area. It looks like poached ivory and other wildlife products from the DRC are being exchanged for arms from France, by way of the Mali-Kuli forest, and all of it being transported in Delacroix' logging trucks. Bashega told me Delacroix has a bigshot Zairean partner. He hasn't given me the name yet, but I'm betting it'll turn out to be connected with the same Hutu group. I suspect Father Loretto knew about all of it."

"He told the Schooley foundation the money being embezzled from our project was being used for smuggling, but he didn't say anything about guns," said Carol.

"And when he contacted us, he focused on the wildlife poaching aspect," said Peter. "I'm guessing he saved the part about the guns for the CIA."

"The CIA?" asked Carol.

"You remember Truman Yates?" asked Peter.

"You're kidding," said Jonathan.

"It's just a guess," said Peter. "But I wouldn't be surprised."

"That could explain why McCallister was so keen to get him out of prison," admitted Jonathan. "But you'd think he'd have told me."

"I think the good Father was looking for revenge, and he figured he had a better chance covering all the bases, bringing each of us in independently. It could have saved us all a lot of trouble if he'd given us the whole picture from the beginning," said Peter.

"Just like it would have saved us here a lot of trouble if you'd let the Embassy know what you were up to," Jonathan put in.

"The Ambassador did know," said Peter. "I gave him a full briefing as soon as I arrived."

"He didn't say anything to me."

Peter didn't try to conceal his amusement. "I know. I told Ambassador McCallister we suspected there was a leak somewhere, maybe here in Rumura. Frankly, Marshall, he thought it might be you."

"Me! That's impossible!" sputtered Jonathan. "I knew McCallister was an idiot, but..."

"It's not really so far-fetched," said Peter mildly. "You're very chummy with Thadeus Maleke, who was one of our top suspects all along. In fact, I'm still very surprised that as far as I can tell, he doesn't seem to be involved in the poaching after all. In fact, I now believe he's probably Father Loretto's anonymous informant. I'm glad, though. I like him."

Jonathan got to his feet, still fuming. "When McCallister gets back, I'm going to give him a piece of my mind," he said.

"Fine. But in the meantime, I may need your help," said Peter.

"Why, what are you going to do?"

"Bashega filled me in on his plan to set up an ambush for Delacroix. Since we've agreed the Commissioner's motives probably aren't pure, I'm guessing he's trying to set Delacroix up in order to get him out of the picture and take over the whole business himself. To make it work, he's got to make sure we catch Delacroix with a hot shipment."

"So you're going to play along with him?"

Peter shook his head. "I can't. Bashega isn't the only one who knows who I am. You remember, David heard all about it last night at the Acropolis. With him in custody, I have to assume Kamanga knows by now too. That could mean trouble."

"But I thought Kamanga works for Bashega," said Carol.

"He does, but I got the feeling he's not all that happy with the arrangement. After Kamanga brought me to his house last night, Bashega dismissed him like some minor underling. I could tell Kamanga resented it. He might be mad enough to sell Bashega out. If he goes to Delacroix with the information, Delacroix will certainly put two and two together and delay the shipment. He might even set up some kind of trap of his own."

"So where do I come in?" asked Jonathan.

"You're still acting for the Ambassador aren't you?"

"That's right. He's due back the day after tomorrow."

"It's just as well. I think you can handle this better than he would."

Jonathan couldn't help looking gratified. "What do you have in mind?"

"You need to bring this matter to the attention of the French Ambassador. You might just drop a diplomatic hint or two that you believe he might already know something about the poaching and the arms smuggling. Whether he does or not, he'll recognize that if this gets out it could be very embarrassing for his government. In exchange for your agreement to keep things quiet, I think we can count on him to get Delacroix pulled out of Rumura, and maybe even to get the French arms suppliers to lay off for a while. With any luck, Bashega will decide to ease off while he tries to sort out the reasons for Delacroix' abrupt departure. "Meanwhile, I'm going to consult with my people back in Washington about how to tackle Bashega and the Zairean."

"Greg and Lisa will be happy to see Delacroix go," said Jonathan. "He's been the main force behind that proposal for a road through the Mali-Kuli forest. With him gone and the French feeling nervous about the whole area, I suspect nobody's going to touch that project for a long time. And according to my contacts, Delacroix' timber company has actually been losing money on the Rumura operation for the past couple of years. They might just pull out altogether."

"But what about the people of Mwatumi?" asked Carol. "They need the road too."

"Maybe we can take another look at the alternative proposal, to put in a new road south of the Reserve, connecting Bola and Rendesha directly with a spur going up to Mwatumi. Anyway, I'd better get back to the office and arrange for you to leave depositions about last night's incident, since you won't be around to testify if anything comes to trial. Not that it will."

Jonathan's departure left Carol and Peter alone in an awkward silence.

"I hope our depositions will help clear David of the murder charge," said Carol. "Although I guess he'll still be in trouble for poaching."

Neither of them voiced what they both knew, that whatever happened to David would almost certainly have much more to do with the strings Maleke was able to pull, and the money he was able to pay, than anything either of them said.

"I'm flying out to Nairobi tonight," said Peter casually.

"I'm on the Air France flight direct to Paris, and then back to Washington."

"I'm only spending one day in Nairobi, and then I'll be heading home through Paris too," said Peter. "Why don't we spend a couple of days in Paris together?"

Carol flushed uncomfortably. "I really need to get back as soon as I can to file my report for the Schooley Foundation."

"Couldn't you do that by fax from Nairobi?"

"I've got to be at the Board meeting in person. There's a lot riding on it."

"When is the meeting?"

Carol hesitated. "Next Monday," she admitted.

"Perhaps you would prefer to go to Paris with Thor Nilssen," he suggested, switching back to his Norwegian accent.

410

"I have to admit, you do that accent very well," said Carol.

"My parents are Norwegian. I've been imitating them since I was a kid. But please don't change the subject. What's wrong? Are you still mad at me for concealing my identity from you? I told you, I didn't have any choice."

"Yes, I am still mad about that," retorted Carol. "And I still think you should have told me what was going on a lot sooner. But that's not it."

"What then?"

"I got a call from Neil last night."

Peter met her eyes and waited for her to continue.

"He said he'd been trying to reach me for days but he couldn't get through to Mwatumi. He was very concerned and very sweet. We talked for a long time. I felt terrible, knowing that I'd...that we'd...while he was so worried about me."

"So, Camilla has dumped him and now he wants to come crawling back to you."

"That's not fair," snapped Carol. "You don't know that's what happened."

"Yes I do," said Peter. "And so do you. You just don't want to admit it. Trust me, you're letting yourself in for a lot of grief if you go down that road."

Carol smiled a bit sadly and laid her hand on his. "And which one are you supposed to be now? The lover who always tells the truth or the lover who always lies? Should I ask you which way you tell people to turn in order to live happily ever after?"

Instead of answering he leaned over and tilted her face gently up towards his. His lips lingered softly, first on one corner of her mouth and then on the other. As he straightened up and drew away, he slipped a card into her hand. "Call me if you should find yourself in a crocodile-infested swamp," he said.

She shaded her eyes to watch him as he circled the pool and disappeared through the doorway into the hotel. The warmth stayed on her lips long after he had gone, even after she had gotten up and plunged head first into the icy blue water.

THE END

Printed in the United States
2094